THE PAWN

THE BOWERS FILES

STEVEN JAMES

Grand Rapids, Michigan

Published by Fleming H. Revell
a division of Baker Publishing Group
P.O. Box 6287, Grand Rapids, MI 49516-6287
www.revellbooks.com

Printed in the United States of America

Library of Congress Cataloging-in-Publication Data
James, Steven, 1969–
    The pawn / Steven James.
       p.   cm. — (The Bowers files ; bk. 1)
    ISBN 10: 0-8007-1896-8 (cloth)
    ISBN 978-0-8007-1896-1 (cloth)
       1. Detectives—Fiction. 2. Criminologists—Fiction. 3. Serial murderers—
Fiction. 4. Magicians—Fiction. 5. Serial murder investigation—Fiction.
I. Title.
PS3610.A4545P39 2007
813'.6—dc22   2007014279

Some of the events in this story are a matter of public record; many are products of
the author's imagination and are not meant in any way to dishonor the victims or
diminish the enormity of the tragedy that took place in Guyana.

In memory of
Gloria and Malcolm,
because your story matters

PROLOGUE

March 5, 1985
La Cruxis, Mississippi
4:13 p.m.

It happened upstairs at her house after school on a Tuesday afternoon. Her parents were still at work, just like always. So Aaron Jeffrey Kincaid and Jessica Rembrandt had the house to themselves. Just like always. Most afternoons found them here, making out, fooling around in the basement.

But today was different. Today was the day.

Jessie smiled at her boyfriend as she unlocked the front door. "Aaron Jeffrey Kincaid," she breathed, "I love you." Her voice sounded so alluring, so alive. It said more than I love you; it said, I believe in you.

"I love you too, Jessie." He stepped past her and swung the door open. "I'll always love you." He said the words smoothly, convincingly, but he wondered if he really meant them. He wondered if he did love her; if he'd ever loved anything at all.

He took her hand as they stepped into the living room. Then, with one smooth motion of his free hand, he shut the door behind them.

They'd been going out for almost three months. At first it'd been like any other relationship for him—after the initial thrill wore off, he'd started to get bored with her; started to wonder if maybe he'd be happier with someone else. But the more time he spent with her, the more he realized she did things to please him. Little things.

7

She went to the movies he liked. She wore the clothes he told her to wear. And she let him do things to her, sometimes whatever he wanted to. So, of course, one day he started wondering how far she would go to please him, how much she would actually do. Who wouldn't wonder those kinds of things?

They headed upstairs to her parents' bedroom. That's where the whirlpool was.

He led her by the hand, and she followed without even a trace of hesitation in her step. Amazing.

Earlier that year another couple had been found in a car. In the garage. Double suicide. So all these counselors had arrived at their high school to talk to the students about death and hope and reasons to live. One of the counselors, a delicate woman with sweet, caramel eyes, had met with him individually. "Aaron, have you ever thought about taking your own life?"

And Aaron had given her a look, wide-eyed and innocent. "Well, just like most kids, I guess." He was playing naïve, searching her eyes for understanding and compassion, toying with her. "I guess I've thought about it—suicide that is. But nothing serious. Nothing specific."

And she nodded and wrote something down in her notebook.

Then he leaned close. "Is there something wrong with me?"

She smiled. "No, of course not, Aaron. It's perfectly normal to think about ending your life sometimes. I'd be a little worried if the thought had never crossed your mind." Then she laughed as if that should have been funny or comforting or something. And she looked across the table at him reassuringly, and he smiled back at her in a boyish, trusting way.

"Thanks," he said. "You've been very helpful."

And after that, the counselors left their numbers on little cards and on posters on the walls of the school for kids who felt lonely or depressed or needed someone to talk to. "They'll be back in two months," the principal had told the students at an assembly in the gym, "to follow up with anyone who needs to talk some more."

Maybe he'd gotten the idea from that—the double suicide and the meetings and the counselor with the eyes of a doe. It was hard to say. Aaron had tried to trace the exact origin of the idea, but finally he'd realized that sometimes ideas just come to you fully formed, as this one had. And in the end it doesn't really matter so much where they come from as it does where they lead you, what you do with them.

"It'll all be over soon," Jessie said as they entered the bedroom. Her voice was more agitated now, excited. Maybe fear had crept into it.

"No, soon it'll all *begin*." He walked over to the window and twisted the blinds shut to close out the warm afternoon sunshine. A few slivers of sunlight cut through the spaces between the blinds and landed on the lightly ruffled blankets on Jessie's parents' bed— streaks of light and darkness lying next to each other, side by side. He walked through the zebra-shadowed room to her arms. "Soon it'll all begin," he repeated. "And then we'll be together forever, and nothing will ever be able to keep us apart."

"I'm ready," she whispered.

"It's a cruel world," said Aaron Jeffrey Kincaid.

"It's a cruel world," echoed Jessica Rembrandt.

"But our love will unite us forever."

"Our love will unite us forever . . ."

Aaron pulled the polished stainless steel hunting knife out of his backpack and led Jessie to the whirlpool. The knife had a serrated edge on one side and a wickedly curved blade on the other. They'd picked it out together last week at a sporting goods store at the mall. The two of them had been planning this for weeks, to make sure everything was perfect. After they found the knife, Aaron had sent her in to pay for it with cash while he waited outside "to keep watch." He'd made her think it was all her idea. He was good at that.

9

Jessie turned on the whirlpool.

The motor hummed, sending jets of warm water churning at their feet.

"I'll go first," she said, "because I love you." Her voice was shaking. Her breathing, fast.

"No, I'll go first. Just like we practiced."

They stripped off their clothes and eased into the whirlpool. Only two heads and a pair of shoulders were visible now above the foaming, roiling water.

It was just like the couples had done in Roman times. Lovers sitting in the baths, letting the warm water help pump the blood from their wrists as they drifted off into the darkness of a sleep that never ends. He knew. He'd researched it. But this was even better. The jets from the whirlpool would help pump the blood out faster.

Steam began to rise from the water.

Aaron carefully placed the edge of the blade against his left wrist.

"It's a cruel world," he said, repeating the mantra they'd practiced together so many times.

"It's a cruel world," Jessie echoed.

"But our love will unite us forever."

"Our love will unite us forever . . ."

People would be surprised if they saw him here. Her parents had never even seen them together. Even at school they were both loners, so no one really paid much attention to them. It was all so perfect. "Everyone will know about us now," he said. "At last."

Aaron drew the blade toward him, deep into the meat of his wrist, and a red spray shot across the pool. A sharp ache bristled up his arm, but he didn't flinch. The cut was angled just so across his vein so it would be harder to stop the bleeding. They'd rehearsed it this way, the best way. The fastest way.

He quickly lowered his hand into the steamy water, and at once the water began to twirl with crazy red swirls. It reminded him of watching his foster mother bake when he lived in California, seeing the food coloring swirl through a bowl of hot water. He thought of her, the smells in the kitchen, the sound of her laughter, until his wrist began to throb. Then, his eyes found their way back to the knife he was still holding.

"Should I do the other one right away?" he asked Jessica calmly. She was entranced, staring at the red water that was now encircling her legs and abdomen.

"No," she whispered. "We need to leave at the same time. Hand me the knife."

He held it to her, handle first, across the steamy, swirling water. "This life is so unpredictable, Jessie." He spoke the words tenderly, evenly, smoothly, as the blood pumped out of his wrist and merged with the crimson water. "Who knows what the future holds? Your dad could get a new job and make you move away; your parents could get a divorce . . ." The blood continued to curl around him. "I could die in a car accident . . . It's best this way. The only way. This way nothing can ever separate us. This way, we're in control of what happens. All that matters is us. All that matters is this moment."

"Our love will unite us forever," she whispered.

"Our love will unite us forever," said Aaron Jeffrey Kincaid.

He held up his hand and watched the blood spill from his wrist. Watched as the patterns trailed down his arm and into the water. Watched as little rivers of blood dripped from his elbow and then twirled into the current, across his legs, around his heart, toward his girlfriend.

She took the knife, placed the blade against her left wrist, looked up at him. "Forever," she said.

"Forever."

She pulled the knife sharply across her left wrist and let out a gasp. He'd shown her how to do it right. The cut was more than sufficient. They'd practiced together using a butter knife to get the angle right. They'd rehearsed it all, down to the last detail. And this cut was not the tentative probing of someone who was unsure. Paramedics called those "hesitation marks." But she wasn't hesitant at all. No, she wasn't just doing it for attention. She believed in everything he told her. He knew she did. She believed in Aaron Jeffrey Kincaid more than anything in the world.

"I'm doing this for you, Aaron," she said. And the look in her eyes told him it was true. She would have done anything for him; had done everything for him. "I love you."

"I know."

Aaron watched her stare at the whirlpool for a moment. Blood was pumping out of her opened wrist now, pouring out. Swirling all around her in crimson currents as her body emptied itself of life. He wondered what she was thinking.

"I'm scared," she whispered.

"Don't be scared. We're going to be together now. There's nothing to be afraid of. Just do the other wrist like we practiced and hand me the knife."

"Nothing can keep us apart," she whispered, pressing the blade against her right wrist. "Nothing."

"Nothing."

She tried to make the cut, but the tendons had been damaged. Her hand trembled. "Help me," she said feebly.

He eased over to her side of the whirlpool, took her hand in his, and held the knife firmly against her skin.

Then he pulled.

She grimaced, then twitched, then relaxed her arm. "Thank you," she said.

He let go of her hand, and the knife dropped into the water—this second cut was even deeper than the first.

"Don't worry about that," he said. "I'll get it."

The water became darker and darker as the jets of the whirlpool chugged on. Curling and pumping. A deeper, sharper red. She had dropped her arms into the water now and was slumping a bit to the side. Her voice was barely a whisper. "Hold me." She tried to reach out to hug him but could barely lift her arms above the water. Blood kept coursing from her wrists.

He leaned close to her. "There's nothing to be afraid of." He held her until her arms dropped into the water one last time.

Then, instead of reaching for the knife, he stepped out of the water and picked up a towel.

She'd done it. She'd done just what he asked. Yes, he'd had to slice his own wrist, that was true, and he'd had to help her, but she had agreed. She had listened. She'd been obedient to the very end.

No one had seen them together. He could easily hide the wound on his wrist until it healed. No one would ask any questions. It was even easier than he'd imagined it would be.

Father would be proud.

"Everything is going to be all right, Jessie," he said softly as he stared at her. He tried to imagine what it was like for her in that moment . . . darkness clouding into the sides of her vision . . . the image of her boyfriend leaving her alone in the whirlpool . . . water and blood dripping together onto the linoleum.

Water and blood. Water and blood.

"Where are you going?" Her words were soft, hardly audible. A whisper.

"Don't worry, Jessie." He was holding the towel up against his wrist to stop the bleeding. "Everything is going to be just fine." Her mouth formed a silent question for him, but the words never came. Her arms quivered slightly and then stopped moving forever as Aaron Jeffrey Kincaid sat down beside the gently humming water to watch his girlfriend bleed to death in her parents' whirlpool.

Oh yes. Father would be very proud.

1

Thursday
October 23, 2008
Somewhere above the mountains of western North
  Carolina
5:31 p.m.

I peered out the window of the Bell 206L-4 LongRanger IV, helicopter of choice for both the Georgia State Patrol and the Department of the Interior, as we roared over the mountainous border of Georgia and North Carolina. Clouds rose dark on the horizon.

The colors of autumn were still lingering on the rolling slopes of the southern Appalachians, although winter had started to creep into the higher elevations. Far below us, the hills rose and fell, rose and fell, zipping past. For a few minutes I watched the shadow of the helicopter gliding over the mountains and dipping down into the shadowy valleys like a giant insect skimming across the landscape, searching for a place to land.

Even though it was late fall, ribbons of churning water pounded down the mountains in the aftermath of a series of fierce storms. In the springtime these hills produce some of the most fantastic whitewater rafting in all of North America. I know. I used to paddle them years ago when I spent a year working near here as a wilderness guide for the North Carolina Outward Bound School. Now, it seemed like those days were in another life.

Before I became what I am. Before any of this.

But as I looked out the window, the waters weren't blue like I remembered them. Instead, they were brown and swollen from a recent rain. Wriggling back and forth through the hills like thick, restless snakes.

I glanced at my watch: 5:34 p.m. We should be landing within the next ten minutes. Which was good, because with the clouds rolling in, it didn't look like we had a whole lot of sunlight ahead of us. Maybe an hour. Maybe less.

My good friend Special Agent Ralph Hawkins had called me in. Just a few hours ago I was in Atlanta presenting a seminar on strategic crime analysis for the National Law Enforcement Methodology Conference. Another conference. Another lecture series. It seemed like that was all I'd been doing for the last six months. Sure, I'd consulted on a couple dozen cases, but they weren't a big deal. Mostly I'd been teaching and researching criminology. Trying to forget.

I'd have to say that despite how disoriented my life had become, the biggest casualty had been my sixteen-year-old—wait, seventeen-year-old—stepdaughter Tessa. After the funeral, I tried to get close to her, but it didn't work. Nothing did. Eventually we just drifted into our separate routines, our separate lives. Case in point: here I was in the Southeast while she stayed with my parents back home in Denver.

Ralph wasn't the kind of man to waste time or words being cordial. He'd jumped right to the point when he called my cell earlier in the day. "Pat, I hear you're back in the game."

"Trying to be."

"Well, you heard about what's going on down here?"

"Yeah." I followed the postings of all the major cities' crime labs and FBI listings. Occupational hazard. I was a regular VICAP junkie—the Violent Criminal Apprehension Program is a way to track crimes across jurisdictions, so I'd read about the murders. Even the details they weren't releasing to the public. There'd been at least five so far, just since April.

"You found another one," I said.

"Yeah. Some hikers stumbled across her about an hour ago. We're out at the site now, and, well, I could email you some stuff, but I gotta say, I could use your eyes over here. There's got to be something we're missing. The signature is the same. It's the same guy, Pat. The press is calling him the Yellow Ribbon Strangler."

Ralph knew that I hated when the press got involved. I'd looked at my watch: 4:02 p.m.

"I don't know, Ralph . . ."

"I can have a chopper over there to pick you up in twenty minutes. You'll be back at your hotel tonight. That's why I could use your eyes right now. Supposed to be some more storms coming through, and I don't want to miss anything here. What do you say?"

And I'd said yes.

Because I always say yes.

"Email me the photos your men took at the other crime scenes," I said, "and video if you have it, and I'll look them over on my way down."

And now, less than two hours after giving the keynote address to 2,500 law enforcement professionals and intelligence agency personnel from around the world, I was on a chopper to meet Ralph and look at the body of another dead girl.

I scrolled through the crime scene pictures on my laptop. Even though I try to stay detached, the images still bother me. They always have. Probably always will.

I glanced out the window. The shadow of the helicopter skirted over a road and hovered for a moment above a parked car on a scenic overlook. A man and a woman who were standing beside the guardrail didn't seem to notice the shadow. They just kept staring at the sprawling mountains folding back against the horizon, totally unaware that a shadow was crawling over them. Totally unaware.

The killer hadn't made any attempt to hide the bodies. Whoever was killing these women wanted them found. After all, there were plenty of places in the hills of western North Carolina to hide a body forever. Or a person. The serial bomber Eric Robert Rudolph had hidden here for five years during one of the biggest manhunts in history and was only caught when he wandered into town to scavenge food from a dumpster behind a grocery store. No, our guy wasn't into hiding; he was into flaunting. And there was something else. Something that hadn't been released to the public. Something very disturbing. Which was why Ralph had called me.

I leaned forward and yelled to the pilot, "How much longer?"

He didn't answer, just pointed at a nearby mountain and tipped the LongRanger toward a clearing.

I closed up my computer. It was time for Patrick Bowers to go to work.

2

A bank of dark, steely clouds churned in the western sky as we pivoted on the edge of the air and the pilot lowered the chopper to the ground.

Someone had strung up a boundary of yellow police tape along the trees surrounding the meadow. It fluttered and snapped in the wind kicked up by the chopper's blades.

I grabbed my computer bag and jumped down, using one hand to shield my eyes from the fine spray of sand thrown into the air by the rotors. It was like trying to ward off a fog of biting flies, but I didn't want to wait one moment longer than I had to.

I could see the hulking shape of Special Agent Ralph Hawkins waving a meaty hand at the helicopter like a traffic cop who'd lost his way and ended up on top of this mountain. Ralph was as thick as a bear. As an All-American wrestler in high school and former Army Ranger he could still break out of a pair of handcuffs with his bare hands. But still, even though he was over six feet tall, I had him by two inches. Bugged him to no end.

"Pat." He threw the word at me along with his hand. Hearing his gruff, thunderous voice made me feel right at home. We'd worked lots of cases together for the FBI's National Center for the Analysis of Violent Crime, back before . . . well, back before everything came spinning apart.

"Good to see you out on the turf again."

"Yeah," I yelled.

Now, the rotors were easing to a stop, and the wind swirling around us found its natural rhythm again as the blades slowed and finally hung limp and still above the dome of the helicopter.

Half a dozen agents wearing black FBI windbreakers stalked around the top of the mountain surrounded by a pack of bored-looking state troopers and four park rangers. It reminded me of a construction site at break time where everyone just stands around expecting someone else to be the first one to go back to work. They were all staring at me. Some were exchanging comments with each other. Others were snickering.

Apparently, it was pretty rare around here to bring in some-one like me—on the other hand, it might have been my age. Even though I've worked fifteen solid years in law enforcement, I won't be turning thirty-six until January. And people often tell me I look younger than I am. That's why I go for the scruffy look. When I shave I look twenty.

Two people stepped forward—a woman wearing a black FBI windbreaker and a rotund man wearing a tie that looked like a bib. He offered his hand. "Dr. Bowers?"

"That's me." I shook his hand.

"Sheriff Dante Wallace, Buncombe County Sheriff's Department." Sheriff Wallace looked like he enjoyed his football games best from the center of a couch. The bristles of hair sticking up from his mostly bald head looked like tufts of gray grass.

"Good to meet you," I said.

"And I'm Special Agent Lien-hua Jiang," said the dark-haired woman beside him. "I'm Ralph's partner." Elegant. Close to my age, maybe a few years younger. Asian descent. Great posture. Like a model. Or an athlete. I wondered if she'd maybe studied dance. She had a tiny chin that made her smile even broader. She reached out her hand and nodded politely. Nice grip. Nice body.

"Great," I said, trying not to look like I was staring. Besides, I was anxious to get to work before the rains came. "It's good to meet you both."

Agent Hawkins rescued me. "All right. Now that we're all on a first-name basis, let's go take a look at our girl. Or at least what's left of her."

—————————■—————————

The Illusionist watched carefully as Patrick Bowers wandered around the top of the mountain with all those other federal agents and idiot cops. Morons! They would never understand. None of them would. Not really.

He knew about Bowers. Oh yeah, he knew all about Patrick Bowers, PhD. He'd read both of his books. For research. Very helpful. A worthy opponent.

The Illusionist grinned as he watched them. He was happy. So happy! He almost started giggling right there. But he didn't. He didn't make a sound. He was in control of everything.

He had a pair of Steiner binoculars in his jacket pocket, but he didn't even need them. He was that close. He was that close to everything! Most of the cops just stood around like the complete and total imbeciles and half-wits that they were. Oh, he was loving this. He was loving every minute of it. They were heading over to the girl. He closed his eyes for a moment and remembered what it was like to be with her. Alone with her. Yes. Oh yes. She'd been the best one so far.

Then he opened his eyes and smiled. He could relive it all right now, as he watched them look over her body. He could relive it all, and they would never even know.

3

I followed Ralph through the maze of onlookers.

I hated to see this many people around a crime scene. The more people, the more likely evidence will be contaminated. "Brought out the cavalry, huh?" I said, nodding toward the crowd.

He shook his head. "Not my choice. Ever since we arrived it's been a jurisdictional nightmare. Bodies in four states so far."

We were near Asheville, North Carolina, a city of about 73,000 located at the nexus of two major highways that crisscross the southeast. Three states, Georgia, South Carolina, and Tennessee, are all an hour's drive away, with Virginia, Kentucky, and West Virginia just another hour or so further north. So far, bodies had been found in North Carolina, South Carolina, Virginia, and Tennessee. It'd taken a while for law enforcement to connect the dots and determine that the killer was probably working out of this area.

Ralph leaned close. "We're doing everything we can to work with these local guys, but just between you and me, they'd do better to fire half their butts and just let us do our job. Plus, somehow, the press found out." He gestured to a pack of reporters herded into a corner of the meadow. He looked at the deepening clouds for a moment. "At least we don't have their choppers flying all over the place."

The storm was rolling in fast. We needed to hurry.

I picked up my pace and tried to think of how I might save some time. "Okay, fill me in. What do we know?" I'd read the notes on the flight over but I wanted to hear it all again. Let it sink in. So I could look for patterns.

"Well, whoever our guy is, he knows how to leave a clean crime scene. We haven't found much of anything so far. He even washes the bodies, sutures the wounds. Our victim has six stab wounds, but she died from being strangled, just like the others. Um, I mean, at least that's the preliminary finding. We're still waiting for the medical examiner to confirm it."

I nodded. The killer had stabbed each of the women ritualistically in the chest and abdomen, but the mechanism of death in all of the murders so far had been cerebral hypoxia—which is just a fancy way of saying the brain didn't get enough oxygen. You squeeze the throat long enough, you choke the brain.

"Wasn't the first one done with the cord of a hair dryer?" asked Sheriff Wallace, who was puffing along beside us.

"Yeah," said Ralph. "The last three with clothesline rope."

"Why would he change his MO?" asked the sheriff.

"He came prepared the next time," Agent Jiang said softly. "He wasn't taking any chances. He brought his own rope."

"I assume you're tracing it?" said Wallace. "To see if it gives you any leads on a manufacturer?"

Ralph cleared his throat. "Already on that."

Sheriff Wallace waddled in closer, struggling to keep up. Special Agent Jiang strode beside us in silence, watching the sky.

"The rope's embedded a quarter of an inch into her neck," said Ralph. "He might have even used something mechanical to tighten it."

I felt my fists clench. After all these years, I should be used to hearing details like this, but it still disturbs me. It used to turn my stomach, now it fuels my anger. I guess in a way that's good. It helps me focus on catching these guys.

"That and we found another chess piece."

I thought back to the case files I'd read. At the first crime scene, the pawn had seemed like a great clue—the piece came from a hand-carved wooden set that the lab guys were able to trace to a woodworker in Oregon who made them out of redwood and shipped them all over the world. The analysts were even able to nail down the dates when the set was made, since the carpenter switched the kind of lathe he was using two years and two months ago. It leaves a different kind of cut on the chess pieces, so the chess set our killer was using was at least two years old. There was no way to know yet which of the eight or nine sets in question our killer had gotten a hold of, but the woodworking guy was being helpful. Right now, some agents were going through his records, checking up on everyone who'd bought one of his sets in the last five years.

"What piece was left this time?" I asked.

"Another pawn. Black. What do you make of that?"

"I'm not sure. Maybe nothing."

"What do you mean?" asked Sheriff Wallace. "It's huge. He's trying to tell us something."

I shook my head. "Maybe, maybe not. These days, lots of killers leave intentional clues at crime scenes to throw off the investigators—someone else's blood, hair, semen. Too many *CSI* episodes and serial killer movies. The smarter we get, the smarter they get. It might be there to throw us off. Or who knows, he might just like chess."

Killers often leave taunting clues or notes at crime scenes. The most common were words scrawled in blood. Sometimes, a handwritten letter would show up. Usually if the killers left anything it was bloody and messy. I'd seen just about everything.

But not this guy. He left a hand-carved, redwood chess piece at the scene of each of his crimes. The first three were white pawns. Now these last three had been black.

What is he trying to say? That this is all a game to him? That everything is black and white? Who's the pawn? Is he the pawn? Is the victim the pawn? Maybe the police. Maybe we're the pawns?

And a ribbon. He tied a yellow ribbon in the victim's hair.

I didn't want to read too much into any of it. The trick is to keep everything in mind as you look at the big picture. That's the secret to nabbing these guys. You assemble all the pieces first, before jumping to any conclusions. Hypothesize, test, revise. Never, ever assume.

We leaned under the police tape. The body lay at the base of a tree about twenty meters ahead of us.

"Did you get soil samples?" I asked Ralph.

"Yeah. Six different ones from around the scene. Just like you taught me."

"Good."

By then, the wind had picked up and the clouds we'd seen on the horizon were boiling over each other, racing toward us. This wasn't good. Our crime scene was going to be wiped out in a matter of minutes.

"Get shots of the hills," I yelled. "I want every angle—I want to see what he saw. And string up a tarp over her body. Don't let her get wet. And the crowd too. I want pictures of everyone here. Video if we have it. Someone get this body covered!"

"Sir, we already checked over the body," someone said.

"I know you have," I said, trying my hardest to remain respectful. "But I haven't." I pulled on the latex gloves I always keep in my jeans pockets. Suddenly, I was glad there were so many people at the scene. We'd need them all to preserve evidence.

I looked around. This is what the killer was looking at. This is what he saw as he left her here. *Why here? Why did you bring her here?*

I scanned the horizon. Layers of dark mountains cascaded back toward the horizon. I figured that in the sunlight you could see twenty or thirty miles in any direction. Today you'd be lucky to see two. I tried to guess which entrance and exit routes he might have used. The nearby forest was thick, the terrain steep. Only a limited number of trails available.

There was no sign of vehicular traffic and no trail marks from a four-wheeler.

Did he know it was going to rain? Had he planned it just like this? That we would be rushing around here trying to collect evidence?

Mists were blowing in now, enshrouding the trees, covering the nearby peaks. Everything began to take on a ghostly, ethereal feel.

Did you carry her up here? Why carry her all the way up here?

Just then, the LongRanger pilot came running over. "Sir, this weather doesn't look good. I've gotta take off or I'm gonna get stuck up here."

"I'll give you a ride to town," Sheriff Wallace offered.

I shook my head. "All my stuff is in Atlanta. The conference finishes up tomorrow."

"Do you have to speak again?" asked Ralph.

"No, I'm done, but—"

"Well, I'll have your bags brought over," said Ralph. "Stay here for a few days. Give us a hand."

I hated being interrupted at a crime scene like this. "All right, whatever." I waved him away. I just wanted to see the girl. At that, the pilot nodded and left us alone.

By then a couple of agents had draped a blue tarp over a tree limb above her. They didn't look happy.

I stepped around them and looked at her.

She was nineteen or twenty. Caucasian. Blonde hair. She lay propped up with her back against a tree, posed, her hands still bound tightly behind her, probably with the same type of rope that was embedded into her neck. She still had her blue jeans and T-shirt on, which was consistent—there hadn't been a sexual angle to any of the previous murders. I was thankful for that much at least. The cotton of her gray T-shirt was stained dark from the stab wounds in her torso.

The killer had tied a length of yellow ribbon in her neatly brushed hair. She was barefoot, just like all the victims had been, and had a toe ring on the third toe of her left foot. Some soil clung to the indentations on the ring. Mud.

I inspected her ankles, gently pulling back the hem of her jeans. No ligature marks or bruises. Her feet hadn't been bound.

"Has she been moved?" I asked Ralph.

"No," he said.

So, this was how the killer had positioned her.

I gently tipped the body to the side. Touching her like this, moving her, felt like some kind of violation. I heard a voice in my head asking her to forgive me, to accept my touch as long as it would help me find the person who'd done this to her.

There was no dirt or debris on her back like there would have been if she'd been raped out here or dragged along the trail. I looked around. *If he didn't drag her, did he carry her? All the way up here? Was this the primary crime scene after all? Did he meet her here, maybe?*

Somewhere behind me the chopper roared to life, but its sound was quickly drowned out by the howling wind of the coming storm.

Daylight was dying around us. I pulled my Mini Maglite flashlight out of the sheath on my belt, flipped it on, and studied the girl's face. Her ocean-blue eyes were open, staring forward. Forever staring forward. No longer bright and alive, now cloudy and opaque. I leaned over and looked deeply into her sightless eyes. The eyes that had seen the man who killed her. Had watched him. There was an old wives' tale that the eyes of the dying record, like a photograph, the face of the killer. But there was no face captured on her eyes.

"She has contacts," I said, still staring at her.

I heard Sheriff Wallace shuffle in close behind me. "Huh?"

"Contacts. This girl wears contact lenses."

"So?"

"The information Ralph sent me didn't mention contact lenses."

Agent Hawkins glared at the crime scene technicians. "I guess we didn't notice."

"Does it matter?" asked Wallace.

"Everything matters," I said. The wind flipped a wisp of the young woman's hair across her face. I pushed it back. "I worked one case where the killer put contacts into a girl's eyes after he killed her. He left fingerprints on the lenses. Everything matters."

I carefully removed her contact lenses and put them into an evidence bag. Then I examined her neck and cheeks and sighed softly. "He tortured her." I didn't realize I'd said the words aloud until Agent Jiang leaned over beside me. I caught the scent of her shampoo. Vanilla.

"How can you tell?"

I pointed. "See those tiny dots? Around her eyes there?"

"Those purplish reddish ones?" she asked.

"Yeah."

"Some kind of hemorrhaging?"

"Petechial hemorrhaging—caused from asphyxiation. Usually, even in strangulation, the dots are small—sometimes only the size of a speck of dust, and only appear around the eyes or eyelids. She has them all across her face, even down here around her neck and shoulders. See?"

"What does that mean?"

"It means," said someone behind me, "he didn't just strangle her, he choked her into unconsciousness and then revived her again. Over and over. It must have gone on for a while."

I glanced over my shoulder.

A strikingly handsome man in his late twenties knelt beside me. "Special Agent Brent Tucker," he said. "Forensics." Dark hair, neat, trim. He looked serious about his work and moved with the confidence of someone who's used to getting things right the first time.

"Yeah," I said to Agent Jiang. "That's what it means."

"You're Dr. Bowers, aren't you?" Agent Tucker asked.

"Yeah."

"It's an honor to meet you."

"You too."

A chess piece lay in the palm of the girl's right hand. A black pawn.

"What do you estimate for her time of death?" I asked Tucker.

He glanced at his notepad. "Hmm . . . They took her temp sixty minutes ago . . . she's clothed"—he was thinking aloud—"it's cool and windy on this mountain, and she wasn't in direct sunlight . . . I'd say sometime this morning. Maybe between eight and ten."

I nodded.

Sheriff Dante Wallace shook his head. "I can't believe our guy carried her to the top of this mountain. How do you know he didn't do her up here?"

Ralph deferred to me, and I pointed to the girl. "There's no sign of a struggle," I said. "The ground isn't disturbed. And look at her hair. It's clean and neatly combed. No leaves. No dirt. She was probably killed indoors." *Probably*, I thought. *But this guy might be toying with us. I'm not sure about anything yet.*

I turned to Ralph. "You said some hikers found her?"

"A couple locals, yeah," he said, "just before I called you. We took them in for questioning. So far they look pretty clean."

"Do we know her name yet?"

Ralph shook his head. "No ID. But there was a girl from Black Mountain reported missing yesterday named Mindy Travelca. We think it might be her. We're checking."

"He wanted her found," I said.

"Then why did he bring her all the way out here?" Agent Tucker asked.

That's what I'm here to find out, I thought. But I didn't say it. I didn't say anything. I just knelt there and stared at the unblinking eyes of a girl who should have been making out with her boyfriend or studying for her college exams or eating a pizza with her roommate or chatting with her friends online instead of lying dead on top of this mountain.

Someone's daughter. Someone lost his daughter today.

Just like me, I thought, even though Tessa was alive and well and wasn't exactly my daughter at all. *Someone just like me.*

I reached down and gently closed the eyes of the girl who might have been named Mindy just as the first raindrops began to fall, like tears from the eyes of God, splattering on the tarp above me.

4

The Illusionist watched as they carefully wrapped and removed the body, as the rain began, as the storm arrived. Everything was going according to plan. Everything!

It would take them at least half an hour to carry the body down the trail to the ambulance. He wished he could stay to watch the show, he really did, but with the storm rolling in and so much work to do, he would have to be going. He glanced at his watch. Oh, yes, he needed to be on his way. There was so much to do yet tonight.

5

After we left the mountain, I rode with Sheriff Dante Wallace to a hotel about eight miles outside of Asheville. Dark sheets of angry rain slanted against the windshield. I was lost in thought, staring at the water running off the windshield wiper blades when he asked, "So how do you do it?"

I turned and looked at him in the dim light. "Do what?"

"Chase these monsters all the time."

I considered my words for a moment. "Well, I try to tell myself they're just as human as I am. It helps some. Makes it more personal."

Tension hardened the lines around his jaw. His voice took on an edge. "How is someone who rapes little babies or dissects his wife and eats her for supper just as human as I am?"

Actually, it was a good question, although I'd never heard it put quite like that. It's hard not to think of these killers as monsters or aliens or subhumans; I struggle with it myself sometimes. "I try to think in terms of the similarities not the differences, Sheriff Wallace. Criminals interact with the world just like everyone does. They have patterns, follow routines, try to save time and money. They eat, drink, sleep, work, get into arguments, avoid the things they don't like, and cover up the things they do wrong so they won't get caught. Just like all of us. I know it sounds cold and unfeeling to say all that, but it helps me catch them. Understanding how people act helps me understand how killers act, and it helps me track them down."

He drove in silence for a few moments letting my words sink

in. At last he turned off the highway and let out a coarse cough. "Well," he said tersely, "you're the expert."

A few minutes later he slowed to a stop in front of a Comfort Inn. "It ain't the Hyatt," he said. "But it should do ya for tonight."

"Thanks for the ride, Sheriff."

"You're welcome . . ." He paused. I could tell he was trying to think of how to address me—Detective Bowers, Agent Bowers, Dr. Bowers . . .

"Pat," I said. "My friends call me Pat."

"All right. See you tomorrow, Pat."

"OK," I said.

Then, I walked inside and tried not to think about what the killer had done to that girl on the mountain.

I dragged myself into my hotel room and closed the door. I could still see her face, her unblinking eyes. Over the years I've tried to forget the faces, but I can't. So many young, promising faces. It seems like it's always the most attractive ones who get killed. Beauty brings out the worst in us. You'd think it would be the other way around—that the twisted, the deformed, the misshapen would ignite rage and terror. But they only seem to arouse sympathy. No, it's beauty that brings out the beast. For whatever reason, elegance and grace always seem to ignite the deepest rage and darkest lusts of the human animal.

I've been to hundreds of crime scenes over the last fifteen years. Probably thousands. I stopped counting a few years ago when I reached nine hundred. At first all the remembering bothered me. It always bothers people at first. Every cop and FBI agent I've ever met can remember their first crime scene.

There's something about seeing your first dead body. It's not like the movies or TV. And it's not like at a funeral where everything has been cleaned up and sanitized. It's dirty and sad and messy and you see the chest that doesn't rise and the lips that don't move and the eyes that don't blink. Corpses are discolored, misshapen, bloated, and reek with the smell of death. There is nothing beautiful or glamorous about a corpse.

Everybody remembers seeing their first dead body.

But after a while the images kind of run together. You remember bits and pieces—a patch of blood here. A bullet hole there. A knife lying discarded on the grass. A torn piece of fabric clinging to a patch of mottled skin. And if you really work at it, you can start to make the connections. *Oh yeah, that was the nine-year-old girl who was kidnapped from her home and found buried outside her dad's fishing cabin in Montana . . . That bullet wound reminds me of the boy down in Arkansas who was showing his friend the shotgun in his dad's office after school . . . Those pliers look like the ones that couple in Maine used to torture their victims . . .*

The details blur together, but the faces remain etched in your mind. You don't forget the faces.

I kicked off my shoes and took a quick shower. Then I flipped on the TV. Images I didn't care about flickered past me. Plastic people flashing fake smiles at a pretend world. I channel surfed past a few home shopping shows, the day's sports highlights, a rerun of *24*, a series of mindless commercials trying to sell me stuff I didn't need, and of course, the political smear ads for the upcoming presidential election.

The last channel I came to was a local news station doing a story on the disappearance of Mindy Travelca. They had footage of her dad standing in his front lawn. Based on the position of the sun in the sky, I guessed they'd filmed the interview sometime late in the morning. If it was Mindy we'd found, she was probably already dead at the time of the interview. "We're just hoping and praying she'll be OK," the dad was telling the camera as bravely as he could, but his eyes betrayed him; they glistened with tears. A girl of about eight or nine ran up and jumped into his arms.

That must be Mindy's little sister.

"We know she's going to be OK," the man continued. "Don't we, sweetie?" The little girl nodded. "We love you, Mindy," he said. "We're here for you—"

I shut it off. I couldn't take it.

They probably would have shown Mindy's picture in a minute or two and I could have known for sure if she was the one we'd found. But I just couldn't watch. Maybe I didn't want to know.

I lay there on my back, listening to the cars rush by on the highway less than a hundred meters away, watching the curtains rustle softly as the heater beneath the window struggled to spit mildly warm air into my room.

Someone lost a daughter today.

I grabbed my cell phone and dialed my parents' number. I heard it ring, and then a frail, familiar voice answered, "Hello?"

"Mom, it's Pat. Is Tessa there?"

"Oh, Patrick. Yes. I'll go and get her. Just a moment, dear." In the background I could hear her calling Tessa's name, and then I heard my stepdaughter yell back that she was *busy!*

I pictured her standing there yelling at my mother. A study in contrasts. Tessa with her shoulder-length, shadow-black hair. My mother with her arctic white curls. Most of the time Tessa liked to wear black long-sleeve T-shirts emblazoned with the skull-shaped logos of bands I'd never heard of. Torn jeans with retro tennis shoes usually rounded out her outfit. My mother always wore a dress. Always.

I waited helplessly as they argued until finally Tessa's voice came on. "What do you want?" she said.

"Don't talk to your grandmother like that, Tessa Bernice Ellis."

"I'll talk *like* I want to *whoever* I want. Besides, she's not my grandmother. My grandparents are dead, remember?"

Ouch.

"I know and I'm sorry, but Martha is my mother, and I'm asking you to treat her with a little more respect."

A pause with ice in it. "So what is it you want, *Patrick*?"

I didn't really expect her to call me Dad, but I could do without the venom in her voice.

"I wanted to wish you a happy birthday."

"My birthday was yesterday."

Of course I knew that. Of course I did. And I should have called. There was no excuse. "I know, but I couldn't call, I was at a conference and then—"

"That is so lame." She was right, and we both knew it.

"Look, I'm sorry. Really, listen—"

"It doesn't matter. I gotta go. I've got stuff to do. I gotta study. I have two tests tomorrow." And then, before I could reply, "You'd know that if you were ever here."

"Listen, Tessa—"

Click.

I stared at the phone. *Oh, that went well.*

Sighed.

Someone lost a daughter today.

Someone just like me.

6

He thought of himself as a magician. A great illusionist. Ever since he'd been a kid he'd liked magic. *Now you see it, now you don't!* It all had to do with disguise and trickery and misdirection.

The first magic show he remembered was back in fourth grade when some guy had come to his school to perform tricks for the students.

"Watch as I make a *red bandana* appear out of nowhere," the guy had called into his portable PA system. And the children had watched, just as they were told, until the cheap sound system squealed loudly and all the kids screeched along with it.

A moment later he pulled out a green bandana and the kids laughed and pointed.

"Oops," he said. "Aha. There!" He pulled out a purple one this time. The kids laughed again. Then it was pink. More laughter.

"Now, watch and be amazed," he said. "As the Magnificent Marty attempts his next trick." He showed them his empty hands and then walked out into the audience, right up to the Illusionist. He looked down at the boy, smiled, and then reached down and pulled a bandana out from behind his ear. This time it was orange.

The kids laughed as the Magnificent Marty walked back onstage, looking very disappointed. He folded the bandana and stuffed it into his right hand. Then with a flourish he pulled out a blue bandana, and the orange one was gone. The children all gasped and clapped and whispered to each other, "How did he do that? It's magic!"

Then he pulled a dove out of a balloon, he escaped from a set of handcuffs, and finally, at the end of the show, as he was bowing, he pulled the *red bandana* out of his nose, and the kids erupted in applause.

And that was when the Illusionist realized that the entire show, from start to finish with all its feigned mistakes and slick banter, had been perfectly planned, carefully rehearsed. The show itself was one big illusion. And the magician had been in control the whole time. He'd crafted each moment to misdirect the children. He was always one step ahead of the audience. One step ahead of the world.

The secret was all in misdirection. *While you're looking over here at this hand, I'm hiding the coin in my back pocket with this one. Watch and be amazed!*

———————————■———————————

The light in the living room flicked off, and the game began. He edged closer to the window and waited. He was a master at waiting for just the right moment. He could wait an hour or a year. And that's what made him who he was. The Illusionist. Always one step ahead of the world.

Time ticked by, and he waited. More lights in the neighborhood blinked out. The dogs stopped barking. Crickets began chirping from everywhere and nowhere. He stood motionless, entombed in the shadows. Always in the shadows. Just like those crickets. A man at home in the dark.

At last the bedroom light went out. Minutes passed. Then hours. He listened to his own soft breathing until the night stopped moving and sleep spread her wings over the neighborhood. Finally, it was time.

The Illusionist pulled on his ski mask and slipped on the latex gloves. Then he glided his leather gloves over the latex ones. He knew that latex gloves can snag or rip. Fingerprints and DNA from the sweat on your fingertips can be lifted from some types of latex. He knew that too. That's why he wore both pair.

He stepped across the footpath to the garden and leaned up against the scratchy brick wall of N3161 Virginia Street. It was an anonymous middle-class house in an anonymous middle-class neighborhood in an anonymous middle-class town.

But it wouldn't be anonymous for long.

He already knew about the alarm system. And he knew how to disarm it. The Illusionist knew where the motion sensors were, where Alice McMichaelson kept the spare key for the neighbors when she left town. He knew it all.

There'd been a break-in at Locust Security Enterprises last week. A flat-screen computer screen had been stolen. Apparently, nothing else had been touched. But he'd gotten what he was looking for. Always misdirection. *Look at this hand while I put the coin in my pocket with this one. Look at the broken window and the missing monitor and don't notice two sheets of paper missing from the copy machine.* No one would notice something that small. And besides, the papers containing the security codes and wiring layout for the McMichaelson home had been put back in the locked file cabinet exactly where they belonged.

He glanced at his watch: 4:03 a.m. Perfect. People usually sleep the soundest from 3:00–5:00 a.m. See? He knew that too. He knew everything!

He walked onto the back porch, past the plaid Martha Stewart lawn chairs, past the gas grill, to the patio door and peered inside the sleepy house.

Lots of people forget to lock their porch doors and just lock the front and garage doors, as if a thief is going to walk down the street and just roam up the driveway and try the front door. Porch doors are the most vulnerable. The Illusionist knew that too. But he was prepared either way. He was always prepared.

He reached out a gloved hand and tried the door. It slid open easily, even easier than he had imagined. Part of him was disappointed. It was always better when it was a challenge.

He stepped across the welcome mat and entered the code to disarm the alarm.

There.

Now he had the whole house and the rest of the night to himself.

7

An oval dining room table loomed before him; beyond that, the living room sprawled back into the darkness. He paused and listened to the gentle sounds of a house speaking to him that all was calm. All was still.

The Illusionist moved quickly and quietly through the dining room and then into the kitchen, letting his eyes adjust to the thick darkness. The vague outlines of the living room furniture slowly materialized to his right. On his left, a large dark opening told him the hallway was there, but he already knew that. After all, he'd memorized the blueprints for the home.

He could hear the sounds of a hamster running on a squeaky wheel in a nearby room. Brenda's room. She was eight years old and had just started third grade at St. Catherine's Catholic School out on Sweeten Creek Road. Her teacher's name was Andrea Brokema, but the students all called her Miss Andi.

The Illusionist entered the hallway and approached Brenda's bedroom. She would be sleeping with Wally, the stuffed walrus she'd received on her fourth birthday.

He stood in her doorway for a moment and watched her sleep in the pool of pale light that found its way through the window. Wally was lying beside her bed.

Hmm. Must have fallen out of her arms.

The Illusionist eased into her room as silent as a dream, picked up the walrus, and slid it gently into the arms of the sleeping girl. He had to lift her left wrist slightly to do it. She squeezed the stuffed animal and rolled over onto her side. The Illusionist smiled and backed out of her room.

There. That's better, Brenda. Much better.

A few steps ahead, the night-light in Jacob's room spilled a green glow into the hallway. *How thoughtful of you*, thought the Illusionist. *Providing me just enough light to see.*

A fifth grader, Jacob liked Spider-Man video games, was good at math, and had been the highest scorer in his soccer league last spring. He played for Andy's Sub Shop. The Illusionist knew everything.

He knew about their mother too.

Because, really, that's why he was here. Not for the kids. For her.

Nobody would notice a missing prostitute. He knew that much already. He'd found that out years ago, as a matter of fact. But a soccer mom who serves on the PTA would be all over the news. Especially one as good-looking as Alice. Just like he wanted. The news media loves a missing beauty. Especially a white woman. They'd be running her story for weeks.

With the help of the night-light in Jacob's room, the Illusionist could see the pictures on the hallway wall . . . a picture of Brenda dressed up like a giant carrot for her school play . . . one of her standing on the beach with a pink shovel in her hand . . . the whole family sitting in a photography studio . . . Jacob holding a largemouth bass beside a lakeside cabin with Garrett next to him.

That picture made him sick.

Garrett.

The man who'd left Alice for that sleazy little tramp six months ago, and then kept showing up again to threaten her and the kids whenever he was drunk. But he didn't stop with the threats. One night he nearly broke Alice's jaw.

Garrett.

The man who'd left a note on his building contractor's desk

last month telling the boss that he was through working for such a lowlife and was leaving to find work where he could be appreciated, somewhere warmer, in Florida. It wasn't uncommon for people who worked construction to move farther south as winter rolled in, so of course his boss wouldn't have been too surprised. He was probably just glad he didn't have to pay that loser Garrett McMichaelson for the last two weeks of work.

Of course, the handwriting wasn't Garrett's.

But the Boss Man wouldn't have noticed that.

Garrett, Garrett, Garrett.

Yet despite how the picture disturbed the Illusionist, it also made him smile slightly. Garrett wouldn't be bothering Alice anymore. He wouldn't be bursting into the house drunk, or pushing her down the stairs, or punching her in the face ever again. No, he wouldn't be bothering anyone anymore. A man who would treat a woman like that didn't deserve to exist. A man that vile didn't deserve to be buried alive deep in the Appalachian Mountains. He didn't deserve a death that gentle.

But the Illusionist was a compassionate man.

It was, perhaps, his only flaw.

He had made it to the end of the hallway now, and of course, there on the left, was her room. Alice's room. The door was shut.

Walking lightly across the amber carpet that lined the hallway, the Illusionist stopped just outside her door. He reached into his pocket and pulled out the plastic bag he would need for the job.

His heart was beating faster now. It was always this way. *Relax. Don't get too excited.*

But it was exciting. It was always exciting!

Beyond the door he could hear the soft rhythmic breathing of Alice McMichaelson, the thirty-one-year-old redheaded receptionist at the Law Offices of Brannan & Seeley. That's where they'd first met. He could remember everything about that day. She was wearing a yellow dress the color of sweet lemonade. And that's what he'd thought of when he first met her—sipping iced lemonade together beneath a spreading tree. Tall cool glasses. Warm afternoon sun. Smelling the summer. Looking into her bright laughing eyes. As they spoke that day, he'd caught the scent of her perfume as it drifted across the counter. And as he inhaled her fragrance it had become a way for him to touch her all throughout their conversation without her knowledge.

It had been exquisite.

He eased the door open and stepped into Alice's room.

Through the faint glow of the streetlight outside the window, he could see her lying on her side, her lush red hair splayed all around her head. In the dim light, her hair took on a darker color, almost the color of dried blood. How odd that he would think of that now, how strange that he would think of blood at a time like this.

He wondered what she was wearing beneath the thin sheet draped so lightly across the curves of her body. He knew she liked to order from Victoria's Secret. Her customer number was N672-9843-G. He knew all of these things from sorting through her garbage. She always left it out the night before it was supposed to be picked up. How fortunate for him.

He wondered what she would look like. Right now. All he had to do was pull back the covers. All he had to do was cover her mouth with one hand and grip her neck with the other. He could do that right now. Right here.

His heart began racing. Everything could happen tonight, in this moment. Just like he'd imagined it happening so many times.

Her breathing never changed. It was so soft and rhythmic. Like music to his ears.

Oh how he wanted to touch her! But he didn't go toward her. He didn't even move. He was in control. Always in control. And he wasn't allowed to touch her tonight. He was here for something else.

I'll be seeing you, Alice, he thought. *I'll be seeing you soon.*

The Illusionist picked up the thing he'd come for, took one last look at Alice McMichaelson, and slipped down the hallway. He heard the hamster squeaking in its cage before he tapped the code into the security system and left the house. Then he eased back into the shadows of the sleepy neighborhood. No one noticed him. No one would ever know he was here. No one would suspect anything.

Because he was one step ahead of the world.

Watch and be amazed!

8

Agent Jiang drove up to the hotel entrance, and I stepped out of the lobby to meet her. Ralph had told me he was going to send someone to pick me up. Great choice.

"Good morning, Dr. Bowers," she said as I slid into the passenger seat beside her.

"Just call me Pat. I've never gotten used to the doctor part anyway."

"Hmm. I would have thought you'd be proud of that." She pulled out of the parking lot and merged into traffic. "First FBI agent in history to earn a PhD in Environmental Criminology."

"So they say. I still prefer Pat."

"OK, then, Pat. Sleep all right?"

"Actually, no," I said. "Not so good."

Why do you do that? Why can't you just carry on a normal conversation like everyone else? Years of taking college classes at night and over the Internet while serving on the force had helped me earn a handful of degrees at a young age while simultaneously working in the field, but hadn't helped so much with my people skills.

She glanced over at me. "You're always honest, aren't you Dr. . . . um, Pat?"

"I suppose so. At least I try to be."

"So, let me guess," she continued. "You're in the business of uncovering the truth. It's tough enough the way it is. You'd hate to make your job even harder by hiding yourself. You don't wear masks, because you know how hard it is peeling them off other people. If you let people see you clearly, maybe they'll take off their masks for you and make your job a little easier."

I blinked. "Yeah. I guess so."

She smiled.

Oh.

"So, Ralph's new partner is a profiler," I said. "I better watch what I say."

She pursed her lips. "Ralph told me about your history with profilers. Don't worry; I won't hold it against you. I'm not petty." She gestured to a cup of coffee in the passenger-side cup holder. "For you."

"Thanks." I might have meant for the coffee or for the truce, I didn't clarify. I grabbed the cup and sniffed at the aroma drifting from the slit in the lid. Nice. Kenyan. I smelled it again. Probably from the Nyeri Highlands. I took a sip. Yes, definitely a SL28 cultivar from the volcanic slopes of the Kingongo Ridge. And somehow she'd guessed right—cream and honey, no sugar. Oh, I could get used to this.

"You chose wisely," I said.

"Mountain Java Roasters. It's in Asheville," she replied. "Ralph said you're picky about your coffee."

"Ralph told you a lot."

"Ralph told me enough."

She was quiet then, and I wished I could think of something else to say to fill the space growing between us, but nothing came to mind.

We drove past a huge stone hotel nestled up against the mountains, and she said, "That's the Stratford Hotel. Built entirely out of rocks from that mountain behind it. Six-hundred-and-fifty rooms. Four-and-a-half-foot-thick walls. Seven presidents have stayed there, lots of movie stars. Huge enclosed atrium with hanging gardens, pools, fountains. Even its own indoor whitewater river. Each of the main fireplaces can hold sixteen-foot-long logs."

"And you know all this . . . how?"

"I took the trolley tour around town my second day here," she said.

I smiled. "Gotcha." The Stratford Hotel looked like a fortress. A world-class golf course lay at its base.

"And by the way, if I call you Pat, you need to call me Lien-hua."

"Sounds good to me."

Beyond that, Lien-hua didn't push the small talk. Whether it was intuition or just politeness, I couldn't tell. Either way I was thankful. It gave me a chance to think through my agenda for the day. I hoped to grab some files at the federal building and then spend the rest of the day visiting the sites of the crimes in this series. Over the years I've found that location and timing of a crime are two of the most important and overlooked aspects of an investigation. Site visits are vital to crime reconstruction.

We pulled to a stop in the parking lot of the federal building, and she turned to me. "It was Mindy," she said evenly, still gripping the steering wheel with both hands, the muscles in her slim arms growing tight and tense. "The girl on the mountain. Mindy Travelca. We confirmed it last night. She was nineteen."

I nodded slowly. At least now I knew what to call her. At least now she had a name.

As I followed Lien-hua into the federal building I thought of Mindy's father being interviewed on TV, the tears wavering in his eyes. And the only thing I could think of to be thankful for was that I didn't have to be the one to tell him the news.

9

Alice McMichaelson groaned, rolled over, and looked at the clock.

6:27.

Good. She still had another hour to sleep before—

Wait a minute. She blinked at the clock. Looked again.

8:27.

What? That can't be right.

She rubbed her eyes, snatched her glasses off the end table beside the bed, and slid them on.

8:27.

Blinked.

8:28.

Oh no. Not today.

"Jacob," she yelled. "We're late. Get up. Brenda!"

"I'm up, Mom!" Brenda's perky voice sang from the kitchen. "I've been up like forever."

"Well, you could have woken me up too!" Only after saying it did she realize how ridiculous it sounded, having your eight-year-old daughter wake you up for work.

Alice jumped out of bed and shook her head. She'd never been great at getting up in the morning anyway, and since Garrett had left her to be with that other woman it had only gotten worse. Trouble sleeping. Bad dreams. And now waking up late for her second day on the job at the bank. Not good.

The law office thing just hadn't been going anywhere. The pay at the bank was better and so were the hours. She could spend more time with the kids. Also, she'd started taking business classes, and the bank gave her Mondays off to go back to school—but none of that would matter now if she showed up late and lost her job.

Alice decided to go without a shower, tossed off her nightgown, and yanked open her underwear drawer. "Jacob, are you up?"

"Yeah," came the sleepy reply from across the hall.

"You don't sound like it."

The creak of his bed.

"I'm up."

Clinking of a spoon and a cereal bowl from the kitchen. "Are we gonna be late for school, Mom?" Brenda had her mouth full.

"I'll write you a note."

"Oh," said Brenda. "OK. I don't want to miss library time."

Alice pulled on some stockings. "Are you getting dressed, Jacob?"

"Yeah, Mom! I'm up, OK?"

"OK, OK."

Alice flew to the closet, grabbed a dress, slipped it on. *Shoes. Which shoes? It doesn't matter. Just hurry. Anything. Black. No. Brown pumps. OK.*

She stepped into the bathroom, held a washcloth under the faucet, rubbed it across her face, smeared on some lipstick. "Get your backpacks, kids. We need to go."

Then back to the dresser. *Hair is a mess. A mess! OK, where is it?* She scanned the dresser. *Where is that brush?*

"Brenda, did you take my hairbrush?"

"No, Mom."

"You sure?"

"Yeah."

Alice shoved her jewelry box aside, opened up the top drawer to see if she'd tossed it in there, scanned the floor. Nothing.

8:39.

Err. "We need to get going, Jacob," she called, but really she was yelling at herself. She glanced into the hallway. Brenda had wandered down the hall and was standing at attention with her pink backpack on. She'd probably been up since six. Jacob, on the other hand, would sleep until noon if he could get away with it.

Alice stomped into the bathroom. She had to brush her hair. Counter. Shelves. No brush. "Are you ready, Jake?"

"I didn't get any breakfast."

"Grab a granola bar or something. We need to get going. Does everybody have their homework?"

"What about our lunches?" asked Brenda.

Lunches!

"I'll, um—" Alice grabbed her purse, pulled out a few bills. Passed them around. "Here. Buy a hot lunch today."

Jake eyed the money. "Can I get pizza?"

"Whatever." Alice scooted into Brenda's room and used her daughter's brush to calm down her hair. It still didn't look good, but it would have to do. She'd find her brush later, no big deal.

She shooed the kids toward the door, grabbed the car keys, and herded everyone into the car, hoping she could make it to her desk before anyone noticed she was late.

———————————■———————————

The main FBI field office for North Carolina is located in Charlotte. Normally that's where Ralph would have set up his base of operations, but in this case, because of the proximity of the crimes, he'd set up shop here at the satellite office in Asheville.

Even in the days when I used to live in the area and work as a wilderness guide, Asheville reminded me a little of Boulder, Colorado—only on a smaller scale and flavored with the music and culture of Appalachia. Just like Boulder, there's an artsy downtown district complete with exotic import shops, dance studios and arts centers, roaming bohemian hippies, indoor rock-climbing gyms, quaint coffee shops selling organic blends, and vegetarian restaurants staffed by women who don't believe in shaving any part of their bodies. And out along the streets you'll find scores of weathered

Jeeps and Land Rovers topped off with kayaks, skis, or mountain bikes depending on the season.

But here in Asheville you also find bearded musicians playing mountain dulcimers, banjos, and fiddles on the street corners at twilight, a large population of retirees, and high-steepled brick churches perched on nearly every street corner. Over the last twenty years the town has become a cultural melting pot where both ends of the spectrum—the religious fundamentalists and the social progressives—meet. Makes for an interesting mix at times.

"Asheville has more art galleries per capita than any other city in North America," Lien-hua told me as we passed through the security checkpoint of the Veach-Baley Federal Complex. "And one of the top independent bookstores in the world."

Apparently, it had been a very informative trolley tour.

Ralph had taken over a conference room just down the hall from the senator's office on the first floor. Lien-hua and I walked in, and I looked around.

I saw that Ralph had brought in half a dozen computers, communication stations, bulletin boards, and dry erase boards. I felt right at home.

The pictures of the previous five victims were posted neatly on the wall. These weren't the crime scene photos, these were the smiling, posed pictures where each victim looks airbrushed and radiant and full of life. Yearbook photos, family vacations, things like that. These are the pictures we use with the media. And thankfully these are the pictures people end up remembering. Rather than the ones etched in my mind. The ones I can't seem to forget.

I placed my computer bag on an empty desk and stared at the photos of the dead girls.

Victim number one, Patty Henderson, twenty-three, smiled slyly out of the corner of her mouth. She was blonde, blue-eyed, had perfect teeth, and looked like she was still in her teens.

Victim number two, Jamie McNaab, eighteen, was sitting on a

paint-splattered wooden stool and holding a paintbrush. Jamie had a playful, girlish face and coy smile. A can of paint lay on the floor next to her. You could tell she was in a studio. The photographer had probably taken pictures of hundreds of smiling teenage girls posing beside those cans of paint.

Make sure we check on this photographer. There might be some kind of link through the studio. Maybe someone who works there or the place that processed the film or something.

Alexis Crawford, twenty, was next. She had stringy brown hair and was pretty in a dainty sort of way, but had a broken, lonely-looking smile as if life had not been easy on her. Which, in the end, it hadn't been.

While I was looking at the pictures, Agent Brent Tucker walked over, pinned up a photo of Mindy Travelca, and then returned to his desk without saying a word.

In her picture, Mindy was smiling just like the others.

Ralph appeared and greeted me with a nod.

"When was Reinita's picture taken?" I asked, looking back at the photos. Reinita Lawson, nineteen, was the fourth victim and the only African-American in the group. She had fine, light chocolate-colored skin and eyes brimming with dreams.

Ralph flipped open a manila file folder. "The day before she was abducted. She'd just posted it on her MySpace page. Why?"

In her picture she was flirting with the camera, her left hand leaning up against her cheek, delicately, invitingly. Her smile held a hint of seduction. She was strikingly beautiful, but something wasn't right. I stared at the picture. I traced her smile, her eyes, her hand. Leaned close. "The day before? Are you sure?" I asked.

Ralph glanced at the file again. "Yeah. What are you thinking?"

"She doesn't have an engagement ring on," I said.

"What?"

"In the crime scene photos you sent me she's wearing an engagement ring."

He flipped through a stack of papers in a manila folder. "Hmm," he said. "She might not have been wearing it that day."

"You get engaged, you show off the ring to everyone." I spoke my thoughts aloud. "Of course, it's possible she got engaged between having the picture taken and getting abducted. But that's unlikely if she took it the day before."

He set down the folder. "So what are you saying? You think the killer might have left it as some kind of symbol? Is he trying to tell us he's engaged to them? Marrying them in some sick, twisted sense?"

"Maybe. I don't know." I stared at the photo for a long moment. "Check it out for me, though, would you? Find out if she's really engaged to anyone. If so, I wanna meet the guy."

"You got it."

Suddenly I realized I was giving orders. "Um, please," I said. Officially, I'd been brought in as a consultant, but Ralph and I had worked so many times together at the Bureau that I just seemed to pick up right where we left off.

He slapped me on the shoulder. Almost knocked me over. "Don't worry, you're cool. Let's just catch this sicko."

Ralph went to make a few phone calls and I looked at the last picture. Bethanie Dixon, twenty-two, was the only other victim besides Patty to be found indoors. She was also the one found the farthest away, in Athens, Georgia. The pawn and the yellow ribbon linked her to our killer, even though the distance didn't seem quite right.

I was jarred from my thoughts by someone calling my name. "Dr. Bowers."

Something about that voice.

No, it couldn't be her.

I turned.

It was.

Special Agent Margaret Wellington.

And my day had been going so well too.

54

10

"Margaret," I said. I knew she would correct me.

"I'd prefer you call me Special Agent in Charge Wellington."

I extended my hand. "Sorry. I guess I forgot."

She flipped back a snatch of her impossibly straight rodent-colored hair and glared at me. I'd forgotten how narrow her lips were, how straight her teeth. Instead of shaking my hand she slid her hands to her hips. "No, Dr. Bowers. You didn't forget."

Well, OK. That was true. I did remember how much she hated being called Margaret, but I'd forgotten that she was stationed here in North Carolina. Slipped my mind entirely. Obviously it had, or I wouldn't have accepted Ralph's invitation to consult on the case. I retrieved my hand. She wasn't going to shake it anyway.

Margaret Wellington had a habit of breathing in sharply through her nose, which made it seem like she was constantly disgusted with you. Which, maybe, she was. "It's been, what, Dr. Bowers? Four years?"

"Has it been that long?" I said. "Hardly seems like it."

She blinked. "Yes. Four years." She cocked her head slightly. "So. How have you been?"

"Busy." It was true enough.

"I heard your wife died," she said. I could feel my anger rising. She continued, her voice even and emotionless. "Very tragic. And then they transferred you to Denver and stuck you behind a desk. Must have been hard."

"I volunteered for the position in Colorado," I said coolly. The National Law Enforcement and Corrections Technology Center in

55

Denver housed the most advanced crime-mapping program in the world. I'd been helping integrate the research from the National Institute for Justice with that of the FBI. "It's important work and this way Tessa could be closer to my parents."

"Yes of course." Finally she backed up a little and even let the hint of a smile dance across her lips. "Well, it looks like I'll be moving back to Quantico again as soon as this case is wrapped up. They'd like me to teach at the Academy again."

"Congratulations. I know how important that is to you."

"Yes." Her voice had turned to chalk. "You do."

I held my tongue. Better to let it be at that.

"See you in the briefing room," she said at last and stalked off to her glass-enclosed office in the corner of the room.

The air around me seemed to breathe a sigh of relief. I saw Lien-hua glance up from her desk, a question mark on her face. "What was that all about?"

"It's complicated," I said. "Ralph, why didn't you tell me she was here?"

He grinned. "Must have slipped my mind."

"Yeah, well, you're going to owe me big-time for this."

"What do you mean complicated?" asked Lien-hua.

I sighed. "We were both working at the Bureau. I was teaching environmental criminology, and she was assigned to counterter-rorism—"

"Wait a minute," Lien-hua said. "I thought that before you moved to Denver you lived in New York City?"

"I did. I'd fly in to teach a couple weeks every month. Anyway, she'd been eyeing the assistant director's position for quite a while and was on the fast track toward getting it when—"

"Some evidence was lost," Ralph said. "There were a lot of accusations, and Pat here noticed some things that internal affairs was very interested in."

I sat down at the desk beside Lien-hua. "Like I said, it gets complicated. Anyway, there was a disciplinary hearing. I had to testify, and she ended up getting transferred here, to the satellite office, to push papers around."

"She's blamed Pat ever since," Ralph added. "And brown-nosed everyone she can to get reinstated at Quantico. Needless to say, she wasn't too happy to have any of us come in on this case, but on the other hand, she wants it all wrapped up as soon as possible because it doesn't look good to have a serial killer running around loose in your neck of the woods when you're trying to impress the director."

I turned back to Ralph. "Wait a minute, what did she mean by that 'see you in the briefing room' comment?"

"Oh yeah. Margaret wants you to brief the team on your investigative techniques."

"When?"

He looked at his watch. "Half an hour."

"What? No way. I haven't visited the crime scenes yet. She knows that. It's too early for any kind of preliminary report—"

"Just walk us through the process, Pat. You know, all that geographical time and space mumbo jumbo."

"I can't, Ralph. I haven't even—by the way, you make my work sound so intriguing and scientific—"

"Thank you."

"I need two days at least."

"We can give you till noon—"

"There's no way I could be ready by—"

"Two o'clock, then?"

"Two o'clock!"

"Two o'clock it is," said Ralph triumphantly. "Good man. I'll go tell Margaret."

"What? Wait a minute." I turned to Lien-hua. "What just happened there?"

"I think you're going to give a briefing at two."

"I didn't agree to that, did I?"

"I'm not sure," she said. "But I can already tell I'm going to enjoy watching you two work together."

I grabbed a handful of files off the desk and stood up. I couldn't believe it. I came in here today planning to visit the crime scenes, and now I was going to be stuck giving a briefing instead. I hate giving briefings almost as much as I hate bad coffee.

She motioned to the screen mounted on the wall. "Before you get started, c'mere for a second. There's something I wanted to show you."

"Listen, Lien-hua. I've got a lot of work to do."

"Wait. This might be helpful." She pulled up the crime-scene photos and started scrolling through them. "He abducts them, tortures them, then kills them and dumps their bodies where we can find them, right?"

"Yeah."

"Where we can find them."

"That's right."

"Most killers either leave a body indoors, at the primary crime scene, or if they move the body at all it's to obstruct the investigation. To hide evidence."

Hmm. And this from a profiler. "That's right. Good point. So why does he want them found?"

"Right. That's what I'm wondering. And one more thing I noticed. He started with blunt force to subdue Patty. Then he progressed to drugging his victims."

"Not as messy," I said, "and more reliable. Sometimes hitting someone on the head has the unfortunate result of killing them right away. Doesn't give you the chance to torture them to death."

"Well, there was some contamination in the original toxicology tests, so we didn't get the correct results in until yesterday. This wasn't in the information Ralph sent you. Look, the drugs used for Alexis and Bethanie are different from the ones used on Jamie and Reinita."

She slid the toxicology reports my way, and I picked them up. "It is a little odd that he'd alternate like that," I said. "Seems more likely he'd progress from one to the other, not switch back and forth."

"That's what I was thinking."

"Let's see what the autopsy brings back on Mindy. If she was drugged too . . ."

She scrolled to Mindy's picture. I glanced back and forth from the bulletin board to the computer screen. In the one picture Mindy looked so alive, so timeless. So enduring. And in the other, so violated, so helpless, so dead; so utterly, unchangeably dead. Life is so terribly fragile. So fleeting. So brief. It's a puzzle I can't begin to understand even after all these years. One minute you're dreaming of writing a novel, or retiring early, or vacationing in Bermuda, and the next you're a slab of cooling meat with a blocked artery or a brain aneurysm. Or a chest full of cancer.

"You OK?" It was Agent Lien-hua's voice. She was staring at me. I had no idea how long I'd been lost in thought.

"Huh?"

She pointed at my hands. I looked down. I'd curled my hands into fists and was squeezing so tightly my knuckles were turning white. I quickly relaxed my hands, flexed my fingers, shook them loose. "Yeah, yeah. Of course. I'm fine. Sorry. What were you saying?" My heart was hammering. *Stay in control. Don't get distracted here. Focus. Stay focused.*

Lien-hua was quiet for a moment and then lowered her eyes, "I know what happened, Pat. Ralph told me. I'm very sorry." It sounded like she genuinely meant it.

"About?" I hoped she didn't know.

"Christie."

Hearing her say Christie's name sent a tremor through me. I could feel the anger rising like a tide. Anger against the doctors or God or fate or destiny or whatever other cosmic forces work together to so effectively screw up our lives and rip apart our dreams. In the first few months after she died, it was just loneliness that gnawed away at me, but lately anger had been giving it a run for its money. I wasn't sure which one was better, anger or loneliness, but the anger didn't make me feel so numb. So maybe that's the one I preferred. I don't know.

"I'm so sorry," she repeated.

I couldn't believe how sensitive I still was, eight months after the fact. "Yeah," I said at last. I should've figured Ralph would have mentioned something to Lien-hua about Christie, but for some reason it still bugged me that he'd told her. "So am I."

"You OK to do this?"

"Of course I am. Yeah. This is what I do." I tried to stretch out my fingers, to shake out the filaments of rage. "So, um . . . let's see what the medical examiner says about Mindy, then we'll see if the killer keeps alternating the drugs. OK?"

"OK."

I fumbled for what else to say. "All right. I'll see you later."

"See ya."

I was still working at uncoiling my fingers when I walked away.

The first victim, Patty Henderson, lived in Spartanburg, South Carolina. She and her husband had twin four-year-old boys. At first the husband had been a suspect. Spouses, lovers, boyfriends are guilty in over half of domestic homicides. They're always suspects. One of the first objectives when investigating a murder is to clear the spouse or boyfriend, then the person who found the body.

Everything seemed to point to him. He and Patty had been having marital problems and were seeing a counselor, and then one day she was found strangled and mutilated in their bedroom. Go figure. But he'd been cleared. At least a dozen people saw him at the time of the murder at a sports bar downtown, and there was no way he could have gotten back in time to kill her. Their sons were at Patty's mom's place for the night so she'd been home alone. Her husband might have hired someone, but I doubted it. The killer had taken the time to pull the sheets up to her neck, as if he were tucking her in bed. Covering a body typically means the killer has some kind of remorse, or that he knows the victim; is close to her. A contract killer wouldn't typically do that, and he definitely wouldn't tie a yellow ribbon in her hair. But if it wasn't the husband, then who?

And then there was the white pawn on the floor of the bedroom closet. At first no one really paid attention to it. In a house crawling with kids nothing is ever put away, you get puzzle pieces, games, and toys scattered across the floor all the time. But then the husband finally noticed it. "That's weird," he'd said. "One of the kids must have brought it home from a friend's house. We don't have any chess games here."

Then a month later an elderly couple found Jamie McNaab in a parking lot just over the state line in the Smoky Mountains of Tennessee. Nothing pointed to a pattern until one of the responding officers noticed she was holding a chess piece in her left hand. That was also the first murder to draw attention to the Asheville area.

You'd think the yellow ribbon would have been enough to tie the crimes together, but that info had slipped through the cracks. VICAP's reporting procedures are a little overwhelming and time-consuming for a lot of cops, and with different people filling out the forms they're never as complete or as uniform as they should be. A lot of investigations suffer because of it.

In the case of Jamie, I couldn't help but wonder if the killer had put the pawn in her hand on purpose because the first chess piece had almost been overlooked. That was a chilling thought, because it might mean that this guy, whoever he was, saw the whole thing as a game. And he was making sure that the police knew every move he made.

Or even more chilling, he might have obtained inside information about the investigation.

Alexis had been found at Grayson Highlands State Park just over the border in Virginia. And Reinita Lawson, in the Nantahala National Forest in the far west corner of North Carolina.

All morning I worked furiously at sorting and sifting the geographic information, comparing it with population distribution data from western North Carolina, downloading cell phone records, inputting data into my computer, gathering all the information that would help me see the overall movement patterns of the offender and the victims.

I skipped lunch, and before I knew it Margaret was standing beside me, tapping her fingers on my desk. "I'm so anxious to hear your take on this case," she said. She wasn't a very good liar. "Are you ready to brief the team?"

"Yeah, I've been looking forward to it."

I'm not a very good liar either.

I gathered my notes and stepped past her toward the briefing room. All the way there I could hear the staccato click of her heels tracking right behind me.

11

Aaron Jeffrey Kincaid did not think of himself as a violent man.

And, truthfully, if you asked the people who knew him best, they wouldn't have described him as violent in any way. *Thoughtful*, perhaps, *quiet*, maybe, *reflective, caring*, maybe even *loving*.

Yes, they might have even used the word *loving* to describe Aaron, but not *violent*.

Because really, it was love that had given him the courage to seal his two friends inside the room fifteen hours ago. His love for his family. His Father. His destiny.

In truth, he was a focused man. A passionate man. Those were good words to describe him. Focused and passionate. And loving.

Less than thirty-six hours.

That's how much time Rebekah and Caleb had left.

Even now as he went to check on them, Rebekah held her hand up to the window, and Aaron placed his hand across the glass from hers, as if they were touching. She didn't look angry. More at peace than anything. He nodded to her.

"Our love will unite us forever," she mouthed to him. And he mouthed the words back to her as if she were his daughter and they were whispering bedtime prayers together.

———■———

She and Caleb had been even easier to persuade than Jessie Rembrandt had been back in 1985.

It had taken him years of searching and waiting and dreaming. Now at last the time had come.

Last year, finally, he'd found the person he'd been searching for all this time, and the plan had been set in motion.

True, it would have been ideal to have everything happen next month, on the 18th, rather than now, in October. That would have been perfect. But only terrorists and madmen assign more significance to dates than to deeds. And Aaron was neither of those. He was simply a focused, dedicated man in love with his family, fulfilling his ultimate destiny.

In a way it was a shame that Rebekah and Caleb would miss the events on Monday. But really, there was no other way about it. What had to be done had to be done.

He took his hand away from the glass and walked outside. The autumn wind felt cool but also fresh and inviting, promising a change in the seasons.

It made him think of all the wonderful things to come.

12

This is why I hate briefings. Usually I'm supposed to summarize all my years of research in environmental criminology and my experience as a detective and FBI agent in twenty minutes. And of course, I'm usually the only person in the room who believes my investigative approach will actually work.

That's the kicker.

Ralph was standing in the corner tapping away at something when I entered the tiny, cramped conference room. "What are you doing?" I asked him. He tried to shove the thing in his pocket, but I saw what it was. "A PlayStation Portable 3?"

He looked slightly embarrassed and shy, which is not easy for someone who can bench-press a truck. "Don't tell anyone. I'm trying to get good enough to beat my son."

"Tony is ten, right?"

Ralph nodded. "I can still beat him at football, hoops, wrestling—"

I stared at Ralph's size. "You wrestle Tony?"

"Yeah, of course," he said. "Why?"

Well, I thought, *you weigh almost three hundred pounds.*

Ralph gave a proud papa smile. "He's a stout boy."

"Oh." I wondered just how much Tony had grown in the last few months.

"Anyway, he's really good at these things, so I'm practicing. Trying to get good enough to beat him at Sorcerer's Realm IV. Don't tell anyone."

"I promise."

He leaned toward me. "I mean it." I could tell he did.

"Gotcha."

It took me a few minutes to connect my computer to the room's overhead projection system, and when I finally looked up, I noticed nearly every seat had been taken. In addition to Agents Hawkins, Jiang, Tucker, and Wellington, I saw Sheriff Wallace and half a dozen other agents and police officers I hadn't met yet.

All at once Margaret stood up, straightened the front of her skirt, and cleared her throat. "I know we all have plenty to do, so let's get started." I glanced at the clock on the wall. Yup, 1:59 exactly.

The chatter and small talk quieted down. Dante Wallace and Ralph took their seats. Brent Tucker sat beside Margaret, and I slid into the chair next to Lien-hua even though I knew I'd be standing up again in just a moment.

Margaret was speaking overly politely. "Dr. Patrick Bowers has been kind enough to join us and offer his . . . unique perspective on this case. I thought it might be prudent if he would outline some of the principles behind his . . . unorthodox investigative approach." Then she stretched her lips into a tight, patronizing smile and motioned toward me. "Dr. Bowers?"

Wow. What an introduction.

I stood and nodded. "Yes, thank you, Margaret." Out of the corner of my eye, I could see Lien-hua doodling in her notebook, smiling.

"First of all," I said, "from what I've seen so far, your work on this case has been thorough, professional, and incisive. So, good work." Stoic nods all around. They knew as well as I did that without a conviction or even a primary suspect, all the praise and backslapping in the world was meaningless.

I tapped my computer's credit-card-sized remote control, and a three-dimensional map appeared on the projection screen.

"My specialty, as Agent Wellington alluded to, is a bit unique. I've worked both in local law enforcement as a detective in Milwaukee, and for the last nine years for the FBI. Mostly I'm interested in where and when the crime occurred and the significance that the crime's timing and location have in the life of the offender, or in our case, the killer."

"Environmental Criminology," Agent Tucker announced. "Which merges the fields of environmental psychology with geospatial investigation."

"Right . . ." I said. "So rather than focus simply on the forensic evidence or the specific pathology of the offender, I'm looking at the relationship the offender has to his victim and his environment. It may seem self-evident, but every crime occurs at a specific time in a specific place."

Sometimes when I'm explaining this stuff I get strange looks, and already the same thing was happening. A few snickers and sideways glances—mostly from the local police officers. I glanced at Margaret. She was staring at me with granite eyes. Agent Tucker nodded and scribbled some notes on a legal pad.

"I know. It seems simplistic, but why that time? Why that place? Why that victim? Locations have use patterns. If we study the sites associated with each crime and the time of day the crimes occurred, it gives us a glimpse into the world of the offender. People typically carry out their routine activities in the most convenient locations. We all do. It's no different for killers. Just like everyone else, serial offenders tend to move in certain repetitive patterns and directions from their place of residence."

I glanced across the room to see how I was doing.

Some of the team members had heard this type of thing before. Most large law enforcement agencies these days have at least one strategic crime analyst, and nearly all of them use some form of crime mapping or apply the principles of environmental psychology to their investigations—even if they don't call the techniques by those names.

Most of the people in the room looked bored.

Well, that didn't take long, and you still have fifteen minutes to go.

"Every murder has at least four scenes," I said. "The place of the initial encounter between the offender and the victim, the site of the attack or abduction, the location of the murder, and the final placement of the body."

I flipped to an active screen that showed a satellite view of North Carolina, and then I used the cursor to zoom in on the western part of the state. As I moved the cursor, the images tipped horizontally, and the cursor glided like a tiny plane over the three-dimensional mountainous landscape.

I heard someone behind me. "It's like Google Earth—on steroids." Chuckles rolled around the room.

"Yeah," I said, "and lots of them. This is one of the most powerfully integrated geographic information systems in the world. We call it F.A.L.C.O.N."

"What's that stand for?" someone asked.

I smiled and glanced at his name tag. "I don't know, Officer Stilton. We haven't come up with that part yet, just the acronym. That's the way government works." I got a couple grunts of acknowledgment for that. Not many, but it softened the mood in the room. "It's a cooperative venture between the NSA and the FBI—with a little help from our friends at NASA and a certain animation company. I'm not supposed to tell you the name yet, though, not until the software is released."

I heard Ralph's voice. "Animation company?"

"We needed someone who actually knew what they were doing to help us with the graphics. They were happy to get a juicy government contract, and we were happy to get the best computer graphics minds in the world. Anyway, using this software, we can pinpoint any place on the earth's surface down to half a centimeter or so. The team is still working on ways to see through cloud cover—don't have that quite nailed down yet, but it's coming. This is just the beta version. We're hoping to have the prototype available to law enforcement agencies worldwide within the next two years."

One of the officers I didn't know spoke up. "Is that a live satellite feed?"

"Not quite," I said. "Four-minute delay."

I tapped the remote control, and a three-dimensional map appeared on the projection screen behind me. As I clicked on the screen, new layers overlaid on top of the previous ones, each layer with another array of circles, diamonds, or triangles. "This first map shows where we found each of the bodies," I explained. "The next one, here"—I clicked the screen again and the diamonds appeared—"has the residencies of the victims. If we know the abduction sites, I've made those appear as ovals." Once again I clicked, and another layer appeared. "And when the murder site has been identified, you'll see those in yellow diamonds."

By now the screen looked a little overwhelming.

"Now, look when I overlay the roads, emphasizing the routes that provide the quickest and most convenient getaway and then compare that to the distribution of homes in the residential areas we're looking at . . ." A series of glowing lines threaded together, connecting the clutter of symbols and figures, making sense of them, bringing order. "Then, if we impose what we know about the victims' life patterns and travel routes at the time they were abducted—"

"How do we know those?" Margaret asked.

"Cell phone companies can track the location of each call placed and received through global positioning technology," I said. "Most new cars also have GPS systems, including Mindy's Corolla. I downloaded the routes Mindy traveled in her car as well as the time, duration, and location of her phone calls over the last couple of days before her murder. I found something interesting."

"What's that?" Agent Tucker asked.

"Based on what we know about the travel patterns of the other victims, you can see that they intersect in four distinct areas: out near the Stratford Hotel, the park next to Mission Memorial Hospital, the downtown district, and over near the university. It's very possible our killer is trolling those locations looking for his prey."

I clicked the screen again, and this time the screen had several pulsing, red, wedge-shaped regions. "We can see that the most likely locations of the initial encounter or abductions are here, here, and here." I used a laser pointer to draw attention to the pulsating areas of the map. "By taking into consideration everything we know about the crime—the observable offender patterns, urban zoning, population distribution, topographic features, traffic flow, weather conditions at the time of the crime—we can extrapolate the anchor point—"

Oh, great word, Pat. That'll really impress them.

"The what?" It was Sheriff Wallace.

"Extrapolate. It means to—"

"No, the 'anchor point' part."

"Oh," I said. "Anchor point, right. That's the offender's home base. Might be his house or maybe a girlfriend's or a relative's place. Maybe where he works. As long as his base is stable, we can use the principles of geographic profiling to pinpoint its most likely location."

I took a drink of water.

Ten minutes and you're out of here.

"Offenders tend not to commit crimes too close to their home base, or too far away from it. Once we've defined his hunting area and drawn a line connecting the two farthest crime scenes, we create the radius of a circle." I did this on the screen with the laser pointer. "Within this circle here"—I clicked on the screen, and a blue-tinged circle appeared near the center of the larger circle—"there's about a 50 percent chance our offender has his anchor point."

"Just like pins on a bulletin board." The officer who said it made sure he spoke loud enough for everyone to hear.

I'd heard all this before, but still I felt my temperature rising. "Yes, the principle is the same. But we're not just looking at crime distribution here; instead we're taking into account sequence, distribution, origination, and timing. The order of the crimes is significant. The first crime in a series often occurs closest to the killer's anchor point. Then he moves out as his hunting grounds get overrun with investigators. However, the body dump sites tend to move closer toward his anchor point as he gets more confident with each crime that he's able to commit without getting caught. So timing and location are significant. Also, places carry meanings for people. We all view the world, our surroundings, through the lens of our personal experiences and perceptions. If I can figure out what the locations of this series of crimes mean to the offender, it'll help me figure out what type of person we're looking for. Instead of asking 'Why did he do it?' I ask 'Why did he do it *here*?' For example . . ."

I pulled up a photo of Jamie McNaab. "Jamie was found beside a parking lot. Now look back behind her, just to the right, there"—I pointed with the laser pointer—"See? There's a sign that reads 'No Loitering.' It's subtle but symbolic." I flipped to a picture of the crime scene of Reinita Lawson. "Reinita was found on a trail leading to Tombstone Caverns—also symbolic. He's taunting us."

"How come no one noticed that before?" Sheriff Wallace asked.

Before I could answer Agent Tucker said, "No one was looking."

I wished he'd stop doing that.

"So, what about the motive?" asked Lien-hua, who had stopped doodling and was looking at me with keen interest and perhaps a hint of antagonism.

"I leave motives to the profilers." I smiled.

She didn't.

"And that means . . . ?" She let her voice trail off and then added, "What, exactly?"

71

I figured someone would ask these questions, but why did it have to be her?

"Well, instead of probing into his mind to try and guess what the guy is thinking, I'm trying to study his life to find where he's living. I think too many investigations get sidetracked by trying to uncover the motive—"

"Excuse me, Dr. Bowers." She set down her pen. "Did you just say *sidetracked* by looking for motive?"

I slid the remote control into my pocket. "Yes, Agent Jiang, I did. Jurors love motives. So do people who read mystery novels and thrillers. Without a motive we feel cheated. The plot needs to make sense. We're addicted to explanations. But in the real world, some things don't have an easy explanation. Motives are never clear, never distinct, never exact."

"What are you talking about?" It was Sheriff Wallace this time. "Without motive, why would we do anything?"

OK. I wasn't exactly sure where my briefing had started to get away from me, but this wasn't in my outline.

"I'm not saying people aren't motivated to do things," I said, "just that 'motive' isn't the silver bullet it's so often made out to be in criminal investigations." I looked around. I got the feeling that with every word I said I was only digging myself in deeper. But I plowed forward anyway, trying not to sound like I was picking a fight. "Why do you get up and go to work each day, Agent Jiang? To make a living? Maybe obligation? Ambition? Passion? To prove yourself?"

"To pick up men?" Tucker interjected. A few people laughed. He said it good-naturedly, and I got the feeling he was trying to help me save face, but Lien-hua just glared at him. I wished he'd just shut up.

"To catch the bad guys," she announced. Her overly simplistic answer was drenched in sarcasm.

"Yes, good. But also to make a living, to pay the bills, to do something you're good at . . . right?"

"Your point is?"

C'mon, man. It's your first full day in town. Don't go making enemies already.

"My point is, everything we do is a tangle of motives, dreams, regrets, shame, hope, desire—all overlapping and competing with each other, vying for our attention, our lives. As soon as we try to force a crime into a neat little package called 'revenge' or 'lust' or 'anger' or 'greed,' we miss the subtle realities of life and tend to overlook the social context of the crime."

Lien-hua shook her head. She wasn't convinced. "But without showing a clear motive, you can almost never get a conviction."

I just wanted to finish this thing up and head out to visit some of the crime sites. I felt anger awakening inside me. *Keep still. Keep still.*

"Yes, that's true," I said slowly. "Showing motive is helpful for getting a conviction, but to show one motive is to ignore the others. Life is never that simple."

"But don't you want to get a conviction?" she said.

"My job isn't to convict them, it's to help you find them. It might make jurors feel better and readers feel more satisfied to name a motive, but I'm not trying a case or writing a novel. Most of the time people don't even understand the things *they* do, let alone what *other people* do. And sometimes things just happen without any apparent reason at all. Life doesn't always make sense." *Yeah. People you love get cancer and die. Families fall apart. You lose your direction, your focus, your clarity. Life spins out of control. No rhyme. No reason. No sense at all . . .*

The room was quiet. Everyone was staring at me. For a moment I wondered if I'd spoken my thoughts aloud, but then I realized I must have caught myself just in time. "When it comes to crime," I said at last, "there may be such a thing as a primary motive, but there's not such a thing as a singular motive."

Wallace again. "So if you don't look for motives, what do you look for?"

Steven James

"Patterns. Habits. Choices. Understanding the intersection of this place and this time and this victim with the life of the offender."

"Excuse me, Dr. Bowers." Ah, yes. I should have known Margaret would join the fun sooner or later. "For centuries investigative work has focused on motive, means, and opportunity. You're telling us we've done it wrong all these years?"

I wonder how long she's been waiting to ask that question.

"Of course not, Agent Wellington. An offender can't commit a crime without the opportunity to do it or the means to carry it out. But what led up to the opportunity? Why did he have those means available at that specific time? That's what I'm looking for. I'm not trying to get into the mind of the killer, I'm trying to get into his shoes."

"Dr. Bowers," Margaret said, breathing through her nose. She took a slow and deliberate look at her watch. "I have a press conference in less than twenty minutes. Do you have anything more . . . concrete to add to this investigation?"

I wished I had something to throw at her. A rottweiler came to mind.

"Actually, I do. I was just getting to that. Let me show you how all this is going to help us catch this killer."

13

"Here"—I pressed a button and illuminated two regions of the map—"are the optimal search areas, the most likely anchor points for our offender. This area just west of Asheville, and this region of city blocks downtown. It cuts out 84.6 percent of the search area. Also, I looked up how many suspects there are so far—2,432 names on the master list. Only 12 percent of them work or live in these regions. I checked. At least this gives us a place to start."

Some of the officers looked stunned that I seemed to know what I was talking about. Ralph looked a little confused. "But why are there two areas?"

Before I could say anything, Tucker answered for me. "In some cases, the mathematics of a geo profile render a bipolar solution; in other words, there are two places equally likely for the offender to reside in or to use as his anchor point."

OK. This guy was really getting on my nerves.

"That's right," I said.

Tucker looked pleased.

"Well," said Ralph, "we can check DMV registrations to see if anyone living in those areas has a green Subaru station wagon like the one those two hikers saw driving away from the trailhead on the mountain where Mindy was found."

"I'm on it," said one of the officers I didn't know.

"Yeah," added Sheriff Wallace. "And we can go through our tip list and suspect list and reprioritize them. We've gotten thousands of tips since this investigation started. It's been a little overwhelming."

"Yes," I said. "Also see if anyone living in those areas has a history of battery or violent assault."

"OK," said Margaret. "Everyone knows their job. Now let's do it right." She gave me a stiff nod. "Thank you Dr. Bowers."

Everyone seemed to be nodding or gathering up their things. Just as I was telling myself the briefing hadn't ended so badly after all, I noticed Lien-hua.

She was glaring at me. Then she rose abruptly and walked away.

Note to self: next time, don't say "sidetracked by motives" to a profiler.

Especially not to her.

Tucker glanced at his watch. "I have some interviews this afternoon. I'm going to talk a little more to the hikers who found Mindy's body and then see if the ME is done with the autopsy."

"All right," said Ralph. "When do you think you'll be back?"

Tucker shook his head. "Probably tomorrow. Big date with the wife tonight. I should be back early in the morning, though."

As he walked away I noticed Margaret lurking in the doorway, arms crossed. "So, Dr. Bowers. Before I go to the press conference, I have one question for you."

"Yes?"

"Where is he going to strike next?"

I shook my head. "Some crime-mapping theorists have tried predictive analysis, but they've only had limited success so far. Sorry, Special Agent in Charge Wellington. I can help narrow down an investigation, but I can't predict the future."

"Too bad." Her voice was ice. "That might actually have done us some good."

Ah, Margaret.

So nice to be working with you again.

I can't believe it's only been four years.

14

I packed up my computer as everyone headed back to work.

I really wasn't sure what to think. Yeah, I'd plugged in some numbers, given us a starting point, but it was all preliminary. I'd just used the info they gave me. Without visiting the sites I had no idea if we were even on the right track.

Lunch. That's what I needed. Food and some fresh air. Clear my head. Besides, there was a certain tree I wanted to check out. See if it was real or if it only existed in the mind of a crazy woman.

I grabbed my computer and headed for the door.

———————■———————

One of Christie's favorite paintings at the Metropolitan Museum of Art in New York City had been a piece called "Hospital Slope," a painting of a huge spreading beech tree done by Zelda Sayre Fitzgerald, wife of novelist F. Scott Fitzgerald, and sometime schizophrenic. According to the tour guide at the art museum, Zelda had painted the picture back in the 1940s while spending time at the Highland Mental Hospital, a sanitarium in Asheville, North Carolina, where she was being treated for schizophrenia. In those days Asheville was famous for the healing power of its fresh mountain air as a remedy for all kinds of diseases, but especially tuberculosis, which they called consumption. The tour guide said the tree was still there today.

Highland Park was less than two miles from the federal building. I grabbed some Mexican food and hit the street, welcoming the chance to stretch my legs.

As I walked through town I tried to get a feel for the vibe of the different neighborhoods—demographics, income level, attitude, that sort of thing. Just like every person, every neighborhood has a different temperament. As I neared Highland Hill, the mood of the neighborhood began to shift from stylish and sophisticated to melancholy and grim. And then I saw why.

As I turned the corner, Highland Hall rose ominously from the hill: brick, square, imposing, institutional. Its dark, weather-stained walls seemed to drain sunlight out of air. And sure enough, beside the old sanitarium grew a beech tree that looked old enough to be the actual tree Zelda Fitzgerald had painted more than fifty years ago. At the base of the tree I found a plaque:

In memory of Zelda Sayre Fitzgerald
1900–1948
"I don't need anything except hope,
which I can't find by looking backwards or forwards,
so I suppose the thing is to shut my eyes."
—Zelda Sayre Fitzgerald

Zelda perished in 1948 along with eight other women when their wing of the sanitarium caught on fire. They all died of smoke inhalation. A bland stretch of gray concrete to the west of the building gave testimony to the lost wing.

I could only imagine what it was like for them. Trapped, dying, knowing there was no way past the flames. Shutting their eyes, screaming for help. Realizing no one could hear them. No one would ever hear them again. Never experiencing the hope they'd been trying so desperately to find.

I sat by the tree for a while, finishing my meal, thinking of Zelda and Christie and this case. I noticed a raven land on the roof of the old asylum, and it reminded me of Tessa. For some reason, she'd always made me think of a raven trying to spread its wings. But maybe instead, she was a dove covered with soot, looking for a safe place to land.

It was hard to know what to think.

After half an hour I walked back to the federal building. There wasn't enough time left in the day to visit the crime scenes, but maybe I could work on a linkage analysis of the crimes and then walk around the killer's downtown hunting grounds. I'd seen a climbing gym there on our drive into town; maybe I could even slip in a workout.

I left the tree behind, but the ghosts of Zelda and those other women followed me. The echo of their screams and the scorched smell of dying hope accompanied me all the way back to work.

15

The Illusionist stared out the window of his van at the girl walking back to her car. He knew her name—Jolene Brittany Parker. He knew her date of birth—June 17, 1989. She'd been a small baby, weighing in at only five pounds and five ounces at birth. But she'd grown up quite a bit since then. He knew everything.

He watched as she arrived at her car and opened up her purse to pull out her car keys. A smile crept across his face as he saw the bewilderment in her eyes.

She set her purse on the car beside her and opened it up, like the jaws of a snake unlocking and opening wide, too wide, to swallow some trembling rodent. She tipped it over, and her purse spit out all of its colorful contents, but still Jolene Brittany Parker did not find her keys.

She replaced the items in her purse one by one and started patting herself down. Feeling her pockets. Turning her head slightly to look at a corner of the ground. The Illusionist smiled. *She's thinking, Where did I put those lousy keys? I know I left them in my purse. Where could they be?*

Oh, this was good. It was so good he could hardly stand it.

She peered in the car. At the ignition. The seat. Nope, didn't leave them in there.

Despite himself, the Illusionist snickered. Not enough to let her hear him, of course. He was a few car lengths away, watching. But he just couldn't help himself. This was so good!

She was distracted, just like he knew she would be. Then, he opened the door of the van and stepped outside. She hadn't seen him yet. She was still looking for her keys. He smiled in a charming way, stepped around a blue pickup, and approached her.

"Everything okay, ma'am?" he asked. The Illusionist was wearing a security guard uniform from the mall. He had thought of everything.

"Oh, I'm just trying to remember where I put my keys," she said absently, giving him a quick glance.

"Maybe I can help you find them?" His smile was disarming, genuine.

"Um, yeah," she said offhandedly, looking back at the ground to see if she might have dropped the keys anyway when she was searching through her purse.

The Illusionist stepped toward her.

But there must have been something about him. The way he stood maybe, or his tone of voice, or his eagerness to help, but something made her uneasy. Maybe she suddenly realized she'd said too much to this stranger approaching her in the mall parking lot because she promptly added, "But I must have given them to my boyfriend. He's coming right now."

She pointed to the mall, toward some guy who was walking their way. The Illusionist let his eyes follow her finger.

It was all so entertaining. So hilarious! He almost started laughing again. There was no boyfriend. Of course not. He knew it all. He knew everything.

This was even better than he'd planned. "Well, then, I'll just wait until he gets here. A nice woman like you shouldn't be standing out in a parking lot all alone. I'll have to have a word with him about how to treat a woman." Then he smiled.

He leaned against the door of the car behind him and folded his arms. Watching.

A moment later the guy turned toward the Jiffy Oil and Lube station on the other side of the parking lot.

"Hmm. Looks like he must have parked somewhere else," said the Illusionist, stepping quickly toward Jolene, so quickly that he caught her off guard.

She was reaching toward her purse again. For the pepper spray?

"Looking for something, Jolene?" Now he had her arm.

She was fumbling desperately through her purse. He could feel her body trembling in his arms. He could almost taste her adrenaline. Smell her fear.

"This maybe?" The Illusionist pulled the bottle of pepper spray from his own pocket with his finger on the trigger, and as a scream froze in her eyes, he emptied it into the face of Jolene Brittany Parker.

She opened her mouth to scream, but he clamped his hand over it and held the cloth tightly against her face before she could. He held his other hand firmly against the back of her head, enjoying the feel of her soft blonde hair feathering between his fingers as she slowly went unconscious. "See, now. It'll all be over soon," he said as she wriggled weakly against his grip.

At last she was still.

He dragged her limp body over to the doors of his van, propped them open with one hand just like he'd practiced so many times, and slipped her inside. A normal man would have struggled lifting a 121-pound woman with only one arm. But he didn't. He was not a normal man. There was nothing normal about him.

He eased in next to her unconscious body. "You shouldn't leave your purse out in the break room." He unwound the duct tape from the roll. "Some psychotic homicidal stalker might slip in and steal your keys." The Illusionist smiled at his little joke.

And then, humming softly to himself, he pulled the doors shut and began his evening's work.

16

The linkage analysis was more complex than I thought it would be.

I rubbed my forehead.

I'd spent the last couple hours poring over the files, searching for those things that either didn't quite fit or fit too well. As my mentor, Dr. Werjonic, used to say, "Life is not precise. The pieces that fit too perfectly tell you there's more to the puzzle. Keep on looking until it doesn't all make sense, then you'll be closer to solving the case."

And, of course, all the while I was trying to avoid the two biggest problems you run into in an investigation this complex. Number one: getting overwhelmed by the details. With this many crimes, comparing the similarities and differences between so many variables can be overwhelming—which is where computers come in handy. And number two: not properly weighing the importance of each of the variables—which is where computers don't come in handy.

And as much as I like to think instinct doesn't play a role in what I do, for some reason, one detail from the fifth murder kept coming to mind, bothering me.

According to the files, Bethanie Dixon had just returned home after attending some kind of private college out west. The killer had left her for dead after stabbing her and strangling her. But somehow she lived long enough to scrawl two words on the linoleum with her blood: *white knight*.

I could understand why a killer who leaves pawn pieces might scribble a chess reference in blood, but why would the victim do it?

I tried to figure out what this might tell us about the connection between the killer and the victim, but I didn't have any idea yet what it might mean.

The phrase, along with the pawn at the crime scene, had sent the whole task force off investigating chess clubs and gaming conventions, chess websites, chess chat rooms, you name it. Hundreds of hours of manpower had been spent chasing the chess connection. But I still wasn't convinced the words and the pawns were linked.

White knight.

What did it have to do with the killer? The rest of the victims?

I sighed.

No idea.

On top of everything else I wanted to patch things up with Tessa but hadn't been able to get in touch with her. I'd tried calling her numerous times all afternoon, but she wouldn't answer her cell phone. I pushed the papers to the side. One more time, maybe.

But maybe not her cell; maybe my parents' landline. Over the last ten years they'd done pretty well incorporating computers into their lives, but when it came to talking on the telephone, they were still stuck in the middle of the twentieth century.

I dialed. My dad picked up. "Bowers residence."

"Dad, it's Pat."

"Hey, Pat. Is everything all right?" He could sense the tension in my voice by just listening to three words. Amazing.

"Yeah, listen, I've been trying to get in touch with Tessa."

"She's in her room. I think she's planning to go out with some friends tonight. Did you try her cell phone?"

"Yeah, all day long. She's not picking up."

"Well, maybe—"

Just then my phone vibrated. I had another call coming in. I glanced at the number. It was Ralph. "Yeah. Listen, just give her a hug for me. All right?"

"All right," he said, and then, "but I don't think I'm the one she needs a hug from."

I stared at the phone. Why did he have to go and say that? I punched a button, hung up on Ralph, and brought the phone back up to my ear. "All right. It worked. Can you go get her for me?"

"Of course." There was a hint of satisfaction in his voice.

I waited until she was on the line.

"What?"

"Hey, Tessa, I've been thinking about you a lot today. I'm really sorry I missed your birthday. I really am."

I paused; she didn't respond.

I could just picture her with her jaw set in that teenage girl sort of way. "Couldn't we at least pretend to get along once in a while?" I said.

"I thought you didn't like it when people pretend?"

Anger on the prowl.

Keep it caged in.

"Listen, I was hoping maybe in the next couple weeks or so we could spend some extra time together."

"Why? Aren't there enough dead bodies out there for you to spend time with?"

I heard it growl. *Easy, Pat. Easy.*

"Your mom's death was hard on me too," I said at last. But only after I'd said the words did I realize Tessa had already hung up the phone.

And that did it. I launched the phone against the wall, and it shattered in a spray of splintered technology.

Just then Ralph burst through the door.

"We might have something!" he blurted. "Why didn't you answer—what happened to your phone?" He was staring at the mess on the floor.

"I dropped it," I said. "What's up?" Last I'd heard, he and Lien-hua were following up on some leads concerning the type of rope the killer used to bind and strangle Mindy.

"About an hour ago a girl left a mall in Charlotte." He looked down at his notes. "Jolene Brittany Parker. Works at some clothing store in the mall. Never made it to her car. A guy says he saw someone with her. He might be able to give us a description."

I was tired, frustrated from my conversation with Tessa, not really interested in a wild goose chase in another part of the state, and annoyed that my phone wasn't wall proof. "What makes you think it's related?"

Ralph paused. "Nothing. Except she wears contacts."

"And?"

"And they match the prescription of the ones we found on Mindy."

"What!"

Lien-hua appeared at the door. "Mindy doesn't wear contact lenses. When we found out about the possible abduction, I decided to check out the prescription. On a whim."

"That was some whim." I jumped up from my seat. "What are we waiting for? Where's this eyewitness?"

"Local cops have him at the mall," said Ralph. "They've sealed off the area. He's still there. Should we bring him in?"

"No. Let's get over there. I want to talk to him on-site."

"It's a two-hour drive," said Lien-hua.

I shook my head. "Too long. How long by chopper?"

"Let's find out," said Ralph.

Lien-hua and I were already on our way up the stairs to the landing pad on top of the building.

17

We landed at a hospital near the mall, and the Charlotte police met us there with a cruiser. A few minutes later we were pulling into the parking lot to Hanes Mall. The road had been cordoned off, but the officers at the entrance stepped aside to let us through.

I could tell which car was hers. A team of crime scene technicians was already hard at work on it, looking for fibers, dusting for prints. Near them, surrounded by a cluster of state troopers, stood a guy who looked about eighteen years old, dressed in high tops, faded blue jeans, and a Detroit Pistons Starter jacket. He was staring off into space like he was either in shock or slightly stoned.

"That's him?" groaned Lien-hua.

"I guess so," said Ralph. "Want me to go at him?"

"Let me," I said.

We walked over to him, and I extended my hand. "I'm Patrick," I said, leaving off my last name. College students tend to become suspicious of those who give both names. It seems like a power play. I didn't want to distance myself from him right off the bat. "Are you Andy?"

He nodded and shook my hand.

"Good." I looked around and then back at him. "You saw something here in the parking lot earlier tonight. Is that right?"

He avoided eye contact. He didn't trust me yet. "I don't know," he mumbled. "I'm not really sure. Should I be talking to a lawyer or something?" He was stumbling all over his words.

"You don't need to talk to a lawyer unless you have something to hide," Ralph interjected, narrowing his eyes. "You don't have anything to hide, do you?"

"No." He answered a little too fast, which meant that he did.

"Well, then, there's nothing to be nervous about," I said. "We just want to know what you saw. That's all. Then you can go meet up with your friends to finish watching the Pistons school the Hornets in tonight's preseason game."

He stared at me suspiciously. "How did you know that?"

I pointed to his jacket. "Detroit plays Charlotte tonight. You keep trying not to look at the four guys in the crowd behind me but doing it anyway, and you've checked your watch three times since I got out of the car. Look, I just want to know what you saw, the best you can remember."

He still looked a little lost.

I looked at my watch. "Probably still in the second quarter."

That seemed to help him focus. "Well, I came out of the mall, right, and um, I saw this girl who looked pretty cute and so—"

"You were following her," interrupted Ralph.

I glared at him, and he backed off.

"No, I mean, why would you say that?" Then he turned to me. "Why would he accuse me of that?"

"Andy, you're rubbing your fingers together. You're shifting your weight back and forth from one leg to the other. You won't look me in the eye. You're nervous, maybe scared that if you admit you were following her, you'll become a suspect. But you're not in trouble with us. We have no reason to think you wanted to harm her; but someone might have hurt her, Andy. Her name is Jolene. The girl's name is Jolene."

He looked back and forth from me to Ralph, then sighed heavily. "OK. I was following her, but I wasn't trying to do nothin'. I was just, you know, I thought she was cute and stuff."

"Tell me about the guy you saw. The one who was standing

over here"—I walked toward the fifteen-year-old sedan—"by her car."

He looked confused. "Yeah, that's where he was standing. How did you know?"

"Sightlines," I said. "Here you're not in the pool of light from the parking lot lights, but you can see both directions on the road, and you have easy access to Jolene's car." I glanced at Ralph. I knew he was thinking, *This is a waste of time, Pat. Get the kid to talk or let me at him. I'll make him talk.*

I walked back over to Andy. "Now, please. Just tell me what you saw—"

"He killed her, didn't he?" Andy started shaking.

At first I thought I should lie, tell him that everything was OK, that the girl was fine. But then I decided to play it straight and give him the God-honest truth. Every minute we wasted meant less chance of finding her alive. "He might have, Andy. Or he might want to. Help us find him. Please. Help us protect her."

A look of horror swept over his face. "Oh, man. She's dead. I can't do this."

Lien-hua put her hand on his shoulder. "My name is Lien-hua, Andy, and I know you think that you didn't see anything important. But I want you to think back. How tall do you think the man was? Was he much taller than her or the same height? Was he Caucasian or black, or maybe Hispanic? Did you maybe see his face?"

He finally seemed to regain his composure. "He looked big. Tall, I mean. And I think he was white. He was wearing some kind of uniform."

"A uniform?" I said. "Like a police officer?"

"Sort of." Andy pointed toward one of the uniformed men nearby. "Like that."

"Mall security," I mumbled. "That's it. That's how he was able to get close to her." I turned to the officers who had driven us here.

89

"Get me a list of all the mall security personnel. And custodians too. Anyone who might have access to their uniforms."

"Yes, sir."

"That's good, Andy," said Lien-hua. "Is there anything else? Anything at all?"

He glanced at the crowd and then back at me. "I don't know. She was looking through her purse, I think. That's it. That's all. She pointed at me, and I saw the guy turn his head toward me, but his face was all in the shadows. When I saw the uniform, I thought maybe I was in trouble or something, so I cut between some cars."

I looked at her car. It was an old beat-up Toyota Camry, typical college student car, probably with more than two hundred thousand miles. I knelt down and shone the beam of my Mini Maglite under her car and then the one next to it. I caught the glint of something behind the tire. I pulled on a latex glove, reached into the shadows, and grabbed the object. Lipstick.

Ralph walked toward me. "Whatcha got?"

I showed it to him.

He turned to Andy. "You said she was looking through her purse?"

"Yeah."

"Why would a girl be standing by her car looking through her purse?" I asked Ralph. "What would she be looking for?"

He shook his head. "I don't know."

Lien-hua spoke up. "Her keys. Maybe she was looking for her keys."

Why? Why here? Why then?

"Her keys. She was looking for her keys," I whispered, "but she couldn't find them because they weren't there."

"So where were they?" Lien-hua.

I pointed to an empty parking spot about five meters away. "He had them. He had her keys. And he was ready for her at her car. Her car is older, probably doesn't have keyless entry. People without keyless entry tend to take their keys out later, when they're right next to their car. The lipstick tells me she was here when she tried to find them. Otherwise, if she had keyless entry, she would have pulled out her keys earlier, maybe halfway across this parking lot. Our guy knew that. Maybe he chose her just because of the age of her car. This guy is good."

"But why would he take her keys?" asked Lien-hua. "If he knew which car was hers, why not just grab her when she was getting into it?"

I slipped the lipstick into an evidence bag and thought for a moment before answering. "Because he wanted to watch her look for them. He's into it for the game. He likes to watch." As I said the words, a shiver snaked down my back. "He likes to watch," I whispered again.

"And?" she said. "So?"

I spun around. A crowd of people stood behind a police line about a hundred meters away. There were already half a dozen plainclothes men sweeping the crowd. So many murderers and arsonists return to the scene of the crime that it's standard operating procedure to photograph the crowds. But our guy would know that. He wouldn't be in the crowd.

Where else? A car, maybe? Was he in one of the cars in the parking lot? I stepped onto the hood of the car next to me and scanned the other side of the parking lot. An Applebee's restaurant. A couple fast-food joints. A Jiffy Lube. "I want this entire area closed down. Do it quietly. I don't want to spook him. He's here."

"In the crowd?" asked Ralph.

"No, not the crowd. Somewhere else."

"How do you know?" said Lien-hua.

"Because if I were him, that's where I'd be." I pointed toward the row of restaurants. "I want a sweep of every one of those restaurants. And we need to make sure there isn't anyone in any of these cars."

That's when I saw it. A walkway leading from the mall to a parking garage. It was perfect. You could look across the whole parking lot but then slide down and escape in either direction, to a car in the garage or back into the mall. Perfect exit route.

As I trained my eyes on the footbridge, a man in a leather jacket and a baseball cap turned suddenly and began to walk back toward the parking complex.

I pointed and jumped down from the car. "That's him."

The guy was hurrying now, almost out of sight.

"Where?" shouted Ralph, pulling out his weapon.

"The walkway. There. Cut him off!" Even as I said the words I was sprinting across the parking lot, barking out orders to the officers standing around us. "Seal off the parking garage. Don't let anyone out!"

A few officers gawked at me for a moment and then joined me in pursuit. "Cut him off in the mall!" I hollered. The officers split off and raced to the mall entrance.

I burst through the door to the parking garage and scanned the area. Nothing. Then I heard footsteps in the stairwell. I leaned over, looked up, and glimpsed movement on the landing above me. "Stop! I'm a federal agent!"

He didn't stop but stepped through the doorway and disappeared.

I exploded up the stairwell and pulled out my .357 SIG P229. I threw open the door and stared at the rows of cars. No one. He had to be behind a car somewhere. Or inside one.

"Step out with your hands in the air!" I swung the gun in front of me, leveling it with both hands, looking for a flicker of shadow, a trace of movement, anything. "I said, step out with your hands up!" My words echoed off the cement walls. No reply. My heart was hammering. He was here. He was close. I didn't know if he was armed or not, but I had to assume he was.

A car door clicked open three cars down. "Drop your weapon and put your hands in the air," I yelled. "Now!"

I could hear the whimpering voice of a young woman. And then the voice of a scared man. "Don't shoot, mister!" A graying, over-weight man in his underwear stepped out of a Ford Expedition with his hands in the air. "She told me she was twenty-one. I swear."

"Get back in the car!" I shouted.

"But you just said—"

He never finished his sentence. Before he could say another word, his neck exploded in a spray of blood as the echo of a gunshot rang against the concrete walls of the parking garage.

18

Confusion swept over the man's face as his hand involuntarily flew up to his neck. He wobbled for a moment, then careened face-first onto the concrete. A moment later the girl was standing next to the car screaming. The shot had come from somewhere beyond them. I had no visual on the shooter.

"Get down," I shouted to her. "Back in the car!" I leveled my weapon. She scurried back inside and slammed the door, probably thinking I was the one who'd shot her friend. I could hear her wild shrieks, muffled only slightly by the doors of their SUV.

"Shots fired!" I shouted. I hoped one of the officers had followed me into the parking garage and could hear me. I raced to the victim. "I repeat, shots fired!"

Why did you shoot this man? Why would you kill this man? Still no visual on the shooter.

I leaned over and held my hand against the victim's gurgling throat. He was shaking slightly, starting to go into shock. The bullet had missed the center of his neck and passed through the side of it. There was a lot of blood, but the wound didn't look fatal. It was a good thing our suspect wasn't a great shot.

"Sir, you're going to be all right," I whispered, hoping it was true, all the while keeping one eye on the cars in front of me. "Lie still. Don't move." With one hand I applied gentle pressure to the man's neck to slow the bleeding, being careful not to press too hard or I might constrict his breathing. With the other I gripped the SIG and surveyed the parking garage. A pack of cops burst through the door.

"Get down!" they yelled.

"I'm a federal agent!"

"Shut up. Drop your weapon!"

Just then one of the men recognized me. "Wait, he's one of us."

"Get me an ambulance," I called out. "And the shooter is still in the building!" I pointed toward where I thought the suspect had run, the most sensible escape route. "Down there. Sweep down toward the exit."

The officers fanned out and began to search the parking garage car by car while I stayed with the injured man.

"Hang in there," I told him. "Help will be here in a minute."

Why did he shoot this man? Was he aiming at me? Did he miss me?

Maybe our suspect wasn't a very good shot. Maybe. But as I considered the possibilities, a chilling thought struck me: maybe he was an excellent shot. Maybe he knew that if he killed this man with a shot to the torso or to the head I wouldn't have had to stop to help him. Or, if he hit him in an extremity, the gunshot wound wouldn't have been serious enough for me to stop. But if he wounded him just right I'd have to make a choice—I'd have to choose between saving this man's life or continuing the chase. Somehow, he'd thought of all that in the brief moment after this man stepped out of his car. Was that possible? Could he be that smart?

Or maybe he knew this couple would be here. Maybe he'd planned it all in advance. I made a mental note to find out why this man and this girl were here on this night at this time in that parking spot. But the more I thought about it, the more I started to believe that the killer had planned it all out. He might have even waited on that walkway until I saw him there. *He's in it for the game. He likes to watch.*

I started to wonder how I could catch a guy who could plan his moves like this. He was smarter than I was.

I stayed with the man who'd been shot until the ambulance arrived a few minutes later. There was a little confusion about which paramedics were going to take him to the hospital—apparently several vehicles had responded. Finally, two of the men lifted the gunshot victim onto a gurney and wheeled him away. We searched the entire parking garage complex, the mall, the parking lot, the restaurants. Nothing.

The girl from the van was still screaming when they took her away. I wondered if she would ever be able to stop herself from screaming when she thought of this night. Some people can put events like this behind them and move on. Most of us can't.

Before leaving, I looked through the Ford Expedition they'd been in. A white pawn was sitting on the center of the dashboard.

19

After the search for the shooter came up empty, I realized there wasn't much more I could do there that night. Local law enforcement didn't really want us around, and even though we could have fought them for jurisdiction, we were already stretched thin trying to investigate all the other cases. It seemed like the best strategy was to let them take the lead on this and keep us updated. That meant I could get back to Asheville and spend tomorrow morning piecing together the overall pattern of the crime series.

Since my shirt was soaked with the wounded man's blood, I turned it in as evidence and bought a sweatshirt from one of the mall stores that was getting ready to close. After cleaning the blood off my hands in the bathroom, I went to sign the chain of evidence papers. That's what I was doing when Ralph walked over to me, shaking his head.

"What is it?" I asked.

"You."

"Me?"

"Yup, you. I need to brief the officers in charge here, Margaret is back in Asheville, and that puts you in charge."

I didn't like where this was going. "In charge of what?"

"Meeting with Governor Taylor."

"What?"

Ralph shrugged his huge shoulders, trying unsuccessfully to look helpless. "He heard about the girl; wants someone to bring him up to speed. Word is he's got a bunch of speeches next week on national security, and he doesn't want to get blindsided by questions about serial killers in his own hometown."

I glanced at my watch: 9:41 p.m. "Does he know what time it is?"

"I'm sure he does."

"Can't this wait, Ralph?"

He shook his head. "Governor Taylor is one person you don't keep waiting. He's spending this weekend at his private residence not far from here, just outside of town. It shouldn't take you too long to brief him."

Great. He just had to say the b-word.

"I'm not good with this kind of stuff, Ralph. You know how much I hate—"

But he'd already turned around. "Take Lien-hua along. I hear he likes the women."

"Who likes the women?" asked Lien-hua.

And before I had a chance to protest any more to Ralph, a car piloted by one of the governor's security detail drove up, and Lien-hua and I reluctantly climbed in.

———— ◾ ————

"He just lives a few minutes away," explained our driver. "'Course, most of the time he's in Raleigh, but a couple weekends a month he likes to come back home."

I listened to him but didn't really listen. Mostly I was thinking about Jolene and the pawn on the dashboard and the killer who was smarter than I was. *He put Jolene's contacts into Mindy's eyes. Why?* I also wondered about the man he shot and the chain of events that had brought me to his side. Time and place.

Time and place.

After a few minutes, my thoughts drifted to the other side of the backseat, where Lien-hua sat silently watching the night slide past the car. I was a little disappointed the car was so roomy. I wished the governor had chosen to send something a tad smaller. A Harley would have been nice.

We didn't talk until we arrived at the front gate to the governor's mansion and one of the sentries waved us through. That's when Lien-hua turned to me. "Good work interviewing that kid back there," she said.

"Thanks. And good thinking to realize she was looking for her car keys. And to check the prescription for the contacts too. Very nice."

"Thank you," she said. "I'm just glad I wasn't too sidetracked by looking for motives."

Yes. Definitely rephrase that in the next briefing.

Governor Taylor's mansion lay back from the main road behind a grove of looming oak trees that sprawled along the drive just barely within reach of the headlights. As we pulled to a stop in the circular drive in front of the elaborate manse, I let out a long, slow breath. "Whew . . . Maybe I'm in the wrong line of work. I didn't know the government of North Carolina paid its public workers so well."

"Tobacco family," our driver said wistfully, pronouncing it *tu-backa famlee.* "They've been in politics forever, but it's cancer sticks paid for this place." He opened up the door for Lien-hua. "I wonder how much of it I paid for before I quit," he mumbled. Then we stepped past him and climbed the steps to the porch.

A young woman greeted us at the door. Mid-twenties, blonde, movie star face, dressed in a skirt that must have taken her an hour to squeeze into. She introduced herself as the governor's personal assistant. "Ms. Anita Banner," she said in a crisp, professional voice. "Please follow me."

She led us down the wide hallway toward the governor's private office. Ms. Banner turned every step into a Spanish dance. I wondered just how personal her assistance to the governor was. Especially this late on a Friday night.

She asked us to wait for a moment in the great room and then slipped through another set of doors to announce our arrival to Governor Taylor.

I glanced around the room. Paintings depicting Civil War battles hung on the walls: Antietam, Fredericksburg, Bull Run, Chancellorsville. Apart from some kind of huge fish mounted above the fireplace, the entire room seemed to be decorated to celebrate the war—and the South. A plaque below one of the paintings read: "First at Bethel. Last at Appomattox." So, a tribute to the soldiers of North Carolina.

Lien-hua picked up a picture that was sitting on the grand piano. "I wonder where the governor's wife and kids are tonight?"

"She took the boys to Barbados for the week," I answered.

Lien-hua stared at me, amazed. "How do you know that?"

"I'm tempted to wow you with my Sherlockian deductive powers," I said. "But actually I heard it on the news last night while channel surfing. His wife loves the spotlight. She's twenty years younger than him and used to be a model. She just might be the first governor's wife in history with her own paparazzi."

"Oh," said Lien-hua. She didn't seem impressed.

Brilliant move, Einstein. Next time try and wow her.

Just then Ms. Banner reappeared and led us into the governor's private office.

He stepped out from behind a vast mahogany desk to greet us. I extended my hand and introduced myself. The governor looked to be in his mid-fifties, but his grip was firm, almost startlingly so. He had cool, calculating eyes that were offset by his wide, practiced smile. He'd loosened his tie but still chose to wear his impeccably tailored suit that moved with him seamlessly as he strode through the room. A small pin with a Confederate flag hung proudly from his lapel.

I was about to introduce Lien-hua, but she beat me to it, stepping forward and taking his hand. "Special Agent Lien-hua Jiang. Pleased to meet you, Governor Taylor." The governor's eyes brightened when he took her hand, and they did not linger long on her hand.

"Agent Jiang," he said with a honey-sweet Southern accent, "the pleasure is all mine."

Yeah, that's an understatement.

"Governor Taylor," I said, nodding toward the room with the fireplace, "you have quite a collection of paintings."

He smiled thinly. "All who are warriors must be students of war." He reached for a bottle on his desk. "Drink?"

I shook my head. Lien-hua said, "No thank you."

"Well, then." He considered a decanter of cognac for a moment and then refilled his glass.

"That quote," I said. "Chekhov?"

He lifted his glass to me with a slight nod. "Taylor," he said, winking at Lien-hua.

OK.

"I especially liked the portrayal of Sharpsburg," I said. The South often used different names to remember the battles than the North did. In this case, I used the Southern name to refer to the battle of Antietam.

He looked mildly impressed. "One of my favorites as well."

But then I blew it. "An interesting way to remember the Civil War." As soon as I'd said it, I realized it. Oh well.

"You're not from the South, are you, Dr. Bowers?" His tone had turned fatherly, patronizing. I was not in the mood.

"Actually, no. Milwaukee, originally." *Go on, say it. I know you're going to.*

He grinned, pleased with himself. "Here in the South, we prefer to call it the War Between the States. Or the War of Northern Aggression . . ."

I knew he was going to say that.

I didn't respond, just waited for him to go on.

He continued, "There's nothing civil about war, Dr. Bowers. The phrase is an oxymoron—like giant shrimp, rubber cement, or tight slacks." As he added that last one, his eyes flickered toward Lien-hua.

"Or act natural," I said.

He shifted his attention back to me, with one eyebrow raised. "Hmm?"

"Act natural. It's another oxymoron. Either you're acting or you're not. But only one is natural." I met his gaze, didn't look away.

"Ah, unless you are a natural actor," he said with a slight raise of his glass.

Or unless you're a true counterfeit, I thought but managed to keep my mouth shut.

"Sir," Lien-hua said, "you wanted to know about the case."

"Yes, yes. Of course." He set his drink on the desk and took his place behind it, in the position of authority. He motioned for us to have a seat in the two tiny chairs facing him. It was a power play, of course.

"Bad back," I said. "Think I'll stand."

Lien-hua sat.

"So," he said, "this girl tonight. What do you know so far?"

Lien-hua leaned forward. "Governor, if I might ask, what's your specific interest in this case?"

"Public relations." He shook his head slightly. "A serial killer? Oh, it's been a nightmare." He let his words hang in the air as if he expected us to agree with him that his public relations concerns were somehow more important than the fact that at least six young women had been brutally murdered. I wasn't sure how much more of this guy I could take.

"I guess no one has informed you about the phone calls?" He asked it as a question even though it seemed like a statement.

"What phone calls?" I asked.

"Let's see, what was her name . . . Bethanie something . . ."

I wondered where he was going with this. "Not Dixon? Bethanie Dixon?"

"Yes. Yes. That's it. From what I've heard, she called our switchboard a dozen times in less than eight hours. That night she disappeared. Two days later she was found dead."

I remembered seeing a series of calls in her phone records when I was reviewing her case earlier today, but I hadn't had time to investigate who she'd been calling.

"Are there transcripts of the calls?" I asked.

"Of course. We tape all incoming calls. I'll have my people fax them to you in the morning. Not much there, though. She demanded to talk to me, said it was urgent. She was afraid her life was in danger. Mine too, it seems."

"What?" asked Lien-hua. "A death threat?"

"I get those constantly," he said, dismissing her concern with a wave of his hand. "This was different."

"She wasn't threatening you," I said. "She was warning you."

"So it seems."

"But about who?" asked Lien-hua.

He gazed at the bookshelf for a moment and then shook his head. "No idea."

Lien-hua shifted in her chair. "Sir, why didn't you tell our team about this earlier?"

"I only made the connection when I heard her name mentioned on the news tonight in relation to this other girl's abduction."

Something wasn't clicking. Something wasn't right.

Lien-hua's phone rang; she looked at the number, excused herself, and stepped into the next room.

"Governor," I said, "does the phrase 'white knight' mean anything to you?"

He stared at me. For an instant his eyes seemed to turn cold and reptilian, then he blinked them back to warm and inviting once again. An amazing transformation. "Does that have something to do with the murder?" he asked. He was searching me, evaluating me even as I was evaluating him.

"She scrawled the words beside her, in her own blood, while she was dying."

I watched him carefully.

"White knight," he said thoughtfully. "Hmm. I don't know. I suppose you use them to play chess. That's the only thing that comes to mind."

Why didn't he react when you said she scrawled the words in her own blood? Why didn't he cringe? He knows something. He's hiding something.

The governor sipped at his drink and then shook his head. "That's all, I'm afraid." He glanced at his watch. "I'll have those transcripts faxed over first thing in the morning. And I would appreciate it if you would keep me apprised of the case. I truly hope you find this girl, Julie—"

"Jolene," I said.

"Yes. Of course."

He rose.

Lien-hua stepped back into the room, and the governor watched her walk toward us, his tongue glancing out to wet his lower lip. I stepped between them and handed him my card. "And if you think of anything, you'll be sure to call us?"

"Of course. Oh—" He raised an index finger and then reached into one of the desk's mighty drawers. "Two tickets," he said gallantly. "One for each of you. I'd be honored to have you as my personal guests Monday for the Cable News Forum's annual awards luncheon. It's at the Stratford Hotel."

Everything he said was another way of patting himself on the back.

"I'll be giving the keynote address to kick off a brief speaking tour on what the states can do to battle global terrorism. I'll be at the Pentagon later in the week."

This guy was unbelievable.

"Well. Congratulations," I said coolly. "And thanks for the offer, but I'm sorry that we'll have to decl—"

Lien-hua interrupted me. "We'd be honored," she said.

He beamed. He wasn't staring at me. "Well"—he gave Lien-hua a slight nod—"then I'll look forward to seeing you Monday morning."

And with that, Ms. Banner appeared at the door and led us back, past the paintings of the war that was not civil, to the car.

———————————■———————————

From his office window, Governor Sebastian Taylor watched the car containing the two federal agents drive away. It had been nearly thirty years since he'd heard the words *white night*. He'd thought that chapter of his life was over for good. Apparently not. He pressed the button on his intercom.

"Ms. Banner?"

"Yes, sir?" It was amazing how much innuendo she could pack into those two little words.

"I'll need some time to make a few personal calls."

"Would you like me to—"

"They're personal calls, Ms. Banner."

"Yes, sir." A note of disappointment soured her reply.

He hesitated for a moment and then added, "Give me twenty minutes. Then, perhaps you can help me, um, work on the wording for my Cable News Forum speech."

"Yes, sir." This time her words sounded just the way he'd hoped they would. He released the intercom button and picked up the phone. Dialed a number. Waited.

A moment later a voice answered, "Reference number please." Governor Taylor smiled. Only three phone numbers actually get you through to a live person at the Pentagon twenty-four hours a day. He knew all three.

"16dash1711alpha delta4," he said.

"Just a moment." A slight pause accompanied by the tapping of fingers on a keyboard on the other side of the line and then, "How may I help you, sir?"

"I'd like to talk to General Biscayne."

"I'm sorry, he's already left for the weekend. He'll be in on Monday—"

"This is Sebastian Taylor, code name Cipher."

"Of course, sir. I'll connect you."

"Thank you."

Governor Taylor waited as the line was transferred, and then a familiar voice came on. "Yeah?"

"Cole, it's Sebastian. I think we might have a problem."

20

Alice McMichaelson rubbed her eyes and glanced at the clock hanging from the wall of her living room.

10:21 p.m.

She tried to focus on the words hovering on the page in front of her eyes, but the more she concentrated the fuzzier they became.

The third yawn in as many minutes escaped her lips.

If only she didn't have to work so much and could spend more time just being a mom.

But to provide for her kids she had to work, and to keep her new job she needed to finish her degree. And to do that she had to study, and when else was she supposed to read these textbooks? She couldn't very well study at work, and then in the evenings and on the weekends the kids had all their activities. The only time she could fit it in was after her kids went to bed.

She yawned again, heard shuffling behind her, and turned. Brenda stood in the hallway holding Wally to her chest.

"What's wrong, sweetheart?"

"Wally can't sleep. He's scared."

"What's Wally scared of?"

Brenda hugged her stuffed walrus tighter. "Monsters."

For just a moment Alice considered trying to convince her daughter that there were no such thing as monsters, but she knew it wouldn't work. She'd tried that before. She'd done what all parents do, opening the closet doors, flipping up the bedcovers to look beneath the bed. "See? No monsters. Now go to sleep." But it never worked. All kids know monsters can turn invisible, so showing them empty closets never does any good. And besides, she didn't have enough energy for all of that tonight. She needed a new approach.

Alice got up and walked over to her daughter. "Monsters, huh. Well, maybe Wally would feel better if he went to sleep in a room where there are no monsters."

Brenda looked confused. "Where?"

"Mommy's bedroom. No monsters are allowed in there when I'm studying my books. It's a rule."

"It is?"

Alice led her daughter down the hallway. "Of course."

"Who made it?"

Alice tried to think fast. "Well, the angels did, honey. Monsters are no match for angels, you know that."

They'd reached the bedroom. "Yeah," said Brenda. "Everyone knows that."

Alice pulled back the edge of the covers. "You see, the angels made a rule long ago that mommies get special protection when they're trying to take good care of their children. No monsters allowed."

Brenda was thoughtful for a moment. "That's a good rule."

"Yes it is. Now climb in."

She pulled the covers up to her daughter's chin.

"Mommy?"

"Yes?"

"Is there a rule about daddies too?"

"What do you mean?"

After a slight pause. "I think sometimes Daddy let the monsters in."

Alice felt her heart hammering. "You know, sweetheart," Alice said as calmly as she could, "all you have to remember is that the angels are watching over you tonight and the monsters are all far, far away. Now, good night."

"Good night, Mommy."

Alice gave her daughter a kiss on the forehead, and as she was closing the door, she heard Brenda telling Wally, "You don't have to be afraid anymore. Mommy says the monsters can't get in."

Then Alice went back to the living room, thinking of Garrett. She couldn't help it. At first he'd been so kind, so gentle, so loving. He'd been a good dad, really, teaching Brenda to read, taking Jacob fishing. Being there for them in the evenings, leaving work at work. But then he started drinking, and it all turned upside down. Everything changed. She tried not to think about the times the monster had shown up in her bedroom. Tried only to remember the other times.

Failed.

How was it possible for an angel and a monster to live in the same man?

And with that question burrowing through her mind, as hard as she tried, she couldn't get any more studying done that night.

As we pulled into the mall parking lot I turned to Lien-hua. "Governor Taylor is something else, isn't he?" I spoke softly enough so the driver wouldn't hear.

"Yeah," she whispered. "And he knows something. I don't see how he could be involved in this case, but there's something more going on here. He's hiding something." And then, anticipating my next question, she added, "Going to that luncheon gives us a chance to find out more about his interest in this case."

She just continued to impress me. "Good thinking," I said. "By the way, anyone important on the phone back there?"

She pointed to the man approaching the car. "Just Ralph. Nothing vital."

Our driver pulled to a stop, and we climbed out of the car. After the driver left, Lien-hua filled Ralph in on our meeting with Governor Taylor. He grunted a little, nodded, seemed to take it all in stride. "All right," he announced. "I have no idea what all that was about, but if we can keep him on our side it can only help. Let's put this thing to bed for the night and get some sleep."

"Good idea," I said. "Hey, listen, can I borrow your phone? I need to make an important call. I'll get it back to you tomorrow."

Ralph grumbled but handed it over. "Battery's almost dead. The charger is back in Asheville—"

"No problem."

"OK. Just don't 'drop' it."

"Don't worry," I said. "I wouldn't dream of it. Thanks."

Ralph and Lien-hua decided to stay the night in Charlotte and bring the local police department up to speed while I flew back to Asheville to get an early start in the morning.

While the chopper pilot did his safety check, I called Terry Wilson, a friend in the NSA who'd worked with me on the satellite-mapping project. I caught him just as he was shutting off the light to go to bed. After a quick greeting, I jumped right into it. "Terry, I need some discreet information on Sebastian Taylor, the governor of North Carolina."

"When you say discreet, do you mean discreet or *discreet*?"

"I mean I don't want anyone else to know you're poking around. Anyone."

"Oh, that kind of discreet."

"Can you do it?"

"It's what I do best. When do you need it by?"

"What do you think?

A sigh. "Yesterday."

"Close enough."

"All right. Let me see what I can do. I'll call you tomorrow afternoon."

"Thanks."

"You'll owe me for this."

"I always do."

I dozed a little on the flight back to Asheville and took a taxi to the hotel. Just as I walked into my hotel room, the phone rang. I couldn't believe it; the day seemed like it would never end. I picked it up. "Yeah?" I said wearily.

"Patrick Bowers." Voice distortion software. I couldn't even tell if the voice was male or female. "Patrick Bowers, PhD."

"Who is this?"

A short, venomous laugh. "He is okay, I trust?"

It's him. It's the killer. The Yellow Ribbon Strangler!

"An inch over and you'd have killed him on the spot," I said, scrambling to think of ways to keep him on the phone.

"Yes, of course. But you and I both know I didn't intend to kill him—although I could have. I had a clear shot at you too, Dr. Bowers."

Considers himself an excellent shot, maybe a sniper. Ex-military. Check gun clubs, gun shows. Narcissist, enjoys controlling others, dominating them. Arrogant. My thoughts raced ahead of me as I tried to stay focused on the conversation.

"Where's Jolene? Is she OK?"

"Oh, Patrick, I was happy to see that you're helping with this case. It raises the stakes, don't you think?"

Even though the voice was altered, I guessed from the underlying speech patterns and pauses that he grew up in the mid-south or somewhere along the southern coast. Maybe New Orleans.

"Jolene. I asked about Jolene—"

"Forget the girl, Dr. Bowers. You can't have her." He laughed again. "I saw her first. It's too late for her."

I was breathing faster now, getting angry. "What do you mean, it's too late?" *Is she dead? Did he kill her already?*

"Forget her!" he continued. "You need to worry about me now."

I tried to conceal my growing rage, tried to control myself. "Then who are you? Tell me your name, and we can talk this through."

"Please, Patrick, don't patronize me. Call me the Illusionist."

"The Illusionist? You're a magician, then. Like Houdini?"

"I'm not like anyone. But you should know that already. You and that stepdaughter of yours, Tessa Bernice Ellis." A slow chill snaked its way down my spine. Before I could respond he finished by saying, "Welcome to the game. I'll talk to you again soon."

"Don't hang—"

But it was too late. The line was dead.

He knew about Tessa? How did he know about Tessa? I frantically dialed my parents and told them to check on her. Now.

A moment later, after they had, I demanded they go to a hotel for the night. Even though they were in Denver, I couldn't take any chances. After a few minutes of arguing, they said they would. I made them promise. Tessa would hate me all the more for doing it, but I didn't care. Somehow this guy knew about her. That meant she was in danger.

Then I transcribed the conversation as closely as I could get it word for word. I called the Bureau to see if they could trace the call, but they didn't come up with anything—not that I really thought they would. I looked over my notes of the conversation again to see if there were any holes, any things I'd missed.

He knows me, who I am, what I do. Is he someone from my past? He said, "You need to worry about me now." Why? Is he after me? Am I the pawn?

"I'll get you," I said aloud. I realized I was clenching my fists again. This time, though, I didn't try to relax them. It felt good to be on fire on the inside. To be back in the game.

I tried to tell myself he was lying, that the girl was okay, that Jolene would be all right and we could still save her if we hurried.

But it didn't work. I knew it was too late. She was already dead.

21

The Illusionist let Jolene hear the entire conversation. He especially liked the look on her face when he said it was too late to save the girl. He hung up the phone and smiled.

He untied the gag and expected her to scream, but she just whimpered instead, "Please, don't hurt me, mister. Please." Her voice was raspy, her eyes swollen and bloodshot from the pepper spray. "I'll do whatever you want," she was crying, blurting out the words, shaking. He liked that. "I won't tell anyone. I promise. Just please, let me go." Oh, he liked that very much.

He put a finger up to her lips. "Shh, now. Quiet, Jolene. I know you will." Her wrists were bound to the chair she was seated on, but he held her trembling fingers between his nonetheless. To comfort her.

Outside the cabin, darkness had long since fallen over the mountains. She might scream, but it wouldn't matter. The walls were soundproof. Besides, they were miles away from the nearest town.

He let go of her hands and walked over to the counter to sip at his coffee. It was late, but he expected to be up for a while. "Do you know how many people are born each day, Jolene?"

"What?"

"387,834 people, Jolene. And every day 153,288 people die. That means that every second 4.5 people are born, and 1.8 people die. Every year, the population of the world grows by more than 78 million people. And do you know how many of those people are remembered after they die?"

"Please, mister." She began to sob softly, but he paid no attention to it.

"Only a handful, Jolene. You live, you die, the world forgets your name. Life is a cosmic joke. But I'm going to make you memorable. Your name will become famous. Your face will become immortal on television and the Internet."

He walked toward her.

"On August 31, 1888, a prostitute named Mary Ann Nichols died at the hands of Jack the Ripper, the world's most infamous serial killer. She was his first. Today, there are dozens of websites in her honor, a fan club, twenty-two songs have been written in memory of her. She lives on. Her name will stay alive forever."

Jolene trembled. "Mister, please—"

"Jack the Ripper was never found, Jolene. Today there are over a hundred suspects. Each has found his place in history." He chuckled slightly. "And despite what some people have claimed, the verdict is still out. No one knows for sure who he was. We don't remember the dead, Jolene, unless they've done something unforgettable." He stroked her hair gently. "Or unless something unforgettable has been done to them." He leaned over to gaze into her trembling eyes. "Oh yes. I am going to give you a gift, my dear. The gift of immortality. I'm going to give you a place in the history of an anonymous world. People will remember you for decades."

"Mister, I'll do anything."

He set down the cup and walked over to his tools. "Have you heard of Boethius, Jolene?"

The girl was crying now, making it harder to carry on the conversation. The Illusionist didn't like that. He picked up a knife from the tray—this one was one of his favorites—and walked back to her side of the room.

"I said, have you heard of Boethius?"

She shook her head no, getting more wide-eyed the closer he came.

"He was a Roman philosopher in 480–524 AD who was falsely accused of treason and lost his place in the senate. He was exiled to a cave until his execution. He had everything one day and lost everything the next. In his moment of deepest agony and confusion, he didn't turn to the gods. Do you know who he turned to?"

Silence.

He held his bracelet up to her face. Inscribed on the metal band was a single word. "Sophia," he read it to her. "The Greek word for wisdom. Boethius turned to philosophy, Jolene. And she taught him a priceless lesson. A lesson that set him free. Do you know what that lesson was?"

Her eyes seemed to light up when he said the word *free*. "Please let me go. I won't tell."

Once again he ignored her. "She taught him that fame and wealth are weak gods because they are so fickle. The best teacher, the greatest instructor to lead us to true wisdom, is pain."

"Oh no. Please. No."

"Oh yes. Suffering is the most faithful teacher, Jolene, for pain leads us to clarity, and clarity leads us to truth. Do you agree with Boethius, Jolene?"

"I don't know." She was shaking.

"Oh, I think you do know. I think you know that Boethius is right, but you've spent your whole life telling yourself that happiness leads to fulfillment. Right? Am I right?"

"I guess so."

"I'm right, aren't I?"

"Please—"

"Aren't I!"

"Yes." He watched her stare at the knife he was twirling only inches from her face.

He leaned closer. "You're answering the questions so much better now. I'm very proud of you. So I have one last question for you—do you think I agree with Boethius?"

She shook slightly, he could see the fear in her eyes. A whisper of terror rippled through her. "Yes."

"Once again you are correct, Jolene. And now I'm going to give you a great gift."

"You're going to let me go?"

"Oh no. I'm afraid not. The gift I wish to give you is two-fold."

"No—"

"I'll give you enlightenment and then immortality. And what is the road to enlightenment?"

"No—"

He cut her then, the first cut of the night, slashing the knife quickly and deeply into her forearm, opening an angry red wound. She let out a sharp gasp. Saw the blood leaking out. Started to hyperventilate.

He wiped the blade clean against his pants leg. Yes, he had special plans for her. Not just the six wounds of the other women. Many, many more.

"What is the pathway to enlightenment, Jolene?"

"Pain." She squeezed her eyes shut. "Pain, pain, pain." Her words sputtered away into strangled sobs.

"Yes. You're right again. I'm very proud of you. Now, let the lesson begin."

And he was right. She did scream. Before the lesson had barely begun.

22

Tessa Ellis waited until she heard the sound of slow rhythmic breathing coming from the adjoining hotel room. Then she waited another couple of minutes just to make sure.

Her grandparents—actually her stepdad's parents—had at least gotten her a separate room at the hotel. She'd demanded that much. There was no way she was going to sleep in the same room with them. Uh-uh. No way.

"We'll get a room with two beds," Martha had offered as she picked up her car keys. "Patrick said it would be best."

Patrick said? Oh, well if Patrick said it, then it must be true. If Patrick cares so much about what's best for everyone, why isn't he here?

"I'm staying home," Tessa said. "And I don't care what *Patrick* says!"

"Please," Conor said gently. He'd always seemed to get along with her better than Martha did. "It'll just be for tonight." He sounded patient but tired.

"I need my privacy!"

And then he surprised her by agreeing. "Yes, yes. Of course you do, Tessa."

She stopped yelling long enough to see what he would do.

Martha Bowers was staring at her husband. He handed her purse to her. "Of course she does, Martha. She needs her privacy. We'll get two rooms. Won't we?" And Martha had given in with a sigh.

The rooms were joined by a door that Conor had said needed

to stay open "just a crack; just for safety's sake. I know you understand."

No, she didn't, but what did that matter. "Fine. Whatever," she said at last.

But it wasn't necessary; it's not like she was in any danger or anything. After all, there were two cops parked outside the hotel in an unmarked sedan. That was probably also the work of her stepdad, Patrick Bowers. Mr. FBI . . . Mr. Serial Killer Hunter . . . Mr. I'll Be Gone Again This Weekend But You'll Be Fine With My Parents . . . It would be just like him to call in two cops to help protect her but not do a thing to come back home himself.

She'd noticed them right away. Over the last year she'd gotten good at identifying cops. When Conor was leading her to the hotel she banged her fist on the window of the cops' car. One of them was so startled he spilled his soda all over himself. That was great. She gave them both the finger. That was even better.

Tessa had listened to Martha and Conor talking in whispers for nearly an hour before they finally slipped into sleep. They'd probably been talking about her, but she couldn't be sure. She couldn't make out the words.

Now she listened again, straining against the darkness, but all she heard were the soft sounds of sleep coming from the adjoining hotel room.

Tessa sat up and slid the blanket to the side.

Pale streetlight seeped through the curtains, giving her just enough light to see.

From the other room, a light rustling sound. Someone rolling over in the night.

Tessa froze.

Waited.

Silence.

She slipped out of bed and padded over to the dresser, grabbed her purse, and pulled out the small case. Then, gently, softly, she slipped into the bathroom. Over the last ten months she'd become an expert at doing things soundlessly in the night, finding her way in the dark.

Tessa closed the bathroom door. Even if Martha or Conor did wake up and decide to check on her, they wouldn't bother her in there. But she didn't want to take any chances. So she locked it. Just in case.

She pulled up the sleeve of her pajamas and stared for a moment at the set of straight scars descending the inside of her right arm.

Last summer she'd thought her grandparents might ask her why she always wore long-sleeve pajamas and even long-sleeve T-shirts, but they hadn't. They'd pretty much left her alone to dress the way she wanted to. So had Patrick. He was as clueless as they were.

She opened up the case and pulled out the razor blade.

At first, when she'd heard about self-inflicting, or "self-mutilation" as some people called it, she thought it sounded weird. Why would anyone purposely cut herself? What good could that possibly do? Then, one night when she was sleeping over at her best friend Cherise's house—back when she used to live in New York City, of course—Tessa found out Cherise was into cutting and had been doing it for two months ever since breaking up with Adam Schoeneck, who'd dumped her for that sophomore cheerleader from East Side High. "It's like, when you have all this pain inside you," Cherise had told her, "it's a way to let it out, you know?"

Tessa had no idea, but she'd said, "Yeah, I know." What kind of pain could Cherise have? She was popular. She had both her parents. She had everything.

"The cut only stings for like a second, and then it's over." Cherise was watching herself brush her rich, cinnamon-colored hair in the mirror. "You have to be careful not to go too deep, though, or you'll start leaving scars. Did you see that new guy at school? Oh! Totally gorgeous. Anyway, want some pizza? I'm starved." Cherise had a way of making the most exotic things sound ordinary and the most commonplace things sound exciting.

Still, for a long time Tessa hadn't even thought about cutting herself. Hadn't even considered it. But then when her mom was first admitted to the hospital, she'd gotten scared and tried to figure out what to do. It all happened so fast. The doctors weren't saying much, but she could tell it was serious. She never expected Mom to get sick, not like that. Things like that only happened to other people, not people like her mom. Not to families like hers.

But then she found out that sometimes they did.

When the treatments didn't help and Mom got weaker and weaker, Tessa had even tried to talk to Patrick—but that didn't help much. It wasn't that he was mean or anything, just distracted. Besides, they'd only known each other for like a year before that, and she'd grown up without a dad anyway, so it'd always been kind of hard for them to talk to each other—to really talk. Then when he got so wrapped up taking care of Mom, well, she had to do something on her own.

So the night her mom started chemo, Tessa had taken an X-acto knife and held it against the inside of her right thigh. Cherise told her the best spots to do it so no one would see, so no one could tell.

"Isn't it kind of weird, hurting yourself like that?" Tessa had asked.

"It's not like you want to hurt yourself or anything," Cherise had explained. "It's more like the opposite. You're actually trying to find a way to let the pain out. Try it. You'll see. It hurts more when you don't do it."

That first time had been the hardest. Tessa wasn't even sure she'd be able to go through with it. Even now she could remember how nervous she was touching the cold steel to her skin, trembling a little, wondering if it would really help, if anything could really help—and then at last pressing the blade hard enough to draw blood and how it hurt more than she thought it would and how her leg twitched and she ended up dropping the knife, just barely missing her foot.

But somehow it did help. Yes. Somehow seeing that small streak of blood made the way she felt inside seem less out of control, less desperate, less awkwardly, gnawingly painful. Even if she couldn't make her mom feel better, even if she couldn't talk to Patrick, at least she could do something. At least she could do this.

Of course, it got worse after Mom died. That's when she moved from her leg to her arm. Everything spun out of control then. Really bad for a while. But Tessa knew she was just doing it to cope. She could stop anytime she wanted to. She knew that much.

So now that she was alone again and her grandparents were asleep in the other room and she had that terrible roaring pain rising in her heart, Tessa fingered the blade and looked at the scars riding up her arm.

She saw her reflection, distorted and angular on the side of the razor blade.

Her heart was racing just like it always did.

How else were you supposed to deal with all this loneliness, this brokenness, this pain that you couldn't put your finger on or hold back or control? You stuff it down, hoping it'll all go away, but it doesn't. It just gets bigger and uglier.

Cutting.

Like burrowing out of your own private little prison one slice at a time. But in this case the prison is you.

It was almost like crying or screaming but without all the tears and noise. That was the best way she could describe it, really. What was that phrase Cherise had used? Oh yeah. Crimson tears.

Crying your way out of prison, scar by scar.

When life spun out of control, you had to do something about it. Something. Even if it hurt for a little while. Even if it left scars.

Tessa pressed the razor blade against her skin and pulled.

23

Aaron Jeffrey Kincaid had barely laid his head on the pillow before the dream came. It was the same dream. The one he always had. The one that climbed out of the nightmares of his past and became the backdrop of life for him even when he was awake.

That's how some dreams are. Whether you're awake or asleep they just won't let you go. They grow thick roots, threading their way through your hopes and desires, your past and your pain, your future and your days, becoming a deep and certain part of you. And even though he'd been dreaming the dream for nearly thirty years, the images hadn't become foggy or clouded by time, just clearer and somehow more distinct. Sharper and more focused than ever.

He was ten when it happened.

The crack of gunshots rang in the air, echoing through the muddy compound before being swallowed by the nearby jungle. Following each blast came a burst of squawks and squeals erupting from the canopy of branches high overhead.

The boy ran with the sound of gunshots all around him. Ran. Trying to forget what he'd seen, what no one should ever see.

Ran. Ran. Ran.

So that's how the dream started—with the gunshots by the jungle. He was out of breath. He heard the loud, loud guns. But those were nothing compared to the shrieks of the children. Mostly it was the younger children screaming. The little ones. The babies. Their cries intermingled with the slow music playing over the sound system; the humming, throbbing music almost like a death march, almost like a church service gone horribly wrong. Some of the people sang along, others were hugging and comforting each other. A few of the mothers cried. But it was the babies he remembered the most. The sound of the little ones crying in the dusk.

He ran, and the shrieks chased after him as he clambered over the fence and hit the ground running on the other side. Behind him, the two guards were yelling for him to stop. That everything was going to be okay! That he should just come back and join the others! That things would be better now! If he would just stop running!

But he didn't stop. He ran like he'd never run before, eyes frozen in terror, down the road and toward the jungle where he could hide. Like an animal he ran. The trees loomed high above him now. He'd reached the edge of the world. He dove into the shadows, a thousand shades of green flashing past his face. Even the sting of branches lashing against his face didn't slow him down.

The branch next to his left ear exploded.

In his dream, Aaron could almost feel the spray of splinters bite into his neck and face, just like they had in the jungle so many years ago. But he didn't stop running. The crack of another gunshot cut through the dusk. Shrieks. Music. Babies. The river.

Just a little farther. Make it to the river.

He was almost out of reach now. Almost to safety. Just a little farther and everything will be okay.

Whatever you do, don't stop running.

———————————■———————————

The boy hadn't been there when it started. Instead he was off playing by himself as he often did, by one of the many rivers that threaded through the jungle surrounding the compound. He liked watching the waves ripple along, easing toward some distant village—toward the roaming sea out of sight somewhere. He would dream of all the places the river might flow, all the shores the ocean might touch. Faraway, exotic lands. Lands he could only visit in his imagination. Because once you came to this town in the jungle, you never left. Everyone knew that. Everyone said so. It became your home forever.

Even though no one was supposed to leave the compound, his parents didn't seem to mind his treks into the jungle. They let him explore down by the river because they loved him. And because he wasn't like the other children. He was different. Special. Destined for great things. He knew it was true. They'd told him so. He would follow in Father's footsteps one day.

Even Father said so.

So they'd let him go to the river earlier in the day when the rumors started.

Everything was so tense, everyone so anxious. Whispering. Shaking their heads and then looking around to see if anyone was watching. And usually someone was. Someone was always watching. Or listening. Things would be different now that the congressman had visited, everyone knew that. The government was coming. It was just a matter of time.

So he'd gone off to be alone for a while. But then the music started and the screams started and that's what brought him back.

It was already happening when he arrived at the pavilion. There were so many people lying in still rows on the floor that at first he thought maybe they'd been ordered to take a nap, and dutifully, unquestionably, they'd obeyed, positioning themselves on the ground.

To go to sleep. Sleep. Sleep.

Then he saw his baby brother and his parents on the ground. But they weren't sleeping. They weren't moving.

He watched for a while, trying to figure out what was going on, why the ones who lay down didn't get up again. Some people lay down quietly and hardly moved again, others shook in ways that frightened him before they stopped moving for good. But none of the ones who drank the medication or accepted the needle got up again.

None of them. Ever again.

Run.

Keep running.

Have to keep running.

He jumped over a log on the edge of the jungle, and a bullet caught him in the left shoulder, sending him sprawling to the ground in a stunning burst of pain. He cried out but then caught himself, clamping his hand over his mouth, tears burning in his eyes as he lay on the jungle floor for a moment and tried to decide what to do. Panting. Breathing. Watching. If he didn't move, they might think he was dead. Yes, that might work. But then again, they might check, just to make sure. What should he do? He wanted to wake up from the nightmare, but he was stuck inside it. You can't wake up when you're not asleep. And he wasn't asleep. He wished he was, but the jungle was real, and so were the tears and the babies and the bodies. So many bodies. You can't leave the nightmare when you're living inside it. When it's living inside you.

If he stood up, they'd shoot him again. Yes, he knew that much. He knew they would. They'd kill him. But he had to get up. He had to! He had to keep going to get away from it all. Away from the screaming babies. Away from the quiet corpses.

So he did. He stood. His breath ragged, a streak of bright pain clutching his arm, he shoved himself to his feet while the gunshot wound screamed at him from his shoulder.

"There he is!" called a voice from somewhere behind him.

The boy flew toward the underbrush as another bullet ripped into the shadows that seemed to be growing all around him. The sounds of the night were beginning to envelop the jungle now that the sun had sunk into the trees. Strange and primal sounds surrounded him: rare insects and wild birds and the haunting cries of the predators who preferred to hunt only in the dark. Heavy clouds hung on the horizon, dark and distant and swollen in the sky, growing more and more gray by the second.

He stumbled to the shore of the river and collapsed, dizzy with pain, the water gently whirling around him, taking his lifeblood downstream toward some distant, unnamed shore.

The voices of the men reached him, but they were fainter now, floating on air. "I got him. C'mon. Let's get back. There might be others who try to run."

He heard the words echo somewhere between consciousness and unconsciousness, somewhere between sleep and death, between night and day. The boy couldn't tell anymore where reality ended and the dreaming began.

And then, with the sky darkening above him, he closed his eyes and let the night climb in with its tawny fingers, sliding back the curtain and worming its way deep into the secret part of his soul.

<hr />

That's where the dream ended. That's where he woke up every night now, dying beside the river, soaked in muddy, bloody water, as the night climbed into his heart.

He lay in bed, shivering despite himself. He wasn't a ten-year-old boy anymore. He was a forty-year-old man. He listened. No gunshots. No screams. Just the gentle sounds of the house settling and sleeping all around him. And the autumn wind outside the house, prowling through the night.

He eased the covers down. A sliver of waning moon hung outside his window, but in the glimmering starlight his eyes found the evidence of the bullet hole on his left shoulder. The scar that told him it was all so much more than a dream. It was a memory.

"Soon," he said to the darkness, "the circle will be complete." With his fingertip he traced the ridge of the scar where the bullet had ripped into him. And to him it felt like evidence of his destiny. After all, he was bound for great things, and nothing could stop destiny. His parents had taught him that much, long ago. And Father himself had told him he was special; told him that he would carry on the work when the time was right.

Aaron Jeffrey Kincaid didn't bother to close his eyes again. He knew he wouldn't be able to sleep anymore that night anyway. Not after the dream.

He rolled out of bed and sat by the window, letting the starlight caress him, inspire him, complete him. In just a few days, everything that he had worked for would be fulfilled. The message would reverberate around the world. Until then, all he had to do was stay alert and aware.

Alert and aware.

Sharper and more focused than ever.

24

"He called your room!" I had to hold the cell phone away from my ear. When Ralph gets upset, his voice is as unwieldy as his left hook. "How in the name of all that is holy did he get the phone number?"

"Well"—I was holding the phone at arm's length by then—"I imagine it's not too tough to call up a hotel operator and get connected to a room if you know the guest's name."

"How did he know you were there?"

"I don't know. He might have followed us from Mindy's crime scene on Thursday, if he was in the crowd."

Ralph cussed under his breath. "Why didn't you call me last night?"

I wasn't really up for this. I rubbed my eyes. I hadn't slept much. Again. "Ralph, it wouldn't have done any good. I called the tech guys; they couldn't trace it. I'm moving into the hotel across the street from the fed building this morning. Wallace is sending some guys to pick me up. He's getting me a car."

Ralph grunted. "'Bout time." He'd calmed down enough for me to slide the phone under my ear as I shoved a sheaf of papers into one of the manila folders on the desk beside me. He must have been processing what I'd just said because after a moment he added, "That mean what I think it does?"

I glanced at the suitcase and the backpack that had been waiting for me when I arrived at the hotel last night. True to his word, Ralph had sent for them. The suitcase was for work, the backpack was for play. I'd been planning for months to spend a couple days climbing in Linville Gorge after that law enforcement conference. Didn't look like I'd get a chance now, though.

"Yeah. I think I'll stick around for a few more days. Nothing pressing on my calendar. And this guy has already made two mistakes—waiting for us at the mall and calling me at the hotel. He's overconfident. We might still be able to save Jolene."

"If she's still alive." His voice sounded grim.

I wasn't sure if I should tell him the killer had mentioned my daughter, wasn't sure if he'd want me off the case. I decided to risk it; after all, this was Ralph. "He knows I have a daughter, Ralph. He mentioned her by name. He might know where she is. I need to make sure Tessa and my parents are safe."

"We'll get them to a safe house out in Denver."

That was Ralph for you. A good man.

"Thing is, Ralph, I need to see her." I'd had a lot of time to think things through last night after talking with the Illusionist. My adrenaline had been pumping so hard I'd needed to do twenty minutes of pull-ups on the door frame of the hotel room just to calm down. It's great exercise. Of course, you can only use your fingertips though. Back when I started working out it took me two years before I was able to do just one fingertip pull-up; another year before I could do ten. That was a decade ago. I've gotten a little better since then.

"What do you mean, 'see her'?" he said.

I took a slow breath. "I need to see Tessa, Ralph. In person. The truth is, we've both been having a hard time. We've never really talked about Christie's death. And now these dead girls, this case . . . it's getting to me. I need to make things right with her. You have a kid, Ralph, you know what I'm talking about. My parents can stay out there, but not Tessa. Either I fly back to Denver for a couple days or the Bureau needs to bring her out here."

"Pat, you know I can't—"

"Get her a safe place close by, Ralph." I eyed the luggage. "Either that or I'm heading back to Colorado right now."

I heard a knock on the hotel room door and peered through the eyehole. Even though it was still dark outside, I could see two very annoyed-looking officers standing outside my door. Neither one looked old enough to shave. One of them held up a set of car keys, dangling them in front of the peephole as if he were trying to hypnotize it. Ah, good. My rental car had arrived. I unlocked the door.

"Well, Ralph? I'm waiting."

He cussed. Sometimes that was a good sign, sometimes a bad one. I figured the timing on this one was in my favor. "OK," he said. "I can't believe I'm saying this—I'll make it happen. But once you two have ironed things out, she goes back to Denver so you can focus on this case. She's here two days max."

"Four."

"Three."

"Deal."

I opened the door and pointed to my bags. The officer who looked older by about three minutes nodded to his partner, who groaned but finally sauntered over to pick up my backpack. I grabbed the suitcase as I told Ralph the flight number I wanted Tessa on. It left Denver at 11:20 a.m. mountain time but because of the time change wouldn't arrive in Charlotte until 6:16 tonight.

Boy Cop grunted, "What 'chu got in this thing? Bricks?"

"Climbing gear," I said to him under my breath.

Then I told Ralph the ticket price.

I had to pull the phone away from my ear again.

The officer shook his head and followed me out the door. I turned my attention back to the conversation with Ralph. "You'll need to have an agent from Denver accompany her. I don't want her left alone for a minute. Not with this guy on the loose. "

"Great. Another ticket."

"Ralph."

"OK." A sigh. "Anything else? Trip to Bermuda, maybe?"

"Hey, that'd be nice. Maybe later this winter."

"In your prayers."

Once I was convinced I'd be seeing Tessa in the evening, I ventured into the case. "So, any progress? Any word on Jolene?"

"Not yet," he grumbled. "I was hoping we'd get video of our guy at the mall, but the cameras only cover the public access entrances, not the employee break areas where her keys were stolen from. We've got some people going over the footage, though, just in case."

"Parking garage?"

"Nope. No cameras."

"Figures."

I unlocked the trunk of the car, and we hoisted my bags inside.

"Ballistics is looking at the bullet, but prelims don't seem to match it with the guns registered to any of the security guards. Local PD is checking out all the guards. So far, two of them look interesting. One guy lives on the same street as Jolene. I thought I'd talk to him before coming back to Asheville."

I nodded my thanks to the officers and slid behind the wheel of the rental car. They walked off mumbling to each other, obviously not happy to be playing Bellhop and Errand Boy this morning. "Hmm. Well, check it out, but I don't think it'll be him. There may even be evidence that points to the guy, but he'll be cleared."

"What do you mean?"

I flipped on my headlights and pulled into the slowly dawning day. "I don't think our guy is stupid enough to go after a girl from down the block or get himself caught on video at the mall. He would have thought of all that. Besides, think big picture. This is just a piece of a complex puzzle. Just one in the series. Remember, predatory killers typically expand their hunting grounds on each subsequent crime; they don't shrink it back toward their neighborhoods. But who knows. Talk to the guard. See what you can find out. By the way, how's the guy who was shot?"

Ralph grunted. "He'll survive. Might not ever speak again, though. If that bullet had gone any further to the right—"

I looked in the rearview mirror and noticed a pair of headlights.

"I know, I know." The taunting words of the Illusionist echoed in my head: *You and I both know I didn't intend to kill him.* "I don't think he meant to kill the guy, Ralph. He might be a sharpshooter. Let's have Sheriff Wallace follow up on that."

I pictured Ralph nodding on the other side of the phone. "We tried talking to the girl who was with him," he said, "but we couldn't get much. She was really shook up."

"Yeah. No kidding." I merged onto the highway and shifted the phone to the other hand.

"She has no idea how the chess piece got in their car—we were able to get that much from her. Anderson's wife was very forthcoming, though—Anderson's the guy who was shot—turns out he's an English professor at UNC. The girl is one of his students."

"Wonderful."

"He told his wife he was playing poker every Friday night. Apparently, it's a regular thing."

A pattern. Yes.

He knew that. The Illusionist knew they'd be there.

"The girl did mention that they'd start in the car and then move to the hotel down the block. She said it was what turned him on."

"That's a little too much information for me, Ralph," I said. "But I appreciate your thoroughness." After that the conversation lulled. We'd both said most of what we had on our minds. Ahead of me, even though the sun wasn't up yet, the edge of the horizon was beginning to glow amber and red.

"That it?" he said at last.

The headlights followed me. Stayed four cars back.

There was one more thing.

I merged into the flow of traffic on the Blue Ridge Parkway. "The whole thing with the contact lenses, Ralph . . ."

"Yeah?"

"It troubles me. He's linking the crimes for us."

"Don't the ribbons and chess pieces do that?"

"This is deeper. It's something else."

"Showing off?"

"Maybe. I don't know. He stole the contacts from Jolene and then planted them on Mindy. He was cross-contaminating the crime scenes with evidence from a *future* victim. I've never seen that before."

I accelerated, passed a few cars. Kept an eye on the rearview mirror.

Ralph was quiet for a moment; I figured he was chewing on everything. "But if it's supposed to be a clue to his next victim, it's not nearly enough to go on. I mean, stolen contacts?"

"That's the thing. I don't think he wants us to stop the killings," I said. "I think he wants us to know we *can't* stop them."

The car I was watching passed a few other cars. Stayed the same distance behind me.

"Look," I said, "I'm heading to the federal building to pick up my laptop—I left it there when we rushed out last night—and then I'm heading back to look at Mindy's crime scene again. The medical examiner placed the time of death somewhere between 8:00 and 11:00 a.m."

"I never understood why it's so important for you to see the crime scenes at the same time as the murder—"

"You notice things. Lighting, maybe. Usage patterns. You see what he saw. It helps me understand the context of the crime. Listen, Ralph, I think I'm being followed."

"What?"

"A car. It's been with me since I left the hotel. He's not being obvious, though. Whoever it is, he's experienced."

"What do you want to do?"

"There's a tunnel up ahead. I've got an idea."

25

About a quarter mile ahead of me the road disappeared into a tunnel that bore through the side of a mountain. I raced the engine and sped toward it. Whoever was tailing me was stuck behind traffic and couldn't pass because the highway narrowed as we approached the tunnel.

I noted how many cars he was back—four—then entered the tunnel and flicked off my lights so the cars behind me wouldn't be able to judge how far ahead of them I'd traveled. I floored the gas pedal and watched the headlights shrink behind me. A few seconds later I emerged from the other side of the mountain, whipped over to the shoulder, and backed up, spraying up a cloud of gravel in the process.

Now I could see the cars leave the tunnel, but they couldn't see me.

I waited. He'd be out any time, and the tables would be turned. I would be following him.

Out came the first car.

I waited . . .

Car number two.

I gripped the steering wheel. My heart began racing. *Is this the killer? Did he wait for me outside my hotel room after calling me last night?*

Number three.

I got ready to follow. I wished I'd been able to get the make and model of the car.

Well, I'd have those in a second.

Waited . . .

The seconds passed. The car didn't come.

I waited a few more moments and then spun my car around and headed back through the tunnel to the other side of the mountain, but he was gone. The road was empty.

He must have realized what you were planning when you sped up. He never entered the tunnel.

I wasn't sure if I should feel disappointed or relieved. It was just another puzzle piece that didn't make sense.

At last I drove back through the tunnel toward Asheville. I dialed Ralph and told him what had happened.

"I'll have Sheriff Wallace check with those two officers . . ."—his voice was getting spotty—". . . see if either of them noticed a car in the parking lot, or someone following you." He was right about his phone. It did need a charge. In a bad way.

Static began to swallow his words.

"I'm losing you," I said.

"I'm sending . . ." Ralph kept talking, but his voice blinked out in the middle of the sentence.

The phone was dead.

Dead.

Well, that was appropriate.

I glanced at the dark mountains looming around me. Above them, the bloated early morning clouds were drinking in the scarlet sunlight that seeped up and over the peaks. For a moment they made me think of giant gray bodies smeared with blood hanging from the sky.

Man.

I need to get a different job.

I turned on the radio and scanned the dial to try and find some music to get my mind off the case. Off death. A few snatches of whiny country music flickered on and then became garbled by static. Mostly all I could get were stations of radio preachers.

I spun the dial, turned them off.

But it was too late. The Bible verses they were quoting brought it all back . . . sitting on the stiff orange chair in the corner of the hospital room . . . seeing Christie on the bed . . . having to listen to the Reverend Donovan Richman go on about the goodness of God when all I could see was evidence of his cruelty lying right there in front of me . . .

She'd asked him to come, Christie had. She'd been going to a small storefront church, and he was their new pastor, and so when she was admitted, she asked him to come.

Reverend Donovan Richman. What a name.

Another man from the church came too, a retired African-American gentleman, Benjamin Grayson. He was one of the deacons, and I gathered from their conversations that he was the one in charge of the "visitation ministry" that served shut-ins and hospitalized church members.

Mostly I sat in the corner in the orange chair while they talked — well, while Richman talked. The rest of us pretty much just listened.

Richman was rife with clichés about why God allows suffering and nodded his head agreeably whenever Christie would whisper something about Jesus or heaven. Benjamin just sat quietly and held Christie's hand and sometimes cried strong, round tears.

I don't know that he meant it this way, but to me Reverend Richman made Christie's pain seem trite, like some kind of cosmic object lesson sent by God to teach her something important about life. I have a hard time believing that God would torture people into loving him. I don't know that much about God or about love, but I do know that torture isn't what brings them together.

—————————————■—————————————

The Illusionist jiggled the mouse, and his computer monitor sprang to life. The first rays of sunlight were sliding through the window, sending streaks of light dancing across his fingers. A beautiful morning. Beautiful!

He cruised to some of his bookmarked websites and skimmed the latest online news concerning the abduction of Jolene Brittany Parker. He even downloaded a couple of articles about her. Mostly boilerplate stuff, but a few were actually interesting. It was always entertaining to see what people were saying about his work.

"Look at this, Jolene," he called over his shoulder. "Your parents are waiting for a ransom note."

No response.

Ah, well, that was to be expected.

He almost giggled. A ransom note! Who did they think he was? As if he were interested in money.

He took a sip of ice-cold orange juice and surfed over to a chat room for true crime enthusiasts, where some of the resident "experts" were taking their stab at profiling the Yellow Ribbon Strangler. How clever was that? Taking their *stab* at profiling him. Ha. And he thought of that right there, on the spot. He was that good!

He scrolled down the list, scanning the inane responses.

Someone named *catchem16* had written that the killer was, "Obviously a unorganized introvert with latented homosexual tendencies since he didn't have sex with none of the women."

Idiot.

Someone named *deadhunter1zero* thought, "The main UNSUB has past military experience and probably has a dishonorable discharge for violent outbursts. He's living out of a mobile home or travel trailer. He works a menial job and has a German shepherd."

In a way it was funny. "He's a white male between the ages of 25 and 40," they would write, "antisocial, divorced, low IQ . . ." Blah, blah, blah, blah. Cookie-cutter profiling. Morons. Imbeciles. They had no idea who they were dealing with.

He wondered what Agent Jiang thought of him. He knew what he thought of her. Oh yes. He knew exactly what he thought of her. What fun they could have together in the moonlight with the ropes and the ribbon and his favorite silver blade.

He could picture it now. Her face. Her body. The workings of her throat as she gasped for breath.

Mmm.

But really, it was better not to fantasize too much about that right now. Her time would come.

And then, of course, there was Dr. Bowers. Despite all his talk about space and time and the geography of crime—see he was a poet too!—Patrick did understand the mind of a killer. Yes, somehow he knew what it was like. Maybe that's why he made such a show of not listening to profilers. Because he was afraid of his own motives, of the dark channels in his own heart. There was something there. Yes. Something to consider.

He read one more asinine paragraph describing how the Yellow Ribbon Strangler probably started fires, wet his bed, and tortured small animals as a child.

Well, one out of three wasn't bad.

Christie died on a rain-soaked Monday afternoon eight months ago today. End of February. Spring was trying to unfold; winter trying to die. She passed away in between the seasons, in the middle of the empty spaces of the year.

The day before she died, Reverend Richman asked how I was doing. When I told him I was okay, he asked politely if I was ready to face death. I said that I was ready for mine but that I wasn't ready for Christie's and never would be. Not ever.

He didn't seem satisfied with my answer. I tried to thank him for coming and told him that right now probably wasn't the best time to talk about all that but that both Christie and I really appreciated his—

The anger had started feeling its way to the surface, and even now I could feel my hands tightening around the steering wheel.

Because he wouldn't let it drop.

He just wouldn't let it drop.

He interrupted me in the middle of my sentence. "Don't take eternity lightly, Dr. Bowers. You never know when your time will come." His concern appeared to be genuine, but his timing was terrible.

"Thanks," I said. "I'll keep that in mind."

As we walked toward the door he said, "You seem like a well-read man; have you ever heard of Pascal's Wager?"

Of course I'd heard of Pascal and his wager. Blaise Pascal was one of the greatest mathematicians to ever live and one of my favorite authors. Without his pioneering work, computers—and geographic profiling—might never have been invented. He's the one who wrote, "The only thing that consoles us from our miseries is diversion. And yet it is the greatest of our miseries." I read that quote years ago and never forgot it. It seemed to tell the story of my life.

"Yes, I know Pascal," I said. "But I've never been a big fan of his wager. I don't like the idea of betting on God."

"But why wouldn't you want to bet on God?"

I took a deep breath. On the one hand I did believe in God, but on the other I wasn't really so sure. I had my doubts, especially in that hospital room with Christie. "Because I know someone who did." I spoke in a low enough whisper so that my dying wife couldn't hear me. "And he let her down."

The sentence tasted like poison on my tongue. I knew they were harsh and hurtful words, but I didn't care. Richman was the one who'd brought it up. He'd pushed the issue. "Now excuse me," I said. I started ushering both him and Benjamin to the door.

"Give God a shot," Richman persisted. "You don't have anything to lose."

And that did it. "Except the truth," I shot back. "That's what really matters in the end—more than what you believe, more than what benefits you. That's the problem with Pascal's Wager, Reverend. It's based on payoffs, either now or in eternity, not on what's true. According to Pascal, if God exists and you believe, you get to go to heaven. And if you believe but he doesn't exist, at least you get to live with peace and hope in this life. Right?"

He nodded.

"But Reverend," I said, "if God doesn't exist, you shouldn't believe that he does, even if it leads you to a happier life—because you'd be believing a lie. Living a lie. I don't want my life based on a lie, even if it's a comforting one. I'd rather bet on the truth."

Richman opened his mouth to say something and then stopped. He looked from me to Benjamin and then back to me. He had no response. Nothing. It was the first time since I'd met him that he was speechless.

And that's when Benjamin smiled and gently patted my shoulder. "You are a man of great faith, Dr. Bowers."

His words floored me. "What?"

"Faith in what's good—faith in the truth. A lot of people don't even have that these days. I admire you." And with that, he left the room.

Somehow he'd dismantled everything I'd just said, every argument I'd just used by agreeing with me. "Thank you," I mumbled.

Richman patted my shoulder too. "He's right," he said. "And you've given me something to think about. Thanks."

Then he left too and I sat next to Christie and wept.

26

The Illusionist slid the keyboard back and pulled out his leather-bound journal.

Enough of the cyberspace imbeciles.

Time to record his impressions of last night while the images were still fresh in his mind. Jolene. Soft, timid, frightened Jolene.

Time to relive the long, delicious night.

His words flowed smoothly, quick and nimble beneath his fingers. It was as if his mind itself were on fire, leaving a trail of cursive thought smoke across the page. Bringing back every emotion, every sensation from the night before. Oh, how he enjoyed this part of the process, this reliving of the night on the page.

And yet . . .

As he thought back over their night together, as enjoyable as it had been, he had to admit that it was somewhat disappointing too. Just like always. She'd been the most exciting one so far. Oh yes, that much was true. But in the end it was just like the others. After it was all done, when the final throes were over, the feelings of disappointment returned.

His fantasies about inducing death were always more thrilling than the actual deaths themselves.

Reality just didn't measure up.

But next time, it would. That's what he told himself. That's what kept him going, the hope—and really, it was a hope—that he would finally find what he was looking for next time.

This time.

With Alice.

Tonight.

It took the Illusionist nearly an hour to record his thoughts about his night with Jolene. He even included some drawings. Crude, yes. But quite memorable and remarkably accurate in their depictions of human anatomy.

Then he carefully picked up the two weighty duffel bags, walked outside, and lowered them into the back of his van. Even though it was a weekend, he had to go to work today. Not the kind of work he enjoyed most, but the kind everyone needs to do. The bill-paying work.

But before heading out to make a buck, he had a couple of important deliveries to make.

As I took my exit off the highway, I thought of Tessa again. On a typical Saturday morning she wouldn't be rolling out of bed for another three or four hours. But if I was going to be spending the morning poking around crime scenes out of cell phone range up in the mountains, I needed to call and tell her about the flight before I left.

But Ralph's phone was dead.

Well, I'd call from the federal building then.

I was sure she wasn't happy about having to go to that hotel last night. She hated being told what to do. Probably even convinced Mom and Dad to get her a separate room. *Well, at least she didn't know you sent a patrol car. That would have pushed her over the edge.* I could only imagine how she'd react when she found out she would be leaving for North Carolina before lunchtime.

After swinging through Mountain Java Roasters and downing a cup of delicately balanced Tizapa from El Salvador, I parked my rental car in the lot beside the federal building.

I sat there steeling myself for a few minutes before heading inside. *Here goes nothing.* Tracking down a serial killer—that I could handle. Waking up a teenager before 6:00 a.m. on a Saturday morning, now that was something scary.

I pushed open the bulletproof glass doors, stepped into the lobby, and handed my ID to the bald guard sitting next to the metal detector. He yawned at me as if it were a greeting and glanced at my card.

The whole case was spinning through my mind. I had more questions than answers.

I set my gun on the conveyer belt.

Mostly I thought of Jolene. I knew the state patrol and the Charlotte police were doing everything they could to locate her. Still, I wished I could find her, help her, save her, make it so that none of this had ever happened. And then take her back to her parents or her boyfriend or whoever and laugh with them as I told them it was just a big misunderstanding, that she'd just gone over to spend the night at a friend's house. See? Everything was fine.

But that was a dream, not a reality. Was she even still alive? . . . What was she going through? . . . Where might her abductor have taken her?

I know it's always best to avoid thinking those kinds of thoughts. Better to keep your distance. But sometimes you can't help but think them. Maybe that's what keeps you human.

And what about this Illusionist character? What kind of game was he playing? Could he really be someone from my past?

I could think of only one guy I'd put away who was smart enough to pull off something this elaborate, but he was on death row in Illinois. Or at least I thought he was: Richard Basque, the man who slaughtered, disemboweled, and then ate the intestines of sixteen women in the farmlands of rural Illinois and Wisconsin back in the nineties. I was the one who'd put him away, early in my career, when I was a detective in Milwaukee. Come to think of it, that was the case where I first met up with Ralph, who was one of the three agents assigned to help us with the case.

Richard Basque. I might want to check on that.

The security guard watched blearily as my gun passed under the X-ray machine, then he handed me my ID and waved me through.

The building was still draped in early morning silence. I headed down the hallway to the conference room, opened the door, and noticed Brent Tucker already stationed behind his desk. *Hmm. He's getting an early start.* He was on the phone and signaled to me with a finger that he would be with me in a minute.

I made the call to my parents and found out they had indeed gotten two rooms. Thankfully I didn't have to wake Tessa—she was in the other room. I offered to pay for both rooms, and of course they declined. But my parents did agree to stay at a safe house for a few days. Yes, they'd make sure Tessa was at the airport on time. Yes, they would take care of everything. Yes, yes, don't worry.

After I hung up and was grabbing my computer, Brent called to me. "Hey, Pat."

"Morning," I said. "How was the big date last night?"

"Fantastic." He gazed at me. "You look tired."

I decided not to tell him about the Illusionist's phone call or the car following me or the strange meeting with the governor. Plenty of time for that later. Right now I needed to get to Mindy's crime scene. "It was quite a night." I yawned. "You heard about the girl in Charlotte?"

"Yeah, from Ralph. Any news?"

"No. Looks like the same guy, though. He shot someone last night too."

"Ralph told me. How is he?"

"Looks like he'll be all right. Eventually." I slipped my computer into its carrying case, then gestured to the empty coffee cup on Tucker's desk. "You must be one of those morning people I hear about."

"I had something I wanted to check on." He pulled up a chair beside him. "Here, sit down; I want to show you something."

"I don't have much time. I'm heading back to Mindy's crime scene."

"I'll be quick." Tucker had set up a chessboard on his desk. The playing pieces were positioned as if someone had stopped suddenly in the middle of a game. "After your briefing yesterday I got to thinking about the significance of the body dump locations."

"And?"

"Well, latitude and longitude are represented by a set of numbers and degrees such as . . ." He glanced at his notepad and read off the numbers, "35°35'42.65'N, 82°33'25.96'W—where we are right now."

I was anxious to get moving. "Go on."

"Well, when chess pieces are moved across the board, chess players represent the placement of their pieces with a series of numbers or letters that record their position. I was thinking—"

"He's showing us the board!" I interrupted.

Tucker nodded. "Right! There are several different chess notation systems out there. I'm trying to see if any of them can be broken down into numeric representations that might correspond to the latitude and longitude of the dump sites."

I was impressed. "This is good work. Let me know if you find anything. I think you might be on to something." I pushed my chair back to stand up and bumped the desk in the process. One of the black bishops fell to its side. I reached over and set it upright on the board.

Tucker watched me. "Now you'll need to take that piece."

"What?"

"If we were playing chess," he said matter-of-factly. "If you touch the piece of your opponent you have to take it on your next turn."

I'd taken two steps when I froze in midstride. *If you touch the piece of your opponent* . . . I spun around. "What did you just say?"

He stared at me blankly. "In tournament play. If you touch your opponent's piece you have to take it on your next move or you forfeit the game."

I smacked my palm down on the desk, upsetting all the pieces on the board, scattering them across the desk. "That's it, Tucker! He's touching our pieces and then taking them on the next turn. That's what he did with the contact lenses. He reached across the board, touched her, and then took her. Don't you see?" I stared at the pictures of the victims on the wall. "Reinita wasn't engaged, was she?"

Tucker flipped through some papers on his desk. He looked shocked. "How did you know? That's in today's briefing. Margaret hasn't even signed off on it yet."

"No, Reinita wasn't engaged," I mumbled, "but Mindy was."

"Mindy?" He started flipping through another folder.

I picked up a pawn and set it upright on the board again, a lone chess piece on the square battlefield. "He touched our piece, Tucker. And then on his next turn, he took her." I snatched up the pawn, held it up to the light.

Tucker let out a long, slow breath. "How long has he been doing it?"

"That's what we need to find out."

27

I was torn.

On the one hand I wanted to get to the crime scene, but on the other hand I didn't really want to go anywhere. If we were right about the Illusionist, we might have found the big break we were hoping for.

Tucker started pulling out the reports from each of the crime scenes. "Yes. Mindy is engaged to a guy from her hometown—Kevin Young!"

"So," I said, "the killer stole the engagement ring from Mindy and placed it on Reinita's finger. Then he stole Jolene's contacts and put them in Mindy's eyes."

"Whew. This guy is good. He's threading everything together for us."

"Yeah. Touching the player he's going to take next. We need to go over everything from the beginning, all the physical evidence. I want to know how long this has been going on."

"Gotcha."

My mind was spinning, flying over all the facts I'd read so far about the cases, wondering what other clues the Illusionist might have left for us. *Does the order matter? What's the significance of an engagement ring or contact lenses? What else has he left?*

But as excited as I was, I also knew there were good people here who could analyze the forensic evidence better than I could. Besides, I had a lot to do today. I needed to get going.

Just then, Sheriff Wallace walked into the room. "Whatcha'll up to?" His mouth was half full of a sausage biscuit; in his hand he held an overstuffed bag from Hardees. Somehow, even though it wasn't even eight o'clock yet, he was already sweating. Damp, yellowish stains emanated from the armpits of his once-white shirt.

"Sheriff Wallace," I said, "I need some of your men to pull all the physical evidence from the previous cases."

"Huh? Why?"

"Focus on anything found on or near the bodies. Anything at all—rings, glasses, jewelry, brands of lipstick, clothes. Tucker can explain everything. We're looking for links. Tucker, you on this?"

"Absolutely."

Sheriff Wallace pulled a cinnamon roll out of the bag and popped it in his mouth. He looked lost.

"He's reaching across the board," I explained, "and he's touching our pieces, then taking them on his next turn." I realized I wasn't making any sense, not to someone who hadn't heard what we were talking about.

Just then his phone rang. He answered it, looked a little confused, and passed it to me. "It's for you."

"Yeah?" I said into the phone as Tucker started bringing him up to speed, trying to summarize our theory in as few words as possible. "Bowers here."

"It's Lien-hua. I've been trying to find you. I tried your phone, then Ralph's phone—"

"Long story."

"I thought you were heading to the dump sites."

"I am. I'm on my way."

"Where are you now?"

"The federal building. I was just leaving." I grabbed my computer and whispered for Tucker to call me if they came up with anything else. I headed for the door. "Where are you?" I asked her.

"On the steps outside waiting for you."

"What? I thought you were in Charlotte."

"Ralph sent me back early this morning. He tried telling you, but I guess your cell phone died."

"Actually, it was his. Never mind."

She yawned across the phone. "I feel like I've been up forever."

"I'm glad I took the chopper last night. When'll Ralph be down?"

"This afternoon after he's done interviewing the security guard. He thought it might be helpful if I joined you since I've been to each of the crime scenes so far and . . ." — she paused for a moment — "I'm the one who's been working on the offender's profile."

Don't say anything stupid, Pat. Don't be an idiot. "Yeah. Good. The profile. I love profiles."

"You're a terrible liar."

"I'll try to remember that."

I stepped outside and closed up my phone. Wait, not mine. Dante Wallace's. Oh well, I could give it back to him later. Nearby, Lien-hua was slipping her phone into her jeans pocket. She had on hiking boots and wore a blue North Face fleece pullover and matching windbreaker to fend off the crisp morning air. With the mountains rising behind her, she looked like she belonged on the cover of an outdoor magazine.

I'd subscribe.

"He's touching our pieces," I said, unlocking the car.

"What?"

"Climb in. I'll explain on the way."

28

Aaron Jeffrey Kincaid finished reading through Governor Taylor's confidential travel itinerary for the week, and then began perusing the guest list for the upcoming Cable News Forum luncheon. It had cost him nearly $80,000 to obtain this information from a woman named Anita Banner, but it had been worth every penny. And when he found out that she would be there too, he was even more pleased. It would eliminate the need of taking care of her in some slightly less subtle way.

He looked through the glass at Rebekah and Caleb.

The effects of the bacterium were beginning to show. Sweating, nausea, sharp mood swings. The rash would start soon, then bleeding from the intestines, the eyes, and then finally, pulmonary failure. It would not be a gentle death.

He glanced down at his hands and noticed that his shirtsleeve had pulled back, revealing the scar on the inside of his left wrist. He stopped and stared at it, gently rubbing his finger across the discolored skin.

The mark of true love.

Even after all this time, the scar was still visible, a reddish gash just over two inches long. The cut had been deeper than he'd originally thought, and without stitches it hadn't healed evenly. Over the years it had even broken open a few times. And sometimes, on days like these, it still seemed to bother him. Still seemed to itch.

Maybe it itched because he was thinking about love once again. Maybe that was it. Or because he was thinking about Monday morning and how destiny would finally play out and about his family and about the babies and about the pawns he'd had Theodore leave beside the bodies of the young women and about how it would feel to watch the newscasts in the days following the luncheon as the disease trickled, traveled, spread family to family, husband to wife, lover to lover, friend to friend. One kiss, one sneeze, one handshake at a time. Around the world, evening the scales.

The Cable News Forum guest list read like a Who's Who of the world's media leaders and also included speeches by senators, congressmen, and dignitaries about First Amendment issues, the upcoming presidential election, FCC guidelines, and a number of other media-related issues. But really, Kincaid wasn't interested in all that. He was most interested in the attendees: Juan Carlos Mendez, president of the Pacific Media Group; Roberta Stratham, CEO of Satellite Broadcast News, along with all the nation's premier cable news correspondents and newscasters. And, of course, Governor Sebastian Taylor.

It was perfect. Especially considering the rest of the governor's schedule for the week—appearances at the Pentagon, National Press Club, and a visit to CIA headquarters in Langley, Virginia. In fact, the governor's speaking schedule was one of the reasons he'd moved the plans to Monday instead of the original date in November.

He grazed the scar with his finger one last time. That afternoon with Jessie had been the first time he'd seen just how far someone would go to prove the depth of her beliefs. Of her love.

But it would not be the last.

Alexis and Bethanie hadn't understood that. He'd had to spend another $120,000 to take care of them and to keep the plans alive. But in the end it was worth it.

Every time he touched his scar, it was as if he were reliving those moments with Jessie, those dreams of youth, all over again. Caressing them.

Some moments are meant to be caressed forever.

He smiled, pulled the shirtsleeve back over his wrist, and headed off to the Alexander Bros. Trucking Company to ship the vats of blood to Theodore.

29

As we drove higher and higher into the mountains, Lien-hua told me what they'd found out about Jolene overnight—which wasn't much. I tried to keep the facts of Mindy's case separate from Jolene. It wasn't easy, but that's the nature of this business. Often you need to juggle two, three, five or more cases at a time. I almost never have the luxury of having only one corpse or missing person on my mind.

I told Lien-hua about how the Illusionist was connecting the crimes for us, and I tried to summarize Tucker's latitude and longitude theory. She listened quietly, then asked, "How does Agent Tucker know about all that stuff? I mean, the chess notation systems and the touching-the-piece thing?"

I shrugged. "I don't know. Maybe he plays chess."

Once again she was quiet, thoughtful.

Ralph had told her about the phone call I'd received last night from the Illusionist. She asked a few follow-up questions about it and scribbled observations in her notebook as I answered.

"How does all this fit in with what you know about the offender?" I asked.

"Most serial killers are sexual predators, but this guy doesn't seem to be. He cares for the bodies, washes them—and I don't think he does that just to get rid of physical evidence. He doesn't rape his victims—either while they're alive or postmortem. It's more about power and control than sex. Calling to taunt you on the phone is consistent with that."

And now for the big question. "So, could you run through the profile for me?"

"You actually want to hear the profile?"

Careful, Pat.

"Yeah. I do."

She hesitated for a moment. "Hmm. OK. Well, I've been revising it all morning in light of Jolene's abduction. It helped me pass the time while I rode back from Charlotte with two very large, very hairy state troopers. I think they were both named Bubba."

I smiled.

"I should mention I don't like doing verbal profiles. Too many details get lost, forgotten, misunderstood . . ."

"I promise that whatever you say will not be held against you."

"Can I trust you?"

"Intimately."

Hmm. I'm not sure that came out right.

Or maybe it did.

"Give me a few minutes to collect my thoughts."

We drove in silence up the winding road toward Arrowhead Mountain. I was anxious to hear what she had to say but forced myself not to bother her. After about twenty minutes Lien-hua looked up from her notes.

"OK," she said. "Here we go. Looking at the style of killings and the demographics of crime in this region of the country, I'd say he's Caucasian. Definitely male. Based on the sophistication of the crimes, the organization displayed, and the intricate way he's linking the crimes for us, I'd say our offender is older, probably late thirties, early forties. He's experienced. These aren't the first crimes he's committed, but he hasn't been caught, hasn't served time. He works alone, no partner."

"How do you know?"

"Our guy is proud of his work, confident, arrogant. As you

noted from his phone call, narcissistic. He wouldn't want to share the limelight with anyone. He works solo. High birth order, possibly an only child."

"What about military service?"

"No, he would look at it as beneath him. Too menial."

Hmm. She was pretty good.

"He's not trying to hide the identities of the victims in any way. He wants us to know who he killed and even when she died—though I don't know why yet. His behavior at the scenes is very ritualistic. The posing, the yellow ribbon, the clues from his next victim, and the chess piece are all part of his signature. It's all very elaborate, very specific. But yet each crime is unique. And everything he's done, including the phone call, speaks of his need to control others."

"Hang on. Back up a minute."

"What?"

"Signature. I've read some conflicting research on it. Apparently, it's not as stable as they used to think."

She wavered her head back and forth to show me she wasn't convinced. "Still inconclusive. Basically, whatever an offender does at a crime scene that he doesn't need to do in order to commit the crime tells us something about him, about his past or his priorities—his goals. That's his signature. Does he commit overkill by stabbing the victim more than necessary? That shows rage. Does he mutilate the bodies in a specific way, take a unique souvenir from the victims, or leave clues for the police? That's all signature. Modus operandi is more the way he commits the crime."

"But neither MO nor signature is completely static or consistent," I said.

"Right." She cleared her throat slightly. "So let me give you a little test, Dr. Bowers. Why do MO and signature change?"

Easy. No problem.

"Well, in every series of crimes you have escalation and adaptation," I said. "In addition, sometimes offenders change how they commit a crime and what they do at the crime because of the victim's reaction. For example, if a woman struggles with a rapist, he might bring a knife to the next crime to threaten his victim, or some kind of restraints to subdue her. Changes in his life situation, personal injuries, traumas, things like that affect killers just like they affect the rest of us. Or he might begin to take steps to destroy or reduce physical evidence after he comes under suspicion or is interviewed or tested for DNA by the police." I paused, thinking. "OK, how did I do?"

"I'd give that a B+."

"What? Why not an A?"

I liked the way we'd slipped into bantering with each other. It felt natural, comfortable to be talking with her.

I aimed the car toward the curve of the road up ahead. A splash of early morning sunlight landed on the windshield.

"You left out experience," she said. "Just like in any profession, he gets better with experience."

Man, and I knew that one too. "OK," I said. "You win."

She consulted her notes again, smiling slightly. "No blitz attacks, which tells me he's able to gain the trust of his victims. Probably a smooth talker, very manipulative. He keeps records of the crimes, writes about them. Maybe in a journal or a diary, or even a blog. His need to control women leads me to believe he's been married and might still be, but if he is, his wife doesn't know about his double life. He's addicted to power, domination, and control, but the irony is that even though he prides himself on being in control, he can't control himself. He can't stop. He can't resist showing off."

So far, despite my natural tendency to discount profiles, I couldn't argue with anything she'd said. It all seemed to fit.

"He's forensically aware, maybe even served in law enforcement. An observation: apart from the first murder, none of the abduction sites were the same as the murder sites or the dump sites. He might be doing that to confuse us, or to show off, I'm not sure yet. His elaborate cat-and-mouse tactics and ability to steal from his future victims and the whole incident at the mall show a high degree of premeditation and versatility—breaking and entering, robbery, stalking, abduction, murder. This man has a high IQ—above average for sure, maybe even genius level. He's familiar with the area and probably lives nearby, or went to high school or college here at some point."

I nodded. "That fits the geographic profile." The turnoff to the trail was just ahead; I slowed down and eased up the dirt road that led to the trailhead. "The farther a body is from a main road, the more likely it is the offender is local and familiar with the area," I said. "It's a pretty stable pattern in geo profiling."

"Dr. Bowers, why do you always say derisive things about profiling but then refer to your work as geographic profiling? You're a profiler too."

Ouch. That hurts.

"No need to get personal," I said. "After all, I thought we were friends."

She cleared her throat. "Based on how he responded to you at the mall, I'd say he works in a job that requires good judgment and quick thinking. And he's able to compartmentalize this area of his life. His co-workers wouldn't even have a clue about the killings. He's been doing it for a long time, Pat, and he's not going to stop until the day he dies or the day we take him down."

Now she was talking my language. I pulled over to the edge of the road and stopped next to a sign announcing that we had arrived at Upper Ridgeline Trail.

We climbed out of the car, and I grabbed the backpack filled with my climbing gear.

"You think you'll need all that?" she asked.

"Never know," I said, heaving the pack onto my shoulders. "There are a lot of cliffs in the area; we may need to get a different perspective on the scene. By the way, I'm impressed with your profile. Really. I am. Usually profilers just repeat what we already know about a crime. I think you've uncovered some of what this guy is really about."

"Why, thank you, Dr. Bowers," she said politely. "So what's my grade?"

"B."

"Wait a minute, I gave you a B+."

I grinned. "I know. I think you grade on the curve."

The sun was blazing through the liquid sky, burning off the low-lying fog and lighting up the patchwork of autumn colors covering the mountain range. A few clouds had found their way into the morning sky and wandered around just east of us. It had rained last night, and the ground smelled damp, pungent. A little musky. All around me the rain-washed brightness of the day seemed solid enough to touch.

Lien-hua stuffed some Forest Service maps into her pocket, closed the car door, and headed for the woods. "C'mon," she said. "The trail starts over here." Then she added, "And that was at least a B+."

30

The Illusionist set down the duffel bag, rang the doorbell, and waited.

He'd delivered the first package earlier, on the way to work, but had decided to wait with this one, just for fun. Just to make things more interesting.

He'd kept it in the trunk of his car for the last couple hours, and only now, during his coffee break, was he slipping out to deliver it. Yes, it was a little riskier this way, but he wasn't worried. Not one bit. Everything was still on schedule. After all, he knew how to plan the perfect crime. He'd done it before. So many times before. And he'd never been caught. Never!

The door creaked open. "May I help you?"

"Yes," said the Illusionist. "You can die." Then he whipped out his Glock and put a bullet through the man's forehead before the guy could even stop furrowing his eyebrows.

The Illusionist picked up the duffel bag, entered the house, and closed the door.

The secret wasn't to be clever. No, clever criminals get caught all the time.

He unscrewed the silencer and holstered his weapon.

The secret lay in misdirection. Make them look at one hand while you hide the coin in the other.

Misdirection and planning, actually. Because when they see the coin isn't in your right hand, they'll immediately look to the left one. So you have to anticipate their reaction and be able to show them that the coin isn't in that hand either. Aha! That's the thing. The coin was really in your right hand all along.

Misdirection. Control. Meticulous planning.

Leaving the duffel bag at the front entrance, he dragged the dead man's body down the hallway and into the bedroom closet.

Where are you going to direct their attention? That's the question. Where do you want them to look? Just like in a game of chess. All of life is a complex game of strategy; moves, and countermoves, taking and losing pieces, setting up for the final endgame. Landing a new job. Getting a date. Negotiating a contract. Life boils down to studying your opponent and thinking through his moves and then finding a way to position the pieces to your advantage. And that's what the Illusionist did best!

After positioning the body, he retrieved the duffel bag and carried it into the bedroom.

Yet only a fool would think he could figure out the whole game before his opponent has moved. No, instead, the best players are the ones who respond to how the other player moves. The key to winning the game isn't in how well you can reason, but in how well you can *respond*. Yes. Because no one can guess every possible future move. Of course not. It isn't possible to predict the whole game. You have to be able to improvise. To adapt. That's where most killers fail.

That's how the Unabomber got caught. He just couldn't stay in the shadows, had to show everyone how clever he was. And then he wrote it all out so the whole world could see. So that his brother could see and turn him in. And then the game was up. No, you must not be clever. You must be controlled.

Anticipation. Calculated response. Self-control.

That's how you stay one step ahead of the audience.

He unzipped the duffel bag and removed the contents. He placed them on the treadmill in the corner of the room and then stepped back to view his handiwork.

Perfect.

After Alice, he would be free to move on. No longer under suspicion at all. Not ever again. The game would simply move to a new place, a new board, with a new set of players. Maybe California next time. Yes, he'd always wanted to visit the West Coast. Or Oregon. That might be nice. Follow in the footsteps of Bundy and Ridgeway. Yes, that might be just the place to go. Have his name mentioned in the same breath as theirs.

No, wait.

Have theirs mentioned in the same breath as his.

The Illusionist smiled. It was almost scary to be this good. Almost frightening to be this far ahead in the game.

He grabbed the empty duffel bag and walked outside. The morning was cool and still. He waited just inside the front door for a few moments, scanning the neighborhood.

The house provided wonderful cover, and he was certain he hadn't attracted any attention, but it was always better to make sure. To be cautious.

He slipped outside, walked the three blocks to the place he'd parked his car, started the engine, and headed back to his day job.

Misdirection.

Sleight of hand.

Watch and be amazed.

The show was about to begin.

31

The 1.5-mile uphill hike from the trailhead to the meadow where we found Mindy would normally take about half an hour, but we were going slowly, carefully. I was trying to imagine the Illusionist walking up this trail with Mindy. *Did you really carry her all this way? Or did she walk? If so, why didn't she fight you? How did you get her to trust you?*

Lien-hua spoke, echoing my thoughts. "She walked with him, didn't she?"

"I think so. It's too far to carry a body uphill."

"Did he force her? Restrain her somehow?" she asked.

"Maybe. There were some bruises on her wrists, but the indentations were shallow. He didn't drag her. He might have tied them postmortem."

"Then how did he subdue her while he strangled her over and over again?"

"I don't know." I'd started panting a little as we hiked but tried to hide it so Lien-hua wouldn't notice. I stopped and readjusted my pack. "He might have used threats of violence. She had a younger sister, didn't she?"

"Yeah. She's eight."

"Maybe that's it. He might have threatened to hurt the girl. I don't know. We may never know." I started walking again. "We can check on it, though, see what her relationship with her sister was like."

Sunlight dangled in between the branches of the trees, dancing across my face. We hiked for a few minutes in silence, and then

Lien-hua said, "I found your views on motives very interesting, Dr. Bowers."

Ah, the briefing yesterday.

"So when you say 'interesting' do you mean 'fascinatingly compelling,' or are you just using the word 'interesting' to try and disagree with me politely, the way most people use it?"

"Hmm. Well, since you put it that way, I choose option number two."

"The 'I don't agree with you but don't want to stir up trouble' usage."

"Yes. Honestly, I'm surprised that you believe motives play such a minor role in life."

We stepped into a sheltered cove protected by ancient trees, some of which must have been over a hundred years old. I could see by the abundance of younger growth that the rest of the hillside had been logged years ago. These hidden coves up in the mountains must have been too hard for the loggers to reach.

"Well," I said, "I think there are only three primary motives, and none of them are very helpful when it comes to solving a crime."

"Just three, huh?" I sensed a bit of amusement in her voice.

"Yes."

"And they are?"

"Desire, anger, and guilt."

"That's it?"

"That's it."

"Just those three?"

"Yup. Think about it. Take them one at a time. Desire: people want fame or sex or money or power. Even revenge is a form of desire. Think of how many crimes result from lust, greed, envy, jealousy, or ambition. All just different names for desire."

"Hmm," she said thoughtfully. "OK. And anger I'll agree with."

"Yeah. And of course there's guilt, which speaks for itself. We all have to find a way to deal with our regrets and our shame, or we implode."

She pushed a branch out of the way. "It may surprise you to hear this, but I agree with those three. However, I think you missed the two most important ones."

"Oh. Well, I find that very . . ." I waited until the branch had snapped back into place before following her. "Interesting. And they are?"

She stopped walking, let her eyes crawl along the trail for a few seconds. At last, she raised them to peer at me, and I could see that they were filled with deep channels of pain. "The first is fear, Dr. Bowers. Sometimes people do terrible things because they've been pushed into a corner. Fear can turn us into different people."

I didn't say anything, but the questions rose in my mind, *What are you afraid of, Lien-hua? What happened? Did you do something terrible too?* "OK," I said at last. "Fear. I'll give you that one. What's the second one?"

She turned and continued down the trail. "Let's see if you can guess the most important motive on your own."

Before I could even venture a guess, we came to an overlook just north of the crime scene. The trail skirted along the edge of a steep escarpment, the mountain ending abruptly at our feet and dropping hundreds of feet straight down to the river. I hadn't noticed this overlook on our hike out to the trailhead on Thursday because of the thick fog that had ushered in the storm.

"Survival?" I asked.

She shook her head, her attention riveted on the view. "That falls under desire—the desire to live. Now, shh . . . don't spoil this. It's beautiful."

I followed her gaze. The valley swept out before us and then rose majestically to become autumn-tinged mountains, endless and alive. The valleys wandered through the mountain range, each with their own unique patchwork of shadows cast by the community of clouds gathering high overhead. A blaze of sunlight ignited each cloud, making them glow even more brightly against the steel blue sky.

I remembered, years earlier, another wilderness guide telling me that "Appalachian" comes from a Native American word that means "endless mountains"; and staring out across these mountains I couldn't help but get the impression that they really did fold back endlessly into space and time. The planet's ancient origami left over from the days when the continents folded together.

The breeze was constant here, rising from the valley, washing up and over us; the gentle morning breath of the hills. I wondered what it would feel like to stand here when the wind was still. What kind of solitude that must be to have the day decide its shape all around you, sky and shadow and peak and valley all draped in deep and primal silence.

"Maybe that's why he chose it," I whispered after a few moments.

"What?" She turned to me.

"Beauty."

"You think he chose this place because of the beauty?"

"Because of the paradox." I looked at her. The wind blowing up and over the peak was whispering through her hair, letting it escape from gravity for just a moment, feathering it around her head in slow motion, easy and free. "Humans can't seem to enjoy beauty without destroying it." I was transfixed by the sight of her. "This trail, for example, cutting through the forest. It's the only way to experience the solitude of this peak. But the trail also mars the very thing it allows us to enjoy—the scenery. I think beauty frightens us into destroying the things we admire most." Our eyes met for a fraction of a second too long, that one tiny piece of time that says more than words can say. "That's the paradox."

She looked away. "The medical examiner placed the time of death right about now." Her voice had become efficient and professional.

She stepped back from the edge of the mountain, and her hair returned to normal. Life returned to normal.

"Yeah," I said softly. "Let's go." And then I followed Lien-hua to the place Mindy died, while thoughts of death and beauty, of Christie's memory and Lien-hua's presence, wrestled in my mind.

32

We entered the clearing where Mindy Travelca had been found dead beneath a tree two days ago, and I set down my backpack.

Lien-hua paced to the middle of the field. "The crime-scene investigation unit was all over this place already. And besides, the storms up here would have destroyed any physical evidence. So, what exactly are we looking for?"

I turned in a circle, taking in the view, the mountains, the perspective, the trail. "Not forensic evidence as much as geographic understanding. Why here, Lien-hua? What significance does this place hold for him? A crime scene is everything related to the crime. The air. The wind. The ground. But a crime occurs in four dimensions, not just three."

Oops, I'd slipped into lecture mode without even realizing it.

"The fourth dimension," she said thoughtfully. "You mean time."

"Yes. Time." I lay down against the tree so that I was in the same position Mindy had been when we found her. I stared out across the mountains. *Why did he leave you here, Mindy? Why did he kill you then?* "A crime occurs in both space and time. And how those two factors relate to each other is what I'm interested in most."

Contact lenses. He left them in her eyes.

Time of death: between 8:00 and 11:00 a.m.

She disappeared Wednesday afternoon.

Died on Thursday morning.

He didn't carry her up the mountain.

She made a cell phone call to her mother at 3:00 p.m. on Wednesday, said she'd be home on Friday.

What did he leave you looking at? What did he want you to see?

Sightlines were important to him.

"There." I pointed to a peak directly in front of us. "That mountain there. Which one is that?"

Lien-hua pulled out the map and spent a few moments orienting herself to our surroundings. "Warrior's Peak. And . . . wait . . . there's a local legend about it . . . hang on." She flipped the map over. "The daughter of a Cherokee chief who lived there was abducted by some members of the Catawba tribe and brought here, to this mountain we're on right now." Lien-hua glanced over the story printed on the map and then summarized. "Her lover snuck through the night to rescue her, but it was some kind of trap. He was killed, slaughtered, and the girl—rather than let herself be married to anyone from the Catawba tribe—threw herself off this mountain, over there where the cliffs are, where we were standing before. According to the legend her tears falling to the ground became the valleys surrounding these peaks. And listen to this"—she paused to find her place, then continued reading—"'some people say you can still hear her crying up on this mountain, when the wind is right.'"

A chill settled over me as I sat where Mindy's body had rested, as I stared out across the valley toward Warrior's Peak. "He knew the story."

Lien-hua was quiet, reflective. "He put contacts in her eyes, Pat. He wanted us to think about her tears."

He wasn't just one move ahead of us, more like two or three.

Lien-hua must have been thinking the same thing. "This guy is good."

"He posed her," I said. "Just like Jamie by the 'No Loitering' sign and Reinita on the trail to Tombstone Caverns."

"Taunting us. Sending us a message. It all plays into his fantasy."

Lien-hua looked around. "Well, right about now is when Mindy died. If they came here in the morning, would that have given him enough time to torture her?"

"No, I don't think so. Not enough hours of sunlight before her time of death. Not with the extensive petechial hemorrhaging she had."

"So he spent the night out here with her," she said.

I looked around. "That's right. But not here. Not in this clearing; it's too exposed."

"So where?"

I pointed to a trail nearby that led to a series of exposed cliffs and outcroppings. "There."

33

Grabbing my pack I followed Lien-hua along the trail. It brought us to the beginning of a series of cliffs that rose twenty to thirty meters above us and stretched back along the ridgeline. Another trail nearby led along the boulder-strewn base of the crags.

"What are you looking for?" asked Lien-hua.

"A cave."

"What? A cave? Why a cave?"

"Mindy had soil caught in the grooves of her toe ring. Yesterday afternoon I compared the soil samples on her toe ring to the samples Ralph collected in the meadow. The soil in her toe ring has a higher clay content than the topsoil does. That and the fact that the killer needed a place out here to be alone with her led me to think he killed her in a cave."

"Soil? Differences in clay content?" she said skeptically.

"What?"

"I thought you weren't interested in physical evidence, Dr. Bowers, just geographical understanding?"

Picky, picky.

"Caves are geographic," I said. "C'mere and look at this."

I pointed to a small footpath leading off to the left. A deep heel depression was visible in the mud. "The kid at the mall said he was a big guy. If he was carrying her to the meadow, he might have left that."

"Why didn't the tech team find that?"

"They weren't looking for a cave."

It didn't take us long to find the mouth of the cave, only forty or fifty meters away. The temperature in a cave remains relatively constant; generally at this latitude it would be cooler than the surrounding area in the summer and warmer in the winter—about 58°F. And today the air leaving the mouth of the cave was condensing in the cool morning. Almost as if the earth were exhaling.

The cave entrance was about two meters wide. I took off my backpack, pulled out my flashlight, and peered down.

She gestured toward my flashlight. "Do you carry that thing with you all the time?"

"A flashlight is a detective's best friend. Especially this one. Precision-machined high-strength aluminum alloy case, waterproof, ergonomically designed grip—"

She shook her head. "Boys and their toys."

The cave dropped vertically into the mountain. I couldn't tell how far. "Well, what do you think?" I asked.

"It's isolated. It would give him the privacy he needed—"

"No, I mean do you want to go in or should I?" I opened my pack and pulled out my climbing rope, a harness, a few carabiners, and some nylon webbing.

"Do you know what you're doing?"

"I sure hope so." I pointed overhead. A stout tree stretched above the entrance to the cave, forking in two near the trunk. "See those branches? See how the bark is worn there?"

"Yeah."

I tied a loop of webbing around each arm of the branch and clipped them together with two carabiners. "That's where he anchored the rope."

"So you're really going in?"

"How else am I going to see what's down there?"

I threaded the middle of the rope through the biners and tossed the ends into the cave, pulled on my harness, and clipped the rope through my belay device.

Lien-hua watched me. "What's that thing for?"

"It's called a Figure-8," I said. "The rope passes through it to create friction, and that friction is what slows my descent. I use my right hand, here, as my brake hand to control my speed."

She stared at the rope. "But how are you going to get back up?"

I held up a couple of ascenders. "That's what these are for. They slide up the rope and lock off. Of course, I could also use prussiks." I pointed to a couple two-meter-long loops of smaller diameter rope. "By wrapping those around the climbing rope with a special knot, I can create loops that I can step into. Then, whichever loop you're not standing on, you slide it up the rope. You take turns stepping and sliding. Kind of like walking vertically."

"Well . . ." She peered at the dark mouth of the cave. "You can go this time. I'll supervise from here."

I double-checked my harness buckles and anchor system, held the flashlight in my teeth, and tipped backward into the cave.

The floor of the cavern lay about ten meters below me. I didn't even need to go all the way to the bottom before I began to picture what the killer had done.

I took the light out of my mouth. "Mindy had pale outlines around her hips, didn't she?" I called up to Lien-hua. "And encircling her upper thighs?"

"Yes." Her voice floated down to me. "The ME couldn't figure out how she got them."

Lividity, the pooling of blood near the skin, begins when the heart stops circulating blood through the body and gravity tugs the blood downward. It might start as early as thirty minutes after the time of death. If she were hanging in a rock-climbing harness when she died, her body weight pressing against the webbing would constrict the blood vessels, keeping the stagnant blood from pooling, creating the outline of the webbing around her upper thighs.

You left her hanging on the rope, didn't you? You lowered her, left her hanging there in a harness, maybe tied her hands off loosely.

Then you could have clipped them into the rope, so she wouldn't struggle too much. You took off her boots so there wouldn't be soil samples, even washed her feet when you were done—but you're not as good as you think. You didn't scrub her toe ring clean.

The floor of the cave had been brushed to eliminate footprints, but the brushing told me a story too—someone was trying to cover something up. A few dark spots stained the clay beside a nearby rock. We would need to test it, but I suspected those stains were Mindy's blood.

He could have wrapped some webbing around her legs, maybe her calves. Outside of her jeans it wouldn't have left ligature marks on her skin. Yeah, just tight enough to control her. She wouldn't have been able to kick or fight back at all. She would be powerless. She would be his. All night long.

"You OK down there?" Lien-hua called.

"I'm good. Hang on." I thought I saw something in the corner of the cave. I scanned the area with my flashlight.

A curl of yellow ribbon.

"He brought her here, Lien-hua. There's water down here too. A pool. I'll bet that's where he washed off the body."

Using the ascenders I worked my way back up the rope to the lip of the cave.

A couple minutes later I had the harness off and was packing up my gear. "We need to get back to the car, get some people up here to work this scene—wait a minute."

"What?"

"Check your maps. See if this cave appears on any of them."

She pulled out the maps, looked them over. "Nope. Nothing."

"It's only known to the locals then. That narrows it down even more. So he knew this cave well enough to know he wouldn't be disturbed here—that he could have all night to do whatever he wanted to her," I said.

"And he knows how to rappel," she said.

"Oh man."

"What?"

I closed the top flap of my backpack and cinched it tight. "The climbing gym on Wall Street. Her car was found half a block away. They lead trips up into these mountains. Climbing *and* caving."

"How do you know that?"

"I paid them a visit yesterday afternoon. Worked out for a while." I hoisted the pack onto my shoulders. "C'mon. Let's go." I turned around, but Lien-hua had already started sprinting down the trail toward the car.

34

It wasn't easy running with the backpack on, but thankfully I didn't have to do it very long, plus it was all downhill. In less than fifteen minutes we'd made it to the trailhead.

I heaved off my pack and shoved it in the backseat of the car. I was still huffing from the run. "Yesterday afternoon . . . I had a few minutes . . . to walk around downtown . . . check out the places from the geo profile." I pulled out the menus and business cards I'd stuffed into the car yesterday along with the brochure from the climbing gym. "I grabbed these."

"You think our guy might work there?" she asked.

I handed her the brochure, pointed to the phone number. "See if you can reach them. See if . . . anyone was missing from work . . . the last couple days."

I threw open the door and pulled out my computer while she tried her cell phone.

"No reception."

By then I'd managed to catch my breath. "Well, let's see if any of their climbing guides were at Mindy's crime scene. Hold that brochure up here, to the computer."

Using my laptop's built-in video chatting camera, I snapped a picture of each of the twelve staff members, then pasted the photos into the face recognition program I'd had installed for my work with the National Law Enforcement & Corrections Technology Center in Denver.

I pulled up the photos and video footage from Mindy's crime scene, and the computer began sorting through the footage, zeroing in on one face after another, calculating, evaluating. A moment later the computer beeped and highlighted a man's face showing a 91 percent probability of a positive match.

"There he is," whispered Lien-hua, pointing to the screen. "The guy in the baseball cap."

"I don't believe it. He wore that cap at the mall too."

"Joseph Grolin," she said.

"Thinks he's a real tough guy." In his climbing guide photo he had a cocky smile and a stubbly beard a few shades darker than his shoulder-length blond hair. Late twenties, early thirties. He wore sunglasses. According to the bio beneath his picture, he worked as a rock-climbing instructor part-time and wrote for *MountainQuest* magazine for his day job. He'd been their outdoor editor for the last four years. Special interests: scuba diving, Native American lore, downhill skiing.

Native American lore.

Lien-hua pointed to the bottom of the brochure. It read: "All our guides are highly trained and certified as Wilderness First Responders."

"The stab wounds," I said. "A First Responder would know just how deep to make them. And how to suture them up."

She pulled out her cell phone again. "C'mon, work. Work!"

"Try this one." I threw Dante's phone to her as I rounded the car and hopped into the driver's side.

"Nothing," I heard her say. "I can't believe he was there in the meadow the whole time. Watching us study the body."

"Yeah," I said. "He likes to watch. C'mon." I fired up the engine. "It's possible Jolene Parker is still alive."

35

We flew down the mountain, nearly careening off the road twice as I took a couple curves too fast.

"Careful," said Lien-hua. "You kill us, and we'll never catch him."

She tried the phone again. Still no coverage.

Asheville lay ten miles ahead of us.

I screeched the tires as I rounded another tight mountain curve.

"Easy, Pat. I want to get this guy as much as you do. But let's do it in one piece."

"Yeah." I eased off the gas a little. "OK, sorry."

She shook her head. "I've never seen anything like this guy. Indian legends, kidnappings, cross-contamination, he's got it all thought out." She tried her cell phone again. Still nothing.

"Betrayal," I said.

"What?"

"The missing motive," I said. "It's betrayal, isn't it?"

"Nope. You betray someone because of desire, and you respond to betrayal with anger. Try again." She set her phone down. No use dialing until we got into flatter territory.

"Curiosity?"

"That's a form of desire—you desire to know what that crime feels like or how it will affect you."

I paused. I was running out of ideas. I thought about saying honor or vanity, but they were forms of desire too. Even duty and integrity are desires—the desire to please, the desire to be virtuous. "Hmm. Remorse?" I said.

"Just another name for guilt."

I shook my head. This was harder than I thought. Maybe if I tried thinking like a profiler, I could do it.

On second thought . . . we all have our limits.

Lien-hua punched the number into the phone I'd borrowed from Sheriff Wallace. "Finally," she muttered and then immediately launched into an explanation of everything we knew so far about Grolin. I could tell she was talking to Margaret.

But the more Lien-hua spoke, the more the expression on her face flattened out, became hard. She tried explaining the situation again, more emphatically this time, but once again she was cut off in mid-sentence.

"What?" I asked. "What is it?"

Lien-hua leaned toward me and whispered through clenched teeth, "Margaret says it's not enough for a warrant."

"What? Give me that phone."

Lien-hua handed it to me.

"Margaret, Jolene might still be alive!"

"Don't raise your voice at me, Dr. Bowers." Each word was a carefully crafted stone.

"Listen—"

"Indian legends?" she snapped. "Contact lenses? Just listen to yourself. There's nothing tying Grolin to these crimes. I'm not calling up a judge to get a search warrant—"

"He was at Mindy's crime scene, Margaret."

"So were fifty other people," she said. "It's not enough."

"He leads trips to this cave."

"You don't even know he was in that cave. All you have is some mud on the girl's foot."

"We have to move on this *now*!"

"Listen to me carefully, Agent Bowers." Her voice had turned to ice. "I'll consider calling it in on Monday when Judge Stephenson gets back from vacation, if you get me some actual evidence instead of just conjecture. Until then—"

"What?" I said. "I'm losing you."

"Just wait for—" she droned on. I slammed the cell phone shut and threw it to the floor. The battery flew out. Along with a few other things.

"Oops," I mumbled. "I hate when I do that."

Lien-hua picked up the various items that used to be Dante Wallace's cell phone. "Nice negotiation skills."

"Um, I'll buy him another one."

"So what did she say?"

"She told me not to waste any time. She said to bring him in." I cruised around a corner and accelerated into a straightaway as the road leveled out. "She said saving a girl's life is more important than jumping over bureaucratic hurdles."

Lien-hua stared at me. Blinked. "No she didn't."

"No," I said after a pause. "She didn't."

I wasn't sure how Lien-hua would respond. I had to do something. I had to. Jolene had a dad somewhere too, just like Mindy did. Crying. Worrying. Hoping. I couldn't just sit by and wait while the Illusionist tortured and killed another girl when we might still be able to save her. I hoped Lien-hua was with me on this, I really did. If she wasn't on board, I didn't know what I was going to do.

Finally, out of the corner of my eye I saw her nod. "Too bad we lost reception right when she was telling us what she wanted us to do."

"Yeah," I said, gunning the motor and flying around another curve. "Too bad."

Lien-hua picked up her phone. It took three calls to find Grolin's address. She pulled out a map and called out the directions.

I merged onto Highway 70 and headed toward Billings Road, breaking every traffic law I could think of on the way.

36

Lien-hua made two more calls. "Unbelievable," she muttered.

"What? Do we have something on Grolin?"

"Two priors. Assault in 2004; he did six months probation and three hundred hours of community service. Domestic violence last winter. Beat up his girlfriend really bad. They were living in Spartanburg at the time."

"The site of the first murder."

"Yeah. And the timing matches. Two days after the paramedics were called in to treat Grolin's girlfriend, Patty Henderson was killed. The girl never pressed charges, just took off. Psychologically, it makes perfect sense—a girlfriend leaving would be a textbook precipitating stressor."

"Enough to set him off."

"Yeah, pushed him over the edge."

"What about the profile, though? You didn't think he'd served time."

"True," she said, "although the history of violence does fit."

I felt myself gritting my teeth. "Why didn't they catch this stuff when they ran the names of everyone at the scene of Mindy's murder?"

"He's a journalist. It makes sense for him to have been at the crime scene."

"So what did Ralph say?" I'd heard snatches of her second conversation but not enough to catch the big picture. "Did he learn anything from interviewing that guard?"

She shook her head. "Waste of time. He's on his way back,

though. I caught him just before he made it to the federal building. Margaret doesn't know he's back in town yet. He's going to meet us at Grolin's place. He said to wait for him."

Suddenly I realized I still had Ralph's dead cell phone in my pocket. "Wait a minute, whose phone is Ralph using?"

"He told me he'd picked up his wife's on the way through town."

I nodded.

"Good. So we go in with Ralph." If Lien-hua and I went after Grolin and saved Jolene, everything would be fine. Margaret wouldn't be able to say a word. But if Grolin wasn't our guy and we moved on this without a search warrant, someone's head was going to roll—namely mine. Ralph was better at fending off reprimands than I was, especially from Margaret. In any case, I felt better about approaching a suspected serial killer with Ralph by my side. Anyone would.

Billings Road lay on the edge of town and wound seven miles up into the hills.

"Isolated," said Lien-hua. "It's perfect. Except . . ."

She didn't have to finish her sentence. I knew what she was thinking. This house lay on the other side of Asheville, nearly ten miles from of the hot spot I'd deduced our offender would live in.

"He could have another base he operates out of—a girlfriend's place, maybe," I said. "A friend's house. Let's have Tucker check on any other residences this guy might've had in the last couple years."

She agreed and placed the call.

As she was finishing it up, we arrived at the dirt road leading to Grolin's house. I drove up the quarter-mile driveway and pulled to a stop next to Ralph's beat-up Jeep about fifty meters from Grolin's house. I could see slivers of Grolin's two-story home ahead of us through the nearby trees.

Ralph stepped out and eased his car door silently shut. "Margaret know you're here?"

"Nope," I said.

"Good. Let's go."

We started toward the house.

"When this is over," said Ralph, "I'll have to remind Margaret that you don't need a search warrant in the case of an emergency, and if saving a girl's life isn't an emergency, I don't know what is." It was typical Ralph. And it was good to see.

"Who drove you back from Charlotte?" I asked.

"Couple state troopers."

"Were they both named Bubba?"

"Probably," he mumbled.

Lien-hua smiled.

"So Ralph," I said, "how do you want to do this?" Lien-hua and I were following him along a trail that threaded through the forest toward the house.

"We go in fast and clean."

I'd seen Ralph's idea of fast and clean before. *Fast* was a word I would use. *Clean* was not.

I had to hurry to keep up with him. Despite his massive size, he moved like a spider through the trees, the result of a four-year stint as an Army Ranger.

The morning was quiet and still. A few birds chattered in the trees. But I felt anything but peaceful. My heart began to hammer. If Grolin was in there, this could end today, or it could spin off in a very bad way. "He's a good shot," I said. "Scary good. Let's be careful."

Ralph led Lien-hua and me up the steps and onto the porch. The place had been painted white years ago, but by now most of the paint was peeling off, curling out into the morning. Wisps of the past, flaking down at my feet.

Ralph approached the door, unholstered his weapon, and peered through the front window. "Anything else I should know?" Someone else might have been scared. He was just gathering information.

"He'll deny everything," said Lien-hua, the profiler. "He's arrogant. He'll probably invite us in, even if he's got her in there. He's sure he won't get caught. He might have her hidden somewhere else." She looked around the yard, then at the driveway where a VW bug was parked. "There's a car here, but not the Subaru station wagon. He might not even be home."

"We'll find out soon enough." Ralph walked up to the door and knocked.

Nothing.

"Hello?" he called. No response. He tried the doorknob. "Oh, look at that. It's locked." He turned toward me with a grin.

"Oh no, you don't," I said. I'd seen that look before.

Lien-hua stared at him. "Oh no you don't what?"

Ralph took a step backward.

She turned to me. "Oh no he doesn't what?"

"You might want to get out of the way."

Ralph judged the distance to the door and then rushed toward it shoulder first. At impact, the door ruptured in half. Instantly, Ralph leveled his weapon and rushed forward.

We heard a creak above us from somewhere on the second floor. "Oh, I love my job," he muttered, swiveling his gun toward the steps and heading up the stairs. "You two sweep this level. I'm going up."

I pulled out my gun and stepped into the Illusionist's home.

37

The Illusionist received the automatic page and slipped into one of the vacant janitor's closets at work. He pulled out his palmtop computer and watched the agents burst into the house on the video feed from the camera positioned in the forest nearby. Oh, it was all so very dramatic with that large agent bursting through the door, everyone drawing their weapons. So very gung ho of them.

He almost giggled. Almost. It was even better than he'd planned it, though they arrived faster than he'd thought they would. He hadn't expected them to connect the dots quite so quickly. Ah well, good for them. A pleasant surprise. All it did was move up the timeframe a bit.

But it was too bad, in a way, that all three of them went in.

Shame to have all of them in there at once.

He sent the email to the woman whose car he had visited earlier in the morning and then sat back and waited. It wouldn't be long now.

The timer on his computer had started the five-minute count-down as soon as the door was breached.

Just four minutes and twenty-two seconds remained before the three federal agents would find even more than they bargained for.

Lien-hua headed toward the kitchen, and I moved slowly, me-thodically, down the hallway, found two doors at the far end, called out, no response, identified myself as a federal agent, pressed open the first door and leaped back out of the range of fire, then burst in, leveling my gun with both hands, sweeping the room. Grolin's bedroom. The bed wasn't made. Rock-climbing gear, harnesses, ropes, and carabiners cluttered the floor. It looked like he was either packing for a trip or had just returned from one.

"Clear!" I heard from upstairs. The sound we'd heard must have just been the house settling after Ralph demolished the front door.

I checked the other room. A small office. Computer. Printer. Bookshelves. Desk. Posters of rock climbers and mountaineers on the walls. A Native American dreamcatcher dangled in the window.

"Clear!" I called.

"Clear!" Lien-hua called from the kitchen.

After the initial sweep, we each started to go over the house again, more thoroughly. I'd seen a small inset window as we approached the house, and started looking for the staircase to the basement. It would be the perfect place to take Jolene.

There.

Halfway down the hall past the kitchen I came to a door. I grabbed the doorknob and twisted it. Locked.

I leaned against it. Listened.

"Jolene?"

---

3 minutes 14 seconds.

For a moment I thought of trying to smash the door open like Ralph had done but decided it was better to keep the damage to the house, and to my body, to a minimum. Besides, that door-smashing stuff is a lot harder than it looks. I glanced around the house. A pile of bank statements held together with a paperclip lay on the kitchen table.

I grabbed the paper clip, straightened it out, hurried back to the door, and slid the paper clip into the lock. I'd learned to pick locks on an undercover assignment back in 2001. Very handy.

The lock clicked, and the door swung open faster than I expected. Since I was leaning against it, I nearly stumbled down the steps. Awkwardly, I ducked back to the side as best I could, in case Grolin was down there with a gun. When nothing happened, I leaned over and called into the dark pit yawning before me, "Jolene?" I slid one hand along the wall, searching for a light switch. I kept my gun trained on the darkness just in case Grolin was here.

Above me I could hear Ralph's footsteps as he scoured the house, systematically searching it room by room.

My fingers found the switch, and I flipped it up. A single bulb flickered on, illuminating the staircase with a jaundiced light. The air curling up toward me was thick with the smell of mold and decay. At the base of the stairs the dirt floor seemed to swallow the wooden staircase abruptly in mid-step.

"Jolene?" I called again, this time softer, my heart hammering in my chest. *This is where he brings them. This is where he does it.*

I stepped forward onto the staircase. Behind me, the door swung creakily shut on its own.

I took the steps slowly, watching for trip wires or booby traps. If Grolin was as good as I thought he was, he wasn't just going to let us walk in here and find her.

"Jolene?"

Step. Step.

No reply. But I did sense a rustle of movement in the darkness somewhere below me. My heart raced.

"Jolene, are you here?"

No reply.

Step.

I reached the bottom of the stairs.

38

2 minutes 25 seconds.

—————————————■—————————————

The dark cellar drank up the light of the single bulb, leaving most of the basement wrapped in thick shadows. I turned on my flashlight.

The air down here was noticeably cooler than the air in the rest of the house.

It reminded me of a cave.

The heavy support beams buried in the dirt floor had long ago started to sway under the weight of the house, giving the illusion that the entire house might collapse at any moment. The middle of the cellar contained a tumble of cardboard boxes and dead furniture. An old mountain bike, a pair of skis, and a torn backpack leaned against the stack. A workbench sat in the right-hand corner of the cellar under a pegboard covered with screwdrivers, hammers, wrenches, ragged handsaws, and chisels. *He might be a carpenter. Or the tools might be for something else. Have those checked for blood. Hair. Prints.*

I turned. On my left, a metal bookshelf leaned against the far wall of the cellar. Even in the dim light I could tell it held textbooks on journalism and English composition, long ago relegated to the basement. *He's a journalist, a writer. A lover of words. He can't part with his old books even if he knows he'll never read them again.*

Above the bookshelf near the ceiling was the small recessed window I'd seen earlier. It was covered with grime. I doubted it had ever been opened.

"Jolene?" I called as gently as I could, hoping not to scare her if she was here and hurt. "Are you here? My name is Patrick. I'm here to help."

Walking into his lair like this made me uneasy. The house groaned, settling onto its foundation, accepting Ralph's weight on the floorboards above me. I steadied my gun and swung the flashlight beam around the perimeter of the cellar, passing the circle of light across the wall.

As I moved through the cellar, I realized that there weren't any spiderwebs lacing across my face even though I noticed spiders skittering across the workbench.

Someone had been down here recently.

"Are you here?" I called. I scanned the walls for evidence of hidden doors or rooms. I listened for a muffled cry, scratching sounds, sobbing, anything to tell me she was here and still alive.

The dirt floor didn't look disturbed. I scanned the room again, walked the perimeter again. The cellar had been cut out of the mountain, and the walls were built with river rock. I inspected the cracks between them but couldn't find any sign of a hidden room or passageway.

There's got to be something here. Something I'm missing. As I looked around, my eyes landed on the workbench.

I walked over to it and trained the flashlight beam on the work space. Pliers. Hammers. Hacksaws. Any of them could be very handy for a sadistic serial killer. Some lay on the workbench, others were hanging from the pegboard, but none of them appeared either bloodstained or freshly cleaned.

Then I noticed an outline on the pegboard where the dust wasn't as thick.

Something's missing. Something was hanging there.

I traced the shape with the tip of my finger.

A saw.

Suddenly his words from last night came back to me: *"Forget the girl. It's too late for her . . . I saw her first . . ."*

He'd actually told me, "I saw her first."

Dear God, no.

Just then I caught a flutter of movement out of the corner of my eye, and I spun around, flipping off the safety of my gun. A scraggly cat jumped down from the top of the bookshelf and scurried up the stairs with an annoyed purr. I took a deep breath to calm myself and listened in the wake of the cat's exit for any sounds, anything at all.

"Jolene?"

As I watched the cat leave, I noticed a woodstove in the corner of the cellar, probably left over from the days when burning wood was the only source of heat for a house out here halfway up a mountainside.

I didn't want to look inside it, but I knew I had to. Over the years I'd seen lots of ways offenders try to dispose of bodies.

A woodstove was one of them.

I crossed the dingy cellar in half a dozen quick strides and held my hand out to see if the stove was still warm.

It was.

I took a deep breath, nearly choking on the thick, pungent air of Grolin's cellar.

I slid the gun under my belt and wrapped the tail of my shirt around my hand. Then I grabbed the stove handle and gave it a firm twist. It snapped up with a click, and the stove's door popped open.

A soft hot glow poured out of the opening. He'd been burning something down here. A pile of embers burst into flame with the sudden rush of air.

Bracing myself for the smell of burnt flesh, I leaned over and peered inside.

39

59 seconds.

―――――――――■―――――――――

Just a pile of ashes and glowing coals. Nothing more. No bones, hair, teeth.

What? A scrap of scorched paper fluttered out. I picked it up. Part of a diagram. Technical drawings.

Technical drawings?

I grabbed a piece of wood from a nearby pile and shoved the coals aside, stirring them, looking for the charred remains of Jolene Brittany Parker.

Nothing. Not even a shred of clothing.

When morticians cremate a body, bone fragments remain. If Grolin had tried to dispose of her body in here, there would be something left of her. But there wasn't. He hadn't burned Jolene's corpse in this stove.

I was relieved but also frustrated. Where was she? What had he done with her?

―――――――――■―――――――――

The Illusionist leaned forward. He'd placed a small camera in the basement on the top of the bookshelf. Dr. Bowers was down there now, poking around the woodpile.

He'd found something by the stove.

They only had 33 seconds left, though.

It wouldn't be enough time to get out.

No.

Not enough time.

———————————■———————————

I set the piece of wood back on the pile, and that's when I noticed the wires.

Wires?

I directed the beam of my flashlight at them.

Oh no.

Pushed the wood to the side.

It was too easy to get in here.

Saw the metal box.

Too easy.

Read the numbers blinking on the timer.

He likes to watch.

14 . . . 13 . . .

"Bomb," I yelled. I spun. I ran. "Get out now!"

Kept the countdown going in my head . . .

. . . 12 . . . 11 . . .

I sped toward the steps.

. . . 10 . . .

Bolted up the stairs, three at a time.

. . . 9 . . . 8 . . .

"Out! Ralph! Lien-hua! Bomb! There's a bomb!"

I burst through the hallway door, Lien-hua right in front of me.

. . . 7 . . .

Down the hall, toward the front door.

. . . 6 . . .

Ralph landed at the bottom of the staircase.

. . . 5 . . .

Outside. Onto the porch.

. . . 4 . . .

Jumping. Landing on the grass.

. . . 3 . . .

Scrambling forward. Lunging to the ground.

...2...

Throwing my body over Lien-hua's.

... 1.

Boom.

———————————■———————————

11:42 a.m., Eastern Standard Time

In Charlotte, North Carolina, Governor Sebastian Taylor caught sight of his reflection in a mirror and tilted his head to see which side of his face was more photogenic.

In Denver, Colorado, Tessa Ellis shook her head and dragged her suitcase up to the next spot in line at the US Airways ticket counter.

In West Asheville, North Carolina, Alice McMichaelson stole a glance at the business textbook on her lap during a time-out in the last few minutes of her son's soccer game.

At the concierge's desk in the lobby of the Stratford Hotel, Theodore punched in the appropriate codes to change the name of the caterers for Monday's luncheon.

In front of his computer, the Illusionist leaned forward with a satisfied grin and watched the house explode.

———————————■———————————

I felt the heat of the explosion wash over me, singeing my hair. Scorching my neck. And then, a shower of debris peppered my back, my legs. A storm of burning slats of wood followed immediately, raining down around us and on top of us, bringing with it a sudden, searing pain in my shoulder.

But I didn't move. I kept my body draped over Lien-hua, and I didn't even turn to see what sort of object had knifed its way deeply into my back, wedging itself against my shoulder blade. Behind me I heard a roar as the house's bone-dry wood exploded into a fireball.

Then Ralph was beside me, urging us forward, yelling for us to get away from the heat and the flames. I helped Lien-hua to her feet, and we hobbled forward toward the trees, then turned to look at the house.

It was completely destroyed.

Any evidence in it would have been destroyed as well.

The cell phone in Ralph's pocket rang.

He fished it out and answered it. Cursed. "They found her," he said grimly. "They found Jolene."

"Where?" I asked.

"The trunk of Margaret's car."

40

By the time we got to the federal building, the crime scene guys had already roped off half of the parking lot. Shock, anger, and sorrow had settled over every inch of the scene. Margaret was stalking back and forth shaking her head, one hand planted firmly on her hip, the other rubbing her forehead. Despite the fury orbiting her, she looked pale.

As we crossed the parking lot, Ralph whispered to Lien-hua and me, "He must have put the body in the trunk of her car early this morning before she left for work. She drove here with it in there. Got an email half an hour ago telling her to look in the trunk."

"Can they trace the email?" I asked.

"Trying to. But the way it was routed, looks like the guy knew what he was doing."

Tucker stood beside the car. He motioned for us to come closer. His face looked pasty, drained. "He blew up the house?"

Ralph nodded.

I looked at the car, couldn't see inside. "She still in there?" I asked Tucker softly. He didn't answer. Just stepped aside. I walked past the crime scene technicians and peered into the trunk.

The naked upper torso of a woman lay in the trunk of Margaret's Lexus—but only the upper half. Jolene had been sawed in two just above the pelvis. She'd also been brutally tortured: dozens of cuts crisscrossed her torso, her face, her arms. *Six cuts aren't enough for him anymore*, I thought.

Despite the fact that she'd been mostly drained of blood a pool of dark liquids leaked from the bottom of the corpse and spread across the carpeting in the trunk.

A metal tent stake was driven deep into Jolene's chest, pinning down a note: "TOO SLOW. YOUR MOVE." A white pawn was in her mouth. A ribbon in her hair.

My mind went numb, spinning, blaming, aching. For the first time in years I felt physically ill at a crime scene. Completely nauseous.

I'd been hoping maybe we would find her alive, save her, rescue her, hoping, hoping, hoping, trying to convince myself the Illusionist had been lying when he said it was too late to save her.

But he hadn't been. Not at all.

It seemed like he'd planned everything, even timed the discovery of her body to coincide with the explosion.

I muttered an excuse to the people clustered around the car and pushed my way through the crowd. I needed some air. Some space. Actually, I needed to throw up, but I couldn't let anyone see me. I slipped off behind a nearby car and just barely made it out of sight before I leaned over to retch.

I emptied my stomach onto the asphalt. There wasn't much there. My entire life tasted like bile. I could hardly believe what was happening. Everything seemed to be spinning apart, the fabric of both my personal life and my career ripping right down the seams.

My stepdaughter hated me. This killer was mocking me. Christie was haunting me. I turned away from the mess of vomit and reached into my pocket to see if I had a handkerchief, anything, and found the jewelry store receipt instead. Evidence that I really had remembered Tessa's birthday, that I really had visited that mall in Atlanta earlier this week, that I really did have a birthday present to give her.

We celebrate the days of our birth, moments of new life.

I was gone on her birthday.

The killer had mentioned her name.

Tessa.

He knew I had a daughter.

Stay focused, Pat. Don't let him get to you.

Jolene was someone's daughter. So was Mindy. So were the rest.

Christie would want me to find this guy, shut him down. To do anything I could to stop him from stealing birthdays from other young women. Other daughters like hers. Like mine.

"We know she's going to be OK. We love you, Mindy," her father had said on TV. He didn't know she was already dead. *"We're here for you—"*

But how could I catch this guy? He was smarter than I was, always one step ahead.

The only way to catch him is to stop playing by his rules. You need to make a move.

I thought of Jolene, what it would be like to lose a daughter like that, to have her mutilated, abused, slaughtered. I couldn't even imagine it.

Right now, the Illusionist was somewhere laughing at us, probably watching us, mocking the pain he was causing. I couldn't let him get away with it. I couldn't.

With those thoughts, rage, white hot and unchained, began to rip through my soul. Howling anger sharpening its claws. Filling me. Boiling inside of me. Chasing away the nausea, chasing away everything and replacing it with a storm of fury. The rage both frightened and reassured me. Over the last eight months, wrath had started to feel right at home in me.

You gotta move out in front of him, Pat. Do what you do best.

I looked back at the people examining Margaret's car.

Everyone was talking in whispers. A tumble of barely audible words skittered across the parking lot toward me. I heard someone mutter something about the media and warrants, and then someone started calling Grolin the names I'd been thinking of but just hadn't gotten around to saying yet.

I had to stop him. And I would. For Christie.

I wiped my mouth on the sleeve of my windbreaker, stuffed the receipt into my pocket, and headed back to the crime scene.

———————————■———————————

I arrived just in time to hear Lien-hua gasp. "He sawed her in half?" Her voice broke in the middle of the sentence, and I wanted to save her from seeing the body and from the images she would never be able to erase from her mind, to protect her from doing her job, from becoming more like me. But I couldn't protect her. I wasn't here for that.

A few minutes later, Lien-hua, Ralph, and I drifted back together on the edge of the parking lot. Margaret strode up to us, jittery and tense. No one said a word. Then Agent Tucker and Sheriff Wallace found their way over to us, and I spoke softly, but to all of them. "When he talked to me last night, he called himself the Illusionist. He told me, 'You can't have her. I saw her first.'"

Ralph's teeth were clenched. "The sawing the woman in half trick."

"That's sick," said Sheriff Wallace.

Margaret turned to Lien-hua. "Where did you say Grolin works?"

"*MountainQuest* magazine. He writes the outdoor column."

Wallace nodded. "I know the place. It's out on highway 25 on the way to Hendersonville."

"Find him. Bring him in."

Dante turned to me. "Dr. Bowers?"

"Yeah."

"Can I have my phone back?"

"Oh yeah. Sure." I reached into my pocket, pulled out the handful of parts that used to be his phone, and handed it to him.

"What on earth happened to it?"

Ralph answered for me. "He dropped it."

"Something like that," I mumbled. "I'm really sorry. I'll buy you a new one."

He shook his head, stuffed the pieces into his pocket, and then motioned to a couple of uniformed officers who followed him to a patrol car.

I felt bad, but then Margaret turned to me and I prepared to feel worse. I was sure she was going to rip into me about disregarding her orders and heading over to Grolin's place. "Get that shoulder looked at," she said. "Have the EMTs check it out."

Now that was a surprise. Considering the circumstances, her concern was somewhat moving.

"I'll be all right."

"Dr. Bowers, there is a piece of wood sticking out of your back."

No wonder it hurt.

"Get that taken out. You get an infection, it costs us more money. I don't want the Bureau to have to spend any more money on you than it has to."

Oh. Well. In that case.

"Ralph?" she said.

"Yeah?"

"I want you to do the questioning." Her voice was iron. Flat and cold.

He nodded.

She tried to stay calm, but her voice began to quaver. "No kid gloves, Ralph. He put that girl in my car."

He nodded again. "I understand."

Joseph Grolin, here we come.

41

Tessa stared out the window of the 737 at the towering castles of clouds surrounding the plane. Glowing corridors of vapor and light split open to encircle the plane, to welcome it into their fairytale landscape. At one time she might have been impressed, even astonished by this journey through gossamer light, but today all she saw was a bunch of stupid clouds.

When she was younger she used to lie on her back in the summer grass and look up at the clouds with her mother, pointing and giggling and finding mystical creatures in the sky; mermaids and dragons and fairies. Just like all children do at one time or another.

"See that one," she would cry. "It's a unicorn!"

"Yes," her mother would say. "I see it. I see it."

Whatever the clouds really looked like, Tessa could always find a unicorn.

But not anymore. No, today there were only clouds in the sky. Shapeless and blank. No unicorns. Just misty haze surrounding her. In fact, she hadn't seen a unicorn in a long, long time. She couldn't even remember when.

She glanced over at the profile of the man escorting her. He'd told her his name: Special Agent Eric Stanton. He didn't really look like an FBI agent, more like an accountant. Hair parted on the side, baby face, clean shave. But he wasn't wearing a ring, and he wasn't really *that* old—maybe twenty-two or so—and he might have actually looked cute if he could lose the tie and the old-man-looking glasses, grow a little soul patch . . . ruffle up his hair a little . . .

"Yes?" He was looking directly at her now. "Did you need something?" He had soft brown eyes.

"Um, no." She looked away, out the window again. She hoped she wasn't blushing.

"You sure?"

"Yeah."

He leaned close. She could smell his aftershave.

Gak. Why did he have to use aftershave?

"You OK, kid?"

Kid!

"I'm fine."

"Well, that's wonderful," he said sarcastically. "As your chaperone I'm very glad to hear that."

She looked at him again. What in the world was wrong with her! The guy was probably over thirty! Old enough to be her dad. She folded her arms and glared at him. She glanced momentarily at the Sudoku puzzle he was working on. He'd been struggling with it for the last hour or so. It was rated "expert." Huh. Yeah, right. He should have probably been doing one rated "toddler."

She studied it for a few brief seconds. "Six, nine, eight, four, one, three," she said.

"What?"

"The bottom row. Fill those in, you should be able to take it from there." After registering his surprise she added, "Though I wouldn't bet on it."

He looked down at the sheet then back at her. "How do you know that?"

She shrugged. "Maybe it's just easy to figure out when you're a *kid*."

Then he made a small sound with his mouth half open, asked her to repeat the numbers, looked down at his puzzle, and started scribbling. While he filled in the squares in his lame little puzzle, Tessa turned back to the wall of the airplane and stared out the window, searching the sky for something. Anything.

But all she could see were miles and miles of clouds.

42

Alice McMichaelson sighed and slumped into her recliner.

After taking Jacob to his last soccer game for the year (they won four to three thanks to Jacob's two goals) and maneuvering through traffic and then stopping by the library to drop off Brenda's overdue books and check out another stack that she'd probably finish by the end of the weekend and swinging through McDonald's to get some lunch and then crawling past that nightmare construction zone on highway 240 West, she'd finally made it home.

Whew.

She kicked off her shoes. Stress. That was the problem. Starting a new job, arriving late for work, not getting enough sleep last night, running around all day with the kids.

She took a deep breath and let her thoughts wander back to work. She really liked this job. The bank was going through a merger — Second National had been bought out by Montrose Intl. Investments last month, and transferring files and accounts had been a nightmare because the two banking companies just happened to use different computer programs — surprise, surprise. But that was one of the reasons they'd brought her on board. They needed extra staff to help with the transition and she needed the money. Garrett had never sent any child support and it was tough enough just making house payments. She had to keep this job. She had to.

She sighed again, then reached down and rubbed her left foot. Ah, that felt good. Tonight, once the kids were in bed, she could do some studying, get ready for her exam on Monday. But for now it just felt good to relax.

Jacob had deposited his soccer clothes in the middle of the hall and disappeared into his room to play video games, and the truth was, she didn't even care. A few minutes ago Brenda had emerged from her room just long enough to find a bag of Cheetos. Alice watched her daughter return down the hallway and then let her eyes wander around the living room. Could use some cleaning. Vacuuming mostly. But then again, it wasn't so bad, really. Being a single mom with two kids, what did you expect? She'd managed OK. And maybe she wouldn't be single forever. She was still young enough to start over again and hadn't lost all of her looks—at least not yet. And there were a few guys who'd shown interest in her, after all.

She brushed at a stray wisp of hair. Never did find that brush, though, and it bugged her. Usually she prided herself on knowing where everything was around the house.

Well, not a big deal. She'd buy another dumb brush. And at least she didn't have to get up for work tomorrow, just take the kids to mass at ten, and after that she had all day to relax. She could make it through until then. Yes. She could manage.

In a few minutes she would get up and straighten the living room. She closed her eyes and whispered a small prayer and rubbed her foot while the weekend drizzled past her outside.

The angels were winning.

At least for now.

43

Ralph suggested we take a breather and then reconvene in half an hour to debrief. It gave us all a chance to collect our bearings, refocus, grab some coffee, whatever. While everyone else went their separate ways, I had one of the paramedics take a look at my shoulder.

He pulled out the blade-like slat of wood that the explosion had buried six inches into my back, cleaned the wound, and smeared the area with antibiotic. "You really should have this stitched up," he said. "There's a lot of muscle damage."

"I'll be all right," I told him. "Just butterfly it shut with some bandages."

"Are you a doctor?"

"Not that kind of doctor. I used to lead wilderness trips, though. Learned first aid for that."

"Might leave a scar."

"It wouldn't be my first."

He gently bandaged the wound and then patted my good shoulder. "You be careful out there."

I thanked him and headed inside for the meeting. On the way past the senator's office I noticed Ralph and Lien-hua standing by the water cooler. Water, good idea. Rinse the bile out of my mouth. I grabbed a cup.

"That shoulder all right?" asked Ralph.

"Yeah. It'll be fine. Little sore though." Actually, it was killing me. "You two OK?"

They nodded.

"Listen," I said, "did you see any evidence at the house before the explosion?"

Ralph took a deep sigh. "A leather jacket in his closet. Looked like the one our guy was wearing last night. I didn't grab it though because we didn't have the search warrant yet, and then there wasn't time to go back for it after you yelled 'bomb.'"

"Lien-hua?" I asked.

She shook her head. "No. Nothing."

Just then Margaret and Tucker walked in. They nodded a silent greeting to us and headed to the conference room. Ralph joined them, but Lien-hua stayed by the water cooler a moment longer.

"So honestly, is your shoulder OK?" she asked.

"Honestly, it hurts like the dickens."

"The dickens?"

"My mom used to say it."

"Oh. Well, anyway. I wanted to say . . . thanks."

"For . . . ?"

"At the house. You covered me with your body. You protected me. You didn't have to do that."

Ah. She noticed.

"I hadn't noticed."

"But . . ."

"Yes?"

"Don't ever do it again."

I blinked. "What?"

"I don't need protecting, Agent Bowers. I can take care of myself. I'm a big girl. Understand?"

"Um, I—"

"Do you understand?"

"Yeah," I said. *No,* I thought. "Wait a minute. Are you saying you don't want me to protect you, but that you're thankful to me when I do?"

"I would give that analysis an A," she said with the flicker of a grin, and walked away, leaving me standing there by myself with an empty paper cup in my hand.

I will never, ever understand women.

I rinsed out my mouth, threw the cup into the trash, and followed Lien-hua to the meeting.

Margaret looked worse than the rest of us. Streaks of mascara scarred her face, and she was staring at the wall, emotionless. A zombie was in charge of our team. Ralph glanced my way and conferred the leadership of the meeting to me with a nod.

"First of all, everyone's OK," I said. "Right?"

Nods.

"I know right now everything seems to point to Grolin, but let's back up for a minute and try to stay objective. Margaret, the CSIU is finishing up outside?"

"Yes," she mumbled. "Then we have to send them to Grolin's house and your cave up on that mountain."

Those guys would be earning their pay today.

"Agent Tucker?"

"Yeah?"

"Did you find any more links between the crimes—like the contacts or the engagement ring?"

He shook his head. "We'll need more time to be sure, but there doesn't seem to be anything else. It looks like he started leaving clues with Reinita."

"But what about Bethanie?" asked Lien-hua. "She came between Reinita and Mindy. Why would he skip over her?"

Tucker shrugged. "I don't know."

"We're missing something," I said.

Just then one of the crime scene technicians burst into the room. We all turned and stared in his direction. I think it intimidated him because he shrank back a little and mumbled, "Special Agent Wellington, you told us to let you know if we found anything . . ."

"Yes," she snapped. "What is it?"

He shrank back even more. "Her purse. It was in the car with her, shoved back into the corner of the trunk."

"Let's see it," said Ralph.

I pushed aside the piles of papers, pens, and empty coffee cups to clear off the table, and the tech guy carefully dumped out the contents of Jolene's purse. Her cell phone tumbled onto the table along with a set of keys, a makeup case, a compact, some crumpled receipts, a billfold stuffed with pictures and credit cards, a few pens, a brush, two tampons, and a checkbook.

All four of us studied the items intensely.

"OK," said Lien-hua. "What do you see?"

Ralph shook his head. "Any of these things could be hers or someone else's. There's no way to know."

We all donned gloves before touching anything. I pulled out her credit cards and shuffled through them, glancing at the names on the cards. "Nope. These are all hers." I uncrumpled the receipts, compared them to the credit cards. "These are all hers too."

"The billfold, maybe?" said Tucker. "Could it be someone else's? He wants us to know. He wouldn't leave something we couldn't link."

Lien-hua flipped the billfold over and shook her head. "It's embroidered with her initials . . . Wait a minute." She pointed to the hairbrush. "Jolene has blonde hair."

"Yeah, so?" I said.

Lien-hua picked up the brush and held it up to the light. "This brush has red hair in it."

"That's it!" said Ralph. He turned to Tucker. "Process that now. I want fingerprints, DNA—" The crime scene technician reached for the brush, but Ralph stopped him. "No offense, buddy." He pointed to Tucker. "You do the fingerprinting. You're the best we have."

"I'm on it," said Tucker.

He hurried off with the brush as the timid crime scene guy scooped up the rest of the purse's contents and followed him to the lab.

"OK, good," said Ralph. "Let's see where that leads us."

"It's possible it might be something else in the purse instead," I said. "Let's not get too excited yet. Either way, he hasn't linked all the bodies for us—"

"I still want to know why he skipped Bethanie," said Lien-hua impatiently. "She was killed between Reinita and Mindy. Did he get started with her maybe, and she resisted, and that's why he didn't leave a clue? Or was he interrupted before he could leave it?"

"Maybe something went wrong," said Margaret, "and he panicked?"

"He didn't panic," said Lien-hua. "The one thing this guy doesn't do is panic."

"Besides," I said, "he would have had the contact lenses with him already; he would have come prepared to leave them no matter what. After all, he left the pawn and the yellow ribbon. Besides, the ring points to Mindy, not Bethanie. It's like he skipped right over Bethanie, like she's not part of the series."

"Yeah," said Ralph. "And if Tucker's right, then he didn't start leaving these clues until Reinita."

"Order matters," I said. "There's something about the order we're missing." *Why did he start with Reinita? What happened?* I stared off into space, processing everything.

I looked up at the faces on the wall. The beautiful pictures of the dead women.

Someone had already added Jolene's picture to the mix.

Patty. Jamie. Alexis. Reinita. Bethanie. Mindy. Jolene.

Alexis and Bethanie were found the farthest away from Asheville.

Maybe he didn't skip Bethanie.

I thought back to the basement at Grolin's house. The workbench. The bookcase. The cat.

Maybe he didn't kill her.

The cat.

Suddenly I remembered something I'd heard years ago. "Only the most foolish of mice would hide in a cat's ear," I muttered. "But only the wisest of cats would look there."

"What?" said Ralph.

I walked around the table to look at the pictures on the bulletin board. "A saying I heard once. It means the best place to hide something is often the most obvious place because it's the last place anyone would look."

Margaret looked at me quizzically.

"We've been looking for what all the victims have in common, right?" I glanced around at the team. "But what if only some of them had something in common?" I pointed to the wall. "Alexis and Bethanie."

Margaret shook her head. "What are you saying?"

"What if you wanted to kill someone but also avoid suspicion?"

"I'd make sure I had an airtight alibi," she answered. "I don't see what this has to do with—"

By then Ralph had caught on. He stood up. "Or you could make sure you wouldn't need one at all."

"Yes," I said. "That's right."

Margaret shook her head. She still didn't understand.

"OK," I said. "Let's say I wanted to kill off Lien-hua here."

"Thanks a lot."

"Just for discussion purposes. If we were friends and then suddenly she showed up dead, I'd be a suspect, right?"

"Well, maybe," said Margaret, glancing at me derisively. "If you had motive, means, and opportunity."

So, she was getting a little of her old spunk back. That was good.

"OK," I continued. "What if I had all those things, but she'd obviously been killed by someone else, say a serial killer. Same MO. Same signature. What then?"

Suddenly it all began to sink it. "A copycat?" she whispered.

"Yeah," I said. "Two killers instead of one. That would explain why the geo profile was off. It would also explain why he started linking the crimes with Reinita—"

"Because someone else killed Alexis, and he wanted to separate his work from the copycat's!" said Lien-hua.

Ralph grabbed the manila folder containing the medical examiner's reports. "Hmm. The wound pattern was the same in each case, but it looks like the cuts weren't as deep on Bethanie and Alexis." He flipped to another page. "And the pawns—the ones found at Alexis and Bethanie's sites—were cut with the same lathe." He studied the photos carefully. "But the graining of the wood might be slightly different. Could be a different set. I'll check it out."

"Why didn't we notice that before?" asked Margaret.

"Because we weren't looking for it," I said. "We were assuming rather than examining."

"Wait," said Lien-hua, "toxicology, remember? Different drugs for Alexis and Bethanie." She hit the table with her hand. "He can't stand that someone else would share the spotlight."

"He's telling us which ones are his," mumbled Margaret.

Wait a minute. Never assume. Theorize, test, revise.

"OK," I said. "I'm hypothesizing here, but let's see what we've got. If someone else killed Alexis—found out about the ribbons and the chess pieces, I don't know how, but let's say he did—then the Illusionist—"

"Grolin," said Margaret.

"Whoever he is, he's following the case on the news, right, Lien-hua?"

"Absolutely."

"He hears about this other body, knows he didn't kill her, and doesn't want to—what did you say?"

"Share the spotlight."

"Right. So he decides to link his crimes for us in another way—a way nobody could possibly copy, leaving clues to his future victims. This way he keeps playing the game even though someone else has reached across the board and started taking some of the pieces."

Everyone seemed to be tracking, following my train of thought.

"OK," I said. "Let's use this as a working theory, but before we jump to any conclusions, let's see if this hairbrush leads us anywhere."

Ralph began to point to each of us like a drill sergeant clicking off jobs on a duty chart. "Lien-hua, revamp the psych profile based on five victims rather than seven—leave out Alexis and Bethanie. Pat, rework the numbers on that geo-whatever computer program of yours. Let's see where that takes us. I'll get the interrogation room set up."

Margaret just stood motionless by the table, stunned. "Two killers," I heard her whisper as I hurried past her to my desk. "And one of them knows where I live."

44

Aaron Jeffrey Kincaid had only met one true psychopath in his life.

As a teenager, Aaron had spent four months in a state-run group home for adolescents in southern Mississippi. The state didn't call them orphanages anymore. Of course not. Much too negative-sounding. Instead, it was a "group home." As if calling a place like that a "home" would turn it into one. As if anything could do that.

Of course, the idea was still the same—children who'd lost their parents and were no longer cute and cuddly little babies whom couples might actually want to adopt get to live together until "they're old enough to move out and become a burden on society." At least that's how the staff at the group home used to put it when they thought the children were out of earshot.

It was their idea of a joke.

So that's where Aaron Jeffrey Kincaid met the psychopath—during his stay at the Oak Island Group Home in La Cruxis, Mississippi.

Sevren was a gray, cold pool with deep currents. On his first day there, he ran into Lucas, an ape-like high school senior nearly six years older than him, in the hallway. Lucas bullied all the other kids and they all hated him, but none of them dared cross him.

The two students stood staring at each other, neither moving. Neither flinching.

"Out of my way," said Lucas, glaring at the newcomer.

Sevren just eyed him. Expressionless. Impassive. Unmoving.

"I said, step aside," growled Lucas, moving closer.

He pushed Sevren against the wall and smacked him hard in the gut. As Sevren gasped for breath, Lucas leaned close. "I heard about your mama, little boy. What she did for a living. She deserved to get cut."

And then, something happened. Something snapped in the wiry little boy who had just arrived. As quick as an asp he grabbed the older boy's throat and squeezed. Lucas beat on Sevren with his massive fists, but it had no effect. It took five other kids to pull Sevren off, and Lucas spent the next four months in the hospital trying to learn how to swallow again.

Of course, the other kids were glad Lucas was out of the picture. So when the administration asked about the fight, they just told them Sevren was acting in self-defense, which was mostly true. And instead of being sent to juvenile prison he was allowed to stay at the home.

Sevren became a coiled serpent, always watching, always evaluating, always calculating. But what impressed Aaron the most wasn't his roommate's physical strength but his ability to manipulate people, to control them. In fact, he was almost as good at it as Aaron Jeffrey Kincaid was.

Almost as good, in fact, as Father.

But of course, that's not what makes a person a psychopath, just having the ability to manipulate others. If it were, someone might actually consider Aaron Jeffrey Kincaid a psychopath. But no, persuasion, admirable though it is, isn't enough. To be a psychopath you need to lack empathy. You need to have a complete disregard for what other people are feeling or experiencing.

Even now, Kincaid remembered watching CNN when Gary Ridgeway, the Green River Killer, was captured back in 2001 after a nineteen-year killing spree in the northwest. After he was finally convicted of killing forty-eight women (and claimed to have killed forty-one more), the investigators asked him what made him different from other people, and he summed it all up in three simple words: "That caring thing."

Psychopaths lack that caring thing. They act on impulse, don't feel guilt, don't respond emotionally the way the rest of the world does, and have an insatiable need for power and control. Some don't feel fear. Some can't find sexual fulfillment unless their partner is in pain, or dying, or dead. Usually it's the agony of others that brings psychopaths the most pleasure.

So that was Sevren. No conscience. No guilt. No fears. No regrets.

They say psychopaths begin exhibiting signs of their pathology at age fifteen.

Sevren was an early bloomer.

———————————————■———————————————

One day after school, Aaron had snuck behind the group home's south wing to grab a smoke out of sight of the host family's window. It was April in Mississippi. Hot and steamy. Humidity you could taste.

Just after lighting up, he heard sounds in the nearby woods. Screeches. High-pitched, primal, something other than human.

The noises were coming from a clearing up ahead. Aaron knew the place. The teens would meet there sometimes late at night to drink or smoke pot around a bonfire.

He heard the sound again. What was that?

And then, laughter. Quiet and calm. And a cold voice oozing through the trees. "You like that, don't you?"

Aaron saw a flicker of movement in the meadow and stepped quietly onto the path.

Another cry, this time sharper. Definitely not human. Some kind of animal.

What was going on?

He had to see.

But then the screech was cut off abruptly, swallowed by a burst of strange, moist, gurgling sounds. "There, now. That's better," said the voice.

Aaron edged forward and peered through the underbrush. He was close enough now to see a figure kneeling, working at something with his hands, humming. Whatever he had on the ground in front of him lay hidden from view.

Aaron took another step closer. Who was that? Only his back was visible.

Maybe it was the movement, visible out of the corner of his eye, or the soft sound of footsteps on the forest floor, but the figure stopped what he was doing. Froze. So did Aaron.

Time crashed to a halt. To Aaron the moment smelled like spring rain and flowers and earth and blood, and then the person in the meadow turned his head slowly and rose in one smooth, serpentine motion. Aaron recognized him right away.

"Hello, Aaron." Sevren was holding a pocketknife smeared with dark blood. More blood dripped from his hands and forearms down onto the leafy forest floor.

Aaron let his eyes follow the descent of the drops of blood. And that's when he saw what his roommate had done to the cat. Somehow the poor creature was still alive. It flopped what was left of its head back and forth feebly, finally facing Aaron. Tried to look at him. Had no eyes left to do it.

"What are you doing, Sevren?"

"A little experiment." Sevren cocked his head slightly and shook out his fingers, splattering warm blood onto the young leaves. "You won't tell, will you?"

For a moment, just a moment, Aaron thought of running. Somewhere deep beneath the gurgles of the dying cat he could hear the sounds of the jungle and the screams and pleading prayers of the dying children. And the babies crying in the dark.

Somewhere beneath the sounds.

The dream called to him. He thought of running from Sevren,

from this meadow, from everything, escaping like he had when he was ten, running and running and running forever, but this time he stood still. Something kept him there, drew his eyes toward the gruesome scene.

Sevren's voice turned dark. "If you tell, Aaron, I might have to explain what happened to Jessica. What really happened."

The words slammed into him like a fist in his stomach, taking all the air out of his reply.

"What?" Aaron searched Sevren's eyes. He couldn't possibly know.

"Jes-si-ca." Sevren said the word slowly, deliberately, savoring every letter. "What really happened to her." Sevren grinned and drew the pocketknife across his wrist, not to cut the skin, only to demonstrate that he knew what Aaron Jeffrey Kincaid was certain no one could possibly know.

Sevren continued. "I saw your scar, there on your wrist, last week when you were changing clothes, and I remembered what happened to Jessica Rembrandt last month. It wasn't too hard to piece together. At first I thought maybe you'd planned to die with her, and then at the last minute you chickened out and couldn't go through with it. But . . . that's not what happened, is it?" He paused, but not for long. It wasn't really a question. "You talked her into it, didn't you?" During the last few words, his voice, his posture, his tone had shifted from cool judgment to warm admiration. "You convinced her to do it."

When Aaron didn't reply, Sevren nodded. Shook some blood off his fingertips. "Yes. I thought so."

Aaron couldn't think of anything to say. He didn't know if it was rage or fear or disgust that swarmed over his soul. "I loved her," he said at last.

Sevren nodded. "Yes," he said simply. "I know." A pause. Then, he continued. "So I won't tell if you won't tell. We'll have two little secrets between us: the girl and the cat." He placed a bloody finger to his lips to signify their pact of silence. "Shh."

Aaron scratched absently at the fresh scar on his wrist. He nodded. "I won't tell."

Sevren looked down at the writhing cat whose paws he'd tied down to four stakes. Then, he looked back at Aaron. "Cross your heart and hope to die?"

Aaron nodded.

Sevren pulled a yellow ribbon out of his pocket and turned back to the cat. Then he glanced back at Aaron. "You can stay if you want. It's just now getting to the good part."

And Aaron had stayed. Until it was over. And then a little longer even.

Long enough to listen to Sevren tell him about his mother.

45

The two boys were sitting together by the campfire pit. They'd built a small blaze and were smoking, swapping stories. Aaron told Sevren about his parents, about the jungle and the babies and his destiny.

And then, as Sevren slid a long stick into the fire, he told Aaron about what he saw when he finally got out of the closet.

———————————■———————————

July 15, 1981
Memphis, Tennessee
7:17 p.m.

The nine-year-old boy watched his mother lean down toward him and felt her smear a wet kiss on his forehead. She smelled sweet with perfume. "Now you be quiet and be a good boy and don't be interruptin' your mama's work. You understand?"

The young boy had nodded.

"You know what'll happen if you interrupt your mama?"

He nodded again.

The air conditioner coughed and sputtered in the windowsill of the double-wide trailer they called home.

She grinned, her mouth big and gaping. She was missing five teeth. "I knew you'd listen to your mama. I knew you'd be a good boy."

Once again Sevren nodded. He didn't want to be a bad boy. He didn't like what happened to him when he was a bad boy. He didn't like having to stay in the closet overnight. He wanted to please her, of course he did, just like any good boy would want to do.

"I'll get you out as soon as I can," she said. And then the change came over her, the strange change that turned her into someone he didn't recognize. Sometimes it meant she hadn't been taking her pills. Sometimes it meant she'd taken too many. Her face turned terrible and red, her voice became angry and hard. "You don't make a sound, boy! Don't you dare let me hear you. Your mama has to work, you understand?"

Another nod. His eyes wide, his heart hammering.

And so, Sevren went willingly into the bedroom closet and sat on the floor. It wouldn't be long if he did as he was told. Then his mama shut the closet door and locked it. Now he couldn't get out. Now she was in control.

He stared at the narrow band of light slicing through the space between the bottom of the door and the floor. It would go black soon, when his mother shut off the bedroom light.

Sevren heard the outside door open and the gruff voice of a man and the girlish giggles of his mama pretending to be interested in him. It was her job. The boy knew that. Then, he heard the bedroom door open and close. A few minutes later the light in the bathroom went out, and his mother began doing her job.

And then came the noises that he didn't really understand. Somehow frightening and beautiful and soft and comforting all at the same time. But he didn't like hearing them, so he sat in the closet doing what he always did: playing games in his mind. At first, when he was younger, it was tic-tac-toe. He would play both sides, first the X side and then the O side, rotating the board in his mind so he could see the game from the perspective of his opponent, which was really just him. But eventually, he figured out that in tic-tac-toe if you know what you're doing, you'll never lose. And since he was playing both sides, he could also never win. That got old pretty quickly.

Then he learned checkers. At first it was much more difficult to keep all the pieces straight in his mind, to remember where he'd moved and which checkers he'd taken. It took him a long time to be able to train his mind to remember the progress of all the red and dark circles as they moved across the board, but in time, he was able to do that too. He had plenty of time in the closet to practice when he didn't do his homework or when he didn't please his mama.

But in time he discovered that the strategies for winning checkers were limited too. So eventually he'd landed on chess. In chess the possibilities were almost limitless. And it didn't matter so much who had the opening move. Yes, white had a slight advantage because it went first, but either side could win. Either could lose. He could actually beat himself.

But on this night, the night with the Angry Man, something was different. Normally Sevren was pretty good at blocking out the sounds, making them seem not so real, but this night, the sounds broke through and found their way into the closet with him. There was a different kind of urgency to these sounds. They turned into gasps and threats, and he heard sounds that he shouldn't have heard. Smacking sounds. Ripping sounds and wet sounds. And then, a slicing, tearing sound that he hoped he would never hear again. He tried humming to block them out, but it didn't work.

And he didn't move. He dared not move until his mama came for him.

He waited, even after he heard the bedroom door open and close, then the outside door slam shut. Even after the soft gasping sounds in the room beyond the closet door went away and everything descended into silence. Still he waited. Playing chess. Winning. Losing. It was all the same in the end. He waited and played and waited and played. He waited until he couldn't wait any longer. "Mama?" he whispered at last. His voice was hoarse, and it didn't even sound like it was coming from his throat. "Are you there?"

No answer. No sound. Maybe she was sleeping? He wouldn't want to wake her. He was afraid of what she might say.

But it was strange for her to fall asleep right then. Usually she came and unlocked the closet as soon as she could, sometimes even before she was done counting her money.

"Mama?"

He heard his voice echo in the closet, but no reply came from his mother, no sound came from the bedroom except the air conditioner sputtering and, with a harsh, grating gasp, dying its final death in the windowsill.

As the hours slipped by, his calls became shouts and then screams and then wails, and then everything just deteriorated into sobbing. He yelled and begged for his mother to come, but she didn't. He banged on the door until his hands were raw, but she didn't answer. Why didn't she come? Didn't she love him?

After a while the tears stopped.

He tried to play chess again, tried to picture the board and the pieces, but in his mind the board had been tipped over. All the pieces were scattered across the floor of his imagination. He couldn't seem to get them set upright again. No matter how hard he tried, they kept tipping over, spilling onto the floor. Scattered. The game was over.

"Mama!"

He flung himself against the closet door, over and over again, screaming with his tired, ragged voice. But his mama didn't reply, and she didn't come to let him out. He tried turning the locked doorknob again and again even though he knew it wouldn't move.

By morning he was no longer screaming. He was no longer pounding. He was just sitting in the corner, smelling the strange and slightly ripe odor coming from beyond the closet door.

He spent that entire day in the closet.

Oh how he wished the air conditioner was working.

It was late that afternoon when he began to notice the flies.

A few crawled beneath the door and joined him in the hot closet. He tried to shoo them away, but they buzzed around him like an angry, dark cloud.

There were a lot of flies.

On the third day, only after he took the umbrella that he found in the corner of the closet and stabbed its tip into the wood and splintered a hole that he was able to kick larger and larger until he could slide his hand through to unlock himself, only then did he emerge into the room.

Only then.

Dim twilight gave everything an odd reddish glow.

"Mama?"

Only then did he see the bed.

"Are you there, Mama?"

Only then.

A form lay beneath the covers, but the sheets were tangled and draped over the still bulge in a twisted, awkward way. Dark pools and splotches stained the sheets and the wall and the headboard of the bed. Flies crawled on his mother's forehead, and he couldn't figure out why she didn't brush them away.

"What's that smell, Mama?"

Beside her bed lay the yellow scarf. Her favorite one. The one she liked to wear on special occasions.

"Let me tuck you in, Mama."

And he did. He even took the yellow scarf from the bedside and tied it gently in her stiff, matted red hair.

Only then.

"There, Mama. That's better. Now everything will be OK." And he lay down beside her and he held her as the flies crawled across his arms.

Only then did he stop playing chess in his mind forever.

The pieces had fallen so far out of reach that no one would ever find them again.

■

Aaron Jeffrey Kincaid remembered hearing this story, remembered meeting Sevren at the group home, remembered seeing what he had done to the cat using only a pocketknife.

He remembered these things when he was in North Carolina last summer researching Q875, because that's when he heard about the chess pieces and the stab wounds and the dead girls with the yellow ribbons tied in their hair.

And when he heard, he knew.

It had to be Sevren. It had to be.

The timing had been perfect, really.

Because when the young women in the southeast began showing up dead, he realized almost at once how to solve the problem that had come up concerning two of the family members.

The solution seemed quite clear. It would allow him to take care of Bethanie and Alexis without drawing undue attention to his family or the plans they'd so carefully laid.

He didn't have to worry that the police would *never* find out that someone else had murdered two of the girls. He just needed to buy a little time. Until October 27th, and after that it wouldn't matter anymore.

Because in the next three weeks there would be so many other bodies to sort through that the world wouldn't even remember those two dead women.

Some scars are meant to be caressed forever.

Oh yes, Father would be very proud.

46

We couldn't find Joseph Grolin.

Sheriff Wallace's team checked the MountainQuest offices. He grunted as he recounted the visit to Ralph and me: Yes, Grolin had shown up for work that morning, but no, they didn't know where he'd gone. Yes, they knew what he was writing: an article about North Carolina raft guides who spend their winters working on the slopes of Vail, Colorado, as ski instructors, but no, they didn't have any idea where he might be. Yes, they would call if they heard anything about his whereabouts. Yes, yes, yes, and now could you please leave the office since you're disrupting the production schedule?

Meanwhile a team of crime scene technicians was combing the remains of Grolin's house for any evidence that he'd taken Jolene there. Anything at all. Last I'd heard, they found a video camera in the woods with a remote cellular feed. I'd told them to look for it. After all, I figured that somewhere out there, he'd been watching.

Unfortunately, they hadn't been able to recover anything substantial from the bomb's timer or ignition mechanism. That was a big disappointment because it might have led us to a munitions manufacturer or distributor.

Brent did some checking and found that four of the bodies had been dumped in popular climbing locations featured in *Mountain-Quest* magazine.

Still no sign of the remaining half of Jolene's body.

They did find Grolin's other car, though—his Subaru station wagon. It was in a Wal-Mart parking lot. The missing handsaw from his basement was in the trunk, Jolene's blood on the blade.

One team was going door to door in Margaret's neighborhood to see if anyone had noticed someone suspicious near Margaret's car earlier in the day. So far, nothing. An APB went out on Joseph Grolin, and cops all over the southeast were looking for him. Despite our efforts to keep a lid on the investigation, once the news stations found out Grolin was listed as "a person of interest" in the case and that his house had blown up, the media frenzy began. Within an hour all the major cable news stations were interviewing everyone involved in his life all the way back to his middle school teacher. "How do you feel to have known the Yellow Ribbon Strangler?" After all, in American newsrooms, you're guilty until proven innocent. And you remain the lead story until the ratings drop enough or the next grisly crime occurs.

I did a cross-check comparing Grolin's vacation days, time off, and days missing from work with the times of the murders. Not surprisingly, he was accounted for during the deaths of Bethanie and Alexis but always seemed to be on assignment researching one of his articles or taking a day off at the times of the other abductions and murders.

Still we had no idea where he was.

Overall, the day had been a wearying roller coaster of excitement and disappointment, discovery and frustration, and right now I could feel my body plummeting into a downward corkscrew; shutting down physically and emotionally. Not a good sign. I needed sleep, and I still had a two-hour drive in front of me to pick up Tessa from the airport in Charlotte.

Also, I still needed to check into my new hotel and unpack the luggage that had been following me around the country for the last week. I told Margaret I was heading out for a little while, and she nodded without saying a word. "Call me if anything comes up," I said. "I got the charger from Ralph. I'm still using his phone."

Another quiet nod.

She was in worse shape than I'd thought.

Of course I could understand. Finding half of a corpse in your car would do that to you.

I left my climbing gear in the backseat of my rental but wrestled the rest of my luggage into the lobby of the hotel across the street from the federal building. A college-aged couple stood hand-in-hand checking in at the registration desk.

The woman was giggling at everything her man said, and when she wasn't laughing she was giving him a slight smile that was oh-so-shy. He stood with his head back, chest out, and ambled toward the elevator like a cowboy ready to drive a thousand head of cattle across the state for his sweetheart.

It was charming. They were in love. It was perfect.

I had to look away.

I checked in and drifted over to the elevator, up to the second floor, down the hallway to room 217, slid the keycard into the lock, shuffled across the threadbare carpet, and collapsed onto the bed. I barely managed to remember to plug Ralph's phone into the charger before I closed my eyes and everything slipped into a dreamy haze.

Sleep came in spurts. Jumbled snatches of dreams mixed with momentary awarenesses of being awake followed by the fading, drifting, helpless tug of sleep once again. I made plans to call the front desk to get a wake-up call . . . plans to set the alarm clock for 4:00 so I wouldn't miss Tessa's flight . . . plans to check my email . . . but then the plans withered and faded away, and darkness, rich and deep, settled over me again.

Sleep.

In my dreams I mostly saw dead bodies. Beautiful, graceful girls with slit throats and manacled wrists. Giggling and flirting one minute, choking and dying the next. Faces of life and masks of death, laughter and tears rolling across each other in a wash of blood and screams and summer dreams. Swollen and distorted, young and attractive. Eyes laughing. Eyes fixed and staring.

Jolene. Mindy. Tessa.

The flirting girl from the lobby.

Lien-hua.

Christie.

During the moments when my eyes flickered open, I would glance at the clock beside the bed and find that the waking world had moved forward a few minutes, or even half an hour. And then I'd slip back into my nightmares of beauty and death.

A fire alarm went off or maybe it was the phone ringing or maybe it was an alarm clock somewhere. My sleeping mind couldn't tell and didn't care. Part of me fought the idea of waking up like it was the thought of dying. *Stay alive. Stay alive. Sleep is the only way to stay alive. Don't wake up. Never wake up.* The sound came again. Persistent. It wouldn't give up. I groaned and rolled over. It wouldn't stop. *Pick up Tessa. You have to pick up Tessa.*

I managed to pry my eyes open.

3:45 p.m.

The room was quiet.

Slowly, space and time began to make sense again. I was in a hotel room with lime-green walls and a creaky bed. Jolene was dead and so was Christie. They weren't coming back. Wouldn't ever be waking up. Not ever. I hadn't set the alarm. There hadn't been a fire. A house had exploded right next to me earlier today. My shoulder really, really hurt.

I noticed a blinking glow beside me. Ralph's cell phone. That was what had been ringing.

Only the cell phone ringing.

I had two voicemails.

The first was from an unknown number: "Yes, um, Dr. Bowers, they told me you'd be at this number. Special Agent Eric Stanton here—the, um, Tessa's escort, that is, chaperone. We were diverted to Chicago because of the blizzards up here in the Midwest—you probably heard about 'em on the news. Anyway, they're not letting any planes in or out. Everything's shut down. We won't be able to fly out until tomorrow at the earliest. I'll call you later when I know more. We'll be in a safe house here in Chicago tonight." He gave a few details about where they would be staying and what number to reach him at, and then he finished by assuring me that Tessa was fine but that she didn't really want to leave a message right now.

Well, that was no surprise.

Actually, I was relieved I didn't have to drive to Charlotte tonight. It gave my shoulder a chance to recover. I listened to the second message on my way down the hall to get some ice for my shoulder. It was from Terry Wilson, my NSA friend.

I returned his call right away. "Hey, Terry, it's Pat. Sorry I missed your call."

"Is this line secure?"

"Yeah. It's Ralph's phone," I said. "Encrypted to level 5-C."

"I'm only 4-D." He sounded a little disgruntled.

I filled the bucket with ice. "What do you have for me, buddy?"

"Pat, listen. Sebastian Taylor was a spy."

"What?" I topped off the bucket and turned toward my room.

"Probably CIA. Maybe NSA. It's a little tough to decipher all that. Back in the seventies, most low-ranking overseas diplomats were agents of some type. Remember, those were Cold War days. The threat of communism was everywhere. The thing is, he was stationed in South America in November of 1978."

Back in my room I sat on the bed with my back against the wall and tied off the bag of ice.

"And?"

"Ever hear of Jonestown?"

"Jonestown? You don't mean the Kool-Aid drinkers?"

"Yeah. Jim Jones and Peoples Temple, you remember all that?"

"Vaguely." I slipped the ice in place and leaned back. It stung, but in a good way.

"Well, listen, Pat. I did some checking, and I stumbled across some CIA communiqués from the Jonestown compound. One came at 3:29 a.m. the night of the tragedy. According to the files, though, no CIA operatives arrived on-site until two days later. So who sent the communiqué? I also found references to a tape, Q875, in connection with Taylor's name. Someone had tried hard to hide the link, though. Pat, listen, this thing is a powder keg. Lots of international black ops went on in those days. I'm not sure how deep you want to go poking around here."

"As deep as I have to go to find our killer. Somehow Taylor is connected to this series of murders. One of the girls called him, apparently tried to warn him—oh!"

"What?"

"Transcripts of her calls. I was supposed to read them this morning. I forgot all about that until just now. It's been . . . how can I say . . . an 'interesting' day."

"Listen. The governor is a powerful man, Pat. The Democrats have the presidency pretty much locked up for 2008; I mean, we're only a couple weeks out from the election, and I know you've seen the polls. Some people say Taylor is already being groomed to be the Republican frontrunner for 2012."

"Don't worry," I said. "I'll be careful. How about I call you tomorrow morning. I've got a few things to check on. Until then, see what else you can dig up. OK?"

"Pat, I don't think I should—"

"Terry, we found the torso of a girl in the trunk of a car today. Someone sawed her in half, and somehow the governor is involved. Get me whatever you can."

He sighed. "All right then, I will. Talk to you tomorrow."

I clicked the phone shut, and pulled out my notebook. I needed to clear my mind and sort through what we knew so far. Even if it took me all night, I had to start getting my mind wrapped around this case.

47

The foothills of the Sangre de Cristo
  Mountains
Northern New Mexico
3:55 p.m., Eastern Standard Time

"We're scheduled to arrive in Tennessee at 5:00 p.m. tomorrow," Kincaid told the video screen. He saw Theodore nod at him from the living room of the house on Larchmont Street in Asheville, North Carolina. "We'll drive in from there." He didn't want to arouse suspicion by flying into an airport in the same state as the luncheon.

"I'll meet you at the airport with the van," said Theodore. "Everything is set."

"And have there been any more problems?"

"No, Father."

"I need to tell you something." There was a stiff reprimand in his voice. "The second girl wasn't dead when you left her."

Theodore shifted in his seat. "I'm sorry, Father."

"I sent you the case files, even found a copy of the right kind of chess set, told you how to tie the ribbon, gave you all the details about the crimes. All you needed to do was make the scenes look like those of the other girls."

"I'm sorry, Father. I did my best—"

"We'll discuss it further when I arrive."

A slight hesitation this time. "Yes, Father."

Aaron Jeffrey Kincaid ended the video chat and walked through his library to the main entrance hall.

Over the years the ranch had shifted from an artists' colony in the sixties, to a guest ranch that catered to movie stars in the seventies and eighties, to the home of Pulitzer prize–winning novelist Olivia Brine in the early nineties—and even served a two-year stint as the weekend getaway for software designer and billionaire Rex Withering, the man Kincaid had purchased it from a decade ago. But as diverse as all of the owners had been, they'd had one thing in common: all sought a place of solitude and inspiration here at the base of the Sangre de Cristo Mountains, Spanish for "blood of Christ."

Kincaid found it ironic that he and his family lived in the shadows of mountains named for the blood of a savior.

He'd originally acquired the four thousand acres of land to use as a corporate retreat for PTPharmaceuticals, but after selling his drug company four years ago for $650 million, he'd made the ranch his home and turned it into the living quarters for his family.

He stepped outside and drank in the desert scents of juniper and pinion. The sandy ground crunched underfoot as he headed toward the building on the edge of the corral. He stuffed his hands into his jacket pockets. At this altitude, October was a brisk and frosty month beneath the lonely, windswept skies of New Mexico.

Aaron Jeffrey Kincaid had chosen this part of New Mexico because out here in the Enchanted Circle, the government let you do your own thing. Yes, officially, the Enchanted Circle got its name from an eighty-four-mile stretch of road that encircled Wheeler Peak, the highest mountain in the state. But all the locals knew that the region really got its name for another reason. Even though the area had originally been settled by Catholic missionaries, over the years it had become the home of a blend of various flavors of spirituality combining Native American beliefs with whatever parts of eastern mysticism were in vogue at the moment. Crystals. Reincarnation. Wiccan rituals. Whatever.

None of that mattered to Kincaid. He didn't believe any of it.

He was just glad the region provided a place where his family could disappear for a few years while the plans were put into place.

In addition, for some reason, cattle in this region were often found mutilated in the fields. Some people said it was just the locals doing it to give the tourists something to talk about. Others said it was from extraterrestrial encounters. For Kincaid it was simply a matter of added convenience since he and his family needed to perform certain tests on the livestock. The rumors made it easier for them to dispose of the leftover carcasses.

Aaron Jeffrey Kincaid walked over to the specially constructed building on the edge of the meadow. It was there that the test room had been set up. It was there that Rebekah and Caleb were dying of tularemia.

Even though at times the ranch and outbuildings had been the home of more than eighty people, Kincaid's group had never numbered more than fifty or so.

Currently, counting Rebekah and Caleb, along with the thirteen children, there were twenty-eight family members.

Bethanie and Alexis would have made it thirty.

It was family. His family.

And since they were family, they would do anything for each other.

Rebekah and Caleb were sitting together on the sofa in their quarantined room. And, just as Dr. Andrei Peterov had promised, there'd been no visible signs of the bacterial infection until about twelve hours ago. "They'll be contagious almost immediately," Dr. Peterov had explained in his nearly impeccable English. "Though they might feel a little nauseous, the true effects of the infection won't be evident until after the first twenty-four to forty-eight hours. By then, of course, it'll be too late to reverse the effects—even if the doctors were somehow able to correctly identify the agent."

After the Cold War it hadn't been tough to find Russian scientists who still sympathized with communism, who still believed in the cause. Many had been devastated in the months following November 18, 1978, when they saw what the capitalistic Americans had driven a small colony of communists to do. Nearly a thousand comrades were dead, and the world remembered them not as believers dedicated to a cause, to each other, to compassion—but only as lunatic members of a killer cult.

That was the fault of the media.

And that's why the media leaders of the world would be the first to pay.

When the Soviet Union collapsed, most of the Russian scientists doing research in biological and chemical weapons fled to the Middle East or North Korea. However, a handful had defected to the United States. Kincaid discovered it wasn't all that difficult to find just the right scientist. Not for someone with money. You'd be amazed what $28 million in cash could buy.

And Dr. Peterov had proven more than worthy of his salary.

Kincaid's pharmaceutical labs had provided the ideal place to perfect the process—all in the name of research and development. Of course, after selling the company he'd brought that research with him to his private labs here in New Mexico.

But for everything to work out as planned, he needed just the right agent. Bacterial or viral, it didn't matter to him. Just something contagious, airborne if possible. Silent for a few days; deadly from the start. And Dr. Peterov had delivered the perfect little bug.

Rebekah and Caleb were holding each other now, struggling for breath. Reading the sacred scripts aloud, bowing in rhythm to the words.

It was Dr. Peterov's idea to use the gram negative bacillus called *Francisella tularensis*. He'd pioneered ways of weaponizing it in Russia before the end of the Cold War. "It's versatile, able to be spread either through ingestion or as an aerosol, fatal about 35 percent of the time, and very tough to identify symptomatically," he'd told Kincaid. By splicing in some genes from Crimean-Congo hemorrhagic fever, he and his team had created something nearly impossible to diagnose. Very exotic. And very deadly.

"What about a cure?" Kincaid had asked him.

"There is no known vaccine for CCHF, and the vaccine for tularemia, the disease caused by *Francisella tularensis*, isn't available to nonmilitary personnel. Of course we developed a way to treat it in case we were exposed, but without our research the Centers for Disease Control and Prevention will never find a cure in time."

It'd taken six years to find a way to make the bacteria contagious human to human and to make it virulent enough to raise the death toll up to 85 percent—a satisfactory percentage to Aaron Jeffrey Kincaid. After all, when you know you'll *most likely* die, it's a thousand times more terrifying than if you know *for certain* that you will—in which case you might find peace; or if you discover the odds are actually *in your favor*—in which case you can survive relatively well on denial.

No, the most terrible thing of all is to face life without the possibility of either peace or denial.

With no place to run or hide.

Distribution seemed to be the primary problem. At first he'd thought about using inhalers to spread it—after all, his drug company produced some of the most popular asthma medicine currently prescribed, but his goal wasn't to indiscriminately infect children, so he gave that idea up almost immediately. No, he needed a more focused distribution system. He'd considered replacing fire extinguishers with an aerosol version of the bacterium and then starting a fire in the Stratford Hotel, but that seemed too elaborate. Besides, the place was built out of solid rock.

Finally, he'd landed on a simple plan. Nearly infallible. Completely unstoppable.

Kincaid looked at Rebekah and Caleb.

The effects of the genetically altered CCHF tularemia were quite evident by now: the trembling limbs, skin ulcers, swollen lymph nodes, orifice bleeding. It was actually rather disturbing to watch.

But, the couple didn't look disturbed or frightened. After all, they'd volunteered for this job. To go ahead of the rest.

A test had been necessary, after all, and this was the easiest way to control it, here at the ranch.

They were holding hands, eyes closed, perhaps in prayer to their Father, Aaron Jeffrey Kincaid. As they mouthed their petitions, Caleb's eyelids started hemorrhaging, seeping blood.

Kincaid spent all afternoon consumed with thoughts of the jungle, watching them die. The babies. The syringes, and of course, Jessie Rembrandt and the whirlpool and the hunting knife twisting slowly to the bottom of the bloody water.

And then, at last, his thoughts turned to Sebastian Taylor, the governor of North Carolina, the one responsible for it all.

48

The further I moved into this case, the more complex and intriguing it became.

After talking with Terry, I spent about forty-five minutes at the desk in my hotel room, jotting down notes, drawing lines to connect ideas, and crossing out entire pages of my notebook as I eliminated different theories.

I hardly noticed how numb my shoulder had become from the ice. Finally, all I had left was a dripping bag of water that I discarded in the trash.

First, we had a serial killer murdering women and leaving their bodies in geographically significant locations. He wanted them found. He was making a statement to us, carefully tying all his crimes together. Besides being an expert marksman, he could tie sutures, electronically scramble the origins of his emails, and might have grown up along the southern coast. Based on the way the ropes were knotted around the women's necks, it appeared to me that he was left-handed. He had knowledge of local climbing and caving areas and knew to leave a clean crime scene and blow up a house.

Quite a resume.

I tried to avoid thinking it was Grolin, but everything kept pointing in his direction.

Second, we didn't know it for sure yet, but the evidence seemed to indicate that somewhere along the line, another killer had started copying him.

But how did the copycat find out about the correct kind of chess pieces, the wound patterns, the yellow ribbons? The two killers could be working together, of course. Either that or:

(A) The copycat knew the Illusionist.

(B) He'd seen the case files.

Since there was no way for me to know whether or not the killers knew each other, I could only look into option B.

But was that even possible? Only our investigation team had access to the case files. Was it actually possible that the killer was a member of the team?

And what about victimology for the copycat? How was he choosing his victims?

So far it appeared that the copycat killer had murdered Bethanie and Alexis, and maybe others we didn't know about. So the real question was, what did Bethanie and Alexis have in common?

I pulled up their case files on my computer and began comparing notes, timelines, relationships. They were both from the East, but from different cities—Bethanie from Athens, Georgia, and Alexis from Roanoke, Virginia. Both had attended college out West for a few months.

Both were killed within days of returning home.

I don't believe in coincidences, so I made a note to follow up on the school they attended. Maybe the killer had something to do with the college.

And then there was Governor Taylor. How did he fit into everything?

I sighed and rubbed the bridge of my nose.

Well, since I wasn't going to Charlotte tonight, maybe I could look into some of these questions and then spend some time reworking the geo profile based on the theory that there were two killers instead of one.

OK. Good. A plan. But first, before anything else, I needed a shower. After hiking up a mountain, dropping into a cave, running to the trailhead wearing a backpack, and having a house blow up next to me, a shower sounded like a really good idea.

■

After stepping out of the shower and toweling off, I pulled some clothes out of my suitcase and noticed a sheet of paper flutter to the floor.

I knew what it was. Of course I did.

Christie's letter.

I've carried her note with me ever since Valentine's Day morning when I found it tucked under my pillow less than two weeks before she died. And now, like an addict, I reached for it. I knew what it would do to me if I read it, but I couldn't help myself. I still read it nearly every day. Even though it feels like someone is pulling nettles through my chest. Because in some strange way, the pain seems to help.

At least I tell myself it does.

I sat down, unfolded the crinkled paper, and let my eyes drink in the words that I already knew by heart.

February 14, 2008

Dearest Patrick,

I can still see the lights of the New York City skyline from my window. And when I look past them I can still see you for the first time, every time.

Patrick, please don't ask why. Don't try to solve this. I'm not one of your cases. There isn't an offender you can track down or a crime you need to solve. It's just the way things are. Our lives are brief, momentary. I see that now. Don't be angry that my moment is going to be over before yours.

Please—I'm not trying to be brave. I'm scared, of course I am. And confused and sad and lost. It hurts so bad to know my biggest dream of all won't come true—the dream of growing old with you. But I can't control any of that. All I can control is what I do with each moment, with this moment, right now. I can either be bitter or grateful. It's the choice we all face, I guess, though I never really thought of it that way before. So I've made my choice. I'm going to be thankful—for this moment and for every moment that I have left with you.

I know things won't be easy. I wish things were different, too. But you'll be great with Tessa. She really loves you. She does, even though it's hard for her to say so. And she needs you right now. I know you'll be able to help each other through this. Don't run from the risk of loving her. Please.

Remember, our choices decide who we are, but our loves define who we'll become. Tell her that, OK? Tell her it's something her mom wanted her to know.

And don't blame God, Pat. Death was never his idea. But life is. Please remember that. Life has always been his idea.

I can still see the lights of New York City reflected in your eyes. I'll always see them. I'll be watching them glitter tonight. And always. I love you, my big scruffy Valentine.

Forever yours,
Christie

By the time I finished reading it, my fingers were trembling. Tears blurred my vision. Her words lacerated my heart and also seemed to comfort me. "I'm sorry," I whispered, even though I knew there wasn't anyone there to hear me. Maybe I was apologizing to her. I don't know. Maybe I was saying it to all the women, the girls, the little boys I've been unable to help, unable to save. "I'm so, so sorry."

I stared down at the note and noticed my hands. My wedding ring was still clinging to my finger; I'd never taken it off. I'd kept her clothes too, bringing them with me to Denver. Her jewelry box rested beside my bed.

Her shadows were all around me. Hints of her followed me everywhere. But she wasn't here. Only her ghost was—lurking in the corner of my life. "I don't need anything except hope," wrote Zelda Sayre Fitzgerald, "which I can't find by looking backwards or forwards, so I suppose the thing is to shut my eyes." Sometimes I felt like shutting my eyes like Zelda did in the burning wing of that sanitarium sixty years ago. Closing them and never opening them again.

"Don't run from the risk of loving her," wrote Christie.

I am so, so sorry.

I put the note away, but I couldn't seem to put Christie away. A counselor once told me that depression is caused by anger turned inward.

I must have a whole lot of anger.

Maybe against God for letting it happen, maybe against myself. I don't know.

So one more thing before going to the federal building. I had to see her face.

I flipped open my laptop and scrolled through her pictures. The beautiful ones of her laughing and alive, just like the pictures of the dead girls we share with the media.

And with every picture came a feeling, a memory—the springy taste of her lipstick, the curve of her thigh, the twinkle that just kept dancing in her eyes even after her laughter had faded away, the way her dusty brown hair turned blond in certain light . . . playing backgammon at that coffeehouse, watching a shy spring rain . . . the way she would get close—a little too close—when she had something important to tell me . . . These were the images I chose to remember even though in the end her hair fell out and her cheeks sank in and her lips became dry and narrow and bloodless.

I chose to publish only the beautiful images in my heart. I guess you can't help but do that when you love someone.

Why did I put myself through this? Why couldn't I move on? Why didn't I just delete the pictures?

Because that would be like deleting her.

And I didn't have the heart to do that.

Only God could be that cruel, a voice inside of me said. And I wondered if it was the anger or the loneliness talking. I guess it didn't matter. Either way, it was still me.

I folded up the computer and headed for the door.

Time to get back to work.

———————■———————

Why didn't he just die? thought the Illusionist. *Why couldn't Patrick Bowers have just wandered around that house for a few more seconds?* It would have made things so much easier.

The game would have been over in such a glorious, memorable way. Now, the plans for tonight needed to be altered. And Alice would have to wait until tomorrow for their little rendezvous.

It was too bad. But he could wait. He was in control. Besides, tonight held its own promises, its own possibilities. And as he thought of these things, an idea came to him unbidden, an idea he could not shake.

The Illusionist smiled and picked up the phone.

49

Aaron Jeffrey Kincaid's phone rang. His private line. "Hello?"

"You got it mostly right, Aaron," said the voice on the other end. "The chess pieces didn't quite match, though. And the knot in the rope was tied on the wrong side of the neck."

"Who is this?"

"At first I wasn't sure it was you, but when the second body showed up, I knew it couldn't be anyone else."

"Sevren?"

A harsh laugh. "I've used a lot of names over the years."

After a brief pause. "Yes. I'm not surprised."

"A name is just another kind of mask."

"Yes, I suppose."

Another pause. "It wasn't easy to find you, Aaron."

"I've been trying to keep a low profile."

"I'll always remember those months we had together at the group home. You remember the first time? In the forest?"

"The cat?"

"Yes. What I did with the pocket knife?"

"I remember."

"I've gotten much better since then, Aaron."

"I have no doubt."

"Practice makes perfect."

"What is it you want, Sevren?"

"I want you to stop interfering in my game. Or maybe I want you to enter it with both feet. I haven't decided."

"So. The two girls."

"Yes. You used my handiwork to hide your own. You remembered from those afternoons in the forest, with the animals."

"There won't be any others. I promise."

"Mmm. Well, before you cross your heart and hope to die, I have to say, I think you used me. And I think you might owe me a favor."

Aaron should have seen it coming. Sevren had somehow tracked him down. He could tell the authorities who Aaron really was, and completely disrupt the family's plans. Everything could be lost. Aaron decided he needed to evaluate this situation very carefully. "What kind of favor do you want? Money?"

"No, Aaron, not for me. I want something money can't buy. I want you to help me tell a little story to a certain FBI agent who just doesn't know when to die."

"I'm listening."

And when Kincaid found out that the agent was in North Carolina, he realized it was destiny after all that was bringing them together.

And he was always glad to fulfill that.

50

As I crossed the street toward the federal building I noticed that the crime-scene investigation unit had finished with Margaret's car. Nothing remained in the parking lot to tell the world a dead body had been there earlier in the day except for a discarded wisp of yellow police tape scurrying across the blacktop. I wondered how the CSIU team was doing with the remains of Grolin's house and that cave. Probably had to hire a local vertical rescue and assist team to help them rappel into the cavern.

As I looked around the parking lot, I glanced back at my hotel and noticed the curtains flutter shut in a room on the second floor.

Wait a minute.

My room was on the second floor.

I counted the windows.

No maids would be in there this late in the day.

Someone was in my room.

For a split second I thought about charging into the federal building and trying to round up some help, but I discarded the idea immediately. *No time. Whoever's in my room will be long gone by the time we arrive.*

I sprinted back across the street, bolted up the stairs to the second floor, and whipped out my SIG.

I opened the stairwell door and scanned the hall. No one.

Eased down the hallway.

Room 231.

Someone followed you this morning on your way into town.

Room 229 . . . 227 . . . 225 . . .

Now someone's in your hotel room.

223 . . . 221 . . . 219 . . .

I leveled my gun.

. . . 217.

The door was closed, locked. I pressed my ear against it, listened. Yes, movement. Someone was definitely inside.

I slid my key into the lock and slowly nudged the door open. I couldn't see the entire bedroom, just the entryway. Whoever was in there was around the corner out of sight, opening and closing drawers.

I cleared my throat. "I'm a federal agent. It's been a really long day, and I'm holding a very wicked gun. So don't move." I don't think those are the exact words we're supposed to use, but it seemed to do the trick.

The sound of the drawers stopped.

"Do something stupid, and you'll end up dead," I said.

I heard whoever it was mumble something.

"Step out slowly." I eased forward, clicked off the safety. "Hands in the air."

A tall, angular man, mid-forties, with a tangled sallow beard and big ears stepped into view. "Don't shoot!" His hands were shaking. "I'm an investigator!"

"What?"

He reached for his pocket.

"Hands up! Keep your hands where I can see them."

He froze. "I'm just trying to get my wallet."

"I'll do that," I said. "Lie down. And watch those hands."

He lay on the floor. I smelled something sharp. Urine. The guy had wet his pants. Not quite what I would have expected from our killer.

He was facedown on the carpet now, his hands spread.

"Was that you this morning following me in your car?"

He nodded.

I reached into his pocket, pulled out his wallet, flipped it open. "Reginald Trembley, private investigator? That you?"

He nodded.

Don't be stupid, Pat, play it safe. Remember, the killer knows how to get close. To gain trust.

I pulled out some plastic cuffs and slipped them around his wrists, yanked them tight. He grunted, but I didn't care. "This is just so we can talk without me having to hold a gun in your face the whole time. All right?"

He nodded again.

I quickly frisked him to see if he was packing a piece or if he'd taken anything from my room. He seemed clean. I helped him up and sat him on the bed, then asked him, "So who are you working for? What are you doing in my room?"

He seemed to have regained some of his courage since emptying his bladder. He sneered at me. "I don't have to tell you anything."

I'd expected as much. "OK. I completely understand." I picked up the room phone and dialed a number. "Yeah, Dante, it's Pat. I'm at the hotel: room 217. Caught someone rummaging through my things. I want you to come over. He doesn't want to talk. Bring the stuff." I hung up the phone.

A wave of fear washed over Reginald Trembley's face. "Who's Dante?" he said. "What's 'the stuff'?"

I walked into the bathroom, pulled down the shower curtain, then returned to Trembley.

"Dante's a friend." I glanced at my watch. "He was right across the street. I'd say you have about two minutes before he gets here. If I were you, I'd talk now. Because when Dante gets here, things are going to get messy. Dante is really good at his job."

I laid the shower curtain on the floor in front of Trembley and spread it smooth. His lips were quivering. The guy was about to cry. "Bethanie's parents hired me," he said.

"Bethanie? Bethanie Dixon?"

He nodded.

I went for some towels. "Why?"

"They think she was murdered. What's that shower curtain for?"

"She *was* murdered. It's to protect the carpet."

"No, by the cult members from the group she was with out West."

I returned with the towels. "Cult? I thought she was studying in a private college in New Mexico."

"That's the line they used to cover things up, to tell the family members." He eyed the shower curtain spread out at his feet. "Please. You don't have to do this."

"I'm not going to, Dante is. What else? You have ninety seconds."

Trembley's rate of delivery began to improve dramatically. "Bethanie joined this group. I'm not sure who the leader is; everyone just calls him the Father. He claims he was there at Jonestown, you know Jonestown?"

I got the iron out of the closet. "I've heard of it. Keep going."

"Claims he was there as a kid and survived. I don't know if it's true or not. You don't need that iron, OK? I'm talking, all right?"

I plugged it in.

"Her parents wanted me to get her out of the group; they were gonna sue, I think." He was talking so fast now I could barely keep up. "But then he let her go, and she turned up dead. They're pretty sure his group did it, but the cops said it was a serial killer."

"What do you know about this guy they call the Father?" I glanced at my watch. "One minute."

"I don't know, I swear! I'm not really that good. I didn't find out very much, and then when she ended up dead and—"

The door swung open.

Trembley was shaking. "No, no, please." He closed his eyes.

Sheriff Dante Wallace walked in munching on a cheeseburger. "What's going—what do we have here?" he said. "Reginald Trembley?"

Trembley opened his eyes. "Sheriff Wallace? You're Dante?" Trembley looked at me. "He's Dante?"

I watched in disbelief as Dante leaned over and cut the cuffs off Reginald's wrists. "You two know each other?"

"Get outta here, Reggie," Sheriff Wallace said. "I don't want you messin' up this investigation. You got it?"

"Yeah, I got it." Reginald Trembley nodded, rose, and stumbled out the door. For his sake I hoped he had a change of clothes in his car.

"What's going on?" I said. "He broke into my room."

"He's a snitch." Dante looked at me. I was still holding the iron. "What's all this here stuff on the floor?"

"I thought I might spill something," I said. "He's a private investigator *and* a snitch?"

"Look, Trembley knows everybody. He's been on our bankroll for the last two years. This region is one of the main drug corridors to DC and New York City up I75 or I95 from Florida, across on highway 26 or 40. Meth dealers, marijuana, dirty cops, you name it. He knows 'em all. That old boy's connected."

"So you just let him go?"

"We bring him in for something like this, we lose out in the long run. He didn't take nothin', did he?"

"No. I don't think so," I said with a sigh. I unplugged the iron. *One step forward, two steps back.* I reached into my wallet and dug out eighty dollars. "Hey, take this for your phone, Dante. I can give you more if you need it. I'm really sorry about that."

He took another bite of his burger, eyed the money for a moment, and then accepted it. "That should be good. I'll swing by and get me one on the way home. Thanks."

"Yeah."

He was still looking at the towels and shower curtain. "Any new leads on the case?"

"Maybe," I said. "I'll keep you posted." Then I glanced down at the floor. "I guess I should put this stuff away. I'll talk to you later."

He stared at the iron for another moment or two before he turned. "Yeah, OK. See that you do." Then he left, taking another bite out of his supper.

As I began cleaning up, I noticed something on the carpet glimmering in the light.

I knelt beside it. A lapel pin of a Confederate flag.

Just like the one the governor was wearing.

Must have pulled off Trembley's shirt when I made him lie on the floor.

I decided it was time to listen to those phone transcripts and see what Bethanie had to say about Governor Sebastian Taylor.

51

Once inside the federal building I didn't waste any time locating the transcripts of Bethanie's calls to Governor Taylor's office. As I read through them I realized she was clearly terrified but also afraid to give specifics. Maybe she was worried someone was listening in.

"Tell him the boy remembers. Tell him the boy is coming," she said over and over. *"You have to tell him!"*

"The boy remembers," I whispered.

Trembley had said the cult leader in New Mexico claimed to be a Jonestown survivor. Was he "the boy"? Terry had said Governor Taylor was a CIA agent stationed in Guyana at the time of the tragedy. Was this cult guy after the governor?

I flipped open my computer to try and figure out what "college" Bethanie and Alexis had attended in New Mexico.

■

An hour later it was pitch black outside, and I was still searching, still coming up with nothing. I heard some footsteps and looked up. Ralph and Lien-hua walked in toting takeout boxes of Chinese food. "It's the best Chinese food in Asheville," Lien-hua was telling him. "Which isn't saying much."

Ralph stopped abruptly when he saw me. "What are you doing here, Pat? Aren't you supposed to be picking up your daughter from the airport?"

"Her flight was delayed," I said. "Comes in tomorrow morning. Remember when I was followed earlier today?"

Ralph set down his food. "Yeah. So you know who it was?"

"Yeah. Mind if I join you? I'm starved."

In between bites of General Tso's chicken and beef chow fun, I filled them in on what Trembley had told me at the hotel and what Terry had told me on the phone.

"Jonestown, the governor, the murders, they're all connected . . . ?" said Ralph.

"Looks like it," I said. "I read through the transcripts of Bethanie's phone calls. She was afraid for her life. And according to the case files, one of the women in Alexis's apartment complex thought she was acting nervous in the days preceding her death."

Lien-hua used chopsticks like an artist uses a brush. "So you're thinking maybe this cult leader in New Mexico is planning something against the governor, and when Bethanie and Alexis caught wind of it and tried to leave and warn Governor Taylor, this man, the Father, had them killed?"

I nodded. The theory explained a lot about the location and timing of the murders but still left some major questions unanswered. "I'll admit it's a work in progress."

"How did the Father find out the details from the case files?" asked Ralph. "Location of the stab wounds, type of rope, stuff like that?"

I shook my head. "I don't know. Some of it was made public, but not all of it."

"But why go through all the trouble of staging a crime to make it look like a serial killer did it?" asked Ralph. "Why not just kill them and then dispose of the bodies?"

"Bethanie's family was already suspicious," I said. "That's why they'd hired Trembley in the first place. If she suddenly disappeared, it would have brought even more suspicion on the group, maybe even put an end to their plans."

"So what do we know about this cult leader?" asked Lien-hua.

"Almost nothing so far. I've been trying to find stuff on the Internet, but I've come up dry. It's like he's a ghost." I sighed. "I even tried contacting Bethanie's family, but they're not returning any of my calls. They might be in hiding. I guess if we had a little more info on Jonestown it might help us see where all these stories intersect."

Lien-hua's eyes lit up. "I thought you'd never ask."

"What are you talking about?"

"I researched group dynamics and cult behavior for my master's degree, spent a couple months studying Peoples Temple."

"You're kidding me."

"Nope. I even had to write up a profile on the Reverend Jim Jones."

"I can give you his profile in one word," said Ralph. "Wacko." He took a bite of chicken.

"If we do not learn from the past—" she started to say.

"I know, I know," he said. "We're destined to drink cyanide all over again."

Lien-hua set down her chopsticks. "You know, there's a lot about that whole incident most people don't know."

"Let's see," grunted Ralph, "vats of Kool-Aid laced with a mixture of potassium cyanide and tranquilizers. I think there were about nine-hundred people there. They'd practiced the whole group suicide thing before. Lined up, drank it, died in the jungle. That about sums it up." He went back to his food.

"Nope, nope, and nope."

"What?" His mouth was full. "What do you mean?"

"The first one's just a technicality—it was Flavor-Aid, not Kool-Aid. Secondly, there were no drills, at least not according to the survivors. And third, while it's true that some of the people did drink the poison, many, if not most, of them were murdered—"

"What!" I said.

She nodded. "Some were injected with cyanide, some were strangled, some died from gunshot wounds, others from crossbow bolts."

Ralph and I exchanged glances. "I thought they all drank it," I said. "Mass suicide."

"Babies don't commit suicide, Pat. Of the 909 who died, nearly 300 were children, another 200 were elderly. Some people were asleep when they were injected. That's not suicide. The babies had cyanide squirted down their throats by their parents."

Just the thought made me physically ill. "I had no idea."

"That's what I mean; most people don't know the whole story."

I pushed my plate away. I'd lost my appetite.

Ralph took a bite of beef chow fun. Nothing seemed to faze him. "All right," he said. "So fill us in."

"Well . . . the Reverend Jim Jones founded Peoples Temple as a mainline Protestant church in the 1950s. They did a lot of social work, crossed over racial lines, attracted lots of minorities, which of course made him popular with the city council of San Francisco. Eventually, though, he stopped teaching about God and drifted into teaching a mixture of pseudo-communism and socialism—of course, he only preached those sermons when the city officials weren't present."

"Of course," Ralph said.

"I knew he was a pastor," I said, "but I didn't know he was a communist."

"Well, he talked like he was, but for him nearly everything he said was to manipulate others. It's hard to say what he really believed. After a while the political tide began to change—lawsuits, allegations of human rights abuse. Jones was even arrested for lewd behavior with another man."

She nibbled at her chicken and then took a sip of bottled water. "Anyway," she continued, "he was paranoid and convinced nuclear war was imminent—also wanted to avoid the lawsuits. He'd researched the best places to live in case of nuclear war and decided on Guyana, South America. Eventually, he and his group moved down there to set up an agricultural project."

"A what?" asked Ralph.

"Basically a commune. They farmed, grew their own food, stuff like that."

"So. A cult," he said.

"Semantics. Call it what you want, but the truth is when you look at what they were able to accomplish in just fifteen months, it's nothing short of astonishing."

I couldn't believe she was saying anything good about Jonestown. "What's so astonishing about a killer cult?"

"Clearing the land, planting, building, even moving toward universal health care. Originally they were planning on having 500 people living there within 6 to 10 years, but in just over a year nearly a thousand had moved down—and that didn't even include the Temple members who were still in California waiting to come down."

"OK, but despite all that, Jones was clearly insane," I said. "Right?"

"Of course. But he was also a genius. And he was able to inspire people to work together toward a common goal, to sacrifice for the good of others, to put aside hatred and prejudice. Most of the people in Jonestown were disenfranchised minorities. He gave them hope, a place to belong. And he had an amazing ability to persuade people. Incredibly charismatic. People even said he could perform miracles—healing cancer, reading people's minds, even raising the dead. Sure, some of the gags were shams and con games, but some of his miracles have yet to be explained."

I ventured another bite of supper. *Jim Jones a miracle worker? You have to be kidding me.*

"Jones wouldn't let anyone leave the town. Soon there were allegations of abuse, torture, kidnapping. Eventually, Leo Ryan, a congressman from Northern California, was told they were keeping people against their will, and he decided to investigate. There was a boy involved, some kind of custody battle with a woman who bore Jones a son and then left Peoples Temple. It gets complicated."

"Simplify it," said Ralph. His mouth was full of rice.

"Ryan was assassinated."

"What?" I said. "Down in South America?"

Lien-hua nodded. "He took a news crew down, met up with Jones, and as he and his team were getting ready to board the plane to return to the states at a nearby airstrip, some men stepped out of hiding and assassinated him and four of the newsmen. It happened at a place called Port Kaituma. A number of others were wounded."

"I don't remember hearing any of this stuff before," I said.

"I remember hearing about it now," said Ralph. "That name, Leo Ryan, but not the details."

Lien-hua continued. "Well, in the aftermath of the tragedy, the media had photos of rows and rows of dead bodies to show the world, and when they latched onto the killer cult angle, most of the events leading up to the White Night were lost in the shuffle."

I sat up straight. "What did you just say? The White Night?"

She looked baffled by my reaction. "Yeah, White Night. The night they all died is called the White Night." As she said the last two words, her eyes lit up. "White night!" she exclaimed. "That's what Bethanie wrote, isn't it?"

I grabbed my computer and pulled up Bethanie's crime scene photos while Lien-hua hurried into an explanation. "Jones didn't like the idea of darkness being associated with something bad or evil because of the large number of African-Americans in his group. So, whenever there was a crisis or tragedy at Jonestown, he called it a 'white night.' Sometimes he'd create his own crisis—even having his guards fire gunshots over the compound—to keep the people following him, believing in him as their savior."

We gathered around and looked at the computer screen. Sure enough, the *K* wasn't a letter at all, just a smear of blood from Bethanie's finger. But because of the chess connection, everyone, including me, had assumed it was "knight." *Never assume. Never ever assume.* I could have kicked myself.

"So that's it," I whispered. "White Night. There's going to be another one. The kid remembers."

———————————————■———————————————

Aaron Jeffrey Kincaid stared out the window at the starry New Mexico sky. Each point of light pierced through the fabric of the night like the tip of a dagger driven through black velvet. So many stars. So many distant worlds. So many daggers piercing the darkness.

He struck a match and lit the scented candles beside him. As he did, the window turned into a mirror, reflecting flickers of dancing candlelight as well as the interior of the room.

He gazed at the reflection. The room still bore the marks of its predecessors, with all their rare artwork and imported Italian furniture. High above him the original aspen beams held up the vaulted ceiling of the main room. Even after eighty years they looked as solid and imposing as ever.

Too bad this place would be a pile of ashes by tomorrow night.

In the dark mirror, he saw the door on the other end of the room swing open. A huge barrel-chested man with a shaved head stalked into the room and stood motionless, at attention, not wanting to disturb the Father. David was twenty-nine years old, had played six years as a tackle for the Bengals, and then started teaching martial arts. His specialty was breaking people's bones with his bare hands.

Kincaid ran his finger along the scar on his wrist and stared at the stoic man's reflection in the dark window. He knew he could have made David wait for an hour, a day, forever. David would do anything for him. Just like the others.

Kincaid approached David. "My son," he said. The words rang with the true affection of a father, even though the two men weren't related.

The leviathan of a man lowered his gaze in deference to his master. "Yes, Father?"

Kincaid laid his left hand on the back of David's neck and gently stroked the corded muscles like a father might caress the neck of his child. "Do you understand what we're doing here? Do you really understand?"

David lifted his eyes to stare at the far wall. "We're creating a better world, Father. We're stepping together into the light. We're completing the revolution, we're—"

Aaron Jeffery Kincaid interrupted his pupil. "From your heart, my son. I know the teachings and the texts. I wrote them."

"Forgive me."

"No need. You were about to say, 'a world where peace can reign and those who have chosen the way of unity can find freedom on the highest plane.'"

"Yes, Father."

"You know the words, but do you understand them?"

A slight hesitation. "I believe so."

Kincaid walked past the window to the array of framed photographs on the wall. He gazed into the smiling, playful faces in the pictures. "David, we are sowing beliefs, and we must all make sacrifices when we choose to follow our beliefs. You know this, don't you?"

"Yes."

"We have to be ready to pay the price that our beliefs demand of us." Kincaid paused and ran his finger along the cheek of one of the African-American girls in the photograph. He remembered her. Ananda, a Hindu name meaning "ultimate bliss." She'd played tag with him in the jungle back when they were children, back before she drank the medication. Before she laid down in the pavilion and began to twitch.

She was one of the children who did not die quickly.

"David, do you know why there is no shortage of suicide bombers in the Middle East?"

David didn't answer quickly. He seemed to weigh his words carefully, as if he were afraid he might let his master down. "Because their hatred runs so deep, Father?"

"No, David. Because their beliefs run so deep. Hatred is the result of beliefs. It is the fruit that falls from the tree of faith. So is love. Beliefs always come first. To change the fruit, you must change the tree; you must change the beliefs. A tree will always bring forth its own fruit. It will never do otherwise. The great prophet once said, 'Every good tree bringeth forth good fruit; but a corrupt tree bringeth forth evil fruit.'"

"Jesus, the Nazarene?"

"Yes. The Nazarene."

52

Ralph, Lien-hua, and I ended up talking about Bethanie's murder and the White Night angle for a few minutes, but then Ralph said, "Wait, we need to stay on track here. What else happened down there in the jungle, Lien-hua? Anything else that might help us with this case?"

She thought for a moment. "Well, it's with the assassination of Congressman Ryan that the conspiracy theories really begin. I wonder if they might be connected."

"What conspiracy theories?" I asked.

"Bob Brown, an NBC photojournalist who was killed on the airstrip at Port Kaituma, got some video of the shooters. Some people who've analyzed the tape say the assassins were lined up in a military formation. The government has always maintained that the shooters were guards from Peoples Temple, but it was never confirmed. No one was ever tried or convicted for the murders on the airstrip."

I thought back to what Terry had told me about Governor Taylor. That he'd been stationed in South America during the Jonestown massacre. That he'd been a government agent at the time. "Could it have been a government job? A professional hit?" I asked her.

Lien-hua had almost finished her rice. She nodded slowly. "Actually, some people think it was. Ryan was no friend of the CIA. A couple years earlier—I think it was in '74—he'd co-sponsored a bill that required the CIA to report classified activities to Congress. At the time of his death he had another bill on the floor of Congress pushing for more restrictions. Two weeks after he was killed, the bill died in committee."

"OK, now this is getting intense," said Ralph.

"There's more," said Lien-hua. "The CIA had a top-secret psychosocial mind-control experiment going on back in the 1970s called MK-ULTRA. Supposedly, it was ended the year Jones moved to Guyana."

"Nice coincidence," said Ralph.

"You gotta be kidding me," I said. "Mind control?"

"A combination of drugs, hypnosis, sleep deprivation, isolation, water-boarding, threats, brainwashing, social pressuring. The CIA has always been interested in seeing what it takes to break someone's will."

"Well, even if the CIA was involved," I said, "those people in Jonestown weren't robots. They made their choice."

"Wait," said Ralph. "Lien-hua, you said some of the people were murdered. Has that ever been confirmed?"

"At first the coroner said the cause of death for the people in Jonestown was cyanide by injection. He came to that conclusion after examining numerous victims with needle marks between the shoulders—the only place on your body where you can't inject yourself. About a week later he changed the official records to indicate they all died by ingesting the cyanide, and that's been the official story ever since—even though firsthand accounts record needle marks on the hands, necks, arms, and backs of the deceased."

"So someone had a little talk with Mr. Coroner?" said Ralph.

"Maybe. No one knows. According to one account, at least 187 bodies had needle marks, then they just stopped counting. You don't get needle marks between your shoulder blades from drinking cyanide-laced fruit punch."

"No, you don't," he said. "Anything else?"

"All personal identification was removed from the bodies before they were returned to the U.S. No one knows why. And only seven autopsies were performed—out of 909 bodies—914 if you count the congressman and reporters."

"This is unbelievable," I said.

"It's history," she responded. "You can look it up. Then in the weeks and months following the massacre, a number of families were found dead in the U.S.—mostly ex-Temple members, some government officials with ties to Jones, a few CIA agents. According to one report, sixteen of the Green Berets that were assigned to remove the bodies from Jonestown committed suicide within three months of the tragedy. That, and there have always been murky ties between Jones and the CIA."

"Spies, mind control, assassins, a suicide cult, a massive government cover-up . . ." said Ralph. "Whew . . . this would make one killer video game."

Lien-hua and I just looked at him and shook our heads.

"What?" he said sheepishly. "It would."

"So anyway," I said to Lien-hua, "do people actually believe this stuff?"

"Some very influential people believe this stuff."

"And what do you think?"

She took a deep breath. "Truth is, no one knows how many died willingly that day. There were armed gunmen surrounding the pavilion carrying AK-47s. Jones's followers were isolated, territorial, paranoid about the government, and, for the most part, loyal to him. You choose—do you want a bullet in the back, or do you join the rest of your family and closest friends and give your children the 'medication'? Do you try to fight off the whole community, or let someone you love press a needle against your arm? For most of them, it was at least coerced suicide, if not murder."

"Wait a minute," I said. "Does the term Q875 mean anything to you? Terry said it was a tape of some kind."

She tapped her fingers on the table thoughtfully. "Well, that would make sense. Jones liked to record himself. The government found hundreds of his messages—talks, sermons, whatever you want to call them. When the FBI went in to clean up the place, they collected all the tapes and archived them. Then, back in 2000 or 2001 most of them became available to the public through a Freedom of Information Act request."

"We need to listen to that tape," I said to Ralph.

"Turn on your computer," said Lien-hua. "It's probably on the Internet."

While I searched online, she continued, "Speaking of tapes and Jonestown and the CIA, Jones actually recorded his final talk as he convinced all the people to die together. It's called the Death Tape. I listened to it when I was doing his profile. Very creepy. He called their action 'revolutionary suicide.' Anyway, on that tape, he tells his men to get Dwyer out of there, meaning away from the pavilion."

"Who's Dwyer?" asked Ralph.

"Richard Dwyer was an official in the American Embassy in the city of Georgetown, Guyana. By nearly all accounts he was a CIA operative sent to infiltrate Peoples Temple. Although when he was asked about it later during the congressional investigation, he said, 'No comment.'"

"Unbelievable," I mumbled. "There's even evidence a CIA agent was there when it all started."

As it turns out, we didn't have to search far to find tape Q875. Someone had posted it online. I downloaded the audio file, hit play. It was chilling. Throughout the tape you could hear radio announcers in the background talking about Congressman Ryan's death and the rumors of mass suicide the day before at Jonestown.

The day before.

Which meant Q875 had been recorded on November 19, 1978. The day after everyone at Jonestown was already dead.

We listened to the whole thing. Twice.

Then again.

Static . . . a radio announcer talking about the tragedy . . . a chair squeaking . . . a few voices in the background, someone saying "Shh!" . . . the sound of people moving around, opening and closing drawers . . . someone sneezing . . . an announcer mentioning that there would be autopsies performed on Ryan and the others, and then the garbled sound of one of the people there in the cabin muttering curses . . . more news reports about Jonestown . . . someone saying "Shut up!" . . . a screen door slamming . . . static.

"That is very, very eerie," said Lien-hua. "Whoever made this tape did it with nearly one thousand corpses lying nearby."

"I wonder if they've ever done a voice analysis on it," I said.

Ralph shook his head. "Speech segments are too short."

"So this tape was recorded on November 19"—I was thinking aloud—"the day after everyone supposedly died. Why?"

"What I wanna know," said Ralph, "is if everyone at Jonestown died on the 18th, who made the tape?"

"What tape?" asked someone in the doorway.

We turned.

Margaret.

Aaron Jeffrey Kincaid, the Father, the Master, removed a black and white photograph of three smiling children from the wall. A blowing ocean of wheat fields stretched behind them and ended at the base of a lush jungle. He tilted the photograph in the gentle, dancing candlelight. These children had been waiting in line when he ran into the jungle. Even now, thirty years later, he remembered their names: Jacob and Isaiah and Emilia. He remembered seeing them giggling and teasing each other as they waited for their turn to drink from the vat, just like schoolchildren might do while waiting in line beside the drinking fountain at recess.

"We are not committing suicide," Kincaid remembered hearing Jim Jones say as the people lined up. "It's a revolutionary act. To me death is not a fearful thing, it's living that's treacherous."

Living is treacherous.

Kincaid turned to David. "We are in the business of sowing beliefs. And we must be ready for whatever fruit those beliefs produce. Both in our lives and in the lives of those we teach." He put the picture down next to one of the candles.

"Yes, Father." David's voice rang with resolve.

Kincaid knew that David was a true believer. He had already made significant sacrifices, had already proven his devotion. Yes. Kincaid was proud of his son.

"And do you know the rest of the verse, David? The rest of the words of the Nazarene?"

A short pause and then, "No, Father. Forgive me."

"'A good tree cannot bring forth evil fruit, neither can a corrupt tree bring forth good fruit. Every tree that bringeth not forth good fruit is hewn down, and cast into the fire.' Matthew chapter seven." As he said the words he stared intently at the photograph. Then he turned to look at his pupil. "We are about to cast the tree that does not bear good fruit into the fire. The corrupt tree cannot be allowed to grow any longer."

"Yes, Father."

Kincaid set the picture back on the shelf. "I'll join the others soon, David. Tell them to begin with the children."

"Yes, Father." Then, without another word, David bowed deeply and backed out of the room.

Kincaid watched him go. Yes, beliefs bring forth fruit, and now the whole world would see the depth of his beliefs. The media elite and the United States government would taste for themselves the bitter fruit they had sown when they hunted down, harassed, and then defamed his family.

For a few more moments he watched the candlelight flicker and reflect. Flicker and reflect. Illuminating his faces of the children.

Then he blew out the candles so that he was once again alone in the darkness, with the stars blinking at him through the night. A family of daggers puncturing the sky. How many stars were in the sky, he did not know: to him there were 909—one of each family member who died in the jungle.

Always 909 points of light piercing the darkness.

Then, he reached up with his hand and felt his shoulder, the scar that had started it all.

Some scars are meant to be caressed forever.

53

Ralph worked at briefing Margaret while I slipped off by myself to get some work done on the revised geo profile. We had twice as much work to do now. The case had split in half: we had the Jonestown angle and the yellow ribbon guy. It's supposed to get easier the more you work on these things, not harder.

I eliminated Alexis and Bethanie from the equation and reworked the numbers. The results weren't bipolar this time. New hot spots appeared, much more focused. New names floated to the top of the tip list.

And Grolin's was one of them. He moved up from 113 to 8.

I tried to remind myself that my role in this case was to help focus the investigation, not nab one specific suspect, but it didn't really help. I wanted to get this guy. When he brought my daughter into it, he made it personal. Her life might be in danger. I hated to think what he might do to Tessa if he ever got his hands on her.

Also I wasn't too happy that he tried to blow me up.

In addition, we still had no leads on where the rest of Jolene's body might be. I was almost afraid to find out. I decided to follow up on the possibility that someone on the team was the copycat killer. I brought up the names of everyone who had access to the case files and medical examiner reports and found sixty-two names. Wonderful.

Ralph stalked over to my desk.

"How's Margaret doing?" I asked.

"Shell-shocked, but I didn't say so," said Ralph.

"Gotcha."

He shook his head. "She told me she's going to take care of investigating this cult."

"What?" I said. I noticed Lien-hua coming over to join us.

"Yeah, it was kind of strange. When I told her about the tape and the connection to Bethanie and the governor, she said we would need someone running point on that part of the investigation and she wanted to do it. Told me she wants us to focus on bringing Grolin in."

"Doesn't that seem a little odd to you?" asked Lien-hua.

He shrugged. "I dunno. Pat?"

"Hard to say. She might want some distance from the guy who put the body in her trunk. Maybe this will help her deal with it. Maybe it just seems like the right political move. Who knows."

"In any case," Ralph continued, "she mentioned that earlier this afternoon Brent interviewed Grolin's girlfriend, a nurse named"—he consulted his notepad—"Vanessa Mueller. Brent said she was acting suspicious, really jumpy. Vanessa said she has no idea where Grolin is, but Brent's been following her all afternoon just in case."

"So that's where he's been all day," I said.

"Yeah. So here's what I'm thinking. Tomorrow we can work with Margaret and see where this whole Jonestown angle takes us, but if there's any chance we can bring Grolin in now, I think that's where we should focus our efforts."

"Agreed," I said. "He's the immediate threat, especially if he's going to go after the woman with the red hair."

"That reminds me," said Lien-hua, "I talked to Brent earlier. They're still working on those prints. We should have them in sometime tomorrow."

"That might not be soon enough," said Ralph. "Since we don't know who the next victim is yet, I think we should stake out the girlfriend's place tonight. See if Grolin shows up."

"Good call," I said.

Ralph scratched at the late-day stubble on his chin. "Only prob-

lem is, Wallace's men are stretched thin—there's a music festival just
outside of town tonight, and the Network of Concerned Evan-
gelicals doesn't like the bands. They've announced they're going
to protest and—"

"I could do it," said Agent Lien-hua.

"Huh?"

"The stakeout."

"You're not here to sit around on stakeouts."

"Um, I could work the stakeout with Agent Jiang," I said.

He looked at me quizzically. "Neither are you."

"No, it's all right," I said. "It'll give me a quiet place to think
things through. Besides, I had a nap this afternoon. I'll be fine."

He still looked hesitant, but then he yawned. He'd been going
nonstop all day. Just the mention of a stakeout seemed to make him
more tired. "Well, I guess that'll work."

"Good," I said.

"All right. Take nine to midnight—that way you can still get a
little sleep later on. I'll get Wallace to find someone for the late shift.
After all, you are driving to Charlotte tomorrow morning."

I nodded.

"Coordinate it all with Tucker," he said. "You want mic patches?"
Ralph was always trying out the military's new toys. The high-tech
mic patches came from some of his friends in the army. Special
ops. Each patch is nearly transparent and the size of a plastic strip
bandage. You wear it just beneath your ear; it works as both a
transmitter and a receiver. It also emits a long-range homing beacon.
Very sleek, high-end stuff. Problem is, the digital router automatically records everything you say. And I wasn't sure I wanted that
on this particular stakeout.

"Naw, twentieth-century walkie-talkies," I said, "if that's OK
by you?"

He shrugged. "Fine with me." Yawned again. "I need some
sleep."

"Go play some video games," I said.

His eyes lit up. "Yeah. I could do that." He nodded. "All right. So Tucker can run point from here, and we'll notify the police department to have a couple cars on standby in case anything goes down."

"Got it."

"I'll see you two tomorrow," he muttered and walked off.

We had just under an hour before we needed to be at the stakeout. Lien-hua went to change and clean up. I called Tessa and left a message that I'd see her in the morning. Then I did a little more work analyzing the abduction locations, and before I knew it Lien-hua had returned and I was climbing into her car to head to Vanessa Mueller's house.

54

Lien-hua pulled over to the curb, flipped off the headlights, and eased the car to a stop, leaving the keys in the ignition just in case we needed to get out of there fast. She had changed into a tailored green silk blouse. I told myself I shouldn't be taking note of things like that, but I couldn't help noticing that she was looking good.

Vanessa Mueller lived in a quaint two-story house with black trim and a wide porch. The house looked like a pale yellow dream in the moonlight. We sat staring at it for a few minutes. The light in the living room was on, and I could see Vanessa sitting on the couch watching television. Thankfully her home was an older design and had only a front door, making it easier to stake out—no rear exit to cover.

I heard the keys jangle as Lien-hua bumped them reaching for her coffee. She cleared her throat slightly. "So, you have a daughter."

I was momentarily confused. I couldn't remember telling her that I had a daughter . . . oh yeah, Ralph had asked why I wasn't picking her up at the airport. "Stepdaughter, actually. Yeah. She's seventeen. Her name is Tessa."

"What's she like?"

"Well, she's smart, street-smart. A survivor. She's tough."

"Tough? Anything else?"

"Um . . . she likes to wear black."

"Well, what does she like to do?"

I shifted in my seat. "I don't know. Listen to music. Hang out with her friends." *Where are you going with this?*

Lien-hua didn't say anything for a few moments. Finally she added, "So you're not too close then?"

I took in a long, slow breath. *Man, Pat, she can read you like a book.* "No. Not really."

A short silence and then, "How did she handle her mother's death?"

I began to fidget with my pen. "OK, I guess. We don't talk about it much. So do you think Grolin's going to show up?"

"Do you talk about it at all?"

I was beginning to regret volunteering for this stakeout. "Christie's death was hard on both of us. Truth is, Tessa and I have never been all that close, and after her mom died, it just got worse—"

Suddenly I felt Lien-hua's hand press gently against my left arm. It unnerved me and somehow comforted me, brought me back to the moment.

"I'm sorry," she said, "I didn't mean to . . . We don't have to talk about—"

"No. It's OK," I said, but I wasn't sure that it was.

She pulled her hand back, laid it on her thigh.

I took a slow breath. "One in every eight women in North America is diagnosed with breast cancer. Did you know that?"

"No. I didn't."

"Neither did I. A year ago." I could feel the familiar tightening in my chest, the desperate helpless feeling you get when you look back over your shoulder at something painful from your past; something that haunts you but is also a part of you. You try to run from it, but it's always right there, breathing down your neck. It's not true what they say. Time doesn't heal all wounds. Sometimes it just throws salt on them and laughs as you squirm.

"What about Tessa's father?"

I shook my head. "She never met him. Christie was in college when she got pregnant. He took off when she told him the news. Never saw the guy again."

I heard Lien-hua mumble a few words about him that I was surprised she knew.

"Yeah. My sentiments exactly." I sipped at my coffee. "What about you?"

"What about me?"

"Ever married?"

"Just to my job."

I tried to think of something fitting to say to that but couldn't. I sipped the really bad coffee and almost had to spit it out. It tasted like hazelnut-flavored motor oil. I set it back down and decided to change the subject. "Work many stakeouts before?"

"Not so many."

"How many?"

"Counting tonight?"

"Yeah," I said.

"Well. That would make one."

I laughed a little. It felt nice.

She turned to face me. "You?"

"Lots in my early years when I was a detective in Milwaukee. I guess some people get used to them. I never really did. I'm too antsy. I hate sitting still. I always need to be doing something, solving something. I like stakeouts about as much as I like briefings."

"But yet you volunteered for tonight."

"Yes. I did."

I looked out the window at Vanessa's house. No change.

A car drove past us, and we watched its taillights shrink into the night. As they disappeared Lien-hua said, "I don't think he'll come."

"Who?"

"Grolin. I don't think he's going to show."

"Oh," I said. "Yeah I think you might be right." I peered at the quiet house. "So, what about you, Lien-hua. You know all about me, what's your story?" It was an innocent question.

"Well, there's not much to tell, I guess." She tipped her coffee back, took a long, slow sip. "I graduated from Washington State

University with a master's degree in criminal science. Then I worked for a while as an officer in DC."

Outside the windshield, the wind fluttered a handful of autumn leaves out of a tree above us and placed them gently onto the hood of the car.

"After a couple years, I applied at Quantico at the National Center for the Analysis of Violent Crime, did a two-year apprenticeship and, ta-da. Here I am."

"Here you are," I said. I was looking at her profile now in the dim light. The light from a nearby street lamp was slipping through the windshield and landing on her face, illuminating her chin, her lips, the gentle slope of her cheek.

She set down her cup and looked in my direction. I didn't look away.

"It's pretty pathetic, isn't it?" she said.

No, not at all. Pretty stunning, in fact.

I caught myself. "What? Your story?"

"No, having to drink this coffee."

"Oh," I said. "Yeah. Painfully bad." I was still looking at her, but I managed to notice the wind nudge the leaves off the hood and drop them onto the road.

We both looked away from each other.

"So you climb, then?" she said.

"A little. You?"

"No, never had the chance. Mostly for me it's kickboxing."

"Kickboxing?"

"Yes."

"Huh. I knew it was something like that."

"What's that supposed to mean?"

"Well, I'm not sure exactly how to say this . . . but . . ." — *Oh, go ahead, just say it* — "your physique, presence, the way you move. At first I figured you for either a dancer or a gymnast."

"Physique?" She was grinning out of the side of her mouth.

Steven James

Oh boy. "I meant it as a compliment."

"You're not supposed to notice things like that."

I smiled. "I'm paid to notice everything." It seemed suggestive when I heard myself say it, but I didn't intend it that way.

She glanced at me out of the corner of her eye. "So I've heard." She located the cup resting beside her leg, lifted it, found it empty, set it back down. "You climb much?"

"Used to. I haven't been to the crags in, well, a while." I hesitated, because the last time I'd been climbing was with Christie. It didn't feel right saying her name just then.

"Hmm," she said noncommittally. "Miss it?"

"Yeah, I do. I miss her—it—I mean, yes, I do miss it. Yes." Only too late did I realize what I'd said, too late to take it back. Thankfully, for reasons I could only guess, Lien-hua decided to ignore it. She started telling me about some of the kickboxing tournaments she'd competed in. I cracked my window open, and a rush of frigid air poured into the car. We'd been sitting here awhile. The windows had started to steam up. I hadn't realized how cold it was getting outside. In the car it seemed warm.

"Maybe we could go climbing sometime," I offered. "When all this is done."

She hesitated and then answered, "Maybe. When all this is done."

"Unless there's someone else you . . . ?" It was a way of asking if she had a boyfriend. She had to know it was. She had to read the subtext. She was too good at reading people not to.

She took a breath but didn't answer. Hesitated. "There used to be," she said at last.

A moment of quiet. There was more to the story. But I didn't pursue it. I stared at the house again. The living room light blinked off.

55

A moment later the light in the upstairs bedroom flicked on. I saw Vanessa pacing behind the curtains, gesturing with her hand.

"She's talking on the phone, you think?" asked Lien-hua.

"Looks like it."

We watched her for a minute, and then the light went out. She was still in the room. Lien-hua picked up her walkie-talkie. "Subject stationary," she said. "No intruders. Will update. Over."

"I'm here if you need me," Brent replied from the other end. "Over."

I waited until she set the walkie-talkie down. "So, what else did Ralph tell you about my life?"

"Nothing much . . . But he didn't have to." She was being elusive. Slightly coy. I was beginning to wonder if she had volunteered for tonight just to be alone with me.

Oh. Wait. That's right, I'd volunteered to be with her.

"What do you mean?"

"I've been aware of you. For a while."

I smiled at her. "Aware of me?"

"Read your books. I heard you present a couple times at some conferences."

"Why didn't you tell me that earlier?"

She shrugged. "Never came up."

"So what did you think?"

"About?"

"The books. The conferences."

"Are you fishing for a compliment, Dr. Bowers?"

I flushed a little and was thankful we were in the dark. "Of course."

"Well," she said thoughtfully, "your presentations are always thought-provoking and professional, your ideas well articulated . . ."

"But?"

"I'd give you a B."

"Not even a B+?"

"Nope. Just a B. I don't agree with your conclusions."

"About profiling?"

"About people."

"People?"

"Yes."

Outside the car, a gust of wind sent a collection of leaves dancing, skittering down the road.

"What do you mean?"

She glanced in my direction. "You still haven't guessed the last motive."

I hesitated. "Are you trying to change the subject? What conclusions did you mean?"

"Trust me. Guess the missing motive."

"OK, but we're coming back to this. Let's see. I'm running out of ideas here. OK, how about this—insanity. Madness. Some crimes are motivated by psychosis."

She shook her head. "That's not a motivation. That's a condition. It precipitates certain behaviors, but it's not what motivates them."

"Depression?"

"That's a condition too, a state of mind. It increases the likelihood of certain behaviors but doesn't motivate them."

The light in the bathroom went on, then a moment later went off.

I sighed. "I don't know, Lien-hua. I give up."

She was silent. I wasn't sure if she was going to tell me what it was or not, and I had no idea what any of this had to do with my conclusions about people. My arm was getting cold. I rolled the window back up.

At last she turned in her seat so she could look directly at me. "We're not just accumulations of choices, patterns, random chance, and mixed motives, Pat. Our movement through space and time isn't just based on expediency, benefits, convenience, and comfort."

In the building tension of the moment I could feel her breathing merging with mine, our hearts beginning to beat in sync with each other.

"So what is it? What's the motive?"

Our eyes met. "It's love, Pat. It changes everything. It's the motive that you missed. It's the root of all the others, the core of all we do. It's the puzzle piece you always seem to overlook, the most important one of all."

She didn't say the next words, but I heard them as clearly as if she had. *That's why you don't know your daughter. That's why you won't let go of your dead wife. Fear and love. The two most important motives. Love and fear, twisting together in your heart.*

My chest tightened, my pulse quickened. I felt defensive and on fire and helpless all at the same time, but it was also alluring to be understood by someone. She knew me in ways I didn't know myself, yet she barely knew me at all. I was overwhelmed with the desire to touch her, to be with her, to hold her. I wanted her to be all that Christie was and more, but didn't want to risk the pain all over again. And I didn't want anyone to replace Christie; I wanted someone to complete me like Christie had, but in a new way. I wanted to love again, to trust again, but I didn't know how. I was afraid to know how.

I was breathing faster.

Normally I know what to do and I do it, I don't hesitate. I don't second-guess. But in that moment I was fumbling around in the dark. Part of me was terrified. Part was in love. Maybe fear and love were just different sides of the same motive, looping through our lives. Sometimes enslaving us, sometimes setting us free. Fear and love. Love and fear. Wrestling. Beauty and death.

Lien-hua and Christie.

My throat tightened.

For a moment I forgot the real reason I was in this car with Lien-hua Jiang.

I waited like a fool, like a schoolboy, hoping she'd take my hand or place her palm on my knee or kiss me. Something, anything. Finally, after an eternity, I watched my hand reach over to brush a strand of hair away from her neck. Maybe I was just thinking it, imagining it, wanting it to happen.

My finger glanced across her skin.

No, I wasn't just imagining it. It was happening. This was happening.

She watched me with quiet eyes. Didn't do anything to stop me. The moment became everything, squeezing out the rest of the universe, sliding outside of time. The air we exhaled met in the space between us, intermingling. Kissing. Becoming one.

She let me trail my finger down her neck toward her shoulder. Her skin was tender and electric and alive. A cool glow slanted through the window. I saw the glistening light ease along her willowy throat, toward the top buttons of her blouse.

I was inhaling all the guilt and desire and longing and loss and fear from the last eight months, and it was too much for me. I hesitated, and in the beat of a heart, in the breath of a moment, everything changed. Somewhere between her words and my tentative touch, a chill settled into the space between us. With gentle precision, she leaned away from me and looked out the window. Time began again. I watched my hand drop out of sight onto the seat beside me. "I'm sorry . . ." I tried to say everything but ended up saying nothing. "I didn't mean . . ."

"We can't." Her words carried a firm finality.

Awkwardly, I retrieved my hand. It landed on my lap with a thud, and I tried to fold my hands, but my fingers were as stiff as bricks. "I don't know what I—"

"No. Don't." She cut me off with a wave of her hand. "Don't say it. Please, don't say anything else." There weren't barbs on her words, she wasn't trying to hurt me or even brush me off, but there was a chill wrapped around them. She had retreated into herself again. Into her shell. The night loomed around us.

I stared straight ahead at the house and beyond it. Inadvertently, I wiped my palms against my jeans. My heart wouldn't stop hammering, my hand wouldn't stop shaking. The finger that had touched her cheek was still on fire, tingling with the taste of her skin.

The moment stretched itself thin. I could sense Lien-hua's heart beating, pulsing someplace beside me, finding its own rhythm again, its own unique tempo. Neither of us looked at each other.

"I'm sorry, Lien-hua."

"Stop." Then she took a deep breath that might have been a sigh. I couldn't tell. "Please."

I peered out the passenger-side window but couldn't seem to find anything to focus my eyes on. I shook my cup. I'd finished my coffee a long time ago—just coffee grounds left. Nothing worth drinking. I didn't feel like drinking any anyway. I felt more like shooting myself in the head.

Somewhere between us lurked a forest of unspoken words. Tension still hung in the air, but the words were going to remain unsaid for now. Because just then, the door to the house eased open and Vanessa stepped outside.

"There she is," I said, leaning forward. Never in my life had I been so relieved and so disappointed to see a stakeout come to an end.

Vanessa glanced up and down the street, pausing for a moment. Her eyes seemed to rest on our car. Then she hurried over to her Corvette, slipped inside, and started the engine.

"She didn't see us, did she?" Lien-hua whispered.

"No," I said as confidently as I could. But she might have. Maybe she did.

Vanessa backed out of her driveway.

"All right," I said. I was glad to be in control of my words again, of my thoughts again. "Time to move."

56

I snatched up my walkie-talkie. "Subject is mobile. Heading eastbound toward highway 240. Unit one in pursuit. Please advise."

"Unit two here," Brent replied. "I'm close. I'll back you up. Over."

Vanessa cruised down Merrimon Avenue and then turned onto East Chestnut.

Lien-hua was keeping her distance, staying just close enough so we wouldn't lose her, sliding and gliding through traffic like a pro.

Suddenly, Vanessa made a sharp left, racing through a red light.

Lien-hua screeched the tires, pulling into the left lane and roaring into the intersection toward an oncoming truck. I was sure he was going to slam into us—into me—but Lien-hua swung the car over the rise of the curb, across someone's no-longer-quite-so-immaculate-lawn, whipped past the truck, and bounced us back onto the road.

"You drive with an attitude," I said.

"Comes from having two older brothers with ATVs."

We'd both taken the events of the stakeout and slid them away into a silent drawer. Closed it tight. Nothing happened. Life was back to normal.

No. It wasn't.

I radioed Brent Tucker. "Subject turned left onto Charlotte. She might have seen us."

"Got her," Tucker's voice came back. "I'm right behind her."

Lien-hua made the turn, and we saw the taillights of Tucker's sedan slide out of sight a quarter mile ahead of us.

"She's really moving," I said.

Lien-hua slammed her foot to the floor, and we swooped around the bend.

"She's entering the Stratford Golf Course," Tucker called. "I've got the east entrance. Go north, cut off the northbound exit."

Ahead of us the road split.

"Which way?" shouted Lien-hua. "Right or left?"

"I don't know," I said.

"Decide!"

I scanned the streets, tree lines, layout of the neighborhood. "Right."

She spun the wheel, and we jolted into the right lane. It led us along a narrow strip of county road and deposited us at the north entrance of the golf course.

"How did you know?" she asked as we jumped out of the car, grabbing our walkie-talkies.

"Travel theory. Urban design. I'll explain later—"

"Male suspect." It was Tucker's voice. "In pursuit."

"Male?" said Lien-hua. "Grolin?"

"Unknown," came the reply.

Lien-hua and I sprinted across the fairway toward hole 17. I started wishing maybe we'd chosen those mic patches.

"Vanessa's on foot!" yelled Tucker. "Heading for the club-house."

"Go east," I said to Lien-hua. "Flare out and see if we can find Grolin before he finds her." Lien-hua bolted out of sight to the left, and I darted through the trees to the right, up and over a sand trap.

I could see a figure about fifty meters in front of me, crouched low and sneaking toward the clubhouse. I hit the button on the walkie-talkie. "Tucker, where are you?"

"West of the clubhouse."

"I think I see him," I said.

"Where?"

"By the golf carts on the south side of the—"

The figure stepped forward, floated into the shadows. Disappeared.

"Wait! I just lost him," I yelled. I raced forward, pulling my gun out of its holster in midstride. "He's gotta be close to you."

"He's by the west entrance," came Tucker's reply. "I'm going in."

"Wait for Lien-hua!" I yelled.

The Illusionist slipped through the shadows along the tree line and up to the clubhouse. He'd had to change his plans for tonight, adapt, but he was confident it would all work out in the end.

Oh, it would work out beautifully.

Look in this hand while I hide the coin in the other.

I remembered the explosion from earlier in the day. *Is this another trap?*

"Wait for backup," I told Brent through my walkie-talkie.

"We've got this guy," Tucker responded. "Let's take him down."

Before I could say another word, Tucker eased through the shadows like a knife and disappeared through a slit in the fence.

Too many people on the scene . . . poor communication . . . someone's going to get hurt.

"Pull back!" I said. "Contain the area!"

The Illusionist unholstered his weapon. Sat in the shadows. Waited.

I heard the glisten of breaking glass and rounded the corner. An alarm began to howl. "He's inside. I repeat, he's inside."

I ran forward, stepped through the shattered window. Listened. "Tucker?"

A gunshot.

No!

The emergency lights burst on, red-filtered, coating the room in pulsing scarlet. The alarm siren throbbed through the night. It felt like I was inside a beating heart.

Brum, brum. Brum, brum . . . Brum, brum. Brum, brum . . .

I flew around the corner.

Brum, brum. Brum, brum . . .

The killer. He's here.

Then movement woven into the shadows. "Who's there?" I yelled. I snapped on my Maglite and swept the room, flashlight in my left hand, gun in my right. "Who is it?"

Brum, brum . . .

Deep grunts. A fight. Two figures in the corner, in the dark. Movement blurring movement.

Blurring movement.

One of them was a woman. Lien-hua. I saw her spin and kick someone. He fell to the floor. She whipped out her weapon, crouched low, ready to move in.

Then a gunshot. She flew for cover.

I ducked into the shadows. "Lien-hua!" I yelled.

Another shot. From the next room.

My adrenaline was going through the roof. "Lien-hua, are you all right?"

"I'm OK!"

"Tucker, where are you?"

Brum, brum. Brum, brum . . .

Then the person Lien-hua had been fighting was standing up, waving two guns, one in each hand, rushing toward me. Everything was a blur, a red blur. "Drop your weapons," I screamed, swinging my gun into position. It was too dark to see him clearly; all I could see was his outline against the window. Muffled sounds. "Now. Drop them!"

No reply. He was aiming the guns toward me, coming fast—

Take him down, Pat, or you're dead.

Before I could pull the trigger I heard two rapid gunshots from my left, and the figure jerked backward into the air and crashed to the ground.

Suddenly the lights were on and Tucker was rushing through the door, waving his gun. "I got him," he cried. "I got Grolin." Red light still pulsing.

Pulsing.

We stared at the other side of the room. Two bodies lay on the floor.

One was Vanessa Mueller, shot in the neck.

The other was Joseph Grolin, bleeding from the chest.

A strip of black gaffer's tape was secured over Grolin's mouth. Both of his hands were tightly taped, thoroughly taped, around the grips of handguns.

Toy handguns.

57

"No, oh please, no . . ." gasped Tucker. "What have I done?"

Lien-hua ran to help Vanessa. I rushed over to Grolin. He was still alive.

"Put your gun away," I yelled to Tucker. "Now."

Grolin couldn't get the guns off his hands. He couldn't drop them. And he couldn't rip the tape off his mouth to tell us. I removed the tape from his face, and he spit out a bloody white pawn.

"Who did this to you, Joseph?" I asked. "Who?"

He swallowed hard, searching for breath. "I didn't hurt her," he managed to say. Tears burned in his eyes. He'd been crying for a while, probably knew the cops were coming and had been trying to get free.

"Who?" I said. "Who did this?"

The crimson light beat around us. Brum, brum. Brum, brum . . . He spit up a mouthful of blood.

"Get an ambulance, now!" I shouted at Tucker, who was standing in shock beside me. I leaned closer to Grolin. He was trying to say something.

But it was too late. He gasped one last time and slumped to the ground.

No!

I started chest compressions, but with two gunshot wounds to the chest like that, it wasn't going to do much good. Brum, brum. Brum, brum . . . "We need that ambulance!"

Lien-hua radioed for help. Tucker was still in shock. "What have I done?" he was mumbling. "What have I done?"

"Why did you have to rush in here, Tucker?" I yelled. "Why couldn't you wait?"

Sirens. The police were on their way.

Brum, brum. Brum, brum . . .

I tried to beat the life back into Grolin's shredded heart. It was no use. Joseph Grolin was dead.

And he wasn't the Illusionist.

Ten minutes later the ambulance was pulling away to take Vanessa Mueller to Mission Memorial Hospital. She might very well die at her place of work. The mood at the scene was grim.

"He rushed me," said Lien-hua. She was stunned. We all were. "I kicked at his hand when it looked like he had a weapon. He wouldn't drop it."

"Each of us is going to have to file a full report on this," I said. "Figure out exactly what happened here."

"You saw him, right?" Tucker said to us. "He was waving the guns at me."

I wasn't sure what to say. In the end, Brent probably wouldn't get into disciplinary trouble. After all, the guy was waving what appeared to be two guns at us and wouldn't verbally respond or drop his weapons.

Of course, he couldn't do either.

He was just another one of the Illusionist's pawns.

I was beginning to think we all were.

"The killer lured us here through Vanessa," I said. "No one shot at her, though, right?"

We all shook our heads.

"All right," I said. "Then he was here, somewhere. We'll have the CSIU guys scour the place and have ballistics check the bullet in her neck to see if it matches the bullet that was taken out of the neck of that guy at the parking garage."

Then I turned to Tucker. "I hate this part, but I have to do it.

As the senior agent here, I need you to hand me your weapon. It was used in a lethal shooting, and until a complete investigation can be—"

"I know." He slapped his gun into my hand. "I know." His face clouded over, and I couldn't tell if it was shock or guilt that was sweeping over him. Maybe it was both. He turned and slouched away. I let him go. I felt bad for him, sick to my stomach about the whole thing. But I didn't really know what else to say.

For the next two hours I answered questions and filled out paperwork for the responding officers until I was bleary-eyed. I was the last one from our team to leave the scene. After catching a ride to my hotel with one of the officers I collapsed on the bed. Tried to sleep.

Ended up doing pull-ups instead.

But my shoulder hurt so bad I had to do them with only one arm.

And with each pull-up I vowed I would catch the Illusionist.

My anger was laced with fresh fire, and nothing short of stopping him was going to put it out.

58

Aaron Jeffrey Kincaid stood outside the gathering room for a moment and listened.

Beyond the door he could hear a man speaking in a measured, calming, rambling way. He knew the voice. It was Father's voice, the Reverend Jim Jones's voice.

And he knew the tape. It was the one in which Father convinced his followers, his family, to line up and die. Over the years Aaron had taught his own family the words. They recited them as blessings over their children, believed in them as if they were holy prayers.

Some people called it the Death Tape.

Kincaid just remembered it as the Final Message.

He opened the door and found his family waiting cross-legged on the lush carpet. A few of the women softly sang an old-time hymn, swaying, their eyes closed.

As he stepped into the room, all the singing stopped. One of the men turned off the recording, and the family members bowed their heads out of respect, lowering their foreheads to the floor, holding their arms out to the side, palms up, like broken wings. He hadn't taught them this gesture; hadn't asked them to do it, but over the years it had just become the natural response. They were only trying to honor him, and he wouldn't deny them that. There was no reason to deny them that.

He loved this group more than he'd ever loved anything in his life—at least it seemed like love to him. It was difficult to tell. They'd taught him so much about himself, so much about his possibilities.

But whether it was love or not, whatever he felt toward them, it was a noble feeling. He was sure of that.

"Thirty years ago a great tragedy unfolded," he began, and as he spoke they sat up again one at a time. "One of the greatest tragedies of that generation. It didn't need to happen. There was no reason for it to happen. Parents died that day, parents who loved their children. Brothers and sisters died that day. Men and women just like us who had done no wrong, who had broken no law, who had hurt no one, died on that day. Good people. People like you and I died on that day. On that terrible day."

His followers nodded in agreement as he spoke. They knew the story well.

"Life was not an option to them if they could not live free. They would rather cross over to the other side than live enslaved by the society that chained them to repression, that hated them for their beliefs." Kincaid drifted among them now, grazing his fingers along their cheeks in an act of silent blessing.

"Their only crime was dreaming of and fighting for and believing in a better world." He paused. It wasn't for dramatic effect, although it served that purpose. He paused because the memories were catching up with him, chasing him just like the Peoples Temple gunmen had done in the twilight. He remembered the babies and the river and the syringes. "But what breaks my heart the most is not that they died but that the legacy of their lives has been stained. All of us must die, but our memories need not be trampled. My family, my friends, were called crazy cultists by the world, left for days to rot in the sun while the U.S. government positioned itself to cover up its role in their destruction."

His voice thickened. His face flushed with anger. "The tragedy that cost them their lives was the fault of the government that hunted them. The culture that lines its pockets with the dreams of the poor."

His followers, his family, voiced their agreement.

Aaron Jeffrey Kincaid stopped walking and stood like a statue, like a god, among his followers, among the true believers. A tremor of pure rage caught hold of him, but he embraced the anger, held it close, let it inform him, become his guide.

He took Marcie's chin in his hand and gently tilted her head up to meet his gaze. She blushed to be singled out in this way by the Master. Some of the women had started to weep softly while the men steeled their eyes and nodded iron jaws. Marcie had borne him a daughter. He knew she would understand about the children. She'd been with him since the beginning. Even worked in PTPharmaceuticals's research and development department before joining the family. The delicate tears in her eyes told him that he was right. She did understand. She stared past him to the door of the library.

"And so, to protect our children from the hands of those who would take them from us, from those who would teach them only deceit and evil and hatred, we have done what we must, out of love. Out of hope for the future. We have sent them to the other side ahead of us to protect them from the pain that I have carried all these years" — he looked down into Marcie's eyes — "the pain of knowing that the memory of those you love has been spat upon by the world."

He watched her face.

"Mercy and love require protecting children from a life filled with such torment."

Marcie began to cry soft, constant tears. Still he didn't let her look away.

"Do we want our children to suffer? To grow up to hear their parents scorned and ridiculed for their beliefs? No. We do not. We will not let it happen, because we love our children too much."

More tears came. A few of the people ventured glances toward the door to the library.

"We have done to our children as our predecessors did to theirs.

But only because we love them as they loved theirs, to protect our children as they protected theirs."

"Yes," shouted one of the men. "Yes, Father!"

And then Aaron Jeffrey Kincaid let go of Marcie's jaw and walked to the library door. He grabbed the handle and opened the door so that he could see the bodies of the children for himself.

59

They were lying in rows. Peaceful and still at last, free from the trials and treacheries of life. Very orderly. Lined up by age, with the youngest first, the babies leading the others.

David had been gentle with them. He could have snapped them in half, but he chose to let them drink the medication instead. His was a pure love full of mercy and compassion. Yes, Kincaid told himself, he had chosen wisely when he'd appointed David to be his aide. He had chosen well.

Kincaid turned to face the group. "They have crossed over before us. They will meet us on the other side. We use the term 'death' to make the transition sound final, but really it is an awakening. And their awakening marks the beginning of a greater awakening throughout the world."

His family shouted their agreement. All of them did, except for Marcie, who stared past Kincaid toward the library with vacant, cloudy eyes.

"The people of Jonestown died because they would rather choose their own destiny than have their destiny ripped from them by the very government that hunted them like animals, that planned to destroy them like dogs!"

The murmur of agreement rippling through the room grew louder, awakening at last into frenzied cheers. Aaron Jeffrey Kincaid, the focused and passionate man, the loving man, the beneficent man, let himself form a fist with his hand. Some acts were so terrible that it was a greater crime to hold back emotion from having its rightful place. "Birth is the death of the old. Death is the birth of the new.

We have planned for this. We have prepared for this journey. The time has come to set destiny right at last!"

Kincaid lifted his hands to the sky. The people stood as one. The anticipation in the room rose to a fever pitch.

"He is our Father!" shouted Aaron Jeffrey Kincaid.

"He is our Father!" the men and women repeated in unison.

"His vision, our vision! His future, our future!"

"His vision, our vision!" they chanted. "His future, our future!"

"It's a cruel world!" In his mind, Kincaid was no longer at the ranch with his family, he was beside the whirlpool with Jessica.

"It's a cruel world!" he heard his family say, and he remembered the jungle and the men with the guns and Jessica's trembling hands and the shore of a hungry river. His first family. The pavilion. Those who laid down and never rose again.

"But our love will unite us forever!" he cried.

"Our love will unite us forever!" Blood curling through the water. Swirling toward the future. Love that cannot die. Distant dreams and dying babies. A journey through the fabric of the night.

Aaron Jeffrey Kincaid handed the needles containing the CCHF-spliced *Francisella tularensis* to his family. This time the world would pay. This time the revolution would find its inevitable completion. And this time so many more would be part of the revolution.

60

I arrived at Vanessa's room at Mission Memorial Hospital a few minutes before 8:00 a.m. to check on her condition. I asked the doctor who was leaving the room when I stepped inside if he thought she was going to be all right.

"Too early to tell." He didn't even look up from his clipboard to see who I was. And then he was gone, and I was alone with her.

I positioned myself in one of the chairs beside a countertop covered with pills and bottles and a Gideons Bible.

I'd called Margaret on my way to the hospital, and the conversation had gone better than I expected. She only swore at me twice. "I'm holding you personally responsible for this debacle last night." Her voice was as taut as a cable.

"I figured you would."

"You were the senior agent on-site."

"Yes, I was."

"Full report. Do you understand? Then we'll see what happens from there."

"Fine."

Click.

As far as I could tell, the killer had called Vanessa and convinced her to go to the golf course. Maybe he threatened to kill her boyfriend if she didn't, who knows.

The preliminary blood tests on Grolin's body indicated that he'd been heavily sedated and then drugged. It looked like the killer had abducted him and then released him at the pro shop in a drug-induced delirium, with his hands taped to those toy weapons.

It seemed like I was chasing a phantom.

I hoped Vanessa might know his name.

She lay still, the monitor beeping soft and regular. Soft and regular. Purring out her heartbeat.

I looked around her hospital room.

The scene looked all too familiar.

A hospital bed. A dying woman. Stiff, ugly chairs in the corners of the room. The only thing missing was a fervent young pastor named Donovan Richman.

Of course, this time the woman wasn't my wife of just five months; instead she was the only person who might be able to lead us to a maniacal killer. That was all.

For a few minutes I found myself listening to Vanessa's soft, methodical breathing and smelling the stark antiseptic smell only hospitals seem to have. And with each passing moment another wave of grief went roaring through my chest. I was sitting there lost in thought when I heard Lien-hua's voice. "Dr. Bowers?"

I turned. "Yeah?"

She stepped softly into the room. "You OK?"

I looked down. I was clutching the Gideons Bible; I hadn't even realized I'd picked it up. "Just thinking. Remembering."

"Christie?" she said softly.

I set the Bible down. "A pastor used to come and visit her, toward the end." I wanted to tell Lien-hua everything and I didn't want to tell her anything at all.

"Did it help?"

I could feel myself getting tense. Thinking back to my discussions with Reverend Donovan Richman made me frustrated all over again. Christie. The doctors. The questions . . .

"Patrick?"

I blinked. "Yeah?" I'd done it again, drifted away.

Vanessa lay motionless beside us. Brum, brum. Brum, brum . . . Lien-hua took a seat in the chair opposite me. "You were telling me about the pastor." She seemed to have slipped into counseling mode. Maybe she was analyzing me, profiling me. But at that moment I didn't really care.

I sighed. "I don't think he really realized how desperate Christie's condition was because more often than not he ended up arguing with me. 'Design is evidence of a designer,' he told me one day, and then recited some of the typical Intelligent Design arguments—irreducible complexity, things like that."

"And?"

"That was the day the doctors told me they'd given Christie a dose of the wrong medication, and her condition was spiraling downward. So when Reverend Richman said that, I laid into him. 'OK. Wings and eyeballs, I'll give you that,' I said. I was trying to find a way to win at something, it seemed like I was losing everything. 'But if design is evidence of a designer, Reverend, then let me ask you a question.' 'What's that?' he said, and I said, 'What's chaos evidence of?'"

"And what did he say to that?"

"I looked from Lien-hua to Vanessa. "At first he didn't say anything. I'd stumped him, so finally he says, 'I don't know, Dr. Bowers. What is chaos evidence of?' But then, before I could reply, Benjamin answered."

"Wait a minute. Who's Benjamin?"

"One of the deacons at their church. He would come in with the pastor. He usually didn't say much, just listened. Anyway, that day he answered my question."

"About chaos?"

"Yeah."

I walked past Lien-hua and stared out the window at the dirty white clouds scampering across the sky. "He whispered the answer kind of softly. But it was like he read my mind."

"So what's the answer? What is chaos evidence of?"

"Us. Human beings."

"Oh."

"Yeah. Well, Benjamin said something about how he knew I'd seen the worst kind of violence humans are capable of, and I mean, he was right. I have. So have you, Lien-hua, its wings and eyeballs, the evil that human beings do to each other . . ." I let my voice trail off.

Vanessa's heart monitor hummed.

"What then?"

"He told me he'd seen evil too: the evil we do to ourselves. In people's confessions and tears and prayers." I hesitated for a second. "He said souls can be just as bloody and torn up as bodies can. He called it the other kind of violence."

"The other kind of violence," she echoed. We both looked at Vanessa. I had the feeling Lien-hua was remembering something, reliving something. "I think I agree with him," she said at last. Something from the past was haunting her.

I wanted to ask her about it, but the time wasn't right. I didn't say anything.

And maybe I should have told her the rest, but I didn't.

Maybe I should have explained that Donovan quietly reached over and held my hand in both of his. Maybe I should have told her that he prayed the simplest prayer I'd ever heard him say, a prayer for hope, a petition for mercy both for himself and for me, and that I just sat there with nothing to say as those two men tried to pass something along to me that my heart had lost—or maybe never had. And all the while Christie lay dying beside us.

No, living.

She was living beside us.

They were living beside her.

I was the one who was dying.

"You're right, chaos is evidence of human beings," Pastor Richman whispered to me after his prayer was over. "But hope is evidence of God. That's the deeper design behind everything, Patrick. Hope despite the pain."

Maybe I should have told Lien-hua those things, but I didn't. All I said was, "Souls can be just as bloody and torn up as bodies ... Yeah, I think I agree with him too."

I glanced at my watch and stood up. I had to get going to pick up Tessa.

"By the way," said Lien-hua softly, "I checked the cell phone records this morning. The call Vanessa got last night didn't come from Joseph Grolin's cell phone." Back to business. Back to the present.

"Do we know whose?"

"No. The number was untraceable—surprise, surprise. But, when Vanessa was talking on the phone back at her house, she was gesturing with her hand. I think that whoever called her was someone she knew."

"Hmm. Good point."

"I wonder why the killer went to all the trouble to set up Grolin, and then sent him in like that just to get shot."

"Maybe he wanted that explosion yesterday morning to end everything, and when we survived he just adjusted, went to plan B. Maybe he wanted to eliminate someone from our team—he knew that whoever ended up shooting Grolin would be taken off the case for a while. Or maybe he just did it because he could, for the thrill. I don't know. Listen. I need to go get Tessa; can you see if you can track down that cult guy in New Mexico?"

"I thought Margaret was on that."

"She is," I said. "But right now I'm not sure who I can trust. So can you?"

She hesitated. "I'll see what I can do."

And with that, I left the hospital to pick up my stepdaughter, the raven who'd been blown onto my doorstep by this chaotic thing called life.

61

Tessa's flight was scheduled to arrive at 11:32 a.m. I arrived at the Charlotte Douglas International Airport about forty-five minutes early, and walked up to the US Airways ticket counter.

The woman behind the counter smiled an automatic smile. Spoke automatic words. "Good morning, sir. Have you tried our automated ticketing kiosk set up for your convenience? Just swipe any major credit card and—"

"I'm meeting up with a subject: Tessa Ellis." I showed her my FBI badge. "Arrives at 11:30 from Chicago. I want her off the plane first and her bags brought around out front, to the curb."

By the look on her face I could tell I'd just overloaded all of her circuits. None of those words appeared on the script she'd been given. "It's a very important case," I added.

"Um . . . yes. Let me see." She fumbled for a moment at her computer keyboard then disappeared into a back room to ask her supervisor what she was supposed to say. A minute later she reappeared with her smile fastened in place again. "Of course, sir. We will have the bags waiting for you, sir."

I nodded. "Thank you."

There aren't many perks to my job. But it turns out there are a few.

The guys at the security checkpoint hassled me a little about bringing in my gun, but when I showed them my paperwork, federal ID, driver's license, and told them my mother's maiden name and favorite salsa recipe they finally let me through.

I grabbed some coffee at Chierio's, the best coffee shop in any airport in the country. Based on the gently nurtured acidity, I guessed their blend came from the mountainous southeastern region of Colombia, the best country in the world to grow coffee beans. And other types of plants too, from what my friends in the DEA tell me.

The coffee was exquisite. And despite all the things on my mind, after three sips I realized that if I were to die right then and there I would die a happy man.

Some people say I take my coffee a little too seriously.

I took another sip of Chierio's South Mountain Blend.

Naw.

Not a chance.

I headed to Gate C-14.

Alice led her two kids out of the Basilica of St. Lawrence in downtown Asheville and over to the car. She'd started taking them to church a few months ago when Garrett moved out. Those were hard, hard days, especially at first. She needed strength, and even from the start, coming here had seemed to help.

The basilica's ceiling had the largest oval-shaped freestanding dome in the United States. The beauty and elegance inspired her, helped her look up toward the heavens again. And hearing the singing and the homilies seemed to help her think more about the things that really mattered, seemed to help her hate Garrett a little less for the things he'd done, seemed to help her feel hopeful about life once again, to trust the power of good over evil, of the future over the past. The angels over the monsters.

It was only after coming here that she'd registered for school to finish her degree. To make a fresh start.

She left the church and aimed her car toward Wal-Mart. She needed to pick up a new hairbrush before going home.

I'd anticipated a long wait, but only a moment or two after Flight 642 landed, the doors opened up and Tessa stepped toward me.

She was dressed in black just like I expected. I'd always thought maybe pink was her color, but with black lipstick, black eye shadow, and even her fingernails painted black, everything about her seemed to convey the tone of her mood, of our relationship. Black.

Don't mess this up, Pat. Don't mess this up.

"Tessa," I said.

She drew in a long, narrow breath, clutched her purse to her side. "Patrick."

"It's good to see you." I stepped closer, held out my arms, offered her a hug. She didn't move.

"Why are you doing this to me?"

I felt my teeth grit. "No, Tessa, when I say it's good to see you, you're supposed to say, 'Oh, it's good to see you too.' Let's try it again—it's good to see you."

A sarcastic, stupid thing to say. Stupid. Stupid!

Why did you say that? Why?

She shook her head very, very slowly. Tears began welling in her eyes. I'd actually driven her to tears in less than thirty seconds. "Why are you trying to ruin my entire life!" She swung her purse around and scootched it up her shoulder and stomped past me.

I stood there in the wake of anger, mumbling to myself, "'I've missed you. I'm glad you're safe.' That could maybe follow. That might be a good thing to say next."

Agent Stanton walked up to me. "And you must be the dad."

No, I thought. *She doesn't have a dad.*

"Stepdad," I said. "Yeah. That would be me."

62

After we picked up Tessa's luggage at the curb, Agent Stanton left us with a feigned salute. I assumed he was flying back to Denver, but I didn't ask.

"Good-bye, Eric," called Tessa with a smirk. "Keep up the good work on those puzzles!"

He ignored her. Shook his head. Kept walking.

"What was all that about?" I asked.

She smiled. "Oh, nothing."

We tossed Tessa's luggage into the car and headed for the highway. I called Terry and listened as he filled me in on the results of his research. I hung up the phone and turned to Tessa. "Well, did you eat yet?"

"Yeah. So, where are we going, anyway?"

"A place called Asheville. But I have to make one stop first."

———————————■———————————

The governor's mansion looked different in the daylight, more Southern somehow. As if it belonged in Mississippi instead of North Carolina.

Tessa stared out the window as we drove up. "Who lives here?"

"The governor does."

"Sebastian Taylor?"

"How did you know his name?"

"It's not that complex, Patrick." She spoke slowly, as if she were explaining something to a five-year-old. "Sebastian Taylor is the governor of North Carolina. We are in the state of North Carolina. It's called logic."

"Yeah, well, I know all that, but I guess I was just surprised you knew his name."

"Why?"

"Because we live in Colorado and most people your age barely know the name of the president let alone the governor of a state on the other side of the country."

"Well," she said, "I'm not like most people my age."

I wasn't sure how to respond to that. "Anyway, I just need to talk to him for a minute. Then we'll get going."

"What are you going to talk to him about?"

"His role in the massacre of 909 people."

———————■———————

Ms. Anita Banner met us at the door, and although her eyes turned to coals when I asked her to stay with Tessa while I spoke with the governor, she agreed.

Governor Taylor was in the great room lounging on one of the leather couches when I walked in. He had reading glasses perched on his nose, a book open on his lap, and was dressed in a stylish light gray mohair suit. "Agent Bowers," he said evenly. He wasn't even pretending to be polite this time.

I decided to follow suit. "You made the tape."

That got his attention. "What?"

"Q875."

He waited, probably to see if I was bluffing.

"CIA. Guyana, South America."

"What are you talking about?"

"Q875. You made one mistake, though. You left it behind."

Governor Taylor took off his glasses and polished the lenses with his handkerchief. He took his time. "I worked for the state department in the seventies and eighties, Agent Bowers, researching trade agreements in France, South America, and Spain. It's all a matter of public record. You can look it up. I'm afraid I was involved in foreign relations, not international espionage."

"Codename Cipher, reference number 16dash1711alpha delta4," I said. Terry is very good at his job.

The governor slid his glasses back onto his face. "Hmm . . . I'm guessing either military intelligence or NSA. Am I right? Is that where you went?"

"I'm not at liberty to say."

"Of course you're not." He set his book aside and rose from the couch. "How long have you known?"

"Just over an hour. I spoke with my source this morning. He was very helpful."

"I'm sure he was."

"How far did it go, Governor? Did you do more than make the tape? Were you there on the airstrip at Port Kaituma?"

The governor stepped around the couch, walked up to me, and stood close enough for me to smell his minty breath. "Dr. Bowers, have you ever been fishing in the ocean?"

"I'll find out, Governor. It's just a matter of time. I already know about Trembley, that you sent him to follow me."

He turned, walked over to the fireplace where the giant fish hung above the mantel. "Swordfish. Or maybe marlin, or like this tarpon here," he said.

"Governor, did you hear what I said?"

"Of course, tarpon tend to stay closer to shore than marlin or sword." He stepped back to admire his fish. "I caught this one off the coast of Tampa. Didn't even realize it at the time, but we were fishing in the most densely shark-infested waters in the world—even more so than the Great Barrier Reef. Most people don't know that." He turned to face me. "Dr. Bowers, do you know what the most dangerous shark in the world is?"

Enough games. Enough banter. "Things spun out of control, didn't they? The place was a time bomb, and you dialed it to zero.

Jones imploded after the assassination, and you needed to give your supervisors proof that you'd cleaned things up. But why did you leave the tape behind? That's the one thing I can't figure out."

"The shark, Dr. Bowers. Try to guess the shark."

"I don't know," I said through my teeth. "The great white."

He smirked. "Yes, you see, most people think so—that's what everyone says, that or the hammerhead; but no. It's the bull shark, actually. Likes to stay near shore, and it can live in both salt water and fresh water, very adaptable to different environments. That's what makes it so deadly."

He turned to me. His eyes narrowed, became bullets. The change was stunning. "They tell me that around there people don't always catch what they expect," he said. "Sometimes the fish at the other end of the line turns out to be a bull shark. Not something you'd want to pull up to the boat."

I cocked my head. "Are you threatening me, Governor?"

He stepped even closer, and his voice leveled off into a flat, metallic whisper. His eyes, cool black stones. "If you're going to go trolling through these waters, you better be ready to reel in whatever fish decides to bite."

"I'm ready," I said. "Bring on the sharks."

"You have no idea who you're dealing with."

"Neither do you."

Just then Ms. Banner and Tessa appeared at the doorway. "The young lady is anxious to get going," said Ms. Banner. My guess was that Ms. Banner was anxious to get rid of Tessa and get back to personally assisting the governor. I watched Governor Taylor's eyes track across the room, and come to rest on Tessa.

I swear, if he even looks at her the wrong way I'm going to take him down.

"And who do we have here?" he asked.

"My name is Tessa. So you're Governor Taylor?"

"Yes, ma'am."

She scanned the room. "Nice tarpon."

You've got to be kidding me.

The governor smiled. "Well, thank you."

Her eyes flickered from one painting to the next, scrutinizing them. "So," she asked at last, "how come you only have paintings of battles that the South won?"

OK. Now that's just plain impressive.

He hesitated for a moment. "That's . . . very astute, young lady. You're a bright girl. I'm sure your father is very proud of you."

"Well," Tessa said, "you'd have to ask him about that."

My heart squirmed inside my skin. "C'mon, Tessa. I'm done here. Let's get going."

The governor grinned. "Dr. Bowers, if you and Agent Jiang can't make it to the luncheon tomorrow, I'll certainly understand."

"Oh, we'll be there," I said. "I've heard they're serving fish."

He breathed out through his nose like Margaret tends to do. Good. I'd annoyed him.

"Ms. Banner," he said, "please give our young guest one of the signed photographs."

And with that, Ms. Banner led us outside without a word, handed Tessa a picture without a word, and ushered us to the car without a word.

As soon as I started the engine, Tessa crinkled up the picture and tossed it out the window onto the governor's meticulously manicured lawn. "I don't like the way he looked at me."

"You're a good judge of character," I said. "Keep that up."

Amazing. We actually agreed on something.

63

All the way back to Asheville, Tessa rode in silence, her iPod plugged into her ears.

I grabbed my stuff from the hotel, checked out, and drove to the safe house.

Tessa and her iPod rode along in silence.

The safe house Tessa and I would be staying in was a dun-colored ranch-style home on the outer fringe of the city, near the French Broad River. Sheriff Wallace had assigned Officers Jason Stilton and Patricia Muncey to guard Tessa. They were waiting for us at the house when we arrived. I recognized them from the briefing I'd given on Friday.

"Getting colder," said Officer Stilton as he tossed his cigarette into the grass and led me inside the house.

Tessa and her iPod walked past us in silence.

"Yeah," I said watching her step past me. "Guy on the radio said something about snow tomorrow morning."

Officer Stilton grunted, which I guess meant he agreed.

"Don't mind the toys," said Officer Muncey as we stepped into the living room. "Haven't quite cleaned up from the last occupants yet."

The living room smelled vaguely of cat litter and baby powder. Toddler toys lay scattered across the floor, making the simplest trek through the living room a challenge. But the bigger challenge appeared to be avoiding stepping on one of the two cats that lurked relentlessly underfoot or appeared out of nowhere and sprawled in front of you, waiting for you to scratch them.

"Domestic abuse case with a city council member," said Officer Muncey. "They brought his wife and kids here to protect them."

"Took the kids," grumbled Jason Stilton. "Left the cats."

Tessa pulled out her iPod ear buds and knelt down to pet the pumpkin-colored furrball. "Oh, they're so cute! What are their names?"

"That one's Sunshine and the black one's Midnight," he said.

I knelt down to pet Midnight.

She clawed at the air and hissed at me.

"You have to reach out toward her with your hand open," said Tessa, demonstrating. "And do it more slowly. That way she knows you're not going to hurt her."

I wondered if Tessa was really talking about the cat.

Midnight purred, rolled onto her back, and let Tessa scratch her stomach. "See?"

"I never would have pegged you as a cat person, Tessa," I said.

"I love cats."

"I didn't know—"

"There's a lot you don't know," she said flatly.

I was beginning to realize just how true that was.

"Hello, there."

I turned toward the voice and saw that Ralph had stepped into the room.

"What are you doing here?" I said.

"Just wanted to say hi to the brains of the family."

"Thank you," said Tessa.

"You remember me, right?"

She nodded. "Special Agent Ralph Hawkins."

"Uncle Ralph." He gave her a hug.

So I made her cry, but Uncle Ralph got a hug. Wonderful.

She pointed at his pocket. "What's that?"

"Um, nothing."

She feinted to the right and then leaned left, stuffed her hand into his pocket, and produced his PSP 3. "Sweet," she said.

"Hey, give me that!" He tried to snatch it away from her, but she stepped back just in time.

"I should have warned you, Ralph," I said. "She's good."

"Why are you playing video games?" she asked. "I thought you were supposed to be like solving murders or something."

"Everyone needs a break sometimes. Now give me that." He reached for it again, missed. Sighed.

"So what are you playing?"

He gave up and leaned an arm against the wall. "Sorcerer's Realm IV. I can't seem to make it past the crypt on Level Five."

"No prob. I can help you."

"You play?"

She did that sarcastic teenage girl jut-your-head-forward-and-tweak-your-voice thing. "Yeah."

"Oh," said Ralph. "Right."

She flopped onto the couch, and he positioned himself next to her. Then she began to maneuver the game controls like a pro while he watched submissively. "See that cave?" she said.

"Yeah."

"Well, there's a secret passage in there, but you need to behead the ogre first."

"I didn't know you could behead him. I always just beat on him with the club."

"No, beheading is definitely better."

I watched them for a few minutes, Tessa pointing. Ralph nodding, his head bobbing up and down above those massive shoulders. Watching Ralph trying to use his thick fingers to press the tiny control buttons made me think of trying to type wearing a catcher's mitt. No wonder he couldn't beat Tony.

And every once in a while Tessa would laugh. For the first time in months I actually heard my stepdaughter laugh.

As she showed my friend how to behead ogres.

64

Before Ralph left he pulled me aside. "Tucker's on disciplinary leave," he told me. "Until they can figure out exactly what went down last night."

I nodded. "Yeah. I expected that. Any word on Vanessa?"

He shook his head. "Last I heard she was the same. Bullet matched, though. It's the same weapon as the mall. Listen, I gotta go, have a good afternoon with Tessa. She's a darling girl."

Darling wasn't exactly the word I would have chosen. "OK, I will."

Then he said good-bye to Tessa and took off. I hung out with Tessa and the cats for about half an hour, and then I checked my messages. Three voicemails from Margaret. Huh, that was even faster than I expected. One message from Lien-hua.

I called Lien-hua.

Maybe I should have been surprised when she told me that two hours ago they'd found the rest of Jolene's body in the home of Reggie Abrams, retired FBI agent, but I wasn't. Maybe I should have been surprised when she told me Abrams had been shot execution style in the head or that he was the former head of FBI in the state of North Carolina, but I wasn't.

The only thing that really surprised me was that Ralph hadn't mentioned any of this when he was with me at the house.

Weird.

"Did we find out any more about this cult in New Mexico?" I asked her.

"A little. The leader's name is Aaron Jeffrey Kincaid. He used to own PTPharmaceuticals but dropped off the map after selling the company a few years ago. I'll email you his picture and bio. Oh, and I have an address. We just called it in to the local police about ten minutes ago. They're heading over to check him out."

"Give me the address," I said, flipping open my laptop.

"What are you doing?" asked Tessa, picking up Sunshine.

Yeah, this is good. She likes video games. "Watch this," I said and booted up F.A.L.C.O.N.

"You're not gonna believe this," Lien-hua said. "Here's the address: 19654 Walnut Road, Taos, New Mexico."

"What's so significant about that?" I typed in the address, and Tessa watched the screen tilt and then zoom in on the coordinates. First the planet. Then the hemisphere. Then North America. The west. New Mexico. Sangre de Cristo Mountains.

"Sweet," she said.

"Well," said Lien-hua, "the phone number for Peoples Temple was Walnut 1-9654. It was retired after the tragedy. It's never been reassigned to another customer."

"Subtle," I said. But as the screen zoomed in closer, I began to regret my decision to let Tessa watch.

"What's that?" asked Tessa.

Deep billows of black smoke churned from each of the six buildings. "The ranch is on fire," I whispered. "The whole place is." I maneuvered the cursor around the screen, tilting it, zooming in and out to observe the buildings from different angles. A fierce desert wind from the west whipped the flames into a white frenzy.

"Are there any people in there?" Tessa asked softly.

I flipped the laptop closed. "Tessa, wait over there for a minute 'til I'm off the phone."

"But—"

"Please."

"Patrick—"

"Now."

She let out an annoyed sigh but finally stepped back.

"What's going on?" asked Lien-hua.

"They torched the whole thing," I said. I zoomed out and saw four police cars racing down the road toward the ranch. Two fire trucks followed closely behind them. I told Lien-hua what I saw.

"How old is the video?" she asked.

I checked the data timer. "About five minutes. We're between satellite passes. Hang on a minute." I zoomed in on something in the corral. An animal. A whole herd, actually.

I zoomed closer.

None of them were moving.

Zoomed closer. Closer still.

It looked as if the livestock were covered with sores. At first I thought it might be insect activity.

No, not that high in the mountains. It'd be too cool this late in the year.

"Listen, Lien-hua, have the police call in a Hazmat team and tell them to avoid the dead livestock in the meadow. If Kincaid is planning another White Night, he might have developed some kind of drug or contagion. We need to isolate it ASAP."

I heard a shuffle of movement behind me and turned around. Tessa was staring down at the screen. "What's going on?" she asked.

I closed the computer again. "Please, Tessa, I'll be off the phone in a minute."

She didn't move.

I pointed to the couch. "Work with me."

She shook her head, slouched away, and situated herself on it with her arms folded tightly.

I heard Lien-hua call out for Dante Wallace to get in touch with the New Mexico state patrol and regional Hazmat teams. Then, her voice came through the phone to me again. "Pat, we're at the Abrams's scene now. Can you meet us here?"

"I need to hang out with Tessa this afternoon."

"Who are you talking to?" asked Tessa.

Lien-hua continued. "Well, I guess we can email you the files."

You really should swing by the crime scene. "Are they done processing it?"

"Yeah."

I nodded. Then I caught myself. "No, I really don't think I can come."

"Come where?" asked Tessa.

"OK," said Lien-hua. "I guess I'll just brief you later on what we find."

Then again, maybe I could leave Tessa here for a little while, let her play with the cats . . . "What's the address?"

"To where?" asked Tessa. "Where are we going?"

I held the phone to my chest for a minute. "*We* are not going anywhere. *I* have to go to a crime scene."

"I've never been to a crime scene."

"I can't take you."

"I thought you wanted to spend time with me."

Oh man, she was good. She was way good.

"I do but—look, it's against the rules."

"But if the cops are done, what would it matter?"

"How do you know the cops are done?"

She rolled her eyes. "You just asked the woman on the phone if they were done, and then you nodded—*hello!*—you wouldn't have done that if she said no. So if they're done, why can't I come?"

"How did you know I'm talking to a woman?"

"Are you kidding me? Tone of voice."

OK, it was official. So she was a better investigator than most of the FBI agents I'd worked with over the last nine years.

"Well," I said. "I'm not taking you, and that's final."

———————————■———————————

I pulled to a stop in front of Abrams's house on Cedar Point Avenue and turned to Tessa. "Stay in the car."

"But then I can't see—"

"I'll be back in a few minutes."

"How are we supposed to spend time together if you're in there and I'm out here?"

"Ha. That's not going to work this time." I pointed to the two FBI agents who were stationed on the porch. "Don't worry, you'll be safe. I'll be back in a couple minutes, and we'll go grab some supper. Maybe steaks or something."

"I'm a vegetarian."

"Oh yeah? Well, I like meat. Nice, juicy catburgers whenever possible."

"That's not even funny."

"Wait here."

She set her jaw and slid down into her seat. As I stepped outside the car my phone rang.

Margaret.

She didn't waste time. "Why aren't you returning my calls?"

"I'm a little busy, Margaret."

"You went to see the governor today?"

Wow. Word travels fast. "I needed some advice."

"On what?"

"Fishing."

"Well, listen," she said. "I've looked over all the reports from last night, and I'm satisfied."

I almost dropped Ralph's phone. "You're what?"

"Satisfied with Tucker's response to the situation," she continued. "Of course, it will have to go through all the official channels, but he really had no choice but to fire his weapon when the attacker refused to comply. You, on the other hand, did not respond appropriately."

I shifted the phone in my hand. "Excuse me?"

"When the assailant was waving the guns in your direction and in the direction of your fellow agents, you did not fire. Standard operating procedure clearly indicates that—"

Anger rising. Rising.

"The man was holding toy guns," I interjected. "And he couldn't have dropped them even if he wanted to."

"But you didn't know that at the time, now did you?"

Don't lose it, Pat. Don't lose it.

"Oh, wait," I said. "I see. Now I get it."

"Get what?"

"Someone from Governor Taylor's office called you, didn't they?"

"Dr. Bowers." She was speaking very slowly, very distinctly. "I hope you are not accusing me of acting unethically?"

"Why not? That's exactly what I'm doing—"

"Bowers, your techniques are not working. We still have no idea who the killer is—"

"Vanessa might know a name."

"Oh, haven't you heard?" Her voice had become chilly. Distant.

My heart sank. "Heard what?"

"She died this afternoon, Dr. Bowers."

No.

"How did she die? Who was assigned to guard her room? What was the time of death?"

"She died from being shot in the neck, Dr. Bowers, when you led your team into an ambush. Now I'd like you to stop all this nonsense about Jonestown and killer cults and focus on finding the man who shot her or I'm pulling you off the case. One more screw-up, and you're going back to Denv—"

"I think I'm losing you, Margaret," I said.

"Don't hang up on me, Dr.—"

I hung up and then shut off Ralph's phone. I was tempted to drop it against the garage door at about eighty miles per hour, but caught myself just in time.

65

Sheriff Wallace met me at the door. "Hey."

"Hey." I avoided mentioning my conversation with Margaret. I just wasn't up for it. I peered past him and looked inside the house. Blood spatter on the wall and doorframe told me where the shooter and the victim were standing at the time of the murder. Abrams's workout bag lay by the door, a racquetball racket leaning next to it. He might've been on his way out when he was attacked.

We followed the dried blood trail through the house to Abrams's bedroom. He'd been dragged into the closet.

"And Jolene's body? Where was that found?" I asked.

"Over yonder. On the treadmill."

"Treadmill?"

"Yeah."

Treadmill?

"By the way, I don't know if this matters now that Grolin's dead," he said. "But I finished going through his credit card statements."

"And?"

"That leather jacket he likes to wear? He bought it from the Gap over there in Hanes Mall last spring. Guess who was working at the Gap that day?"

"Jolene."

"Yup."

I thought for a minute. It was all too perfect. Someone had been framing Grolin and planning it for close to a year. "Any other leather jackets purchased that day?"

"Other jackets?"

"From the Gap. Were any other leather jackets purchased that day, or maybe later that week?"

He looked perplexed. "I don't know."

"Find out."

Lien-hua entered the bedroom. Ralph was right behind her.

"Ralph," I said. "What's going on? Why didn't you tell me about this crime scene when you were at the safe house?"

"I thought you'd appreciate a little time away from the case."

"Why?"

He glared at me. "I flew Tessa in so you could straighten things out with her, right?"

"Yeah."

"So do it."

I felt my fingers tense. Anger began to curl through me. At Margaret for being Margaret. At Tucker for rushing in last night. At the Illusionist for winning. At Ralph for being right. "But you should have known I'd come out here after talking to Lien-hua on the phone—"

"Yeah," he said icily. "You're right. I should have known."

"Listen, it's important for me to be here at this crime scene." I said it loud enough for everyone to hear, but I knew I was saying it for myself. Silence in the room. *There are some things more important than crime scenes,* I heard a voice inside of me say. At first I thought it sounded like the voice of my dead wife. But then I realized it sounded more like the voice of her only daughter.

I tried to shake the thoughts from my head, get focused again. No one responded to my comments. I continued, "So, he was shot yesterday morning, right?"

"Yeah," said Ralph. I could tell by his tone that he was still upset.

I turned around and scanned the room, expecting to see a pawn somewhere. When my eyes came to rest on the treadmill, I wasn't disappointed. A white one. "But why Abrams?" I asked, exasperated. "How does he fit into this whole thing? What do we know about him?"

"He made a name for himself back in 1991," explained Lien-hua. "That's when North Carolina signed on to become part of the FBI's Violent Criminal Apprehension Program."

"VICAP," I said.

"Yes. He was the one who signed North Carolina in."

It seemed like the case was spinning off sideways, getting skewed. I was starting to doubt I'd ever be able to catch this guy. "Did we get anything on that brush yet?" I was asking everybody. "Get any prints off it? DNA? Anything?"

"Hmm." Ralph scratched at his chin. He seemed to be lightening up. "Far as I know, Brent was taking care of that. We should have had those back by now. Maybe with him being on mandatory leave right now, something slipped through the cracks. I'll check on that."

"I'll do it," said Sheriff Wallace. He stepped away to make the call.

I walked over to the closet. Abrams's body had already been removed. A patch of dried blood stained the carpet.

"Dragged him into the closet," I said. "Why a closet?"

"I think it's part of his narrative, his fantasy life," said Lien-hua. "The first pawn was found in a closet, he strangled Mindy in that cave . . ."

"Maybe he feels at home in tight places," said Ralph.

"Or maybe he likes the dark," added Lien-hua.

I had to let that sink in.

The phone in Ralph's pocket rang. He looked at the number. "It's the police in New Mexico," he said. He headed into another room to take the call in private.

I turned to Lien-hua. "So what's he telling us here?" My approach didn't seem to be working all that well. Maybe hers would.

"He's escalating quickly," she said. "He's shifted from being a serial killer to a spree killer, not taking time to cool down anymore. He left Jolene's body with key FBI leadership from both the past and the present. Maybe he's saying you couldn't catch me then and you can't catch me now."

"You think he's been active since 1991?" I asked.

Lien-hua leaned down, pointed to the bloodstain in the closet. "Maybe. The execution-style murder tells me it wasn't anything personal for him. This was to make a statement, nothing more. Just like Vanessa and the guy in the parking garage, it's all part of the game to him. Anyone and everyone is expendable."

I looked at the treadmill. "So why did he leave her legs on the treadmill?" I asked.

A voice came at us from the doorway: "Legs on a treadmill—*hello!*—running but not going anywhere."

We both turned. Tessa.

"What are you doing here?" I snapped. "I told you to wait in the car."

"I got bored."

"Tessa?" said Lien-hua.

"Yeah. And you must be the woman on the phone."

Lien-hua glanced at me and then back to Tessa. "Yes. I must be. And I think you might be right."

"About what?" I said.

"Running but not going anywhere," she said. "He's summing up our investigation. That's what we've been doing—running but not going anywhere."

I sighed. "C'mon, Tessa. Back to the car." *Well, at least she didn't contaminate the scene. At least they've finished processing it.* "What if there'd been a dead body in there?" I said to her. "What then?"

"Ew. That would've been gross. I would've thrown up."

"That's right. You would have. Now, c'mon."

As we left the room, I had a thought. "By the way, how did you get past those two agents on the porch?"

"I can be pretty convincing when I put my mind to it."

I couldn't argue with that.

"Did you hear that lady?" Tessa was staring at the bloodstained carpet as we walked back to the living room. "She said I was right. About the treadmill. Did you hear that?"

"Oh. Well, she's a profiler," I started to say. "She can't help it—"

Stop, rewind.

Reach out with your hand open . . .

"Um . . . it was a good observation, Tessa. You might have nailed it."

She grunted. "Wow, I'm writing this one down. On Sunday, October 26, 2008, Patrick Bowers actually offers his stepdaughter a compliment."

"Tessa," I said, a slight edge climbing into my voice, "do you know what the word *acerbic* means?"

"No."

"Well, you have an acerbic wit."

She stopped, folded her arms, and cocked her head. "That is *so* not right."

"What?"

"Telling me I'm sour, bitter, and vitriolic."

I stared at her. "I thought you didn't know what acerbic meant?"

"I lied."

This cannot be what all teenagers are like. It just can't be.

"Comes from the Latin," she said. "*Acerbus*. Means bitter, gloomy, and dark."

"Oh," I said. "That's just great."

"I took two years of Latin instead of Spanish in middle school. Latin is a dead language. I thought it'd be cool to study a language that was dead."

Man. Did I really want to take on parenting this girl?

Wait. Stupid question.

Yes.

More than anything else in the world.

Before we made it to the front door, I heard Ralph cussing in the other room. And this was one of those times I didn't think it was a good sign.

"Bodies," he said loud enough for my stepdaughter to hear. "They found fifteen bodies."

66

The color drained from Tessa's face. "What did he say?"

"Tessa, this is why I didn't want you to come along."

"Don't do that," she said. "I hate when people say I told you so!"

"OK. Listen, I'm sorry. Please. I want to make things right between us. It's just that, can you wait outside? Please. For a couple minutes."

"Don't call me names then."

"I won't. I promise."

She plopped onto the front porch swing, and I went back inside to tell Ralph what I thought of him cussing within earshot of my stepdaughter.

From his vantage point, the Illusionist watched the girl swing back and forth, back and forth on the porch. He recognized her right away from his research. Tessa Bernice Ellis, Dr. Bowers's stepdaughter. So, he'd flown her in, brought her to North Carolina to protect her.

How nice.

The Illusionist closed his eyes and let his mind wander, his senses dream, his desires explore the possibilities. Yes, this could mean an even more fitting conclusion to the game.

He scanned the front of the house with the binoculars, studied Bowers's rental car for a moment, made a note to himself that the good doctor had his backpack with him. Probably his climbing gear. Hmm.

He allowed himself one more lingering glance at the girl and then headed back to his house to get his supplies.

Before I could lay into Ralph, I saw the look on his face. "Thirteen of 'em were children," he said.

My mouth went dry. "Thirteen kids?"

He nodded. "No smoke in their lungs."

"They were dead before the fire began."

"Yeah."

"They killed their kids?" said Lien-hua.

"Just like at Jonestown," I said.

"The building next to the house had two adult bodies," said Ralph. "One male, one female. And Kincaid's private plane is gone from the regional airport. Filed a flight plan to Seattle."

"Seattle?" I said. "What's in Seattle?"

"They're checking."

Suddenly the door flew open, and Wallace came ambling into the room, waving his new phone.

"What is it?" I asked.

"The prints," he exclaimed.

"Who?" asked Ralph. "Who is it?"

Wallace shook his head. "If the killer touched the brush he didn't leave any prints. But I think we might have found his next victim. Every bank employee in the country is fingerprinted, so if there's a robbery it's easy to see if it was an inside job—there's a national database of their fingerprints, and we—"

"Yeah, yeah, I know," barked Ralph. The stress of the case was getting to him, to all of us, wearing our patience razor-thin. "Who is she? What's her name?"

"Alice McMichaelson. She works at Second National Bank. Lives in West Asheville."

"She's next," I said.

"Do we have an address on her?" said Ralph.

Sheriff Wallace told it to us.

"Get some cops there *now*," I said to him. "But make them plainclothes in case he's watching the house. This just might be our chance to finally move out in front of him."

67

Alice McMichaelson was sitting in her living room balancing her checkbook when the doorbell rang. Before she could even get up it rang again. *Probably some kind of salesman. Don't they ever give it a rest? I mean, give me a break, this is a Sunday.*

Maybe if she ignored him he'd go away.

Ring. Ring. Ring.

Oh, all right already.

She crossed the carpet and peered out the window. A man wearing khaki pants, a golf shirt, and a maroon windbreaker stood on her porch. When she pulled the curtain to the side, he nodded at her.

Alice opened the door, kept the chain clasped in place. "Yes? May I help you?"

He held up his wallet to show her his badge. "Ma'am. I'm Officer Lewis with the Buncombe County Sheriff's Department. May I come in?"

"Is there some kind of problem?"

"It might be better if I explained it to you inside the house, ma'am."

She looked past him to the car in the driveway. A sedan. Maybe he was off-duty or undercover.

"Please," he said. "There's a very dangerous man on the loose. We think he might be after you. He's unpredictable. He could show up at any time. We need to get you out of here as quickly as possible."

"Who is he? What does he want with me?"

The man glanced over his shoulder and then back toward her. "Think of the worst thing you can. That's him getting started."

She made no move to open the door any wider. Why was this officer by himself? Why didn't he have a partner with him? He must have noticed that she was hesitant. "Look," he said, "we believe you and your children might be in some danger. But I can't force you to do anything. I'll wait here on the porch for you to decide." He handed her a card. "Here. Call this number and they'll confirm I am who I say I am."

68

After I drove Tessa back to the safe house, Sheriff Wallace called to inform me that his men had contacted Alice, but she refused to leave her home. "We can send a squad to surveil her house, but other than that our hands are tied."

I thought back to the hairbrush and the fingerprints and made a couple calls. When I found out Alice had only been working at the bank for less than a week, it gave me an idea. I called Lien-hua and put things into play.

Then I got a text message from Ralph telling me Governor Taylor was scheduled to speak in Seattle to a consortium of tech companies next Monday.

Aha. So that's where Kincaid is planning to strike.

At least we had a week to find him.

------■------

Governor Taylor stood in front of the mirror and tried to concentrate on his speech for Monday. Tried, tried, tried, but the words just wouldn't come.

"We are on the brink of a new chapter in our nation's history," he said to the well-groomed man in the mirror. "A chapter defined not by the throes of terrorism, but by the footnotes of freedom."

No, that wasn't it. The "footnotes of freedom"? Horrible. He'd have to fire his speechwriter tomorrow. He pulled out a pencil. Um, the banner of freedom? Clarion call of freedom? The resounding shout of freedom? Yes. That was good. He liked that.

He scribbled some notes across the page. He liked to use pencil instead of pen since he often wrote, erased, and rewrote phrases dozens of times. He was a precise, careful man. When Sebastian Taylor did something, he did it well. He did it right. It was one of the reasons he was such a good leader.

The presidential election was less than two weeks away, and he was actually glad the Democrats were polling so well; if the Republicans lost this election it would give him a better chance in 2012. Two years to plan, two years to run.

Actually, four years to run. Starting now. With the video bloggers and nearly everything you do showing up on the Internet these days, every speech, every word mattered.

So why did the distant past and his previous career have to come up and haunt him now, right when everything else was coming together?

Kincaid peered out the plane window at the countryside far below. "David," he said without turning to the man beside him.

"Yes, Father?"

"I never told you what happened on November 19th after I woke up by the river. It's time you know." Kincaid rubbed his finger over the scar, caressing the moments, remembering them all. "As you know, a Peoples Temple guard shot me in the shoulder. When I awoke I was in shock, too weak to find my way through the jungle. The only thing I could do was head back to the compound to look for help. I figured there would be others like me who'd fled in the night, who would be returning then, in the daylight. I thought maybe they could help me."

Governor Taylor snapped the pencil in half.

It had been nearly three decades since the assignment. Yes, of course, he'd been in charge of the wet work on the congressman, but he was only doing his job. When Dwyer blew his cover and then

Jones spun out of control, he'd needed to make some split-second decisions to diminish the fallout, to make sure all the evidence pointed where it was supposed to point.

That's when the problems began.

———————■———————

"And were there others left alive, Father?"

"No. I waited all morning. No one came back. I was alone with the bodies. Nearly everyone I knew was dead. I went to the hospital—really, it was only a small cabin—and found some painkillers for my shoulder. I didn't want to go near the pavilion, but I didn't want to leave either . . . I had nowhere to go, so I spent most of the morning waiting, trying not to look at the pavilion. I hid when some looters from the tribes living in the jungle came through. And then . . ."

Kincaid's voice slowed. Became even and hard. "The members of the Guyanese Defense Force arrived. They were laughing, my son, joking about the bodies; about my family and my friends. 'Their brains were asleep before, and now their bodies have joined them.' That's the kind of thing they were saying. But the word they used for 'asleep' could also be translated 'dead' or 'lifeless.' They were saying those things about the people I loved, David."

"Your first family."

"Yes. My first family."

———————■———————

He'd almost finished editing the tape when that stupid kid showed up.

———————■———————

"After they left, three Americans arrived—two men and a woman—and I was about to run up to them when I heard them talking. 'Not quite what we planned, huh?' and then one of them laughed and said, 'No big loss, though.' Then one of the men said something about cleaning out the files, and they headed to Father's cabin. I hid in the shadows and watched them. They started pulling files, grabbing notebooks."

"Destroying evidence?"

Kincaid nodded. "Yes. The links to the CIA's involvement in the shooting, I assume. A radio was on in the background; I could hear news reports of the killings. I wanted to see more, so I pushed open one of the screen doors, and I think they heard me."

No witnesses. Those were his orders. No survivors.

So when the kid opened up that screen door, what was he supposed to do?

"He grabbed a needle, David. And he started chasing me."

The kid ran like a freakin' rabbit through the compound.

Remembering it now, Sebastian Taylor realized he should have grabbed one of the AK-47s that he'd given to his contacts to pass along to Jones's guards. Instead, he'd thought he could cover it up by using one of the needles. But the kid got away. Escaped into the jungle.

"I hid by the river, and watched him through the trees."

The memories came back to him now in fits and starts, one image opening up the next like pages of a book he hadn't opened in years.

He saw the two other agents step out of Jones's cabin. "What were you going to do with that needle?" Felicity said in between sneezes. She was allergic to half the plants in the jungle.

"We have our orders," he told her. "Cole was very clear about our mission."

"You were gonna kill a kid!"

"We need to get out of here." It was Tad.

"I'm not quite done with the tape," he replied.

"I'm not going anywhere," said Felicity. "I can't believe you were going to kill a little kid. This whole mission is a disas—" And she never finished her sentence. Tad had embedded a needle into her neck and depressed the plunger. She was drifting to the ground, shaking.

"What did you do?" yelled Sebastian.

The convulsions began. Felicity was not dying delicately.

"She's nearly compromised this mission three times already. We can't let them know a kid survived," said Tad. "She would have told."

"But you just—"

Tad reached over and grabbed Felicity's armpits; she wasn't dead yet but would be soon. "Help me drag her over to the pavilion. No one will know." She was trying to speak, but her head was jerking back and forth uncontrollably. It wasn't pretty to watch. Tad continued, "We'll tell Cole that Jones's men got to her first. As long as we limit the number of autopsies, we should be all right. And we just won't mention the kid, OK? He was never here. Remember, no survivors. Got it?"

Tad might tell too. He might mention the kid.

"Yeah," said Sebastian, fingering the needle in his hand and eyeing the space between Tad's shoulder blades. "No survivors. I got it."

———————————■———————————

"They killed the woman. Injected her. I saw them do it. Then Sebastian killed the other American."

Kincaid paused, reached into his suit coat, and produced a half-full syringe in a plastic bag. "Sebastian tossed the syringe. I'm not sure why I picked it up, but his fingerprints are all over it. It's time the world knows exactly what kind of man Sebastian Taylor is."

"Is the cyanide still potent, Father?'

"Quite. I had it tested just to be sure."

Kincaid put the plastic bag away. "He was on his way back to Father's cabin when the helicopters arrived."

———————■———————

Then the Rangers and Green Berets showed up, and he had to disappear. Fast. If they saw him there, six other missions in two continents would go down in flames. And so, he never finished editing the tape.

All because of the kid.

———————■———————

"I knew some of the Temple members who came down to identify bodies. They took me back to America with them, said I was one of their children."

Finally, Kincaid turned to look at his faithful son. "David, when I arrived in America, the media was saying the same kinds of things the looters had said about my family. The world has had thirty years to apologize, and no one, apart from a few fringe websites and a couple of self-published books, has tried to imbue compassion and humanity into their tale, has treated them with the respect and dignity they deserve as human beings, as children of our common God."

"And that's why the media leaders are going to pay."

"Yes. That's why they're all going to pay."

———————■———————

Governor Taylor looked at his face in the mirror. His was not the face of a murderer, but of a patriot.

That's all he'd ever been. A patriot. A man who would do what needed to be done for his country. Just like the soldiers of the South had done in the War of Northern Aggression. They'd fought for freedom—freedom for states to make their own laws, to govern themselves. A real freedom. A true freedom.

He'd always done whatever he needed to do to promote freedom. That's what a patriot does.

And now. What needed to be done?

It took him only a moment to decide.

He made the call.

"Yeah?" said the voice on the other end of the line.

"It's me. I have what you want. Meet me in room 611 tomorrow morning at the Stratford Hotel. Ten sharp, before the luncheon. We can take care of things then."

"It'll look like an accident?"

"Don't worry. I've got it all planned out."

Click.

Yes, Sebastian Taylor would do whatever needed to be done.

He was a true patriot.

He scribbled some notes onto the page and set to work finishing his speech.

69

Aaron Jeffrey Kincaid's jet pulled to a stop on one of the corporate runways skirting the edge of the Tri-Cities Regional Airport in northeast Tennessee. It was a small enough airport for him to bribe his way in without the proper paperwork, yet large enough to handle his jet. And it was close to Asheville, less than a ninety minute drive.

He stepped off the jet and onto the tarmac. Drank in the damp autumn air.

This was the last time he would ever use this plane. Well, it had served its purpose. Just as the ranch had. As Rebekah and Caleb had. As Jessica had. As his family had. Everything had a time and a place and a purpose. That was what destiny was all about.

David stood beside him, pocketing his cell phone. "Father, the house is ready."

"Good. It'll give us a chance to rest and prepare for tomorrow's activities."

Just then a van appeared on the edge of the runway and pulled to a stop a few feet from the hangar. The driver's door swung open, and a slim, worried-looking man with trendy glasses stepped out, bowing reverently. "Father."

"Theodore," said Kincaid. "Has everything been arranged?"

"Yes. The uniforms are waiting at the house."

David edged toward the van.

"And the shipment? Has it arrived?"

"Already at the hotel, Father."

"Good." Kincaid scratched at the scar on his wrist. "Now I

believe it's time to discuss Bethanie. She wasn't dead when you left her, Theodore."

A slight pause. "Yes, Father. I know."

David slid into place behind Theodore.

"I gave you specific instructions."

"I'm sorry, Father."

"And so," said Kincaid, "now you have a choice."

He bit his lip. "A choice?"

"Would you like to do it yourself or have David help you?"

Theodore swallowed hard. "Father, please, I did my best."

Kincaid waited silently.

"Please I—"

"All right, David then."

David stepped forward and unleashed a barrage of tightly controlled kung fu moves that broke ribs, crushed the windpipe, and then snapped the neck of the young man who'd first invited him to join the family. It was over in a matter of seconds. Helping people make the transition was, after all, David's specialty.

Kincaid watched the pulverized body twitch on the damp runway.

Thought back to the pavilion.

To the ones who lay down and never stood up again.

To the whirlpool.

To Jessica.

To the words of the Reverend Jim Jones: "To me death is not a fearful thing, it's living that's treacherous."

"Put him in the back of the van," said Kincaid. David and the other men obeyed, dragging the fresh corpse over to the back of the vehicle and hoisting it inside.

"Hide the plane," said Kincaid. "Lock it in the hangar."

Then he climbed into the van with his family and set out to fulfill his destiny.

70

Alice walked down the hallway and entered the bathroom. She was a bit nervous, but at least her children were safe now. That's what mattered most. The children. She'd sent them with Officer Lewis earlier in the day. He'd promised they would be safe with him.

She turned on the bathroom light and caught sight of her jaw line in the mirror. A faint scar was still visible from the time Garrett had attacked her and sent her to the hospital. Yes, she knew what it was like to be threatened by a dangerous man.

She had her instructions and she would do them. She would follow them to the letter.

Alice McMichaelson would do anything to protect her children.

She opened the shower curtain and turned on the water.

The Illusionist grinned.

So now.

Grolin was dead, and Vanessa had expired earlier in the day — how unfortunate. He'd been there when it happened. So very tragic.

True, he'd hoped to stage Grolin's demise a bit more elegantly, a little less obtrusively, but he could only keep him drugged so long.

Besides, sending him into the pro shop delirious had been a stroke of genius. The guy had actually started a fight with Agent Jiang! And inviting Vanessa to the golf course had been risky of course, but he needed to get the agents to a place that was isolated enough for him to control what happened, and where the shooting could take place without any clear witnesses. The idiotic investigators had acted just like he'd predicted. They would never be able to piece it all together.

These were the things the Illusionist thought of as he watched from the shadows outside Alice's house. He remembered the first time he was here, just a few days ago, how hard it had been at the time to say no to himself, to his urges, his desires.

But now the moment was here.

At last.

A few minutes ago Alice had entered the bathroom. He could see steam cloud the windows. As he thought of her showering, his breathing became deeper, quicker.

Yellow lemonade in the sweet summer sun.

Soon. Soon.

He waited. The bathroom light blinked out. With his imagination he watched her step into the hallway and then from the hallway into her room. And, as if by magic, he saw the bedroom light come on, not just in his imagination but for real, and her lithe figure behind the curtains, shedding the towel. Lithe. Yes. That was a good word to describe her. The right word. The perfect word.

Lithe.

He would use that word later, when he wrote about tonight.

Sweet, sweet lemonade.

After a few moments the bedroom light went out. He waited a bit longer but then grew tired of the wait. He'd waited long enough for Alice. Too long. It was time to reward himself for a game well played. Time to enjoy the spoils of war.

He glided up to the house as smooth as a serpent. Donned his gloves. Pulled on the ski mask.

Back door again. This time it was locked. Ah, good. He picked it in less than thirty seconds. Disarmed the security system.

Inside.

He caught the scent of the house, slightly familiar, yet slightly foreign. Sweet and clean with a hint of cigarette smoke from the days when Garrett lived here.

He listened. Nothing but the sounds of a sleeping home. He crept down the hallway. Past Brenda's room. Past Jacob's room. No time to pause and look at the pictures. Not tonight. This was the last move of the game. He'd reached across the board and touched her, and now it was time to take her home, to make her his.

The Illusionist eased the bedroom door open and saw Alice lying on the bed. A still form beneath the covers.

He heard a voice in his head, a little boy crying out from inside a closet: *"Mama?"*

No.

"Are you there, Mama?"

No.

He wouldn't think of those things.

He didn't have to, and he wasn't going to. No. No. No!

"What's that smell, Mama?"

Stay in control. One step ahead. Always one step ahead.

Alice had left the window open a crack and pulled a wool blanket up to her neck. Red hair sprawled across her pillow. He slipped his hand into his pocket, pulled out the cloth with the medication on it, and tried to tune in to the gentle rhythm of her breathing. Couldn't quite. Closed his eyes for a moment to drink in the dainty perfume that lingered in the air. Her perfume. Her lovely perfume. A way to touch her.

Reached down. Grabbed the covers.

Checkmate.

Threw them off.

Found only a pile of pillows and a wig. Heard a woman's voice behind him.

"Don't move. You move and you die."

———————————■———————————

Checkmate.

We had him.

I heard Lien-hua tell him not to move. I flipped on the hall lights and rushed out of the bathroom where I'd been hiding. I could see her standing in the bedroom two meters behind the killer, her weapon trained on his back. "On your knees," she commanded. "Now."

He stood frozen beside the bed, both of his hands in the air.

He was dressed all in black. He wore a ski mask. I couldn't see his face.

"Spread your hands!" I yelled. "All the way out. Slowly." I took a cautious step forward.

He remained perfectly still, his chest the only thing moving.

Why isn't he moving? What's going on?

"We have him," I said into the mic patch I was wearing, heard Ralph reply, "We're coming in."

Outside the house, searchlights burst on, and the agents and officers we'd hidden throughout the neighborhood stepped into position. Alice had agreed to help us. "Whatever you want me to do," she said, "to protect the children." So we'd put our people in place, leaving just enough space for the Illusionist to make his move. Air support would be here any minute. He was not getting away.

"On your knees," Lien-hua yelled. "Now!"

The Illusionist knelt slowly.

I stepped forward and leveled my gun. "I said spread your hands."

"Nice move, Patrick." He kept his voice to a low whisper. I couldn't tell if it was the same voice I'd heard on the phone or not. It sounded vaguely familiar but was too soft to recognize. He was moving his hands evenly toward his head, carefully. "But the game's not over yet."

Just as his fingers touched the side of his head, the lights went out.

A thrash of movement by my feet.
A flash of gunpowder. Someone crashing into me.
I was on the floor.
I heard a gasp.
A thud.
A soft moan from beside the closet.
The sound of breaking glass.
A scream.

71

Tessa was sandwiched on the couch between the two officers, pretending to watch some lame TV show with them.

Sitting on the couch like a family. Watching TV with two cops.

How pathetic.

Like a family.

She thought of Patrick and being at that crime scene earlier in the day. And picturing the legs of a dead woman—*her sawed-off legs!*—on a treadmill. It was too much. Flying in here, meeting up with Patrick. Hearing about those people in the fire. Too much. Way too much.

She'd seen those buildings burning on his computer.

There were bodies inside the buildings.

Dead people.

She needed to cut herself. Tonight.

She stood up.

"Where are you going?" asked Officer Muncey.

"Just to the bathroom, OK!"

As she walked away she heard Officer Muncey mumble, "I thought I was done babysitting when I got out of high school." She whispered the words, but Tessa heard her. She heard every syllable.

Tessa locked the bathroom door and pulled the razor blade out of her purse.

■

I turned on my flashlight. Leapt to my feet. Scanned the room. He was gone.

Lien-hua was down.

"Lien-hua!" I ran to her.

She stirred. Rubbed her head. "Blindsided me," she muttered. Her eyes slowly came into focus. He'd just knocked her down. That was all. "But I got two kicks in first."

She'd had less than a second. Two kicks? Amazing.

"I heard a shot," I said.

"It wasn't me."

I turned around. The window was shattered. I had no visual on the suspect. "He's mobile. I repeat, the subject is mobile," I yelled into my mic.

Did he get past me?

Alice!

I ran back to the bathroom. "Alice?"

"Did you get him?" her voice quavered.

"We're going to."

She stared at me from the shower, fully clothed, a bulletproof vest on. All part of the plan. Lien-hua had staged the shower, slipped into the bedroom to lure him out. At least Alice's kids weren't here; that was good. Federal protection. She'd be joining them in a few minutes. I heard shots fired outside and made it to the window just in time to see a dark form leap over a fence three houses away and disappear. Someone lay facedown in the backyard. A police officer.

"Officer down!" I yelled. We were ready to contain the killer, had roadblocks in place around the whole neighborhood, but I hadn't expected him to move so quickly.

"Suspect heading south along Virginia Street," somebody said.

"Any word?" I yelled into my mic patch. "Anybody?" I heard shouts and confused voices. Then Wallace's voice: "Cherokee Avenue heading west."

He's left-handed... Left-handed subjects tend to turn right when fleeing, but when they meet an obstacle, they move to their left...

Wait, he would know that.

"Get to the fence," I hollered. "Suspect will head west through the field, then north at the fence. Cut him off. I repeat, west then north."

A voice came back. "Unit three in pursuit."

I ran to the bedroom window and stared out across the neighborhood, trying to orient myself to the landscape again, to map out the streets and overlay them against the topography. "All units on the perimeter," I said, "suspect is male, white, six foot one, two-hundred pounds, wearing black pants, black sweatshirt. Armed and dangerous. Approach with extreme care."

If only there were square city blocks here. It would be so much easier to contain him.

"Get to Richmond Avenue," I yelled. "He'll be heading for the strip of woods running south by southeast. Hurry. If he gets to the subdivision beyond the river, there'll be too many places for him to hide. Hold your positions. Control all exits."

I stared out across the street, saw the outlet roads being shut down by our roadblock, saw the string of slowing taillights as the streets leading into and out of the subdivision were sealed off. A few police cars raced to the scene, an ambulance flashed by and then nudged through the roadblock, bringing help to the injured officer lying on the lawn. Just then, the helicopters came roaring in. Too late. Everything was too late.

Still no electricity. "Can we get these lights on?" I yelled. I heard the shuffle of feet as some officers headed to the circuit breaker. Then Dante's voice in my ear. "He's not here. It's like he disappeared into thin air."

I smashed my fist into the wall.

Ralph burst through the door.

"He made it to the subdivision," I muttered. "We can search house to house, but there are too many places for him to hide in there. My guess is we lost him."

Ralph began filling the room with curses. "What happened to these lights?"

I shook my head. "He must have used a small electromagnetic pulse device. Maybe planted it in the dining room or connected it to the security alarm on his way in. He had the trigger hidden beside his ear."

I heard an officer from the living room. "I've got it, right here!"

"A trigger by his ear?" said Lien-hua.

Someone must have found the breaker; the lights came back on again.

"It's not that uncommon," I said. "Suicide bombers sometimes thread a detonator cord up their shirt and tape it to the back of their neck or hide it behind their ear so if they're told to put their hands on their head they can still detonate their device. I shouldn't have let him move his hands in close like that."

He got away. Again.

He was ready for us.

Ralph turned to Lien-hua. "You OK?"

"I'm fine." She kicked the closet door with a yell, splitting it in half. Her voice was on fire. "We had him. I can't believe he got away!"

Ralph was admiring her work on the door. "Nice kick."

I glanced out the window. "Thank God that officer was wearing a bulletproof vest." One of the paramedics was helping her to her feet, leading her to the ambulance.

"All right, people, listen," Ralph shouted to the pack of officers now entering the house. "We go door to door. Let's move!"

72

I shoved my suitcase into the backseat of the car next to my climbing gear and stared up at the methodical gray slabs sliding across the sky. Dark continents hanging from heaven. The temperature hovered right around freezing; the air was wet and heavy. Freezing rain — or maybe even snow — was on its way.

Here's what I knew:

(1) I was off the case. Last night was it, the last straw for Margaret. She was holding me responsible for Joseph Grolin and Vanessa Mueller's deaths; and of course last night when the killer got away — well, that was my fault too. So Tessa and I were flying back to Denver today. And when all the internal investigations were over, I'd be lucky to get a job as a truancy officer in a middle school — at least according to Margaret.

(2) Alice and her children were safe, at least for the moment. Everything had turned so explosive that Ralph had kept her location top secret. He didn't even tell me where he sent them.

(3) The Illusionist was still on the prowl. We hadn't found any sign of him last night, even after searching the entire neighborhood.

(4) Aaron Jeffrey Kincaid and his group never arrived in Seattle. It was like they'd dropped off the planet. That worried me a little, but it looked like the team still had a few more days to find him.

344

(5) The safe house had run out of Mountain Java Roasters coffee beans. All we had left was tea.

I could tell already, it was going to be another rough day.

———————————◾———————————

I still had some things to pick up from the federal building, but maybe I could get those on the way to the airport. My emotions? Honestly, they were mixed. Maybe I was better off at a desk job in Denver. I'd helped narrow the suspect pool here and focus the search area, but still, I felt empty, useless, like a failure. Yes, it would give me more time with Tessa, but I wanted to catch this guy. Wanted it bad.

I wasn't sure if I would see Brent Tucker again before I had to leave town, so I gave him a call to encourage him. After all, I was beginning to understand how he felt. "You're a good man, Brent Tucker," I said as I walked into the kitchen and found Tessa foraging for some breakfast. "I appreciate all your hard work on this case."

"Thank you, Dr. Bowers," he said. "It was an honor to work with you. I look forward to the day our paths cross again." After a couple minutes we both said our good-byes and hung up.

"Is there any coffee?" Tessa asked groggily.

"You drink coffee?" I said. "Oh, right. A twenty-first-century teenager. Of course."

"What's that supposed to mean?"

"Nothing," I said. "I think we're out."

"Aha." She held up a coffee can she'd found in the cupboard. "Want some?"

I read the label. "Hmm. I think tea this morning. But I'll brew it for you if you want."

"I can do it," she said.

"I know. Just let me. Please. Have a seat." I pulled out the chair for her. She hesitated for a moment and then eased into it. "Want some cereal too?"

"Whatever."

While the coffee percolated I searched for some cereal. "So," I said to her. "Almost packed?"

"Almost. So, the guy got away, huh?"

Great. Make me feel even worse.

"Yeah, but they'll get him. There are good people on the case . . . and I guess this will free me up to spend more time with you."

Silence. I waited.

Nothing.

"How does that sound?"

"Whatever."

"Well, are you glad you got to miss a day of school?" I opened the fridge and pulled out some milk and OJ.

Tessa shrugged.

C'mon, Pat, think. You can do better than that.

"Tessa, do you know what the most dangerous shark in the world is?"

She grunted in a teenage girl sort of way. "That was random."

"Well, do you know?"

She rolled her eyes. "The bull shark. Everyone knows that."

Kincaid led his family through the staff entrance to the Stratford Hotel. He recognized the faces of some of the guests who were milling around. Even though most attendees had come last night for the opening session, the most prestigious guests were arriving this morning by helicopter, trying to beat the snowstorm that was predicted to hit the area.

Security was tight. As tight as a glove. Metal detectors had been set up at every public entrance. But no one was the least bit suspicious of Kincaid and his family.

After all, they'd been hired as the caterers for this morning's event.

It was time to prepare the food.

I opened the cupboard and pulled out a box of peanut-butter-flavored cereal. "How's this?"

She shook her head very, very slowly. "I'm allergic to peanuts. I've always been allergic to peanuts."

Oh boy.

"I must have forgot."

"I thought you were supposed to notice everything."

"So they say."

Silence again.

So notice something already.

"Um, right now, I notice that your left eye is slightly darker brown than your right one."

She grunted. "Brilliant."

I heated some water for tea and poured myself a glass of juice. "Do you want some OJ?"

"I guess."

The coffee was ready. I poured her a cup, and then I studied her for a moment. "I notice you're wearing long sleeves again, and I remember seeing scars on Cherise's left arm back when we were living in New York City, and I'm wondering if . . ."

She stared past me quietly, wouldn't look at me.

Careful, Pat, don't blow this.

"Sugar and cream?"

"Black."

You can get into all that later . . . Reach out to her with your hand open . . . Do it slower . . . that way she knows you're not going to hurt her . . .

I set it on the table. "That's all. Just long sleeves."

After a brief silence she said, "Well, so far your powers of perception are unparalleled. 'The girl is wearing long sleeves.' That oughtta crack the case wide open. No wonder you get the big bucks."

347

I took a slim breath. "Do you ever think about wearing a color other than black?"

"Like what?"

"I don't know. Pink, maybe."

"I look better in black."

"How's your coffee?"

She drank some. "Horrible."

Well, at least she had good taste.

I found some puffed rice cereal and poured it into a bowl for her.

"I notice that you're wearing your mother's perfume."

She paused with the coffee cup halfway to her lips. Just then the phone—Ralph's phone—rang. I glanced at the number on the screen: unknown.

—■—

Kincaid walked around the magnificent enclosed courtyard of the Stratford Hotel. It was absolutely breathtaking: hanging gardens, verandas, walkways, fountains. And winding around everything was an indoor whitewater river with a pool at the base of an eight-foot waterfall. Even though the temperature outside was dropping, in here it was still over 60°F. Right now the hotel staff was busy setting up fifty round tables on the east side of the courtyard for the luncheon.

And in less than two hours the tables would be full.

Yes, his family had been infected and would be breathing the airborne bacteria on the guests as they served them, but he wasn't going to take any chances.

He went back into the kitchen where his family was preparing the meat. As Marcie walked past, he nodded to her. She lowered her gaze and nodded back deferentially.

Humans typically contract both tularemia and Crimean-Congo hemorrhagic fever through ticks, but either can also be contracted through direct contact with the blood of infected livestock. He'd opted for the cattle rather than the ticks. In fact, he'd infected his whole herd. Even now the roasts that the conference attendees would be eating were soaking in the infected blood he'd shipped on Friday.

Governor Taylor arrived at the Stratford Hotel and went up to his suite of rooms. The presidential suite. *Aptly named*, he thought as he slid his key into the lock.

Anita Banner followed the governor closely, wearing her favorite skirt, enjoying the turned heads of all the young men she passed. Soon she'd be able to afford an even better skirt. In fact, a whole new wardrobe. A whole new life.

A life finally free from the groping hands of Sebastian Taylor.

Tessa watched to see if I'd answer the phone.

It rang again. I reached for it.

She ventured a bite of cereal.

I flipped the phone open and then snapped it shut, turning off the ringer when I did.

She'd been following my movements out of the corner of her eye. "Why didn't you answer that?"

"I was busy."

"Doing what?"

"Noticing you."

Suddenly I remembered the words from Christie's note: *Don't run from the risk of loving her . . .* "We need to be here for each other," I said. I wondered if Christie had left a similar note for Tessa. I'd never asked her. *Make it right, Pat. C'mon.*

Tessa was toying with her spoon. "I found it in the dresser."

"Found what?"

"Mom's perfume. It's OK, isn't it? That I'm wearing it, I mean?" For a moment she almost looked shy. A shy raven.

"Yeah. Of course. I'm glad you're wearing it. Really."

"Yeah?"

"Yeah. It's cool."

"Cool?" she said with a slight grimace. "Did you just say *cool*?"

"Is that OK? Is it still cool to say cool?"

"I guess," she said. "It just sorta surprised me . . ."

I picked up the jug of milk and a jet of pain shot through my shoulder. I flinched and set the jug down again.

"What's wrong?" she asked.

"Nothing."

"You're lying. Don't lie to me."

"You're right." My back was throbbing. "OK, honestly, I hurt my shoulder pretty bad yesterday."

"Doing what?"

"Someone tried to blow me up."

"Really?" She sipped her coffee.

"Yeah."

"Who?"

I stirred some honey into my tea. "I'm not certain, but I'm reasonably sure it was the serial killer."

"Oh," she said, and then, "How many people has he killed so far?"

"At least six. Maybe more. Probably more."

"So, not up to the average of eight victims yet? I mean, for North American serial killers?"

I hesitated. "You know, in some families this kind of conversation would seem a little odd."

"Not in this one," she said.

I blew on my tea. "Not quite up to eight yet. As far as we know."

We ate our cereal.

"So, why do they do it?" she asked after a few minutes.

I gave her my stock answer. "Well, I try not to ask why. You get sidetracked doing that."

She scoffed. "Yeah, right. That's a cop-out if I ever heard one. I know you wonder. You have to. You're too curious about stuff not to."

My cup of tea trembled in my fingers. Her words struck home. "Well, I guess maybe I have, but in the end I think the why is easy: killers want the same things out of life everyone wants—fulfillment, accomplishment, a sense of worth, acceptance, power—"

"Love."

I fumbled for what to say. "Yeah. That too. But they don't know the right way to get it."

Neither do you.

"No one does," she said. "Not all the time, at least."

I couldn't tell if she was saying that as a simple observation, or as something more personal. After a moment she added, "So then what makes us different from them?"

I was about to say something trite, clichéd, stupid. But the truth is, there's only a fine line that separates us from them, and sometimes it wavers back and forth like a snake in the sand. Sometimes we step over it, all of us do. Curiosity, maybe. Desire. Anger. Who knows. But the ones who step over with both feet are still just as human as we are. All of them are: those people in Jonestown, the killers I track. They're searching for hope, looking for love, trying to figure things out. Just like us. In so many ways they're just like us. That's the scariest truth of all.

"Sometimes it's hard to tell the difference," I said. "I guess a lot of it boils down to the choices we make." Then I remembered a quote I heard once. "I think it was Goethe who said that all of us have within us the potential to commit any crime."

"Something like that." She sipped at her coffee. "What do you mean?"

"Goethe wrote, 'There is no crime of which I do not deem myself capable.' At least that's the most popular translation."

I took a long look at her. "How do you know that? How do you know all this stuff?"

"The Internet," she said, as if that explained everything.

"Oh yeah," I said. "I've heard of that." I waited to see her reaction.

"And I like to read too. I read a lot." She took a bite of her cereal. "I read your books."

"You did? What did you think?"

She shrugged. "They're OK, I guess. Kinda boring."

Well, then.

I reached into my pocket. I wasn't sure if now was a good time, but I couldn't think of a better one. "Hey. I got you a birthday present. Sorry it's late."

She eyed me. "What is it?"

"I'm not telling. It'd take away the surprise." I set the small rectangular box on the table. She looked at the present but didn't reach for it. I slid it to her. "You'll have to open it."

She picked it up abruptly, tore the gold foil wrapping paper away, flipped open the fuzzy gray box, and then stopped. She didn't even remove the necklace.

"It's got your birthstone," I said.

"Tourmaline."

"Yeah. They had other colors, but I thought you'd like black the best."

She set the box back onto the table.

"Do you like it?"

Tessa shoved her cereal bowl to the side and blinked, letting her eyelids rise very slowly. "So that's what this is all about."

"What?"

She looked around the room. "This. All this."

"What are you talking about?"

Her eyes became razors. "Why didn't you ask me if I wanted to move to Denver?"

"What do you mean?"

"After Mom died. We just picked up and moved. Why didn't you ask me if I wanted to move?"

"Well, I just thought it might be best for both of us to get some space—"

"For both of us?"

"Yeah."

"And how did you come to know what would be best for me?"

"Tessa, I—"

"We're supposed to be a family. Families make choices *together* about what's best for *everyone*, not just for the one in charge."

Her words seared the air between us. I had no idea what to say. "Listen, I—"

"You took me away from all my friends." Her lips quivered for a moment, and then the dam broke. "My mom dies, and you make me leave everyone I know and move across the country, and all I ever wanted was a family like Cherise has—a mom and a dad—and when Mom met you, I thought maybe it would happen, just maybe I'd finally have someone to teach me the things dads are supposed to teach their daughters—I don't know, like about life or guys or whatever and maybe come to my volleyball games and make me do my homework when I don't want to and tell me I'm pretty sometimes and give me a hard time about my boyfriends and take a picture of me in my prom dress and then stand by my side one day when I get married . . ."

My heart was breaking, wrenching in half, but I felt powerless. "I never knew—"

By then tears were rolling down her cheeks. "You never asked!" Her voice was ripe with pain.

"I'm so sorry, Tessa, I—"

She grabbed the necklace box and threw it at my chest. The

tourmaline necklace clattered to the floor. "You can keep your stupid necklace, *Patrick*!" She rose from the table. "You can't buy my love!"

Tessa swept out of the room, and I sat there, stunned, suspended in time. A cold silence swallowed the room.

Go to her. Tell her you're sorry. Do something!

I stood up and started for her room. Stopped with one foot in the hallway.

Wait. You need to give her some space. Right now that's what she needs . . . remember? Reach out to her slowly . . . That way she knows you're not going to hurt her.

Maybe I could drive over to the federal building, retrieve the rest of my things, and then come back to straighten things out. I didn't want to push her, pressure her. I wanted to respect her, show her I really did care.

I slipped into the master bedroom, grabbed my wallet, and then plugged Ralph's cell phone in so that when he picked it up later it would be charged. As I passed Officers Muncey and Stilton on my way through the dining room, Patricia Muncey asked what was up. "I'll be back in a few minutes," I mumbled, preferring not to explain what was really up.

The black cat nearly tripped me as it jumped out of the way when I threw open the front door. Once outside, I had to turn my collar up against the freezing rain that had begun to splinter through the dark morning clouds.

I climbed into the car and headed to the federal building. All around me the day seemed soaked with the foretaste of death.

73

Tessa collapsed onto the bed, sobbing. Her heart screamed out, ached for love, but no one heard. No one at all.

She hated Patrick and she loved him at the same time. Both! She wanted to hug him and she wanted to slap him. It didn't make any sense, but it was true. It didn't matter though. Nothing mattered.

She pulled out the razor blade.

She couldn't stand this anymore. Nothing had changed. She flew all the way out here, and nothing was any different. Patrick wasn't her dad. Of course he wasn't. No one was. What was she really hoping for, anyway?

She heard a car engine outside her window and looked up from the bed just in time to see Patrick backing down the driveway.

Going off to work again. Running away. Leaving her alone.

There'd always be another killer out there somewhere. That's what really mattered to him, anyway. That's what he loved. Not her.

If only she wasn't in his life, they could both be happy.

In that instant she knew what she had to do: go back to New York. Hitchhike to the City. Maybe she could move in with Cherise or one of her other friends. She was old enough to get a job, to live on her own. All she had to do was slip out and get away before he came back. It's what he really wanted, anyway. It's what they both really wanted.

After all, it wasn't his fault he'd fallen in love with a woman who had a stupid teenage daughter. What was he supposed to do? Suddenly know how to take care of a teenager? Suddenly care about the daughter too, just 'cause he loved her mom?

Tessa wiped at her tears and looked around the room.

She could solve everything by leaving. That's what she needed to do.

She slid the blade into the back pocket of her jeans and flopped her suitcase open. She couldn't bring the whole thing, way too obvious. Just the knapsack. That's all she would need. She yanked it out of the closet and began to stuff her clothes inside it.

74

Ten minutes after leaving the house, I walked up to my desk in the federal building. The office chatter drifted into silence as I walked in. No surprise there. I gave a slight nod to the people staring at me and maneuvered between the tables to my makeshift work station. I didn't see Ralph, Lien-hua, or Sheriff Wallace, just Margaret watching me from behind the glass door of her office.

I ignored her.

I stared at my desk. Not a whole lot here. A couple notepads, a framed picture of my wedding, the mic patch I'd been using and must have forgotten to turn in. As I was grabbing my files, papers, notes, I noticed a manila folder—today's briefing. There was really no good reason for me to look at it now except that Margaret wouldn't want me to.

I flipped the folder open.

The Hazmat team in New Mexico had sent in the tissue samples, and the lab found a bacterial agent, just as I'd feared they might. Pathogen type: unknown.

■

Aaron Jeffrey Kincaid made sure the preparations for the meal were going well and then slipped quietly away from the family. He had a special role to fulfill in today's narrative. There was someone he needed to meet.

■

The phone on my desk rang. I looked around. No one else nearby. I should just let it ring. After all, I didn't work here anymore.

But then again, maybe it was Lien-hua calling to say good-bye.

I snatched up the receiver. "Bowers here."

"I wanted Alice." The same voice distortion software as before. I waved to Margaret, pointed frantically to her phone. She scowled at me but at last picked it up.

"Well," I said. "I guess last night *you* were the one who was too slow."

"How did you know I'd run down Richmond?"

"Fleeing suspects follow standard patterns. You're not nearly as clever as you think."

I heard his breathing grow heavier. Good. I was getting on his nerves.

I decided to test him. See how much he really knew. "You killed an officer last night. They're not going to be satisfied bringing you in alive anymore. Turn yourself in. Save us another funeral."

"All of us are on our way to a funeral, Dr. Bowers. Don't you see that yet? It's just a matter of timing and location. You of all people should know that."

He doesn't know the officer lived. He thinks he killed her.

"So that's it, then?" I needed to get him to stumble. To give something up. "We're all just pawns waiting to die?"

His voice became acid. "Dr. Bowers, my mother was murdered in cold blood. No reason. No design. She was a prostitute. You know what that means, don't you? She was expendable. How many hours do you think the cops spent tracking down the killer of a trailer-trash hooker?"

I had no idea if he was telling the truth or not, but I played it like he was. "No one is expendable," I said. "And I'm sorry about your mother, really—"

"No you aren't. No one was sorry. No one is sorry."

"Was she a pawn too then?"

"We're all pawns."

"Then who's playing the game?"

"God is. He's knocking us off the chessboard one at a time, littering this pathetic little planet with the corpses of his beloved little children. Just passing the span of eternity killing us off to entertain the angels."

His words chilled me. They could have come from my own lips a dozen times over the last few months.

I thought of Christie.

Remembered her note. *All I can control is what I do with each moment, with this moment, right now.*

"None of us are pawns," I said. "Not you, not your mother."

He snickered. "If I kill someone I spend the rest of my life in jail or maybe I get the needle, but if God beats me to it, he gets to stay in heaven and be worshiped by his faithful little minions. You tell me—is that fair?"

"Death wasn't his idea." I could almost hear Christie speaking to me, the words of her note finally making sense after all this time. I could hardly believe I was saying this, wondered if I really believed it myself. "But life is. Life has always been his idea."

"Pain was his idea. It shapes us. Defines us."

"No, we're defined by our choices, our priorities, the things we love—"

"Well," said the killer. "I know what I love."

"And what's that?"

A pause. "Bethanie and Alexis weren't mine."

I'm tired of playing it his way. "I know."

"I'm not sloppy like that."

Push him. Get him to play a card. "What then? Did you call me to confess?"

"I know who the other killer is."

It's another one of his games. His tricks. "Yeah, well, I'm off the case. Tell somebody else."

"You're the only one I'll talk to—"

I slammed down the phone.

There. I made my move. Let's see what the Illusionist does now.

———————————■———————————

Tessa finished stuffing her clothes into her knapsack and overheard the two cops talking in the living room. "You all right with the kid?" the guy said.

"Of course. What's up?"

"I'm gonna run out and grab some cigarettes." It was Officer Stilton again.

"Can't you wait half an hour? They're leaving in a few minutes, anyway."

"Half an hour?" he scoffed. "Obviously you don't smoke."

Tessa listened intently.

Officer Muncey sighed. "All right, then. Whatever."

"I'll be right back." He walked out the door.

This would make it even easier. All she had to do was slip past one cop to be on her way to New York City. She watched out the window as the guy climbed into the car and backed down the driveway.

———————————■———————————

"Bowers," screamed Margaret from her office. "What did you just do!" She burst through the doorway.

Call back, c'mon, call back . . .

I stared at the phone. "He'll call back."

"You hung up on him!"

Call back. "He has to be in control, he'll call back."

She was fuming, ready to explode.

"Let me stay, Margaret."

The phone began to ring.

"Pick it up, Bowers!"

"Let me go after this guy."

She reached for the phone.

"He won't talk to you. You heard him."

Ring, ring. Ring, ring.

"Answer it!" she yelled.

"Let me go after him. Tell me I'm on the case."

"No."

Ring, ring.

"Then I'm leaving." I turned to go.

"All right! Now ans—"

"Say it."

"You're on the case!"

I snatched up the receiver. "Yeah."

"You do not hang up on me, Dr. Bowers!" Each word was soaked with the killer's slow, distinct rage.

"I don't think you know who he is," I said. "Why would you tell me his name?"

"I don't like sharing center stage."

"No. Too obvious. You wouldn't give him to me. You'd go after him yourself." *There's something more going on here . . .*

"He's an old friend, Dr. Bowers. It wouldn't be right to kill him. Let's just say I made a promise."

"Who is he then?" I was testing him, of course. I already knew Kincaid was the man.

"I can't tell you that. Fact is, he probably convinced someone else to do the dirty work for him anyway; he's good at that. But I can tell you this: he'll be at the Stratford Hotel, ten o'clock this morning."

What? Not Seattle next week?

The luncheon.

Kincaid is going after the governor today!

Then the Illusionist hung up the phone, and the office became a frenzy of activity as people tried to trace the call. *If he really knows Kincaid, then Kincaid can lead me to him.*

Margaret stormed over to me. "Don't ever do that—"

I grabbed the things off my desk. "I'm going to the Stratford Hotel."

She seemed to ponder my words, the killer, the body in the trunk of her car, her prospects at Quantico, all in one condensed, career-defining moment, and finally gave me a brisk nod. "All right. I'll have Ralph and Lien-hua meet you there. Be careful."

"I will be. And thanks."

She turned and walked away, and that was that.

Before I left, I called Officer Muncey to tell her I wouldn't be back right away and to make sure Tessa was OK. "Don't worry. She's fine. She's in her room. I think she's packing."

"OK."

I hung up and patted my SIG P229.

Bring this guy in, Pat.

Next stop, the Stratford Hotel.

75

Lien-hua beat me to the Stratford Hotel and met me at the door.
"Just got a call from the Tennessee Highway Patrol," she said as we
stepped inside. "Someone saw two guys fighting on a runway at a
regional airport not far from here. Security found Kincaid's plane.
It had over a dozen meal trays."

"So he's got some helpers." I thought for a moment. And then it
hit me. "They infected their livestock; you think they might have
infected themselves?"

"I hope not," she said.

I hated to even think about the consequences if they had.

Ralph burst in. "Let's go." He pushed his way to the front of
the line by the registration counter. "We need to see the president
of the hotel, now!"

━━━━━━━━━━━━ ■ ━━━━━━━━━━━━

Nell Prescott, president and CEO of Stratford Enterprises, wel-
comed us into her office and listened to us intently. After hearing our
hurried explanation, she immediately led us to the hotel's security
center. A bank of video monitors stared down from the walls of
the confined, dimly lit quarters.

A tightly muscled bulldog of a man bustled up to us. "What's
going—"

"Mr. Williamson," said Nell Prescott. "These people are from
the FBI. We have a situation."

His whole body seemed to snap to attention. "What kind of
situation?"

Tessa waited until Officer Stilton had driven away, then she grabbed her knapsack and opened the bedroom door.

She could hear Officer Muncey watching TV in the living room.

Tessa crept down the hallway toward the front door. She eased forward, reached for the doorknob, and then heard the cop's voice right beside her: "And where do you think you're going, young lady?"

Tessa whipped around and saw Officer Muncey standing beside her. "I'm just going to do some homework at the table. *OK*?"

Officer Muncey gestured with a nod. "Kitchen is over there."

"I know!"

Tessa stomped into the kitchen and threw her bag onto the table. She didn't see the necklace Patrick had tried to give her anywhere around. Well, good for him. He must have taken it with him. Who cares.

Aaron Jeffrey Kincaid scanned the lobby. He didn't like that they were cutting things this close, but it was part of the deal he'd made with Sevren to assure that his former roommate wouldn't pass his name along to the authorities.

Just then, he heard a man whisper his name.

He spun around and recognized his contact from Trembley's description. Kincaid accepted the package and handed over the envelope of cash. The man hurried away.

As he watched him leave, Kincaid noticed a scurry of activity behind the check-in counter. Two security guards were talking into their earpieces, staring suspiciously around the lobby.

So, they knew already. He hadn't expected this until after the meal at least.

But it didn't matter. They were too late. People were already sitting down to eat. Still, he needed to tell his family that the plans had changed. They'd need to be ready for his signal.

And he needed to find the governor.

------■------

After we briefed Mr. Williamson on the basic facts of the case, he shook his head. "We already swept the whole place. Believe me. The ballroom, the lobby, the gardens, everything. We even brought in the dogs. It's secure."

Lien-hua shook her head. "It wouldn't be an explosive device, maybe something chemical or biological. Closer to what happened at Jonestown."

"Jonestown?" Williamson gasped.

I didn't have the time or energy to explain everything to this guy. "What about air vents, air-conditioning ducts, things like that?"

"I told you," said Williamson flatly. "It's secure. Do you have a suspect?"

"Aaron Jeffrey Kincaid," I said. "Wait. That's it." I flipped open my laptop, pulled up the picture of Kincaid that Lien-hua had found yesterday while researching him. Then I opened the face recognition program and asked Williamson, "Where can I hook into your video feeds?"

------■------

Officer Muncey sat down at the table next to Tessa's knapsack.

"What are you doing?" asked Tessa.

"Seeing if you need any help. What subject are you studying?"

"Algebra." Tessa tossed her hair to the side. "Oh yeah. I need my calculator. It's in my room." She hurried past the officer and went to her bedroom, grabbed a calculator, and then dialed Cherise's number on her cell phone. *Please pick up. Please pick up. I know you're there. Please.*

Voicemail.

"Cherise! I need you to call me back in like one minute. Please. I know you're there. It's important."

Tessa slipped the phone into her pocket and hurried back to the kitchen only to find Officer Muncey unclasping the buckles on her knapsack. "Hey," yelled Tessa. "What are you doing?"

Officer Muncey met her with a cold gaze. "Did you find your calculator?"

"Put down my knapsack!"

The computer screen flashed with faces, names, comparisons, and then . . .

Nothing.

"He's here," I mumbled. But I wasn't sure, couldn't really be sure.

"He could be a guest, maybe?" said Williamson. "In his room?"

"Pull up your guest list."

He typed in Kincaid's name, then shook his head. "No one staying here under that name."

"He would almost certainly use an alias," said Lien-hua.

"Any ideas?" asked Williamson.

"Jones," I said. "Try Jim Jones."

Williamson typed, shook his head. "No. Wait—"

"What?"

"Someone named James Warren Jones is working with the catering."

"That's it," I said. "The food. They're going to contaminate the food. Don't let anyone near the food!"

"Too late," someone whispered.

We all gazed up at the video monitors. The room became stone-still.

On the screens surrounding us, the servers were spreading out like fingers on a hand, delivering poisoned food to the elite media leaders of the world.

76

Tessa's cell phone rang. "Just a minute," she told the cop. "And don't touch my stuff!" She slipped to the other room and answered. "Hello? Cherise?"

"What is going on, girlfriend? I haven't heard from you in like three weeks, and then you're all of a sudden, like 'call me in one minute' and—"

"I might be in trouble."

"What?"

"Hang on." Tessa peered around the corner and saw Officer Muncey standing with her hands on her hips.

"You don't have books in here, do you?" said Officer Muncey.

"I'm on the phone," Tessa snapped.

Then Officer Muncey unclasped Tessa's knapsack and dumped Tessa's clothes onto the table. "Tessa," she said. "Hang up the phone."

"Stop those servers!" I told Williamson. "And call the Centers for Disease Control and Prevention. Tell them to get a team in here now. And, Ms. Prescott, we need to shut down the hotel, quarantine these people. We have to. No one leaves."

She pursed her lips but only for a moment—probably calculating the losses in tens of millions—and then nodded briskly. "I'll do it." This was a woman who wasn't afraid to make a decision.

"We have to control this," I said. "Shut it down."

"We don't even know what the contagion is," said Lien-hua.

367

"I say we take Kincaid out," said Ralph, cocking his gun. "Fast and clean."

"Wait, everyone. Wait!" said Lien-hua. "Remember Waco? Jonestown? When these cult leaders get scared a lot of innocent people die. These guys are paranoid, delusional. The more you raise the threat level, the less likely they are to back down. I think we need to negotiate."

Ralph cracked his knuckles. "Ready to negotiate."

"Hang on," I said. "We need Kincaid. He's the only one who can stop this. Wait a minute. His main target is Sebastian Taylor." I turned to Ms. Prescott. "Where's Governor Taylor now?"

"Probably in the presidential suite. He checked in this morning. Room 611." She pointed. "The elevators are down the hall."

I took off for the door. "Focus on containing this meal," I called back. "I'm going after Kincaid."

Aaron Jeffrey Kincaid knocked exactly four times on the door to Suite 613, and Anita Banner opened the door. "There you are," she said. "Do you have the rest of my—"

He handed her an envelope of cash. "You're sure I can get to his balcony from yours?"

She nodded, flipping through the bills. "Positive. I checked it out myself."

He headed for the balcony. "Be sure to join us for lunch downstairs," he called back to her. "The roast is to die for."

"Sit down, Tessa," said Officer Muncey. "You and I are going to wait right here for your father. He shouldn't be very long."

77

"Governor Taylor!" I pounded on the door. "It's urgent. Open the door."

The governor swung the door open, eyed me. "Agent Bowers," he said, "how's the fishing been?"

"No time for all that." I rushed past him to search the room. "Has anyone been in here, Governor? The kid remembers. The kid from Jonestown. Aaron Jeffrey Kincaid. We have to stop him—"

"That's far enough," said a voice, but it wasn't the governor's. Wait a minute, I knew that voice. Whiny. Repulsive. Annoying. I turned and saw Reginald Trembley aiming a .40 caliber Glock at my face.

Tessa snatched her knapsack from Officer Muncey. "All right, I'll wait. Whatever! But keep your hands off my stuff!" She began to jam her clothes back into her bag when she heard the front door open.

"Jason," called Officer Muncey. "Tessa was planning on leaving us."

Footsteps from the hall leading to the living room.

Tessa glanced out the window. Something wasn't right.

"Wait a minute," she whispered. "No car."

"What?" said Officer Muncey.

Tessa pointed outside. "He left in a car. It's not here. Besides, we would have heard the engine, the car door slam." Officer Muncey looked at her curiously. Tessa shook her head. "It's not him." She began backing down the hallway toward her bedroom. All she could think of was that treadmill. Those legs.

Footsteps.

"That's not Officer Stilton," she whispered.

"What's going on?" Officer Patricia Muncey had a bewildered look on her face. It was the last expression she would ever have.

━━━━━━━━━━━━━━ ■ ━━━━━━━━━━━━━━

"Listen to me," I said to Governor Taylor and Reginald Trembley. "Both of you. We need to search this suite. Governor, there's someone who wants to kill you."

"I know," he said.

"You do?"

"Oh yes," said the governor smoothly. He closed the door and slammed the deadbolt into place. "I've been doing a little trolling myself."

I noticed a tray of half-eaten hors d'œuvres. "Did you eat those? Governor, please. Listen to me—"

"Shut up," Trembley sneered. "How does it feel to have a gun pointed at you this time, Mr. Federal-Agent-With-The-Bad-Day-And-The-Wicked-Gun?"

"Gun, huh?" said the governor. He reached into my holster and retrieved my SIG. "Hmm. Very nice."

OK. This was not playing out exactly like I'd envisioned it.

I needed to forget about Kincaid for a minute and just keep from being shot.

Keep them talking. You have to keep them talking.

So that's what it's come down to: die or give a briefing.

Wonderful.

"So, you were playing both sides, weren't you, Trembley?" I was stalling, of course, trying to think of a plan. "Started off investigating Kincaid for Bethanie's parents, but then Kincaid found out, didn't he? He offered you a better deal if only you'd find out some information for him about the crimes. How am I doing?"

He smiled a wet, slimy grin.

"Enough," said Governor Taylor.

"Kincaid needed details, though, right?" I continued quickly. "In order to stage the murders. So that was you? You used your contacts at the police department to get access to the ME reports and crime scene photos. It all makes sense now."

"Jason Stilton has always been a good friend," he said smugly. "Do anything for a buck."

What? Stilton?

"What did you say?" I asked.

Stilton's name was one of the sixty-two. He had access to the case files.

"Enough!" repeated the governor.

OK, deal with Stilton later. Right now, stay alive.

I pointed at Sebastian Taylor but kept talking to Trembley. "Then you found Sebastian too, didn't you? Through Kincaid, maybe? Did you threaten to expose the governor's role in Jonestown unless he—"

"Let's just say that Mr. Trembley and I have reached an agreement." Governor Taylor turned to Trembley. "Haven't we?"

Grinning that moist grin. "Oh yeah."

"Blackmail," I said.

"A business transaction," said the governor. "Now, Dr. Bowers, it's time for you to die."

———■———

Tessa's back found the wall as Officer Muncey turned to look down the hallway to the front door.

And what happened next happened so fast it seemed like it was all one action and that all the movements were connected through space and time by a deadly, invisible cord.

The sound of a gunshot ripped through the house. Officer Muncey jerked backward, glanced down at her chest, brushed her hand against her sweater, sighed softly, crumpled to the ground anticlimactically, and sprawled onto the carpet. Alive one moment, dead the next. Just like that. Tessa watched it all happen. Felt the tug of the cord on her soul.

Then she heard a man calling from the other side of the house. "Do you know how many people are born each day, Tessa?"

———■———

All the time that I was blabbing I was desperately trying to figure out how to get out of this mess. I looked around. We were in the multi-room presidential suite. To my right, a veranda overlooked the fountains and gardens of the atrium. The doors to it were closed. I couldn't jump, anyway. We were on the sixth floor.

"Mr. Trembley," said the governor. "You may shoot him in the head now. Aim carefully, please."

Trembley leveled his gun at me. It was all happening too fast. I didn't even have my escape plan figured out yet. This was not—

Blam.

I jolted. Expected to feel the bullet tear into me. Felt at my face, scanned my chest. What? Nothing.

Then I looked up.

Trembley lay dying on the carpet.

"Nice shot, Dr. Bowers," said the governor, holding my gun. The barrel was smoking. "It looks like you killed him."

And in that moment I realized I might have underestimated Sebastian Taylor.

———■———

Tessa ran down the hallway, locked the bathroom door, then slipped into the master bedroom instead and left its door unlocked.

"387,834 people, Tessa," called the man who'd shot the woman cop. "And every day 153,288 die. Where are you, Tessa? Today is your day."

She heard the killer coming down the hall, trying the doors. Heard him open the door to the room she'd slept in last night.

"I know you're down here, Tessa." He moved to the next door in the hall. The bathroom. Found it locked. "Aha. There you are."

She crouched in the corner of the bedroom, next to the dresser, trembled, pulled out her phone, dialed 911.

"Hello," said a bored-sounding voice, "please state the nature — "

Her heartbeat was going through the roof. Her words came out in spurts as she tried to breathe. "There's a man . . . in the hall . . . has a gun."

"Where are you calling from, ma'am?"

"I don't know. I don't know. I'm in a house, a FBI house. Call the FBI office. Ask for Patrick Bowers."

"Ma'am, I can't — "

He was bashing on the bathroom door, hollering her name. "Tessa, open the door."

"He's coming," Tessa whispered urgently. "He killed the cop who was supposed to be protecting me."

Then she heard a car pull into the driveway and a car door slam. Officer Stilton.

"Well," said the governor. "I guess I won't have to pay Mr. Trembley after all. Shame." He set down my gun, picked up Trembley's Glock, and aimed it at me. "And now it's your turn, Agent Bowers."

No, no, no. This was not good.

My heart began to jackhammer in my chest. "So you're going to shoot me? Is that it?"

"Oh no. I wouldn't do that. No need. Trembley already did, right before he died."

Not good at all.

Tessa heard the bathroom door burst open. The clatter of splintered wood. Cursing.

Then the killer stopped. He must have looked out the window in the bathroom and seen the car there.

Oh no.

She glanced out the window. Officer Stilton was walking up the driveway.

She had to warn him. If she didn't, the man in the hall would kill him too. She pulled the window shade back and tried signaling to the cop, but he was fumbling with his pack of cigarettes and didn't see her.

She tried opening the window, but it was either jammed or sealed shut. Oh duh, she was in an FBI house! The windows were probably bulletproof and sealed shut for her protection.

Great.

She looked back at the phone. The screen read "Call Ended." Either she'd lost the signal or they'd hung up on her when she stopped talking. Either way it meant she was dead meat.

Wait. If you can't get out, how did the killer get in? Did he pick the lock? Was the door left unlocked on purpose? Why would someone have left it unlocked?

Officer Stilton paused and then turned back to his car. He must have forgotten something.

78

"Someone definitely heard that shot," I said to the governor. "They'll be coming for you."

He shook his head. "Don't think so." He let his gaze wander around the suite. "Presidential suite, remember? Bulletproof glass. Soundproof rooms. Welcome to the waters where the big fish swim." Then he tapped the Glock's barrel against his palm. "Let's see . . . So, how does this sound? Stressed-out FBI agent who lost his wife and got stuck behind a desk for six months finally gets back into the field but hasn't quite recovered from his bouts with depression. Everyone in the office has noticed his erratic behavior and angry flare-ups. He concocts a wild conspiracy theory about the governor of North Carolina being involved in the Jonestown tragedy some thirty years earlier and despite being warned off the wild goose chase by his superiors, he takes things into his own hands and tries to assassinate the governor in his hotel room just one day after threatening him at his private residence. But thankfully, the private investigator who Governor Taylor had hired to investigate the rogue agent killed him before he could carry out his deadly plans." Sebastian Taylor looked down at Trembley's body. "Unfortunately for the PI, Dr. Bowers was able to squeeze off one final round, killing him, before expiring."

OK, that actually sounded kind of believable to me.

"It'll never fly," I said.

"Oh, you seem to be forgetting, I'm very good at what I do."

"Gunshot residue," I said. "It's all over your clothes, your face, your hands."

"I was in the room when you shot him. It would be natural for some residue to be on me."

That was actually a good point. How ironic. Location and timing of a crime were going to be the death of me. Literally.

Keep him talking.

"I still can't believe that even you would be willing to sacrifice nine hundred innocent people," I said.

He shook his head. "Never part of the plan. You should have figured that out by now. Ryan was the target. We knew we could pin the assassination on Peoples Temple, shut Jones down, show the world how crazy and unstable communists are. His followers were just collateral damage." He smirked. "We weren't sure exactly how Jones would react, but we figured he'd self-destruct—which he did. In the end it just went further than we thought it would."

"That's what you call the death of all those people? Going further than you thought it would? Collateral damage?" I felt anger pacing back and forth inside me, ready to pounce. "You used him. You used them all."

"We did what we had to do. Ryan was a threat to our country, always fighting to limit the way the CIA did its work. We did it to protect freedom, not to limit it. We just created the perfect storm and waited to see how it would play out. I wasn't sent in to make sense of it, just to help recast the story."

"Remove the evidence, leave the rumors."

"Eloquently put."

"So what about the truth?" I said. "That doesn't matter?"

He wet his lips with the tip of his tongue. "Rumors, Dr. Bowers, not truth, are what matter in the end. Rumors start wars, topple regimes, ruin marriages, end careers. The driving force behind world commerce is innuendo, not truth. Everything from the stock market to the futures market to the price of oil is determined by guesswork and gossip. Control the rumors, Dr. Bowers, and you control the world."

"And in the case of Jonestown, you controlled the rumors."

A smile writhed across his face. "We *influenced* them. After all, those people really did kill themselves off; we had nothing to do with that. All we did was shape the way their story was told." He raised the Glock, pointed it at my chest. "Just as I'm going to shape the way your story will be told."

Think fast . . . think fast . . .

"But then why'd you leave the tape behind? At least tell me that much."

"I was interrupted before I could finish editing it." He shook his head. "It's that simple. Someone just showed up in the wrong place at the wrong time. Gotta hate those interruptions." He took aim.

Faster. Faster.

"Ralph and Lien-hua know."

The governor scoffed. "They can't prove anything."

"No," said a voice from behind me. "But I can."

Governor Taylor and I turned to see a gentle-looking man in his early forties step into the room from where he'd apparently been hiding on the balcony.

"Hello, gentlemen," he said. "My name is Aaron Jeffrey Kincaid. And I have something to give you."

Tessa faced the door, her heart ready to explode. It was the last door in the hall. The killer would try it next.

911 hadn't helped. Who? Who could she call?

She saw a cell phone recharging on the dresser. The phone Patrick had been using. It would have the phone numbers of the other FBI agents! She grabbed it.

It was turned off.

Pressed power.

Waited.

Heard the killer moving through the hallway.

Waited.

There.

She scrolled to the recent calls. The first name listed was Brent Tucker.

79

The governor swiveled on smoothly oiled joints and fired the Glock at Kincaid, hitting him square in the shoulder, sending him reeling toward the balcony where he smacked into the railing and flipped over backward. A moment later I heard the splash as he landed in the river six stories below. A series of screams echoed through the courtyard from the delegates who saw what happened.

"I should have done that thirty years ago," said the governor, gazing toward the balcony.

While he was momentarily distracted I scrambled over, grabbed my gun, rolled across the carpet.

"That, Dr. Bowers," said Sebastian Taylor from somewhere behind me, "is how you handle a shark."

I positioned myself behind the couch. Flattened my back against it.

"Sebastian," I yelled. "Put down the gun." I peered around the edge of the couch and then ducked back. He was scanning the room looking for me, trying to conserve bullets now that the balcony doors were open and the room was no longer soundproof. He'd need to choose his shot wisely; security would be here any moment. "You ate the hors d'œuvres," I called. "You're infected. We need to treat you."

"Wasn't me, I'm afraid," he said. "I gave those to Anita before sending her to her room. I suppose I'll have to find a new personal assistant. Ah well, she was getting a little old for me anyhow."

I couldn't see him; he was on the other side of the room. "Governor," I said. "It's over. I recorded everything you said. I'm wired."

I touched the mic patch to make sure it was still in place beneath my ear. I'd put it on after grabbing it from my desk before leaving the federal building. No one was monitoring the other end at the moment, but everything the governor had said was automatically recorded.

Every word.

Despite the interruptions.

That is how you handle a shark.

Brent Tucker ... Brent Tucker ... Tessa had overheard Patrick talking to him on the phone earlier this morning. What had Patrick said again? Something about him helping with the case, being a good man.

So he was a friend of Patrick's. He could help. She punched the number. Waited while it rang. Hurry, hurry, hurry.

She heard the catch of the lock as the cop who liked to smoke opened the front door of the house.

I heard the door bang open and ventured a glance. Governor Taylor had fled.

Shouts and screams rose from the courtyard. I ran to the balcony.

Kincaid had landed in the foaming water near the base of the waterfall. It must have cushioned his landing enough for him to survive the fall. He was hobbling to his feet. "It's a cruel world," he was shouting. "But our love will unite us forever!" And one by one, his people, the caterers for today's luncheon, were taking capsules out of their pockets and popping them into their mouths.

Endgame.

Tessa couldn't believe that the killer didn't open the door in front of her, the last door in the hall. Instead, she heard him run back toward the center of the house.

Officer Stilton, no! He was going to kill him too.

The cell phone in her hand was ringing, still ringing.

Answer, Agent Tucker. Answer!

———————————————■———————————————

Aaron Jeffrey Kincaid looked around the courtyard. The world was spinning. People screaming.

He was standing in water. Swirling water. Blood weeping from his shoulder.

Blood and water. Curling together.

The river.

The whirlpool.

Jessica and the days of true love.

"His vision, our vision!" he yelled. "His future, our future!"

———————————————■———————————————

I watched as the hotel security guards raced into the lobby and then fumbled around trying to figure out what to do: arrest the people who were killing themselves or try to calm down the panicking guests who were paying $1,200 a night?

"Arrest them!" I shouted. The room was erupting in confusion. People were trying to leave, stampeding everywhere. "Stop them," I yelled. "It's a suicide mission! We need them alive to identify the virus!"

You have to get down there.

I knew the elevators would be jammed with people, so I ran to the stairs, descended to the main floor, and bolted into the courtyard of hanging gardens and pools.

All around me, chaos.

———————————————■———————————————

Tessa held her breath, waiting for the gunshot she was sure would come, waiting for the killer to shoot Officer Stilton too.

No shot came, and when the phone in her hand vibrated, she almost screamed.

"Hello? Pat?" a voice said.

"No, it's me," she cried. "It's Tessa!"

"Tessa?"

"I'm his daughter." By then she was crying.

"Are you OK? Where are you?"

"I need your help. I'm at the house. She's dead. Someone's dead. Hurry."

"OK, calm down. I'll be right there. I'm close by."

80

Off to the right I saw four security guards trying to tackle a mountain of a man near the east entrance to the courtyard. He was wearing a caterer's uniform and was throwing the guards around like rag dolls. Four to one, but they were hopelessly outmatched. Ralph must have seen them the same time I did because he rushed into the middle of the melee and called to the guy doing the pummeling, "Pick on someone your own size, you freakin' pansy."

Just then I located Kincaid. He was about twenty meters from Ralph. I ran toward him but found my way blocked by the crowd.

Ralph waved the security guards to safety and then pointed to the capsule the guy had pulled out. "Don't take the sissy way out. Fight me. Right now. If I win, I don't let you die today." Ralph was rolling up his sleeves. "I take you in, we prosecute you, put you away for the next forty years, and you get to experience all the joys of the American penal system. If you win, well, I'll swallow your little pill."

What are you doing, Ralph?

I wanted to help him, but I had to get to Kincaid. I pushed my way through the crowd, struggling to get to him before it was too late.

Kincaid was right in front of me. "His future, our future!" he was shouting.

He slipped his hand into his pocket.

He's going for a capsule. Don't let him die. You need to find out the name of the contagion.

I rushed him, tackled him, and sent the capsule he'd pulled out spinning across the cobblestone path. But not far enough. It was still within reach.

As we crashed onto the ground, he wrestled free, squirming and fighting like a madman. "Don't do this," I managed to say. "These people are innocent." But he brought his elbow down with crushing strength into my gut. I gasped for breath. This guy was tougher than he looked.

He snatched up the capsule, shoved it into my mouth, then punched me hard in the jaw.

Don't swallow, Pat. Whatever you do, don't swallow!

———————◼———————

Tessa waited one moment. Then another. Her heart wouldn't stop pounding. Still no shot. The killer must have slipped away. Then she heard Officer Stilton gasp when he saw the body in the other room . . . the sound of him shouting her name . . . sirens blaring toward the house . . . the bedroom door crashing open. "Tessa!"

It was him. The cop who liked to smoke.

So then. She was safe. It was going to be OK. Everything was going to be OK.

———————◼———————

I could taste the bitter tablet dissolving on my tongue.

I tried to spit it out. Couldn't. Kincaid was on me with a vengeance, clamping his hand over my mouth.

Just then I saw a blur beside my face, and Kincaid's jaw snapped back, and he flew off me.

I spit out the capsule.

Lien-hua swirled around with the grace of a gazelle, leapt into the air, and cracked her heel into the side of Kincaid's head a second time, this time hard enough to swipe him off his feet. His body torqued around backward, and he slammed into the ground, unconscious. She landed softly on her feet, ready for another kick.

"An A," I said. I was trying to catch my breath. "I would definitely give that kick an A."

"'Bout time," she said, rushing off toward a woman holding a capsule.

Marcie watched as the others slipped the capsules into their mouths and bit down . . . watched as the people she loved collapsed onto the floor with mouths full of foam . . . watched as they convulsed . . . as they gasped for breath . . . as they died.

Being captured alive had never been part of the plan.

She stared at the capsule in her hand and heard shouting all around her, voices telling her what to do. "Take it . . . Drop it . . . Swallow it . . . Stand down . . ." A thousand voices coming from everywhere at once.

She had a choice. She had to make a choice.

"Wait." An Asian woman came running toward her with open hands. "Please. Don't. No more people need to die."

I scrambled over to Kincaid to cuff him and see if I could find out the name of the virus, but when I was only a few steps from him, he pulled out a syringe inside a plastic bag, thrust the tip through the bag, and plunged it into his heart.

No!

He fumbled for something in his pocket. "And this is for—" he started to say, but then he began to convulse.

In all my time in law enforcement I'd never witnessed such a terrible death.

In the end I had to turn away. I couldn't watch. I looked up just in time to see Ralph punch the gorilla in the stomach. The man was gasping, backing up as Ralph went at him, bashing him with his shot-put-sized fists.

Roundhouse.

Uppercut. Finally a left hook. Ralph hit him so hard in the face that he spun around in an instant and, with a meaty crunch, collided face first against the stone wall of the hotel and toppled to the ground. Ralph wiped his hand across his face to get the blood out of his mouth as he cuffed him. "Ah," said Ralph. "Just the way I like it. Fast and clean."

Tessa looked around the living room.

Police and a bunch of ambulance guys had arrived, and half a dozen people she didn't know were milling around asking her questions. They'd put the cop who'd gotten shot on a gurney. Maybe she was still alive.

"Tessa!" Agent Tucker came running in. "Are you OK?"

She blinked. "Where's Patrick?" she said weakly.

"He'll be coming in a minute," he said. "Don't worry, Tessa. I'm here to help you."

"We would rather die free than live as slaves," said Marcie.

"That's what he told you, isn't it?" asked the woman, coming closer. "Kincaid, right? Or maybe Jones? But what do *you* think? You get to decide. That's the thing. A slave is someone who can no longer choose."

"Stay back!"

The Chinese woman stopped. "What's your name?"

After a pause. "Marcie."

"I'm Lien-hua. Please, Marcie, help us protect these people. Please."

Marcie watched as the security guards tried to corral people into conference rooms, control the panic, calm people down.

She thought of her daughter lying still on the floor. Saw the look in the little girl's eyes as she'd told her to drink the "medication" back in the library. "Will it hurt, Mommy?" her daughter had asked.

"No, sweetie, it won't hurt," Marcie had said—had lied. She'd lied to her only daughter because Aaron Jeffrey Kincaid told her to. "Of course it'll hurt," she'd wanted to say. But she didn't say it. She just told her it wouldn't hurt, and then her daughter nodded and closed her eyes and opened her mouth, a trusting little girl.

Marcie backed into the retaining wall of the fountain, lifted the tablet. "There's nothing left for me here. My daughter is dead. I killed her."

The woman, Lien-hua, was still talking to her. "Please. I know you loved your daughter. I know you did. Sometimes when people are afraid, they do things they later regret."

"You don't know what it's like—".

"No, I don't," the woman said, and it surprised Marcie that she agreed with her. "None of us can know what it's like for someone else. It's what makes us individuals. We each have our own pain, our own mistakes. But we can reach out toward each other, help each other. That's what makes us human."

"It's too late . . ."

Lien-hua pointed to the line of people being herded out of the courtyard, guided into conference rooms to be quarantined and treated. "It's not too late for them, for their children. You don't have to do what Kincaid says. He's gone. You get to decide. Please help us."

The capsule was in Marcie's hand.

She raised it to her lips.

She got to decide. It was her choice.

She saw them: the children in the library. The poison still moist on their lips. Moist on their lips.

Her daughter's trusting face.

At last, with her little girl's smiling face drifting before her, Marcie let the last fragment of her old life fall from her fingers and onto the floor. "Francisella tularensis," she whispered. She sensed a man beside her, a big man with a rough voice. It was almost as if she were somewhere else watching, a spectator observing a woman getting handcuffed. "Genetically enhanced . . ." she said in case anyone was listening. This was good. She could finally do something good with her life. Something right. "We spliced the genes . . . Crimean-Congo hemorrhagic fever . . ."

81

Tessa tried to drink the glass of water Agent Tucker had gotten for her, but her hands were still shaking. She heard purring and noticed Midnight stretching out on the floor at her feet. She hadn't seen Sunshine since the craziness started.

She set down the glass and looked in her lap. She had two phones—hers and the one Patrick was using. She slipped them into separate pockets in her jeans and gently stroked Midnight's soft fur.

She just wanted to get out of here. To go home.

Mr. Tucker was talking on his cell. "Yeah, Agent Wellington?" he was saying. "This is Brent. I need to get a message through to Pat. Tell him I'm with his daughter, and she's fine. Yeah. Make sure you tell him. All right. Thanks."

———————■———————

I overheard Lien-hua talking with one of Kincaid's people about the contagion. Ralph was cuffing the woman. I ran to them. "Wait, ma'am. What did you say?"

"Crimean-Congo hemorrhagic fever," she said.

"What's that? How do you know?"

"I have a degree . . ." Her eyes were blank. "In microbiology . . ." She spoke to us from another place. "I used to work for Father at PTPharmaceuticals . . . I was a researcher . . . that's where we met."

I looked her in the eye, tried to help her focus. "Can we stop it? Do you know how to treat it?"

The woman nodded. "We altered the genetic makeup, but I worked on the project. I can help you."

"Let her go," I said.

"It's another trick," said Ralph. "She'll kill herself just like the others."

"I believe her," said Lien-hua. "I believe you, Marcie."

So her name was Marcie. I looked at her. Tried to read her eyes. Couldn't. "Why would you help us?"

"The children," she said, "my daughter." Mists began to form in her eyes. "No more children need to die."

"She could be lying," said Ralph.

"She's not lying," said Lien-hua softly.

Marcie's eyes found me. Searched me. "Do you have any children?"

A rush of emotion overwhelmed me. "Yes. I do," I said. "A daughter. She's seventeen."

The woman nodded, smiled. "My daughter was seven. I loved her." She looked directly at me. "I killed her," she said, her voice as fragile as glass, "because I loved her."

Fear and love, the two missing motives that drive all the others. Set free in some hearts. Twisted in others.

Then Marcie began to weep, and Lien-hua reached out for her, cut off her restraints, took her in her arms. Ralph's cell phone sprang to life and he flipped it open. "It's the CDC," he said. He told them about Marcie and then grudgingly he handed the phone to her. "They want to know what you know." Then he glowered at her. "No games, you understand?"

She nodded and stepped aside with him to a quieter corner of the courtyard.

Just then Margaret came hurrying over to us. I didn't even know she was here. Probably just came when she heard about all the media people present. "Sit down, Pat." It didn't sound like anger in her voice. Something else. Fear? Concern?

"What is it?"

"Sit down."

"Tell me."

"A few minutes ago there was a 911 call from the safe house."

"What?"

"Listen, Tessa's OK. An officer was shot, though. Officer Muncey."

"Where's Tessa?"

"She's still there. Don't worry—"

"Jason Stilton has always been a good friend," Trembley said. "Do anything for a buck."

"Where's Stilton?"

"Officer Stilton?" She looked at me curiously. "He's there, Pat. They called an ambulance. Brent Tucker's there too. I just talked to him. He told me he's with Tessa. He wanted you to know."

Oh no.

Suddenly, everything began to spin and click. The pieces of the puzzle slid together with grim accuracy, shattering my mind, my world. "He knew we were leaving for Denver," I muttered. "That's why he called me this morning. He wanted me here. That's why he gave me Kincaid . . ."

"What?" said Margaret.

"The first murder," I whispered, "was two days after Grolin's girlfriend moved out, after he beat her up . . . Right?"

Lien-hua nodded but looked confused.

"She was treated for her injuries, wasn't she?"

"Yes," she said. "What are you thinking? What is it?"

"He knew," I said. The world was getting bleary. Whatever was in that capsule was starting to affect me. *How does the killer get away? He always slips away. At the mall . . . at the golf course . . . Alice's house . . .*

"He knows how to cut them . . ." I said, "to keep them alive . . ."

"What are you talking about?" asked Margaret.

"It's the drugs," said Lien-hua, eyeing the half-dissolved capsule on the floor. "Get a doctor over here!" And then to me, "Take it easy, Pat. Sit down."

Only the most foolish of mice would hide in a cat's ear, but only the wisest of cats would look there. I felt weak. "The Illusionist," I whispered. "He's been hiding in my ear the whole time."

And that's when I saw that Kincaid, before he died, had pulled something out of his pocket. It lay hidden in the grip of his left hand.

"I have something to give you," he'd said to Taylor and me.

He had something to give me.

And I knew who it was from.

82

Tessa was on the couch, trying to relax, trying to catch her breath. Agent Tucker sat beside her. The house was a little quieter; a bunch of the cops had left when they wheeled that woman away.

Agent Tucker placed his hand on her shoulder. "You OK?"

She nodded. "I'm shaking, though."

"It's shock," he said. "We need to get you out of here."

"Is she dead?" asked Tessa softly. "That police officer?"

Agent Tucker nodded slowly. "I'm afraid so."

A paramedic appeared in the doorway. "Is everyone in here OK?"

Agent Tucker slipped his hand around Tessa's shoulder. "I'm taking her with me."

"The CDC team is on its way," announced Ralph. He had left Marcie with Mr. Williamson's security personnel.

"Good," I mumbled. I was walking over to Kincaid's body.

Ralph pointed to Marcie. "They think they can control this thing with her help. Treat it." He looked at the gruesome scene around us. The bodies of Kincaid's group lay scattered around the courtyard. Only the big guy and Marcie had survived. "With a little luck, no one else is going to die today."

I heard his words but only faintly. They were fading into the distance of space and time.

It couldn't really be what I thought it was in his hand. It couldn't be.

Showing us the board . . . he's been showing us the board . . .
I reached Kincaid's body.

———————————■———————————

The paramedic looked confused. "The guys outside told me to come in and take a look at her."

Agent Tucker stood up. Stood toe to toe with the paramedic. "C'mere for a second," he said.

Then Tessa watched him lead the paramedic into the hallway and around the corner out of sight.

———————————■———————————

Brent Tucker is with Tessa . . .
I knelt down, noticed a ragged scar across the inside of Kincaid's wrist, probably from a suicide attempt a long time ago.

He shot the man in the neck but didn't kill him . . . made sure he didn't kill him . . . he knew where to shoot them . . .

I reached out to open Kincaid's hand. My heart was screaming. *No, no, no!*

My fingers began to tremble.

He reaches across the board, touches a piece, then he takes her.

———————————■———————————

Tessa heard a muffled gasp and a soft thud.

———————————■———————————

I uncurled Kincaid's fingers.
Saw the item.
Tessa's necklace.

———————————■———————————

"Agent Tucker?" called Tessa.

———————————■———————————

I spun around, yelled to Margaret. "Get Tucker on the phone! Now!"

Tessa strained to see around the corner. "Are you OK, Agent Tucker?" Her heart began to slam against the inside of her chest.

A voice inside of her told her to get up. To get out. Something was wrong.

She tried to stand but was still dizzy from shock.

Her legs felt wobbly.

"Agent Tucker?"

Margaret put her hand on my elbow to calm me down. "Don't worry, Pat, Tessa's all ri—"

"I know who it is!" I yelled.

"Hello, Tessa," said the killer, the Illusionist, the boy who had snuggled up to the corpse of his mother, the man who was at home in the dark. He stepped around the corner, holding a dripping blade, and grabbed Tessa, shoving a cloth over her mouth, quickly, so quickly that it swallowed her scream and sent her reeling into a terrible, terrible sleep. Terrible and dark.

But before the shadows closed around her she saw one last thing—one last grisly thing—a man trying to crawl around the corner of the hallway, trying to get to her. To help her. Failing. Falling. Collapsing onto the carpet, his throat slashed.

A man.

A dead man.

Special Agent Brent Tucker.

83

"Don't worry, Pat," said Margaret. "She's OK. The paramedics are looking after her." But her words were barely audible, floating somewhere beside me. They meant nothing. Because I was holding Tessa's necklace in my hand, and nothing else mattered.

He leaves an item from the next victim.

My daughter is next.

"Phone!" I yelled, pocketing the necklace. "Give me a phone!" Lien-hua handed me hers. I dialed Tessa's cell phone number. *Please answer. Please, please.* The room was twirling; I was about to collapse, dizzy from the drugs.

It rang.

Someone answered. "Hello, Patrick." I knew that voice: it was the paramedic who'd treated my shoulder. The paramedic who'd waited patiently for us to finish examining Mindy's body, the one who helped the injured officer to the ambulance outside of Alice's house last night. But no one noticed him because he was supposed to be there. Because paramedics are always supposed to be there. Even in Charlotte, in another city, he could blend in and disappear in the chaos following the shooting in the parking garage by just wearing his uniform. It was the perfect disguise because it wasn't a disguise at all. He became invisible by the cleverest misdirection of all—by fitting in.

By hiding in my ear.

"Checkmate," he said.

Dizzy . . . dizzy . . . swaying . . . I handed the phone to Lien-hua and mumbled, "GPS . . ." The world was closing in. "Track her cell location with GPS . . . It's the param—" I started to say, but before I could tell them who the Illusionist was, everything went black.

84

Tessa opened her eyes.

She had no idea how long she'd been unconscious.

Something was stuffed in her mouth. Some kind of gag. It made her want to retch, but she was afraid that if she threw up she'd choke on the vomit and die like that kid from school did last year at that party when he got so drunk he passed out and never woke up.

Never woke up.

Calm down, Tessa. Calm down.

Never woke up.

Calm down.

She was on her side. Her hands stretched behind her back, tied together. It felt like duct tape. When she tried to move her legs, she couldn't. Her ankles were tightly bound too. At least she still had her clothes on—thank God.

Her mind felt fuzzy, unclear. She looked around.

Where was she?

An ambulance. She was in the back of an ambulance, and they were driving up a curving road, into the mountains.

Drifting. Drifting. She blinked, tried to focus.

Slipped into unconsciousness again.

I woke up, looked around. A huddle of faces surrounded me.

"The guy tossed the phone," someone was saying.

"The paramedic," I managed to say.

"He's back!" Ralph's face loomed into view. "You OK?"

I nodded feebly. "It's the paramedic." I tried to speak, hardly made a sound. "The Illusionist. It's him."

"Put out an APB on the ambulance!" Ralph shouted. I saw Margaret calling it in.

"If it's a paramedic, where's his partner?" asked Lien-hua.

I knew the answer from my days as a wilderness guide, and I wanted to tell her that in isolated mountainous regions, EMTs and paramedics drive their ambulances home, so that when a call comes in they don't have to drive back to town first, but can respond faster. And they don't always arrive on the scene with their partner. I wanted to explain it all, tried to, but voices and visions whispered to me, blurred my thoughts, curved reality around me.

What kind of drug was that?

"Where's that doctor!" yelled Ralph. Then he looked at me. "That was a good idea to track her phone, but he discarded it."

"Where?" I managed to say. "Where did he toss it?"

"240 West."

Location and timing . . .

"How long ago?"

Location and timing . . .

"'Bout two minutes."

What was that paramedic's name? I tried to think, tried to remember.

He never told me his name. Just told me it might leave a scar. "Find out who responded to the 911 call at the safe house," I said.

"I'm on it," said Ralph.

"He'll probably switch vehicles, Ralph." I felt so weak. "We can't chase him . . . gotta get out ahead of him . . ." I felt weak and nauseous. I must have looked it too.

"We need to get you to the hospital," said Lien-hua.

I slapped myself in the face to wake up. Some of my thoughts were positioning themselves in a straight line again, but not all of them. "Not before I find my daughter," I said. "Get my computer. It's still in the security room."

"Pat—" she said.

"Please," I begged. "Please. Hurry."

She left for it.

"His name's Sevren Adkins," Ralph announced. He asked them where Sevren lived and then scribbled down an address. "We can't track the vehicle, though. It's an older model. No GPS." Then he said something into the phone and turned back to me. "I've got Asheville EMS on the phone, Pat. Anything else you need to know?"

"Is he on their high angle rescue unit?"

He asked them.

"Yes!" he yelled.

That explains the cave connection.

"Find out if he used to work in Spartanburg, if he was the one who responded to the domestic abuse call from Grolin's girlfriend. I want to know how long he's been playing this game."

A minute later Lien-hua returned with my computer. I fired up F.A.L.C.O.N. "Showtime," I said. I typed in the address Ralph had given me. The image focused, zoomed.

Onto clouds.

Useless.

We haven't found a way yet to see through the clouds.

———————————————■———————————————

Tessa was dreaming, dreaming, dreaming. The world was a blur. A blood-drenched dream. She remembered arguing with Patrick . . . the necklace . . . her knapsack . . . seeing that cop get shot . . . Agent Tucker trying to help her . . . the paramedic.

And then everything was swallowed by the clouds.

She shook her head to clear her thoughts. Her mind was filled with visions of puffy clouds floating overhead, forming into fairies and unicorns and dragons with wispy, bristling teeth, and she could hear her mother's laughter from somewhere nearby and then she was coming home from her mother's funeral and she could see her reflection in the bathroom mirror where she was pressing a razor blade against her arm and the blood was dripping, falling, spreading out across her arm and then down the hall and onto a treadmill and across the carpet, and then it was flowing from Agent Tucker's neck, forming into shapes on the floor, clouds on the carpet, coloring the world red with crimson tears.

Bloody rain.

Calm down, Tessa. Calm down.

A terror still and deep settled over her, descended into her. She was tied up. She was with a killer. She was going to die.

She was afraid to make a sound, afraid of what he might do if he found out she was awake, but despite herself, she let out a muffled gasp.

The man driving the ambulance turned around and smiled. "Tessa," he said. "So glad you could join me."

━━━━━━━━━━━━━ ■ ━━━━━━━━━━━━━

Ah, so she was awake. Good.

It was more fun when they woke up early and had more time to contemplate what was about to happen to them.

He heard a cell phone ring.

What? He'd tossed the kid's phone earlier. Whose phone was that?

Another ring.

He hadn't checked both of her pockets, just the one.

She was carrying a second phone.

━━━━━━━━━━━━━ ■ ━━━━━━━━━━━━━

"Sevren lived in Spartanburg," announced Ralph, hanging up his phone.

I tried to pull together everything: Grolin had been set up from the start. He was Sevren's perfect little pawn, writing about locations in *MountainQuest* magazine that Sevren could later drop bodies into to make all the evidence point away from himself. And as a paramedic, Sevren would have known Vanessa from working at the hospital, could have convinced her to come to the golf course.

He's showing us the board.

I thought of Tucker's longitude and latitude theory and pulled up the geo profile and the computer's chess game, grabbed the image of the chessboard, overlaid it onto the geo profile, resized it to fit. Locations, abduction sites, crime scenes. I added the golf course. The safe house.

Patterns . . . patterns . . . patterns . . .

I had to find him. I had to predict where he was going to go.

You don't predict the future, Pat. You can't.

But I had to.

Sevren stopped the ambulance by the side of the road. They hadn't quite made it to his destination yet, just a little farther before he could switch vehicles, but he needed to get rid of that phone. He climbed into the back with the girl.

He fished the phone out of her pocket, stepped outside the ambulance, and hurled it into the gorge through the swirl of damp snow that had started descending on the mountains. Then he returned to her side.

Yes.

Maybe he could have a little fun with Tessa now that she was awake. Why not? He'd earned it. He watched her squirm for a few moments and then removed her gag.

85

"We got him," announced Ralph.

"What?" I said.

"Sheriff Wallace just called in. State troopers are at his house. He probably switched vehicles like you said; his van is parked out front. They're going in."

"No!" I hollered. "Tell them to stand down. Remember the bomb in Grolin's place? If they breach the door, that house might blow. He might have Tessa inside. It would be the perfect ending to his game. Stand down!"

———————————■———————————

As soon as the paramedic took off her gag Tessa spit in his face.

For a moment he looked like he might slap her, but then he just grinned and wiped off the saliva. "Tessa, do you know who Boethius is?"

Calm, down. Tessa, calm down.

Outthink him. That's what she needed to do. Stall. Until she could get free.

She nodded. "Of course." Tried to tug her hands free, failed, but felt something in the back pocket of her jeans. What was that?

Her razor blade.

His eyes narrowed. "Tell me."

Boethius . . . Boethius . . . the name was Latin . . . masculine.

"A Roman," she said. "He was that famous Roman guy." He

had to be famous, after all, or else the killer wouldn't have even bothered to ask.

"Yes," he said suspiciously. "And what did he write about?"

She slid out the blade and began working it against the tape binding her wrists as she tried to figure out who in the world Boethius could be.

Ralph called off the raid. "What do you want us to do then?"

"Hang on a second." I was still groggy.

The capsule. You swallowed half of that capsule.

I had no idea what kind of drug was in there. Something powerful. I glanced at the bodies of the dead cult members scattered around me.

"Give me a shot of adrenaline," I said to the doctor who had finally responded to Ralph's call for help.

"We need to get you to the hospital," she said.

"Not yet," I splashed a handful of water from the fountain into my face. "I gotta find my daughter."

Ralph walked over. "Do as he says, doc," he thundered. "Do it now."

Reluctantly, the doctor gave me the shot.

I stared at my computer screen. "Tell them to wait for me," I told Ralph under my breath. "Tell them I'm on my way but not to make a move until I get there."

"But no one is supposed to leave the hotel—"

I pulled out the necklace and spoke in an urgent whisper. "Ralph, he's got Tessa."

"You've been exposed."

"Marcie will help us, you said so yourself."

"Pat—"

"Ralph, he's going to torture her, and then he's going to kill her. I have to stop him. You know I do. I'm going."

His face wrinkled up, then turned to steel. "Yeah," he said at last. "OK. Go. I'll tell them to wait for you."

I pocketed the necklace and slipped into the hotel kitchen, figuring there'd be a delivery entrance I could use that wouldn't be heavily guarded. After all, most of the guards were busy controlling the panicking guests. Thankfully I only met one security guard on my way. "I'm sorry, sir," he said, "you've been infected. I can't let you out—" My fist found his jaw. He fell to the ground.

"Nothing personal," I said, stepping past him. "But this concerns my daughter."

I pushed the door open and ran through the driving snow to my car.

—————————————■—————————————

Tessa thought and thought hard.

The guy said Boethius was a writer. OK, so what did he write about? . . . What would a Roman guy write about? The wars? Was he a historian? A philosopher? Playwright? Had to be one of the four, really there weren't that many other choices, not from some stupid Roman author.

Then she noticed a bracelet dangling from the guy's wrist. It had a word inscribed on it: "Sophia."

Sophia means wisdom . . . A philosopher, maybe? . . . Was Boethius a Roman philosopher?

Her hands were almost free. Almost.

"Wisdom," she said. "He wrote about wisdom."

The man gently stroked the back of her head. "I'm impressed."

Then his fingers intertwined in her hair. She cried out. He pulled her head back by her hair, exposing her throat. His voice seeped into her ears. "And what is the secret to true wisdom, Tessa?"

Oh no. Now he had her. The secret to true wisdom? Tessa had no idea.

The secret to true wisdom . . .

She tried to speak, couldn't. He loosened his grip slightly.

Say something. Guess!

"Love," she whispered. "The secret is love."

"Close," he said. "The answer is pain."

Sevren curled his lips into a dark smile and told the girl, "Of course we'll get more into that lesson when we get to the house." Then he climbed into the cab of the ambulance and pulled onto the road to take her to his workshop.

There. Her hands were free.

Now for her legs.

Almost as soon as I'd peeled out of the parking lot I realized Sevren wouldn't head home. Of course not; it would be too predictable, too obvious. He always tried to stay one step ahead.

So he would have another place to take the women. But where?

I thought through the geo profile, the chessboard.

I was still missing something . . .

The tempo and timeline of the crimes . . . the crime distribution pattern . . . road infrastructure . . . the time-benefit ratios . . . optimal travel routes. Asheville is shaped like a football, outlined by interstates 26 and 40 . . . bodies in three states . . .

The pieces were scattered all over the board . . . There was no pattern! None . . . The sites were scattered all over . . .

Except for one place.

Nothing happened in that one place.

Exactly.

The answer wasn't where the pieces were placed—it was where they weren't. All the locations, all the chess pieces, were clustered around one location where nothing happened. No murders. No abductions. No dump sites. Everything else orbited around this void, this abyss on the map. He'd tried to hide his tracks but left the biggest one of all. By trying so hard to stay away from his anchor point, he'd shown me right where it was.

Warrior's Peak.

I whipped the car around and aimed it up into the mountains.

———————■———————

By the time Tessa had freed her legs, she'd made a decision. There was no way she was going to let him get her back to his house. She could only imagine what he would do to her there. She crawled to the back doors and tried opening them, but they'd been locked from the outside. She threw her weight against them. Nothing.

No, she had to get out. She had to. Even if she died in a car accident, she couldn't let him get her to his home.

Tessa looked around the back of the ambulance. Her eyes fell on one of the huge first-aid kits. She flipped it open, pulled out a pair of razor-sharp scissors, and headed for the cab of the ambulance.

———————■———————

Icy snow bit into the windshield as I cruised up the serpentine road toward Warrior's Peak. All the state troopers were looking in the wrong place, but there was no way for me to get word to them. No phone with me, no radio in my car. Maybe they could follow the homing beacon on the mic patch I was still wearing. I wasn't sure how far it would broadcast. I could only hope.

As much as I wanted to race up the mountain, I had to be careful. The visibility was low, and the road was spotted with patches of black ice. Twice my tires lost their grip on the pavement, and I almost went skidding off into the gorge.

Then I saw the ambulance about a quarter mile ahead of me, but it was swerving back and forth like the driver had lost control.

What's going on?

I accelerated.

The adrenaline was wearing off. I was feeling nauseous again, sleepy. My vision grew blurry. I couldn't trust my senses. I needed to get to her fast.

I was only about a hundred meters behind them when it happened.

The ambulance spun sideways, glided along the icy road, smashed through the guardrail, and then disappeared off the edge of the cliff.

No, that couldn't have happened. It couldn't be real. I was seeing things. Hallucinating.

I crushed the accelerator to the floor, slicing through the snow, through a dream, through a new reality I was trying to construct around myself, and by the time I reached the spot where they'd gone over I'd almost convinced myself it hadn't happened, that I was only seeing things.

Almost.

But when I jumped out of the car and staggered to the edge of the precipice, I saw that it was real after all.

Headlights stared up at me from three meters below. My daughter and the killer were caught on a ledge. "Tessa!" I couldn't keep the terror out of my voice. "Are you OK?"

Sevren's voice came back to me, like poison blackening the day. "Patrick, is that you? I should have known you'd find—" But before he could finish his sentence the ambulance tipped back over the outcropping and dropped into the heart of the gorge, encased in the screams of my daughter.

86

"No!" I howled.

I listened for the sickening crunch of metal on rock or the roaring screech of the vehicle tumbling down the cliff, but it didn't come.

I leaned forward but couldn't see much. I scrambled a few meters down the cliff, toed out onto a ledge using stray roots for handholds, bent over, and then I saw them. The ambulance was caught in the branches of a towering fir tree that jutted out about twenty meters farther down the cliff. Beyond the tree, the gorge dropped off a hundred meters straight down into the valley carved by a hopeless Cherokee girl's tears.

"Tessa!"

"Patrick," she called. "Help me, Patrick!"

Something powerful and deep stirred within me. Something bright and wild and right. *Nothing else matters. You have to save her.*

"Throw down a rope," yelled the Illusionist.

"He's hurt, Patrick. His leg!"

"Shut up!" And then a smacking sound and a feeble cry.

"Keep your hands off her!" Fire rose inside of me. The beast of anger roared, broke loose, ran wild.

Even though the snow had let up a little, I couldn't scramble down the cliff to help her—it was too steep and icy for anyone to free climb. No time to drive around looking for help.

"Drop a rope," Sevren yelled. "You have gear in your car. I saw it when you were at Abrams's house."

I tried to think. Everything was becoming fuzzy again. "She comes up first," I yelled.

Laughter, dark and vicious. "I go first, or I start to play with her while I wait." I thought of what he'd done to the other women before killing them. "I have a knife," he said. "I'm good with a knife."

"Help me!"

"All right!" I heaved myself up and over the ledge. "Don't touch her. I'm getting a rope!"

I hurried to the car and pulled out my climbing gear. His voice found me. It was calmer now, full of dark desire. I imagined him eyeing Tessa as he spoke: "Hurry, Patrick. I'm not a patient man."

A river of emotion churned through me. Anger. Fear. Love. Hatred. I had no idea which would win. Somewhere behind me I heard the tree creak and a branch snap off and crash into the gorge.

Hurry!

I took off my gun and laid it on the hood, pulled on my harness, grabbed some webbing, and scanned the area for something to tie into. Some kind of an anchor. Anything. There were no trees close by. I had to hurry.

The only thing available was the guardrail, but a long section of it lay crumpled from the ambulance's impact. No other choice. I tied the webbing around a section of the railing that still appeared to be intact, threw a carabiner through it, and clipped the rope into that. It was dicey, but it would hold our body weight. At least I hoped it would. No time to wonder. Just time to trust.

I pushed the pack with my other rope and the rest of my gear out of the way, and then attached a couple of prussiks and ascenders to my harness's gear loops.

"Hurry!" Sevren yelled. "Or I start giving her lessons. Drop a rope and some ascenders."

I wasn't about to back down. Tessa was the only reason I was willing to help him, and he knew it. If he killed her, there was nothing to motivate me. "I'm coming down for her, Sevren. Or you get nothing."

A short silence and then a blinding shriek that sliced all the way through me. "Patrick!" It was a cry of acute pain and final terror.

"I just cut her, Patrick. Cut her good. The brachial artery, right there on the inside of the arm. Oh, it looks deep. It's spurting. Based on my medical training, I'd say she has about four minutes before she bleeds out. I'm pretty good at estimating time of death. Trust me."

Dear God, please. No, no, no.

Tears of white-hot anger blurred my eyes. "Press your hand against it, Tessa," I yelled. "Listen to me! You have to stop the bleeding!"

Hurry, hurry, no time.

No time.

I grabbed two extra harnesses and clipped them to my harness. Then I sprinted toward the edge of the cliff and launched myself away from the ridge and into the gorge. The rope sailed through my brake hand. I was on the brink of losing control and freefalling into the valley when I managed to catch myself, and control my descent. I tapped my feet off the rock face, hopped over a rocky overhang, and zoomed headfirst toward the ambulance.

"Tessa, I'm coming. Hold your hand against the cut!"

87

A moment later I arrived at the ambulance and locked off, so I could hang in place. I stepped gingerly onto the hood, trying to use my weight to steady the vehicle. It was tilted but still horizontal enough for me to stand on the hood. Only then did I realize I'd left my gun sitting on the roof of my car at the top of the cliff.

The windshield stared at me like a giant splintered eye. A web of spidery cracks withered across it, emanating from the place on the driver's side where Sevren's head had smashed into it. He stared through the glass at me like a snake eyeing a mouse on the other side of the aquarium. A smear of blood oozed down his forehead, making his face look wild, primal. Beside him I saw Tessa, pale, crying softly, her left arm awash in blood. Her right hand pressing against the wound.

"Give me a harness," said Sevren.

"I'm taking her up."

"OK, let's discuss it then." He looked at his watch and then at Tessa's arm. "A couple minutes from now, it won't really matter, will it?"

Anger boiling. Boiling.

"All right. All right."

Tessa groaned softly.

I cursed him in my heart, but I didn't say anything for fear he might hurt Tessa worse. I lowered myself toward the driver's door. The impact from the fall had jarred it open, and it swung loose on broken hinges. I handed him a harness, and he started pulling it on. His face wrenched in pain as he did. *Tessa said his leg is hurt.*

I saw a bloody scissors on the floor of the cab and a crimson stain spreading across his pants leg.

Good for you, Tessa.

She was squeezing her arm, stopping the flow of blood.

"Hang in there," I told her. "It's going to be OK." She nodded. She looked so fragile. So broken. "I love you," I said. "I love you, Tessa Ellis."

He clipped in. "All right. Hand me the ascenders."

I did.

Think, Pat. Think!

At that point we were both attached to the rope, but I was above him, balancing on the hood, locking off the rope with my right hand. He wouldn't be able to ascend until I got out of the way. "Now," he whispered, and seemed to be weaker from the effort of struggling with his leg. "Get out of the way and then unclip."

C'mon, Pat. Think. Do something.

Then he added, "Toss that other harness, or I'll sit here for a while."

"You have to let me take her—"

Tessa moaned and slumped back against the door.

"You're killing her," he said softly. "It won't be long now."

I dropped the other harness into the gorge. Now I had no way to take Tessa up the rope. I had no idea what to do; she was bleeding to death within reach of me, yet I was powerless to help her.

I slid onto the hood and unclipped. The storm had picked up again, and the metal was slippery with snow. I was staring through the cracked windshield, just inches away from my daughter, watching her die. I heard a weak cry and then she said, "I love you, Patrick." Then her eyes rolled back. She went unconscious.

"No!"

Sevren laughed as he eased out the door. "Looks like you were too slow once again, Dr. Bowers."

88

"I'm coming for you," I said to him. "Wherever you go, I'll find you." I was getting dizzy again. The world was spinning. Sounds were eating into colors. The drugs. Oh no. Not now. The scent of a thousand snowflakes overwhelmed me. If only I hadn't left my gun on the car.

"So, then." A smile slithered across his face. "A rematch."

He slid one of the ascenders up the rope.

Nausea swarmed over me.

"I think I'll pay Agent Jiang a visit tonight . . ." he said.

Everything was a blur. *You can't let him get up that cliff.*

"I have a couple lessons I'd like to share with her."

Get him closer.

I whispered to him.

He stopped. "What?" he said.

He loves to control others. Lien-hua said he has to be in control.

I said it again, softly, ever so softly. Then I smiled and laughed at him.

He leaned toward me. "What did you say?"

I was struggling for breath. I felt myself slipping toward the edge of the hood. Toward the edge of the world. I reached back behind me for something to hold onto. Nothing. But instead of thinking about how I was going to die, all I could think of was how I'd let Tessa down. Let Christie down.

His leg is hurt.

My fingertips found the ridged outline of the windshield, and I curled them around the thin lip of metal, willing every pull-up I'd ever done into the tips of my fingers.

I whispered once again. He leaned close and sneered. "You're pathetic. Begging like a little baby. I expected more out of you. Good-bye, Patrick Bowers."

Yes, he was close enough.

This time I didn't whisper: "Checkmate!" With one motion I twisted my body toward him, swiveling my leg and smashing my boot full force into the wound on his leg. His scream was bright and searing and very satisfying. It was a good, solid, bone-crunching kick that even Lien-hua would have been proud of. I'd hit him with his brake hand loose on the rope, and he hobbled backward, teetered on the edge of the hood for a moment, and then spun off into the valley. I heard the rope sailing through his Figure-8 and waited to hear him rip off the end of the line and plummet to his death, but somehow he was able to grab the searing rope in his palms.

"Bowers!" he screamed. His voice was thick with hatred. He barely sounded human anymore. "You're mine!"

He'll be back in a minute.

You have to save Tessa now.

89

I clenched the ridge of the windshield, my feet hanging over the edge of the hood. My shoulder was exploding in pain, but I somehow managed to pull myself up. As I did, the wound in my shoulder ripped open, and the pain cruised up my neck and blistered apart inside my head. I felt warm blood oozing from the wound, drenching the back of my shirt. I tried to ignore the blast of pain but almost blacked out.

The ambulance was slipping, everything was slipping. I needed something to tie into, quick, before we went down. I felt along the icy rock face beside me. It was cluttered with fissures and cracks. I needed something to jam into one. Anything that would hold my weight.

And I only had one thing with me. My flashlight.

I pulled it out and pounded at it with one of the carabiners, smashing its precision-machined high-strength aluminum alloy case into a slim crack.

Using one of the prussiks, I flipped a lark's head knot around it. Clipped in and then smacked my hand against the windshield. I had to wake her up. "Tessa!" I smacked it again. Nothing. "Please! Wake up!"

I eased closer, saw her chest rise and fall. Rise and fall. She was still alive, thank God. The ambulance tilted beneath me. Below us I could hear Sevren enraged into madness calling out my name, making his way up the rope with the catch and click of the ascenders. Catch and click. Ascending the rope. Catch and click. Getting closer by the second.

Tessa! You have to wake up!

I reached through the open window and grabbed her shoulder. Shook her. "Tessa!"

Her eyes fluttered open then closed.

"Wake up!"

I whipped off my belt and as gently as possible, tucked it around her arm above the cut artery and then cinched it tight. A crude tourniquet. She might lose the arm, but at least the tourniquet should keep her alive.

Then I whispered a prayer to the God I wasn't even sure was listening. I begged the heavens to hear me, a guy who had no right to expect any divine favors. *Please. Please, she doesn't deserve to die. You took Christie, don't take her. Please let her live. I don't care about me, just let her live.*

I shook her. I loved her. "Tessa!"

Snow fell past us, all around us. She blinked and looked up, confused. Behind her I saw the back doors of the ambulance burst open.

Sevren.

The cluttered contents of the ambulance spilled out all around him. He put his good leg on the bumper.

Tessa's lips formed words that were faint, barely audible: "Help me."

I hooked my hand under her right armpit. As I did, I noticed the rope had flipped over the body of the ambulance and was now jammed in the crack between the open back doors. Sevren was on the bumper, bouncing it with his leg. The ambulance began to rock.

"Stop," I yelled to him. "The rope. It's caught!"

Tessa looked down at her bleeding arm. "My arm," she whispered. Her voice was soft, fragile, that of a child. *She's a little girl, and I'm her daddy.*

Sevren jumped on the bumper again, and the ambulance tilted one final time. I clutched Tessa's good arm. *I'll never let go . . . I'll never let go . . .*

We were moving, moving. I slid down to the end of the prussik. My anchor held. My trusty flashlight.

I tightened my grip, and Tessa snaked up through the open window as the ambulance spit her out and slid away from us and into the gorge. As it did, it met Sevren Adkins's body, jerking him into the slit between the doors. Pinning him. Crushing him. His piercing cries told me how tightly his body was wedged in place. The entire weight of the vehicle was crunching down on him.

Tessa and I swung into the cliff. "Patrick!" She was dangling over nothingness, and I was holding her.

"I've got you, Tessa," I yelled. "I'm not letting go. I promise!"

But the ambulance was still moving.

How? The rope tied to the guardrail should have held it in place.

Oh. The guardrail.

"Against the cliff!" I yelled. I hoisted Tessa up into my arms and embraced her as the twisted chunk of metal that used to be a guardrail rushed past us on its way to the bottom of the gorge. A long narrow scream cut through the valley. Sevren's cry seemed to stain the day, a dark scar blacker than midnight arcing up toward us from his descent into hell. It lasted longer than I thought it would and then ended with a sickening crunch as the ambulance sandwiched his body against the boulders at the base of the cliff.

I hugged Tessa close. "It's OK now. He's gone. You're safe." And in that moment, I was neither angry nor afraid. Somehow, somewhere, I found a fragment of hope that I could hold onto, buried deep beneath the months of rage. A new anchor.

Chaos is evidence of human beings.
Hope is evidence of God.

High above me I heard the unmistakable gruff voice of Ralph. "Pat!"

They'd found us. The mic patch!

"Tessa's hurt," I yelled. "Hurry!"

I heard the clink of carabiners as someone pulled out the rest of my climbing gear and got ready to throw down another rope.

I was starting to get dizzy again.

"Hold on," I said. She clung to me, and I took my last prussik, tied it into a quick field harness around her waist, and clipped her into the anchor.

"Patrick?" she whispered.

"Yeah?"

"Where did you learn all this rock climbing stuff?"

"Something called experience."

"Oh yeah," she said with a faint smile. "I've heard of that."

"Now," I murmured, "I need to say good-bye."

"Good-bye? Why?"

"I think I'm about to pass out."

"Really?"

And before I could answer, I did.

90

I heard voices all around me speaking in hushed tones, respectful tones, and for a moment I wondered if I was dead.

"Looks like he's coming out of it," said a voice from somewhere nearby. A husky voice. "'Bout time."

When I opened my eyes and saw Ralph's massive form next to me, I mumbled, "If I'm dead and this is heaven, what are you doing here?" I mumbled.

"Who ever said we're in heaven?"

I blinked my eyes and then squinched them shut, overwhelmed by the sharp white glare of the room. I grimaced. "We better not be in a hospital. I hate hospitals."

"At least this time, no one's dying," said Tessa.

I turned. She sat beside the window, her face outlined by daylight. She might have been an angel sitting there—a beautiful black-haired angel wearing a T-shirt with a cobra slithering through the eye socket of a human skull.

It was a beautiful sight, slightly twisted and macabre, but adorable nonetheless.

"I knew you'd wake up." It was Ralph again. "I told the docs not to worry." Then he added proudly, "While you were asleep I made it past the crypt."

"Beheaded the ogre, huh?"

"Yup. Fast and clean."

"I showed him how," added Tessa.

"Well, that's nice," I said in a fatherly sort of way. I noticed that

Tessa's arm was thickly bandaged in the place the Illusionist had cut her. She didn't seem to be in too much pain, maybe the cut wasn't as deep as I thought. I'd ask her about it in a minute.

I rubbed my head. "So, how long have I been out?"

"A whole day," said Ralph. "I guess you really needed your beauty sleep."

"Wow, I guess I did."

"They gave you some pretty nasty stuff, Pat." I looked toward the voice. Lien-hua was the third and last visitor in the room. She was seated in the corner in one of the prerequisite ugly chairs.

"Phencyclidine, aka PCP," piped in Tessa. "It's a disassociative hallucinogenic analgesic, kinda like its cousin—the ever popular but not as potent club drug Ketamine. A dose as low as 20 milligrams can kill you, and doses as high as 150–200 milligrams are considered not compatible with life."

"Let me guess, the Internet?"

"Do you even have to ask?"

"So how much was in the capsule Kincaid tried to stuff down my throat?"

Lien-hua answered, "250 millgrams. If that capsule had dissolved any more in your mouth you wouldn't be here talking to us."

"Which reminds me," said Ralph soberly.

"Yeah." She lowered her eyes.

"What is it?" I asked.

Ralph's voice stiffened. "Pat, I don't think you heard about Tucker . . . He didn't make it."

The news took the air out of my lungs, the moment out of my heart.

"He died trying to protect Tessa."

We were all quiet for a few minutes. It seemed like forever but still not long enough.

"How's his wife?" I asked.

"Taking it pretty hard. They didn't have any kids. He was all she had."

I hated hearing all this. Brent Tucker had been a decent man. A good man. Annoying at times, overly enthusiastic, but dedicated. I couldn't have found Sevren without his ideas. I didn't know what to say.

"We're going to see her this afternoon," said Lien-hua. I don't know how long we sat in silence before a nurse came in to check my heart rate, and life eased forward again.

"Did you find Sevren's body?" I asked Ralph at last.

"Not yet."

"What?" I gasped. "He was in the ambulance when it fell!"

"Those things are built like tanks," said Ralph. "If he slipped inside it, it's possible—"

"No," I said. "He couldn't have survived."

"We'll find him."

The nurse finished up and disappeared again.

"Any word on the governor then?" I asked.

I saw Tessa smirking. "The tape," she said.

"What?"

"From the mic patch."

Ralph grinned. "Yup, it's made quite a splash on the Internet."

Tessa tapped her chest. "I posted it for him."

"In one day Sebastian Taylor went from being a presidential hopeful to the top of the FBI's most wanted list. I think that's a record. You should see the cable news coverage."

"No thanks."

"His wife returned from Barbados last night only to find out her husband used to be a CIA assassin. She's been thrown right into the middle of the international media spotlight."

"I'll bet she's right at home." Then I had a sobering thought. "Sebastian will be tough to find. He'll know how to drop off the grid."

"Yeah," said Ralph, "but he likes the media too. I have a feeling we'll be hearing from Sebastian Taylor again."

"Enough about all that," said Lien-hua. "Are you OK, Pat? Seriously? You were in pretty bad shape."

"I'm all right, but I could use some coffee."

She reached behind her and then handed me a cup of the good stuff: shade-grown Yrigacheffe from Ethiopia's Sidamo region. I could almost smell the bananas growing above the beans.

Now I *was* in heaven.

"Cream and honey, no sugar," she added. "It's a little cold, though. I didn't know when you'd be waking up."

I tried to sit up, cringed, fell back.

"You sure you're OK?"

"You want me to be honest?"

"Always."

"Come here, then."

She leaned closer. The scent of vanilla.

"Yes?" she said.

I spoke quietly, so no one else would hear. "I'm sorry about that stakeout."

A pause. "Let's not be sorry, let's just be careful."

"OK."

"I was really worried about you, Pat. I was afraid we might lose you. And, well . . ." She was searching for the right words to say. Never found them. "One more thing. When I was talking about motives and I mentioned fear, you could see it, couldn't you?"

"See what?"

"The history. In my face."

I lowered my voice. "Something happened to you, didn't it?"

She was quiet.

"When you're ready," I said, "if you want to tell me, I'll listen. You can trust me, Lien-hua."

"I know I can."

"What are you two whispering about?" asked Tessa.

"Nothing," I said.

"Yeah, right," she said in her wonderfully sarcastic teenage way.

Lien-hua returned to her chair. "Hey, come here, Tessa," I said. I patted the bed next to me and, somewhat reluctantly, she joined me. "There's something your mother wanted me to tell you, but I never did. I'm sorry, I just didn't know if I believed it before."

"What is it?"

"'Our choices decide who we are,'" I said, "'but our loves define who we'll become.' She wanted you to know that." I paused for a second and then said, "I'm sure she would have told you herself if only . . ."

"She did."

"What?"

"She did tell me. And she said you would too, someday. When you finally understood what it meant."

Tessa waited for you, Pat. She's been waiting for you this whole time.

I took a deep breath. "Thanks for sticking with me until I got the chance to say it."

"Like I had a choice," she grumbled. But she let the wisp of a smile flicker across her face as she did.

■

Over the next couple minutes Agent Jiang told me that Alice and her children were doing fine and that Alice was even getting some reward money for helping us corner the killer. "She'll be able to cut back on her hours at work to spend more time with her kids. She seemed thrilled by the deal."

"What about the people at the hotel who were exposed to the contagion? What about all of us?"

Ralph answered as he punched at the keys on the PSP 3, which he'd started playing when I was talking to Tessa. "With Marcie's help the CDC was able to vaccinate us. Lots of people are sick, but no fatalities so far." Then he looked up from his game. "Without her help, though, we'd all be goners."

"And, oh yeah," said Lien-hua, "Jason Stilton won't be seeing the outside of a jail for a long time. He was found with an envelope full of cash and a short list of excuses. He's facing corruption charges as well as conspiracy to commit murder."

"He's the one who delivered the necklace to Kincaid, isn't he?" I asked.

She nodded. "Of course, Stilton is saying he didn't know anyone was going to get hurt, just that Trembley had offered him a way to make some easy money by delivering something of Tessa's to a guy at the hotel, a guy Trembley had worked with before."

She paused to collect her thoughts. "Oh, I almost forgot, Margaret called a couple hours ago to tell us she'll be returning to teach at Quantico. It seems the director was very impressed with how quickly the team that she'd assembled was able to solve this case."

"Wonderful." I shook my head. "So, what's next for you and Ralph?"

"I'm looking over a case from San Diego. A series of arsons. They want me to work on the profile."

"And I gotta testify at a hearing," Ralph said with a heavy sigh. "Seems an old friend of ours from Illinois is up for parole."

I gasped. "Not Richard Basque?"

"One and the same."

"But how? He has sixteen consecutive life sentences!"

"DNA. He's been fighting for years to have it reevaluated. Finally got his wish. Samples didn't match. Looks like it might clear him."

Great. If there was one man I wouldn't want to see walking the streets again, it was Richard Basque. He was one of only two people I'd ever met who made me genuinely, deeply, insanely afraid. Thankfully, the other one was dead. Ralph shot him in a hostage situation back in 2004. The Illusionist came in a close third.

"By the way, Pat," said Ralph, "where's my phone?"

"Oh," mumbled Tessa, "so it was yours."

"What do you mean *was*?"

"The killer . . . well . . . he dropped it."

I saw Ralph getting ready to cuss. "Not in front of Tessa, you don't," I said. He caught himself, sighed, and shook his head. Then he mentioned something to Lien-hua about the arsonist case and a string of grave robberies somewhere in the Midwest, but I didn't really hear him. I was too busy watching my daughter look out the window. She was still dressed in black, but I saw she had painted one of her fingernails pink. She saw me staring. "It's a start," she said, glancing at her fingertip. "I'm getting used to it, but don't get your hopes up."

I decided to ask her about her arm. "So, how are you feeling? Is your arm OK? Where he cut you?"

"It will be." Her voice faded to a whisper. "It's gonna leave a scar, though."

"Yeah, well, that's not so bad. Back when I was a wilderness guide, we used to have a saying: 'Scars are tattoos with better stories.'"

She smirked. "I like that." She held her right arm out to me. "Here, help me. Pull up my sleeve."

I gently nudged her sleeve up to her elbow and saw the series of straight scars on her forearm.

Cutting. So she is into cutting.

"Do they have good stories?" I asked softly.

She thought for a moment. "No. And for most of them, it's the same story, over and over again."

I struggled for the right words to say. "Well, maybe we can write a better one," I said at last.

She nodded. "OK."

Then I remembered the words of Zelda Fitzgerald: "I don't need anything except hope," she wrote, "which I can't find by looking backwards or forwards, so I suppose the thing is to close my eyes."

No.

Zelda was wrong.

The thing is to finally open your eyes. That's the only way to find hope.

The only way to find anything that really matters.

"And what about you, Pat?" asked Ralph, interrupting my thoughts.

"Me?"

"What's next for you? You going to stay in Denver or go back to teach at the Academy?"

"I don't know," I said. "I'll have to talk that over with the rest of the family."

Tessa nodded ever so slightly to me, and I nodded back.

Moments passed by, and that was OK.

She leaned forward and peered out the window. I tried to see what she was looking at but couldn't quite get the right angle. At last I asked her what she'd found.

"You wouldn't believe me if I told you."

"Try me."

She pointed. "A unicorn. Up there in the clouds."

I leaned over as far as I could to follow her gaze. I didn't see the unicorn, but I did see the tourmaline necklace dangling from her neck, collecting sunlight with wide-open arms. And the glistening black necklace looked right at home as it swung across the skull on her shirt.

And then landed again.

Right beside her heart.

EPILOGUE

The Pentagon
Department of Defense
Sublevel 4
4:58 p.m.

General Biscayne scratched his signature across the last two forms and was just pushing back from his desk to head home when his phone jangled to life.

"Yeah," he snapped. "What is it?"

"Hello, Cole. It's Sebastian."

A chill ran down the general's spine. Sebastian Taylor frightened him. Always had. He'd suspected Sebastian was responsible for the disappearance of two operatives back in '78 and a couple of others in the '80s but had never been able to prove it.

General Biscayne tried to mask the fear in his voice. "What do you want?"

"You called Margaret Wellington, didn't you?"

"Sebastian, I—"

"You told her to keep everything quiet. To make the case go away. But you made one mistake. You mentioned my name."

A pause. A decision to lay down all his cards. "So maybe I did. You're a fugitive. What are you going to do about it now?"

"I think, General, that I'm going to go fishing."

The line went dead.

And with trembling fingers, the general set down his phone.

And so.

Now it begins.

Look for the next Patrick Bowers thriller,
The Rook, in spring 2008.

ACKNOWLEDGMENTS

The Internet, great repository of knowledge that it is, has various attributions for the quote about the foolish mice and the wise cats. So, my thanks go out to either Andrew Mercer or Scott Love or whoever else might have thought of it in the first place.

In addition, I'm indebted to the following friends for their ideas, support, research, and encouragement: Wayne Kirk, Chris Haskins, Lara and Pam Johnson, Michelle Cox, Dr. Todd Huhn, Tammy Edwards, David Lehman, Dr. Godwin, Dr. Morse, Von Roebuck, Dr. Kim Rossmo, Tim Carter, Becky Cox, Steve Kipperman, the Asheville Chamber of Commerce, Dr. John-Paul Abner, Lee Garner, Shawn Scullin, Alton Gansky, George Hill, Deb Van Horn, Lonnie Hull DuPont, Pamela Harty, Jennifer Leep, Cat Hoort, Kristin Kornoelje, the Black Mountain Writers' Group, the Jonestown Institute, and finally, my daughters and my wife for their unending patience and encouragement, and, oh yes, the kind folks at Oasis Coffee Shop for staying open late.

Steven James is a critically acclaimed author and award-winning storyteller. He has written many collections of short fiction, scripts, and inspirational books that explore the paradox of good and evil. He lives at the base of the Blue Ridge Mountains with his wife and three daughters. This is his first thriller.